BETTER MAN

by

Robert O'Grady

This is dedicated to all those who helped along the way. You know who you are. Many thanks. Love ya's.

I.

Discoveries

Chapter 1

The sun was near bled for the day. Blackness painted over the life of the land and land itself and he rode through the obsidian sheet piercing like a dying star. He atop his horse amidst the encroaching stillness. The rancher chewed and threadbare on his spotted horse, fleeing from the dogged predator behind him. He glanced aback and squinted in the fading light. His pursuer a thousand yards out.

He yelled and dug his spurs into the slackened horse. The animal grunted. He hollered again and spurred it again. The horse squealed, but obeyed the command. "Come on! Come on!" he said to it, patting its neck. He was perspiring despite the drop in temperature and the breeze whisking across his face. His shirt caked with dirt and sweat carried the unwanted passenger of blood near his rib cage. The red flowed rendering the stain a work in progress. The edges of the blood trails browned, but the rancher's own color mimicked that of the half moon in the sky above.

The night now fully blanketed the terrain. He strained his neck to peer behind. His pursuer was gone from sight, now one with the opaque meridian of the land. He spun his head forward and felt a shooting pain in his side. "Whoa," he said much quieter than the commands before and the horse slowed to a mild trot. He pressured the wound with his hand and then lifted his palm to his face. The moonlight was faint and challenging, but the rancher saw his hand was blackened by blood and darkness. "Stuck me good," he whispered. The horse snorted and its feet became restless. "What is it boy?" The rancher clicked his tongue and teeth and the horse moved right of the direction they previously headed.

The man could make out a large rock formation shaped somewhat like a cactus ahead. The arduous smell of dust and heat had vacated and gave way to the cool crisp of the evening. They scampered beside the mammoth stones. "Good boy," the man said to the horse and rubbed his wound. The full weight of his right foot entered the stirrup and he swung over the horse. He hollered in pain then teetered forward before landing on his back with a thud. The wind left his throat. He coughed from the deep places of his body and strived to inhale. He shook his head rapidly and used his diminished leg strength to push himself sitting congruent with the ground and rock. He mustered a deep breath sounding like air through a straw. He coughed long again and felt flecks of liquid propel onto his lips and drip to his chin. He wiped his face with an already fouled shirtsleeve and it came away with moist redness. "Son of a bitch lunged me for sure." He leaned over and spat. The dusty earth darkened on his mark.

Just then his horse squealed. The rancher tensed. He swiveled his head left and right and repeated and nervous tears filled his eyes. He used his remaining strength to push himself a few feet against the rocky construction. His chest inflated and reversed hurriedly. His breath was audible and he firmly grasped a neighboring weed in attempt to redirect the stress. The plant was dead and crumbled between his fingers. "Sunna-bitch," he huffed. Rich blood escaped the corners of his mouth. He gently palmed his wound. He turned in the direction of his horse. The animal was gone. He nodded as though accepting the fruition of a grand plan beyond his comprehension. Breath rippled through his windpipe. He closed his eyes and forced himself calm. The effervescent noise of the critters around him saturated the night. His wound pulsated beneath his shirt and his muscles ached. He opened his eyes, adjusting to the blackness. He let both hands fall helplessly to the dirt for respite. He leaned his head back on the rock and saw the stars above shining indifferently. He swallowed hard and closed his eyes again, this time with expectations of permanence.

**

The rancher was awoken by the shrill call of a raven in the distance. The moon was where it had been. Little time passed. The excruciating pain in his side seemed a contagion, slithering through his limbs like an oily serpent. His eyes were thirsty and creased. He peered at the overriding night sky; the stars and moon connected in his vision, unyieldingly draining into one another as his glazed over pupils strained to dilate. He was stiff all over, muscles atrophied. His body jackknifed at the waist. He blinked progressively and creaked his head forward. He squinted. The muted shape of a man idled before him. The figure was a barely a silhouette, his edges inconspicuous with the black around him. The stranger ignited a match. The flame danced on the end of the stick bathing the lower half of his face. The rancher recognized this shadow, his pursuer. The image of the stranger's face, smooth and sharply handsome, had been ingrained in his mind from the moment the knife entered his body. The stranger's breath extinguished the flame, and then he rolled down his sleeve and stuck the scalding ember into the flesh of his own wrist. The rancher winced, awestruck, but the stranger made no sound.

"What the hell are you?" the rancher finally spoke. He awaited an answer and sighed when none came. "Are you death?"

"I'm yours," the stranger said calmly.

"How'd you find me?" the rancher said.

"Generally when a man's desperate, he reaches out for something." The stranger gestured at the rocks. "You would have been better off in the open."

"You're some kind of demon."

The stranger tilted his head upward, his hat brim no longer concealing his eyes. "I understand it must be easier to accept this viewing me as some ghastly apparition or some supernatural being, but the fact is I'm as real as what's coming. I'm a man. Just like you."

"Not just. Not like me."

"I suppose not quite like you. I lack your cowardice."

"Fuck you, cowardice."

"Vulgarity won't get you anywhere. You left your wife alone to be taken by my hand. What sort of man allows this to happen?"

"You stabbed me goddammit, outside 'fore I could do anything!" The rancher coughed up more blood. Tributaries forming on his chin.

"This is true, but you made no attempt to save her. I did my work without interruption and when complete I left to see you flee by horse."

The rancher moaned and began to cry. "I saw blood spray on the curtains from outside and I knew what you done."

"You were wise to know, but still a coward."

"I couldn't have saved her."

"Maybe not. Perhaps we weren't meant to know though I wouldn't want that transgression on my conscience." With that the stranger rose from his crouch, blotting out the moon. The rancher's eyes were poorly adjusted, but he could make out the slight glimmer of the pistol as the stranger removed it from his holster.

"Why are you doing this?" the rancher questioned. His blood loss growing aggressive with each word.

"It would seem an act of compassion at this juncture." He cocked back the hammer of the pistol.

"Why don't you just leave me? I'm finished anyway." the rancher pleaded.

"You need to take solace in the fact that you never had a choice. All of the things you've done, the decisions you made, have led you here to this moment. I know what I am and what I need to do. What are you? I judge that what you'd say would be different than what you know. You would speak meandering typical thoughts of duty and righteousness; we now know to be inaccurate in your case. This is the blueprint. This is our fate."

"This ain't right," the rancher said.

"Right's of no consequence." The gun barrel stared down at the stranger containing his past, present, and future. The pistol spoke but once and the bullet struck the rock through the rancher's eye. The shot resonated in the open. The surrounding creatures hushed for that brief moment almost sympathetically and then continued their cacophonous song like they were members of the same unwitting chorus. The stranger holstered his weapon and then stared contemplatively at the night sky. He cracked his neck and rubbed his barren face with his hand. From beneath his coat he unsheathed his knife, a Bowie stained since the previous encounter. He walked forward to his prey and went to work. The land, enduringly parched, was reticent to drink the foreign blood pooling beneath the lifeless body, yet after a time like most things it reformed and took it without restraint.

Chapter 2

Tim Collie was laying eyes closed in his bedroom soon after sun up. The rays pounded through the window nudging his consciousness. The thumping illumination was unsuccessful and his mind brought him to thoughts of his wife.

He sits upright and turns his head toward her. She opens one eye and gives a crinkled smile. "You had a good night," he says quietly.

"Yeah," she answers.

"Better than some at least I reckon," he says moving out of bed.

"I still got the day to go through."

"Nights are tougher though."

"You keep repeatin' that to yourself."

"I do believe I will. Some lungs take no heed to night. You're improving." Tim says. He begins dressing himself. He stares into the mirror and the reflection of his lying face stares back. From behind he hears a cough tear through her throat. His eyes dart in the mirror to her direction and he moves quickly by her side.

"Will you just let me be?" she says.

"Are you alright?" He stops a few feet from the bed.

"I don't need you to dotin' on me every sound that takes your offense."

"I don't mind doting. It's part of my sworn duty." Tim walks to her side of the bed and sits down slowly. She turns onto her side, facing him. A slight smile warms him.

"I bet when you sworn that duty you didn't account for no situation like this," she says.

"My accountin' never was that good anyway. I pay no mind to this situation or any other that would have you believing I'd want no part of it. I'm part of you or us or whatnot."

"Well you got some kinda way with words Tim."

He pulls a clean white handkerchief from his pocket. "May I?" he asks. She nods and he soothingly wipes the outskirts of her mouth. The handkerchief comes away a pinkish-red and Tim puts the cloth away quicker than he retrieved it. He rubs her forehead with the back of his hand. She lets out a tone of appreciation and he kisses her head. He takes his weight off of the bed and begins to stand.

She weakly grasps his wrist before he can finish the motion. "I 'preciate all you're doin' for me," she says.

"I know you do."

"No you don't. It's gotta be hard to be gone for days and nights and have to come home to worrying." He completes his rise and turns away from her then pinches the bridge of his nose. "Tim, I can see your look even if you're not looking. I ain't getting better at all."

"I don't want to hear talk like that." He twists to her with a slight vengeance in his voice. "It's not doing anyone any good to sit there conversing at such things." She recoils into the pillow and grips the sheets as if they are her only solace. "Aw hell I'm sorry for yelling," he says, yelling.

"It's fine Tim," almost muted. "I know this hasn't been easy. I guess I just lose hope sometimes."

"Well goddammit stop doing that."

"Ok I will."

"Well good then."

"There is hope then? Is there Tim?" Her voice sounds childlike.

"There surely is. There always is."

"We just need money?"

"That's right. I told you if I could get enough money together, we could maybe get us a superior doctor or travel to one."

"And then I'll be fixed?"

"I reckon Maggie. Now let me get on to work so my promises don't make a liar out of me."

"Alright then Sheriff Collie. You go. I'll be here waiting when you get back with a good supper. You'll be home for supper?" She is upright now on the bed, the meekness subsiding from her as their conversation progresses.

He walks to the still shaded part of the room and opens the dresser drawer. Maggie watches him do this in silence as she always does. He pulls out his black gun belt and routinely notches it around his waist. He shuts the drawer and opens another. The Colt 45 Peacemaker reveals itself to him and then to Maggie as he places it in the holster without reticence. "I don't see what could possibly keep me," he says and shoots her a contrived smile.

"You be careful."

"Always am," he says. He leaves the room and she hears the front door shut. He closes it softly like he always does as if disturbing his already woken wife is sinful. The sun continues to beat through the window and the temperature rises a few degrees. Maggie lays prostrate on the bed for a short time before getting up to look outside. She sees Tim Collie's shape ebonized by the sun as he rides into town with his back to her. She presses against the glass and graces an uncontainable smile. She moves into the living room, but cannot help notice that the rays approaching through the panes dye a shaded X over her husband's side of the bed; and then the smile leaves her face.

His eye twitched and the color behind his lids brightened. Awakening was uncontainable. He sat up in the bed, remaining on his side of it despite the other being empty for over six months now. Collie yawned and then grazed his hand over the barren half. It was cold and he vacated the mattress entirely. It chirred relief when he did. He was slow to start burdened with apathy, but then began his routine as it played in his dream, his unconscious faithful and symbiotic to its proprietor.

Chapter 3

Silence cast over the nominal crowd in Bollard's Bar and Billiards just as Morgan Nutley's life was fleetingly snatched from him without time for himself or onlookers to ponder just about anything. His neck spit its remaining essence onto the dirty floorboards. Arterial spray had vengefully tarnished his dubious enemy and the reachable décor. Porter rose from the floor, freshly bleeding above his eye. He surveyed the patrons. The room paused with an aura of considerable shock. Six witnesses on their feet and Bollard himself stared, mouths agape, at Nutley's corpse.

Bollard spoke first. "What the hell did you do Porter?"

"What do you mean what did I do? He shot hisself. You all seen it."

"You forced him you simple prick."

"He called me...he said I was a sucker of cocks and a liar. You heard him. I had provocation. A sucker of cocks. I can't abide that. The gun went off. I'm a victim here. Look at my head. My head's caved in."

"It ain't caved," Bollard yelled. "You statin' your side don't change the outcome for Morgan."

"Well I's just saying, I didn't mean to do that and it wouldn't have likely happened if he didn't strike out at me." Porter's voice was trembling and his hands shook. His body rickety as he peered over the audience. He dropped to his knees next to the product of the dispensed bullet. His ducts began to well up with tears and he reached out to the corpse.

"Don't you fucking touch that body Porter. It stays that way 'til the Sheriff arrives," Bollard said. He pointed to two shaken looking men in the bar. "John and you there, grab hold of him." They remained still and Bollard raised his voice. "Do it." They jolted at his tone and scrambled to Porter who was now plagued with tremors and mucus draining from his nose.

"Don't," Porter said. The two men grabbed him by the arms and dragged him across the room. Porter's scruffy pants and boots left two thin trails as they cut across the soiled floor.

"Sit him down there in that chair," Bollard said. The two men placed him in the chair then turned to Bollard for more instructions. "Make sure he don't move," he said. He ran a hand over his own perspiring bald head and then itched his strong apparent beard.

"Let me the fuck alone," Porter pleaded. The two men put hands on his shoulders.

Bollard stomped from behind the bar and leaned over it as best he could with his stout frame. "You keep your mouth shut. I don't want you fucking anything up here 'fore Collie arrives. You upset a working fuckin' business. A man comes in here for whiskey and his feet tarnished in blood? I contradict that notion. You came in here riled like a red heathen looking to stir up some kinda mess from the get go. You and that big fucking mouth of yours. The man was down already in the game and you kept to prodding him. For what? So you could smear that pompous grin across your face you ignorant son of a bitch? I believe you to not be a cocksucker but a damned stupid fool. You know a man can only take so many words against him 'fore he ends it. Leave you alone? Yeah I'll leave you alone. I'll leave you alone when Collie gets here." Bollard leaned back from the bar and patted his face with his apron. The crimson in his features began to fade as he shook his head staring at Morgan Nutley's dead body.

***

The Sheriff's office of Little Creek stood anew yet imperfect in the corner of the L shaped town. Two parallel stretches of businesses lined the road like they were built on the edge of an unbending stream, while between them loomed alleyways and side paths to the homes of the people who lived there. The town was currently alive. Horses and people possessed the road. Merchants and shop owners wandered about peddling their latest products and skills and some perfectly situated the displays at their building exteriors to draw the largest crowd. However, to their misfortune the principal numbers were huddled outside of Bollard's Bar, straining their necks in an effort to peer above or below the saloon doors while Bollard himself guarded the front entrance dissuading people to enter.

"What's the difference if we lay eyes or not?" A thin man from the crowd asked.

Bollard planted at the door, swayed his upper body blocking the various fields of vision. "We're not quite ready for opening yet this morning sir."

Another man among the dozens spoke up. "I ain't interested in drinkin' just post sun up, but I reckon we got a right to know the reason of gunplay in our town."

Bollard used both hands in a pleading, but effectual manner. "Now I'm not saying you don't get to know, but I can't have people rummaging through here at the present. This here was a turn of events, got outta hand. That's all. Its getting taken care of as I stand. Most important thing for you all to know is we will be open for business as early as an hour I add up." He stepped backwards and his back nudged the entrance doors. "And first round of liquor is half price for everyone today."

A small number of eyebrows rose in approval. Bollard backed inside and kept close watch on the congregation. They remained peeking and craning like a group of buzzards until they lost interest and ambled away, occasionally looking back for change.

By the time Collie approached the main road of Little Creek, the throng of people at the bar had dispersed. He had ridden slowly to town this day adding a further ten minutes to a ten minute journey, thus allowing him to consider life and his state of affairs in life. As the horse trotted down the road he atop of it tipped his hat and bid a proper morning to any passersby that paid him mind. There were a decent many, but less than usual. Collie could see a despondency and inquiring demeanor in the people's faces and he doubled his horse's pace to the station.

"Mornin' Sheriff," a man yelled from the livery.

By the time Collie heard this, his back was to the man, but he still responded in the suitable manner with a pleasantry masking his concern. He approached the hitching post outside of his station. He slowed the horse and swung down from it. His right foot hit the ground with more than a slight impact and he patted down his jacket. He hitched the horse and long strode into the office.

He pushed open the door with force and Upton shot up from his desk startled. Collie scanned the room quickly and saw the three vacant cells at the far side of the room.

"Upton," Collie said and nodded hello.

"Mornin' Sheriff," Upton responded. "Must admit that I got to wondering when you might be comin' in."

"Oh yeah? Virgil ain't in yet?"

"No sir, Tim. Virgil left late last night and I ain't seen him since. I been here all night though. It was quiet up 'til this mornin'."

"Seems unsettling out there today." Collie said and saw the younger man's hands shaking. "Why don't you take a minute." He saw Upton noticeably breathe deeper to slow his intake. The young man's hands steadied slightly.

"Sorry Sheriff. It's not that I'm scared or nothing. Just unsure."

"Unsure of what?"

"Well, on account of the shootin' and me not having been to one by my lonesome I determined it best for me to wait, being that you usually get in a few minutes after this particular shooting occurred." Upton spoke rapidly and appeared relieved as if the words were burdensome to hold.

"Shooting?" Collie questioned. His body stiffened.

"Yeah a shooting. From over at Bollard's. Well one shot only from what I heard. But still from over Bollard's." Upton sat down in his chair halfway through his statements.

"And Virgil ain't been in yet. You sure he isn't over at the bar?"

"Well hell Tim, I'm not sure." Upton stood back up with nerves returning to his voice. "I done messed this up."

"How long ago was this?" Collie said. There was a calming nature to his tone.

"Not ten minutes ago I reckon."

"Seems like the mess is relegated to Bollard's. No use harping on "should've.""

"Yessir, Sheriff," Upton sighed and looked at the floor.

"Grab that shotgun from the rack and let's go." Upton lifted his head and nodded. He moved to the gun. Collie turned and left the building and Upton followed.

The two men walked summarily through Little Creek in direct route to the bar. There was a presence about them. Upton saw the reverent gestures from the townsfolk as they nodded and tipped their hats to the sheriff. Collie paid no mind to any of it and carried forth his purposeful gaze. Upton's peripherals gave way to local shopkeepers and tradesmen carrying on with the business in a pseudo manner. Their curiosity and watchful methods singed his flesh. Upton's head swiveled about at multiple stimuli as he carried the Perkins double barrel. The pistol on Collie's side continued to reside in the holster, while his fingers occasionally tapped the butt with reassurance.

The wooden boards of the porch emitted a hollow boom as the two men stepped to the saloon doors. "You first," said Collie to Upton and the younger man shoved the flap of the door with the shotgun.

"What the hell took so long?" Bollard said as he moved to the door. "If he hadn't been dead already he'd of bled out by your time keeping." Upton moved inside, gun up, and Collie went in behind him, moving left to counter his deputy. "Collie, tell that boy to lower his gun. Ain't no cause for tensions."

"Deputy Smith," Collie said.

"Repeat," said Bollard.

"Call him Deputy Smith, not boy," Collie spoke again.

There was friction between Bollard's upper and lower teeth at the instruction. He made a motion to talk, but only grunted. Collie kept eyes on Bollard until he saw his comment accepted. "I apologize for what might have been thought as dawdling. We came as soon as we could," the sheriff said. He scanned the room and his expression dropped. He saw Porter held down in the corner bleeding profusely from his brow. The two men exerted little effort in restraining him. Porter like an animal snared in a trap raised his good eye at the sheriff. Collie stared back in a fusion of anger and disappointment. He looked at the blood on the floor, which had begun to congeal in the thin parts of the splatter. Emotion welled up in his face, but he forced it back. "Stay here by the door. Make sure no one comes or goes," he said to Upton. He brushed passed Bollard, careful not to step in the aftermath of the shooting. "Jesus Christ." His voice trembled. "Why don't you tell me what happened."

"What the fuck you think I've been waiting to do," Bollard said louder than necessary.

"Not you," Collie said, approaching the confined man in the chair. "You, Porter. What happened?"

"What you need him to recollect for? He was drunker than hell when it happened," Bollard said.

"I ain't askin' you Bollard for Christ's sake," he said half turned.

"Well I got myself a business to operate here and Nutley down there isn't worth much at pushin' a drink in his state. If he was we'd be running already."

Collie twisted toward Bollard. "I can appreciate your situation here and need for us to be prompt, but there ain't no outcome until there is one and you're not helping matters boasting in the background. Why don't you grab a bottle and wait outside with Deputy Smith there."

Bollard wore a look of consternation. "A bottle? What the fu-

"Yeah. Whiskey's your drink right Kenneth?" Collie said knowingly.

"I don't need no drink. I gotta open."

Collie strode right at Bollard almost confrontationally. He was inches from his face. "It's been a difficult mornin'. All I'm sayin' is you could use yourself a drink. Calm those nerves a bit and then I'll hear your side. Upton'll be out there with ya and I got hold a' this matter inside. You in agreement?"

Bollard took a step back and looked down at the floor and shook his head. "Yeah a drink'd be good." He went behind the bar and emerged with a clear unlabeled bottle.

Collie watched him the whole way. "Good, now go get hold of your nerves and settle yourself. Upton will be right behind you." The big man swung the doors out violently and took a large swig from the bottle. Collie motioned Upton to the bar. "You go out with him and make sure he gets his eyes glazed."

"You need him drunk?" Upton asked.

"No, drunk ain't no good. But liquor's got a way of 'splainin the truth. Just get his side with no bullshit. There's a

man of fictitious nature. If his hands ain't tarnished on this, that may well be, but I'd like to make sure."

"I understand Tim," Upton said. Collie saw that he did and sent him to go outside.

"Upton," he said quietly and the deputy halted at the doors. "That bottle passes your lips one time. No more." Upton nodded and the doors swung shut behind him. Collie walked back to the end of the bar where Porter sat with Bollard's pressuring companions at his side. "Why don't you boys go sit quiet at one of them tables yonder."

"Yes sir Collie," one said and they left without hesitation. Collie looked down at Porter whose eyes drifted refusing contact. Collie saw the man's hands were blemished with dirt and blood, but not gunpowder.

"Look at me," Collie said. Porter did with reticence, a sad hatred inherent. "We got a peaceful way in this town. We ain't had a killin' outside of Sioux in roundabout a month and now I see Morgan Nutley dead sober for the first time and you with your head leakin' from the top. Now I understand you to be a constant fuckin' drunk, Porter, and assuming that whatever brains you have ain't spilled out that wound on your head I'd like to know just what happened in my town this mornin'.

Chapter 4

Porter walked the route with feet like anchors. He was crying and holding a bandage to forehead as if his very insides were melting. Collie and Upton followed behind him each on horseback. The cemetery was in view. They would reach it in a few short minutes. The plot of land stood upon a hill overlooking the town not too far away. As their procession was near breaking from the town line Collie saw an old woman outside of the bank staring at Porter and then to the deputy and sheriff himself. He looked back at her and tipped his hat. She shook her head and crossed herself religiously. Her weathered face had surrendered to rivulets that ran through the skin forming a map of having lived through all sorts of times regardless of their nature. When she finished signing she broke stare and turned and walked opposite the sight. Collie ran a hand over his own face and then kept on riding.

Upton was holding his pistol. "Sheriff, I'm sure you got the proper notion of justice here, but I'd like to be kept informed."

"Upton, why don't you go ahead and put that piece away."

"Sorry sheriff, I just ain't too comfortable escorting prisoners when the destination ain't been revealed."

Collie kept his watch on Porter as his deputy spoke. "The destination is the cemetery yonder and we're not escorting a prisoner as far as you know."

"Pardon?"

"What I'm sayin' is that he's not a prisoner because he didn't shoot no one." Upton looked perturbed. "You said yourself what Bollard told you. Morgan Nutley shot himself in the throat accidently when he pistol whipped our man here."

"It just doesn't feel right having a body and no one accountable for it."

"It ain't supposed to feel right, but that's the way it is. We can't hang a man for being stupid. Porter there's a repeat offender and woulda got a neck stretch some time back if we could. But this situation here's an occurrence we simply need shake our heads at and deal with."

The deputy snickered. "I reckon you do got the right notion here not telling him his consequence yet." Upton holstered his piece. "I mean he looks like hell right Tim?"

"Surely does."

The two lawmen rode behind Porter and he never once looked back. With each ineffectual step, the gravesite seemed to add three more. He took his hand off of the bandage and it remained glued to his wound. Sweat dripped and burned his retinas. His shirt was tainted with two different bloods and the perspiration made his clothes an extension of his own skin. He wiped his nose with his shirtsleeve and the mucus transferred to his arm. "You ain't gonna bring me outside of Little Creek to simply shoot me are ya Collie?" The words clawed through his throat. The sheriff gave no answer. "I mean I know I'm at fault here at least partial, but he hisself did the shootin'. Blaming me for that is like killin' your dog cause a wolf ate your chickens."

"Keep walking Porter," Collie said.

"Now godammit I wanna know what's in store. I got words that some oughtta hear if you're gonna put the lead in me."

"We're gonna put lead in you if you don't shut that mouth of yours," Upton yelled, a tonal shift from Collie. The sheriff made no remark or gesture toward Upton and the three men finished their march to the graveyard silently.

When they reached the top of the hill, they on horseback dismounted and Porter fell to his knees. A small cloud of dust formed beneath his legs and it was quickly stirred away by the intruding wind. Collie walked with his gun away to the fallen man. "Get that shovel out the pack," he said to Upton.

A middling tree with limbs like talons grew center the cemetery and the sun blazed through it projecting emaciated shadows over the headstones, scratching for souls that had long since vacated. Collie squinted at the sun and then down to Porter. Upton handed him the shovel and Collie dropped it on the ground. "What the fuck am I doin' with that," Porter said staring at the tool.

Collie's shadow invaded Porter. "You need to dig the grave," the sheriff said.

"I ain't diggin' my own grave. If the law don't wanna do right and hang me proper, then it's on them to dispose of and break their own sweat doing it."

Upton wore the expression of a confused man, but Collie stood tall and impeccable. "The grave ain't for you."

Porter raised his head. "You want me digging for the sunnabitch that cracked my head?"

"Healin' out don't seem like a probability for Nutley whereas I reckon it might have some effect on you," Collie said.

"I ain't doing it," Porter said and he spit on the ground.

Collie's jaw clenched and the bones protruded in his face. From behind he heard Upton cock his pistol. He gave the deputy a halting signal. "The hell you ain't." There was abhorrence and fire in his voice. "You have the opportunity to get off easy here. You think other peacekeepers about this land would bother to give a damn what drunken degenerate shit like yourself would have to say when he's covered in another man's blood and that other man happens to be dead? I know most of them and they'd surely be sooner inclined to let you nibble on the end of their gun barrel or drop you with a noose 'round that ungrateful neck of yours." He paused and called behind him. "Deputy Smith."

"Yes sir," he said caught off guard.

"There was a Sioux attack last night in the outskirts?" Upton stared bewildered at first. Collie turned and raised his brow to him and then saw that the man understood the fiction.

"Yes sir. Deputy Wells rode out last night to reconnoiter."

"How far," Collie said.

"Oh not far by horseback," Upton answered.

Collie focused on Porter who was still kneeling. He crouched next to him. "You ever seen a Sioux attack?" The wind spoke between the words. "Gone hand to hand with the red man? It's fascinating really. You never see the perpetrator of the first kill. One in your party usually ends up falling with a spray of blood and you either hear a shot or nothin' but a slight rustle in the brush. Three or four more tend to fall depending on the size of your party before the first pistol leaves the holster. Then the savages storm down one after another from all sides and the picture disappears in smoke. The sound of hell is everywhere and your imagination covers the scene. You see if you're lucky you take a bullet and close your eyes for the duration. But chances are you don't die right away. There's pretty good odds that you get stuck with a stone made weapon deep in the flesh." Collie patted his own shoulder when he said this. "And sometimes when the heathen sticks you, he gets close enough for you to feel his breath on your face and he pushes the blade in 'til it scrapes the bone. They fight like hell they do. You see them peel the skin off the tops of heads. Man or woman doesn't matter. Even children if the mood catches 'em right. Now and again the skin pulls back easy like bed linen. But when it don't, you'll hear it in the scream 'cause sometimes they do this before death, and the last look in the eyes of those at the receivin' end comes across like they were at odds with the devil himself." Collie then stood up. "Deputy, you fine in town by your lonesome for a few hours?"

"Ready as always sheriff."

"That's real good. I may be takin' a ride out to the woods with our man here. It may take time getting out there, but the load will be lighter on the way back."

"Oh Christ," Porter said from the ground.

"Or maybe Porter, you might wanna reconsider this mornin's events in your head and realize that a man died from your words. Your finger may not have even grazed past a trigger, but his blood's on you for the wrong reasons. And maybe you'd go as far as to even thank Deputy Smith and myself for our kind intentions in regards to our handlin' of said events. Maybe you could do that, and then dig the hole for him who wouldn't be dead if you hadn't run your mouth. Maybe these things could happen."

Porter reached for the shovel and hesitated to stand up. He was full of grime and appeared more like the occupant of a grave than the digger of one. Collie and Upton walked to the horses. They watched as Porter excavated the appropriate site. The sun moved across the sky and the shadows of the tree's claws grasped at ghosts in other directions. The two lawmen stood silently like pillars for the most part, never bothering to sit in rest.

Upton viewed Sheriff Collie, whose hat brim now shaded a portion of his face. "You know he's had his head in that earth this whole time. Ain't bothered to look at us once."

"You're surely right Upton. I'd venture a guess that he wouldn't cast his sight in our direction again any other day either."

"You may be right sheriff." The three men remained at their posts until the job was done and then went in the directions they best saw fit. With their backs now to the cemetery the lawmen reentered Little Creek without words and approached their station with a disquieting essence.

Chapter 5

The piano downstairs bumped painstakingly at the door of room three without answer from either inhabitant. The stranger could feel the laughter and boisterous prattle scurry across the floorboards as his feet buzzed irksomely from the sound pollution. He sat silently in the chair watching the girl sensually peel the clothes off of her body. He removed a book of matches from his pocket. His appearance was a combination of machismo and dapperness. His stark white hat contrasted his black vest and jacket and sat on the arm of his chair peering unmistakably through the vague light of the room. He lifted his foot and sat cross legged before striking the match.

The whore flashed her eyes from the bed at the sudden flicker from the darkened corner. He brought the flame close to his face and the end of the cigarette ignited an orange glaze at the tip apparent in the duskiness. "You liking what you see mister?" she asked, now horizontal on the mattress. She was still adorned with a slight bustle and garters atop each stocking. The stranger, preoccupied with his own actions did not commit to an answer. "Mister, you want me to keep going?"

The stranger made no eye contact with the woman. She saw the illuminated cigarette tip glow richer as he sucked in the tobacco. He exhaled and the smoke cunningly departed his lungs. He nearly stopped his breath and the fumes slithered upward past his face. He continued the exhale and quietly puffed his lips to form smoke rings. The grey reptilian vapor collided with itself and pirouetted up along the walls, dispersing and thinning above him before disappearing as if by its own will. He sat and watched the process as the whore's cackle continued to exist. "You want me to strip mister, or you gonna smoke that cig all night?" she said.

"I never asked you to strip," he said without moving and the cigarette brightened again. "That was of your own accord."

"Well I'm sorry mister. I've just never been in no transaction here where the buyer didn't want the ride he paid for." She sat up on the bed.

The stranger glided his head from an upward angle to directly face the woman. "They say patience is a virtue. We'll complete our transaction in due time."

"I didn't mean to offend you mister, all's I wanted to know is how I'm supposed to be getting you off?"

"There's no need to worry about that. I'm not offended." He took one last drag on his cigarette and then held it between his thumb and forefinger and he let the charred air cloud around him. He gently dropped the cigarette on the floor in front of him. It fell and he uncrossed his legs and stepped on it. He leaned forward from behind the hazy darkness and the woman could see his face for the first time. He was freshly shaven with a prominent chin and chiseled jaw. He cocked his eyebrow up toward his black hair, slicked and parted to the side and then whittled an impressive smile across his cheeks. The woman remained sitting, but her posture lightened at the sudden change in demeanor. "You find this interesting? The work you do?"

Her brow furrowed in misunderstanding. "Interesting?"

"Yes interesting."

"Whorin' isn't interesting," she said shaking her head.

"Then why do it?"

"Money isn't free."

"Working solely for money takes the wonderment out of life. It becomes the singular purpose causing all else to fade into the background. It is truly a sad state of affairs when one cannot enjoy the work they do."

"Well I've known a lot of women in my days in the same line as me and I can't think of a single one that took any joy out of this other than the payment."

"The payment." He leaned further. "I saw quarters downstairs through the hallway past the bar."

"Yeah, so?" she said, beginning to become disinterested.

"Is that the women's quarters?"

"Yeah we sleep there."

"Does the lodging come out of your end?"

"No, it's part of the deal for working here."

"Then what do you do with your payment?"

"You asking me how I spend my money?" she said rather angrily.

"Dope?" he queried.

"Shit mister, I didn't come up here to be interrogated. This isn't any business of yours. Now if you ain't gonna pay or have no need for snatch, I need to go back down and find myself a customer with the proper agenda for this establishment. Then maybe I can get that payment that has caught your fascination." She stood up from the bed and bent down to the spread garments on the floor.

"Don't go," he said almost whispering. She continued the move so he repeated louder. "I'll pay." She stopped moving. "I'll pay. Please stay." She stared at him unconvinced and he picked up on her feeling. He reached into his pocket opposite the matchbook and pulled out a roll of money. He did not uncoil it, but rather placed the roll on the arm of the chair accompanying his hat. "I have the money here. Please have a seat and stay."

She sat back down on the bed upright and tense. "I've now offended you and I'm sorry." There was great life outside of the room. "I'm sorry. I was rude with my questions. I tend to overextend my welcome in regards to conversation. I find other people to be quite captivating and I found you particularly bewitching. I take it as an oddity that a beautiful woman like yourself does not have a line of suitors at her step each moment of the day."

She unsuccessfully attempted to fight back the smile. "Well heck mister, you're the first guy in here that ever called me beautiful."

"You must be joking," he said.

"No sir. I gotta confess something to you."

"Well this is interesting indeed," he said playfully.

She giggled. "When I saw you sitting there all handsome and proper, I was thinking that I would've done you for free. And I surely haven't ever said that before, not even to the other girls or had the thought cross my mind. Most fellas, I mean customers, treat us not much different than the horses they came in on, but you have a flattering way about you. Kind of noble like."

He exhaled through his nose and removed the smile. "I sincerely appreciate you saying that. It concerns me to hear that about the other men though. I suppose that's why I questioned your motives previously about working in this profession. Subjecting yourself to such negative treatment is a shame."

"I guess we have to use what God gave us," she said.

"Indeed."

"If you wanted to come near me I could show you exactly what he gave me." She lowered her head with a 'come hither' stare and pushed up the cleavage from her bustle. "What do you say to that mister?" She paused with a questioning expression. "What's your name anyways."

"Why don't we just keep it at mister. Revelations often lead to disappointment."

"Well alright," she said puzzled and then grinned. "Why don't you call me Guinevere if we're being mysterious?"

"Guinnevere is a fine choice, wife of Arthur. Undoubtedly noble," he said distantly.

She lied down on the bed lifting one leg to remove her garter. "Come on over here mister and I'll show you my ladylike qualities."

"You'll use what God gave you?"

"Oh absolutely," she said low and desiring.

He turned away and looked at the window across the room. Then he sat back in his chair as if to remove himself from the conversation. The shadows in his corner again engulfed his body and he recurrently crossed his legs. "What God gave you," he said pondering her phrase out loud. "Is that to suggest that that is all he has given you?"

"What? You at talking again?" she said.

He began tapping his finger on the arm of the chair. "Is that to suggest that that is all he has given you," he repeated softly yet sternly. "A womanly figure and nothing else? Or do you think it possible he awarded you with greater qualities and you yourself chose to abandon them or ignored setting out to ascertain them in the first place? It pains me when people make no attempt to know themselves. There is so much to explore about this world of ours, which is to say that each of us is our own world. A multitude of worlds crashing into one another and each is more than slightly different and the fragileness of each world is apparent. Ours are worlds that do not endure, and we have the power to end other worlds and that is the ultimate power in existence. We can constantly discover new and mind bending things about our nature and the possibilities of our nature. For one to stop looking or ignore the aspects of one's self puts me at great unease."

He rose from the chair and crossed the room to the window. The woman recoiled when he drew near and then got up to leave. "Mister I don't understand what you're conversing at with yourself. I got a mouth to feed and I'd as soon let you keep your money." She pulled her dress up from the floor and began refastening it. The stranger peered out of the window and spoke.

"I'm sorry Guinevere. I'm sorry for my digression. And I'm sorry for insinuating previously that you lacked patience for it is superficial now that you most certainly employ this virtue."

"Well I surely don't at the present."

"But you do even now. I am unsure as to how long you've been in this establishment and I assume you will not tell me now, yet your time continues to reside here. You collect payment from each customer that enters you and then you spend or save the payment depending on what you see fit. If you do save your money, you probably establish a time frame or a monetary amount for a goal. And when you reach this goal you will be free. However like so many, when the goal is obtained it calls the bluff of the maker, and is postponed in hopes of reaching a new goal not far from the first. It is true of most everyone. People spend most of their life waiting for moments that they let willingly pass. They wait for their own inevitable demise. That is the one universal equalizer to mankind; the existence and knowledge of an expiration on each soul. That is why you remain here waiting for what is coming."

He caught her reflection in the glare of the window and turned fully in her direction. She placed the shoes on her feet and headed toward the door. She opened it only to have it blocked inches from the frame. The stranger's foot closed the gap between the door and the adjacent wall. The woman was startled and he pushed the door and bolted it shut.

"What are you doing?" she said and reached for the door handle frustratingly. The stranger struck her with his elbow near her temple and unconsciousness overtook her. The force of the blow made her slam into the wall and she collapsed to the ground like an ancient unkempt building. He stared down at the body and saw her skin was bloodless. He backed away from her body and stepped back over to the window. The night sky stretched over the town and he nodded at it with admiration. He unbuttoned the shirt cuff of his left wrist and rolled the sleeve up his forearm. The flesh on the under part of his arm revealed a family of small burn marks like a string of beads all in a row. Those closest to his hand were a muted flesh tone and each became richer as they ran further toward his body.

He left the window and proceeded to his chair in the corner. The Bowie was now unsheathed. The blade cast no glimmer in the dead light and he placed it on the cushion. The stranger removed the matchbook from his pocket. The tip changed from red to black. The flame empowered that corner of the room and his eyes stared through the flicker at the faux Guinevere lying on the floor. He brought the match near his face and doused it with his breath. With no averseness to the result, he completed his ritual and watched on as the family welcomed the new addition.

Chapter 6

When Deputy Virgil Wells arrived at the Sheriff's office in Little Creek, he entered to see his boss and fellow deputy sitting slumped and alone at their separate desks like two opposing islands. Collie's head rose at the deputy's homecoming, but he revealed no elation on the matter. Upton's head rose as well and he gave a welcoming nod before inviting another sip of coffee.

"You boys at a stalemate?" Wells said with little inflection.

"Takin' in the quiet," Collie said.

"I's up in the hills on the outskirts on account of the shooting last night."

Collie sipped from his mug and placed it on the desk. "Upton mentioned it. You find anything?"

"Damned odd." Wells placed his coat on the rack and relieved himself of his gun belt before making way to his desk. "I went up there to reconnoiter after the shootin' broke out and I's up there through the night and the better part of this mornin' as you likely noticed and I couldn't find one damn thing, like the whole event took place and evaporated quick as it happened."

"Sioux you reckon?" Upton said.

"Could've been, but can't say likely or not." Wells let out a sigh and then sat. The rims below his eyes were ashen and his face wore two days' worth of stubble. "Coulda' been road agents too, though I'm inclined to say no without spotting ransackin'. Even could've been a few nice travelers met with some wolves or such. Or maybe just the two biggest guys in town proving who's what. This place takes a toll regardless."

Upton looked intrigued and anxious. "Still could've been those heathens though. They ain't looking to relent 'specially on us towns so close to Yankton and the railway."

Wells smirked admiringly at the man's statements. "You got yourself an active mind Deputy Smith."

"I'm just sayin'," Upton said.

Wells yawned and began to speak through it. "What you're saying is possible, but what I'm saying is that it ain't necessarily that way. And if we go into looking at every shootin' takes place in the miles around this town then we best go on praying for a pair a' wings on our backs to navigate us."

Collie leaned forward in his chair. "Why don't you take Upton back up there tomorrow in the full light?" Upton looked at the sheriff and Wells at Upton. "Take a look with fresh eyes." Upton was excited at the prospect.

"Well I suppose I could if he thinks he's ready," Wells said.

Upton was about to speak only to be cut off by Collie. "He's ready. You're ready right Deputy Smith?"

"I-I'm ready," he answered off guard.

"He did good today," Collie said.

Virgil measured up the young deputy. "Today?"

Collie swung his chair and faced the newspaper on his desk. "Got a statement from the barman after a shootin'. Controlled a troubled looking crowd after such an event. No nerves in the fingers and no misspent lead."

Wells's eyebrows pinched his nose in confusion. "Shootin' today? I been gone one day. What the hell did I miss?"

"Upton will tell you later on your ride. He's got a grasp," Collie said and drained his coffee.

"Then I am impressed," Wells said slowly. "Our young deputy was called upon to perform a duty and he did so outright without regards to fear and he stood upright in the name of duty. I says that deserves a drink." He pulled a whiskey bottle from his drawer. "Tim?" Collie nodded and Wells pulled out two glasses. "I believe I'll have to get myself another glass today." He poured the liquor into each glass and handed them to the men. Wells kept the bottle uncorked in his hands. "I myself don't have many poetic inclinations so I leave this opportunity of silence here to our own Deputy Smith."

The young man smiled. "Oh it ain't right to cheers yourself."

Wells laughed. "Hell I'm not askin' you to gloat on yourself. Why don't you tell us the rendition a' how you got your name." Upton's smile dissolved.

"Aw shit you already know that." Wells let out a boisterous laugh and Collie could not help but crack a smile. "And you never woulda if I hadn't been legless with whiskey my first night.

"I know we know it, but I damned sure like hearin' it," Wells said. "Remember that this job entails listenin' to orders."

"Sheriff?" Upton said.

"I'm afraid he's right. Without leadership, man reverts to chaos," Collie said. "You better listen to your senior."

"Alright fine. But I'll say it once more as the last time. Then it disappears like this drink here."

"Drink it first and repeat. Just speak up," Wells said. Upton did not hesitate. He put the whiskey back in his throat and held out his glass for another.

"Goddammit," Upton said. The other two looked on in anticipation, Wells more so. Upton cleared his throat and began. "Keepin' short as possible." He cleared his throat again.

"Quit your damn stalling," Wells said loudly through his chuckle.

The young man sighed and Wells filled his glass again and swigged from the bottle. "I was born to Catherine and James Smith twenty years back," Upton said with his nose to the floor. "They both had their minds set on me bein' Jack or Jenny as a girl, but when my mother went into the havin' stage, she saw me and my pa saw me and they figured that Jack Smith was too common a' name and I was too darn special of a boy to be so ordinary so they named me Upton on account of them thinkin' I was special."

A howl of laughter erupted from the other two men. Wells leaned over and slapped his own leg. Collie wiped away a small tear. Wells made an effort to be upright again and tried to calm himself. He held the bottle of whiskey out to the deputy. "Here's to our man Upton and to James and Catherine Smith. The sheriff and I thank them for sending us their special boy." They all laughed again including Upton. He tried to mask his pleasure with an arm in front of his face, but the others saw through his attempt and he quickly gave it up and allowed the humor to get the better of him.

The men drank one more shot a piece and the laughter subsided after a short time. "We best put this bottle away so we can keep our worth," Wells said.

"Agreed," Collie said and handed back the shot glass. "You look damn tired Virgil. Why don't you head on home and get some rest. Come on back in the morning and take him with ya' out there."

Wells signaled agreement. "Yeah some sleep'd do me."

"Upton, why don't you take a stroll round town and then get home yourself. Stay fresh for tomorrow," Collie said.

"You ain't ridin' out with us sheriff?" the young man said.

Wells observed Collie and then turned to the deputy. "Let's get on outta here like he said. We'll see ya' tomorrow Tim." Upton raised his hands in befuddlement and grabbed his gun and followed Wells out of the door. Collie saw the door shut and heard their boots thump across the porch before crunching on the grainy road ahead of them.

The sheriff sat in his chair silently looking at the door for a minute before leaning forward to rub his temples. He closed his eyes and continued the motion without any noticeable relief. He rose with his mug and refilled it from the pot across the room. The coffee was lukewarm, yet potent. He stared through the window of the station at the main drag of Little Creek. The wind picked up and delicate pillows of dust floated about before ascending and disintegrating in the sunlight. He looked on as the residents carried forth like worker bees, hindered only for a short time by the interruption of the morning's event. He stood there drinking coffee and saw Mrs. Purnell from down the road slide gracefully across each business front; she in her white dress, the outfit sweeping the ground making her a ghost through the airborne flakes of earth. He watched as the wind then stole her hat and toyed with her its retrieval. He looked on as two young boys chased each other with wooden pistols. The boy in front tripped and collapsed causing the other to fall headfirst in the dirt next to him. Their motions quick and airy like two straw stuffed dummies. When they arose, Collie saw the whites of their eyes accentuated by their swarthy faces. The second to fall gave words and pushed the other boy down.

He watched as the two boys scuffled near the hitching post of the bank prior to being snatched up by the shockingly overbearing arms of their mother. He watched as Mr. Fairclough stood outside of his shop assembling a coffin from freshly fallen pine. The hammer fell and rose mechanically on the mark each time, thus swiftly establishing the new home of Morgan Nutley. Collie sipped his last inch of coffee and viewed the passing of a saddled rider-less horse trotting down the way, unmindful and uncaring of its surroundings. To say it had a purpose would have been accurate.

Collie absorbed the scenes. They checkered through his mind and he shook his head in amusement. He placed his cup down and dressed himself with his jacket and hat. He reached the door and stopped abruptly. The star on his chest removed with little force. With his mouth agape, he exhaled two short breaths on the unpolished metal and rubbed it on his sleeve. The shine was still faint, but improved. He reattached it to his vest. It was alien against the black material, but not against the man. He pulled open the door and exited the building to lend a hand.

Chapter 7

The road leading out of Little Creek was beaten and weathered. Within it lied the hopes, histories, and asperities of travelers from years past. An unchanging route would lead journeyers near seven miles to Yankton. Though ancillary paths wiry and uncertain loomed ahead and coiled out in the distance on each edge of the passage forming the branches of an omnipotent and ever reaching timber. Each branch represented a gamble over tribulation or prosperity.

The deputies rode parallel with their backs to the town. Their horses kept a mild trot and the men's upper bodies swayed in unison with each step of the animals. Their route was introduced with a steady incline leading past the cemetery. As they went by it, Wells spoke. "He'll be interred there?"

"That's right. In front of that mound of dirt," Upton said.

"So he shot himself," Wells asked.

Upton coughed and spit on the ground. "Yes sir. Musta' had his thumb near the trigger when he hit Porter with the butt."

"Huh. Don't strike me as unusual to subtract one drunk from any particular situation. Usually on someone's intention though."

"Yes sir."

"Damned unfortunate," Wells said. "Collie's kept town tranquil for a time now. Must've been broken up about it."

"He seemed it. Not that he'd say anything on the matter. His voice gave way. Started talking about a Sioux massacre to our man. Threatened to drop him unarmed up in the hills. I can't recollect each word bein' out of earshot and all, but his speech seemed to test 'em both."

"What happened to your man?"

"Haven't seen him since. Tim said we couldn't arrest a man for not killin' the dead one. We left him at the grave site and rode away. Sheriff said Porter'd be punished enough once he sobered being he hadn't supposedly ever killed a man before. Says he was a drunk, but sure no killer."

"Sounds like a scene," Wells said.

"Surely was. Felt odd not to arrest him at first, but he broke down when he was diggin'. We saw him and let him to it. I knew then and course Tim knew that what we done was just."

"It's a rare occasion," Wells said.

"What is?"

"It's a rare occasion that you feel just."

Upton looked to say something, then opted not to. He spat again. They pushed forward for awhile in silence. The trail opened up beyond the incline to a flat and barren landscape. The hills kept watch on them from the left and to their right the land was stretched and dry like an old drum head. A vast expanse of grass filled pastures waited ahead pastoral and welcoming.

"Ridin' up here, it seems God couldn't make up his mind," Virgil said. Upton took notice of the pictures around him and agreed. "We'll be turning off up here."

Upton snickered and shook his head. "I figured them fields up there were too good to be true." They approached the desired trail. It curled slightly backward from the road and up into the hills before disappearing in the terrain. Sharp and jagged rocks protruded sporadically from the ground like teeth on the fringe of the path rendering the comment more tangible. "This one here, Virgil?" Upton said. Deputy Wells barked the order to his horse and the two men spurred their animals up the way.

The secondary trail dipped out of view from the main drag as did the deputies when they reached the first series of hills. The land became bumpy beneath them and the mounds spawned wild growth in each direction. Solid trees stood proudly while young wildlife either scattered or continued mindfully their business unscathed by the human presence. "You reckon we're on the right course?" Upton said.

"Shots seemed to come from this direction," Wells said.

Upton's body tensed up and he spun his head in succession. "You don't think we'd be walkin' into any kinda ambush right?"

"We most definitely are," Wells answered.

"Jeeeeeesus," Upton said concerned. He strung out the word quietly to himself and cocked the pistol in his holster.

Wells turned and raised his brow at the younger man. "Boy, what in the hell you doin'?"

"Getting' ready. For a jump that is." He removed the gun from its holster and pointed the barrel in the air.

"I figured you being so special and all that you'd be smart enough to know when I's foolin'." Wells waited a moment and bellowed a laugh from his stomach.

"Aw hell," Upton said. He frowned and withdrew his sidearm.

Wells calmed and wiped the sweat from his forehead. "Shootin' occurred over a day ago. Can't imagine those who done it had an inkling to stick around."

"They wouldn't probably."

"Let's push on," Wells said.

They strode in a concentric circle for the better part of an hour. The air was crisp despite being weighed down by the humidity. Their conversations were limited and seemed so without effort. The beauty surrounding them at points was staggering and the growth was rich. Aside from the cutting trail, the land was virtually unharmed, a testament to the idea that nature would prevail if ignored. There was small game in each direction and had the men been so inclined, they could have feasted well on rabbit or squirrel. The deputies were a small part of the earth around them. Its grandness could have opened up and swallowed them as a minor conquest.

They continued their search to no avail. Upton conveyed frustration and he hunkered down on his horse with fatigue. Wells lacked emotion to the younger man and alluded to perseverance with his own silence. They continued to move. A short time lapsed and a vulture shrieked announcing itself in the sky above. "Buzzard," Wells said.

"I can't see nothing, Virgil." The sun peeked through the trees, but gave way to hindered vision.

"Watch for shadows through the thicket. Sounds about near." Both men craned their necks and remained in position. At Wells's words the sun was blotted and they lowered their heads. "'bout twenty yards thataway you reckon?" Upton nodded and they rode to their mark. They halted, but stayed mounted.

"For our own satisfaction we best find something dead or dying," Upton said.

"Wishin' for such ain't advisable."

"Sorry," he said. "I-

"Quiet," Wells commanded.

"What is it?"

Wells dismounted and loosely tied the rein on a tree limb. Upton observed Wells's activity and kept his hand on his pistol. The older deputy walked past Upton with a look of curiosity. "I don't believe you'll be needing that," he said. "Come on down off that horse." Upton did as ordered and sidled next to him.

"Whatcha see?"

He did not answer and sauntered forward with Upton at his back.

Upton rolled his eyes in disappointment. "Shit. How did I not notice that."

"It's alright. Missed it myself yesterday." A large swarm of flies clustered in front them zipping erratically over a dead fawn. They took on the shape of a moving black oval, their buzzing pierced through the air and would have been intolerant if amplified.

"Smells like a slice a' hell over here," Upton said covering his mouth and nose with his hand. "It's been there some days."

"It ain't our casualty."

Upton moved forward, leaned down, and waved away the flies with his free hand. He gave the incapacitated animal a once over. "Buzzards and such been at it a while. Not much meat left. Wouldn't likely shoot a deer small as that and not take the meat or the hide. Skin's pulled back near the legs and up the center. Torn away. Maybe coyotes. Not sure what killed it though. Can't tell from these here remnants." He got to his feet and backed away from the carcass. "Coulda been wounded and starved. Maybe got by a bobcat. What you thinkin' Virgil?" He turned and saw Wells had his pistol out. He reciprocated the action.

"Stay calm," Wells said without making eye contact. He was staring straight past the body of the fawn at a thick patch of shrubbery some twenty yards ahead.

"We okay?" Upton said.

"Up ahead in them bushes next to the tree. Them look like a pair of boots to you?"

The young man squinted and cocked his pistol. "With a pair of legs occupying them."

"That's what I thought. Move forward, gun up."

"And you?"

"I'm behind you."

"Don't seem fair."

"You're a bit more agile," Wells said and winked. They walked forward stealthily. Their feet crept over the ruinous bark and twigs that littered the soil. The fallen items popped and cracked under the weight of their legs. The pair of boots in the distance idled.

They arrived within ten feet of the sight. Their field of vision increased as they approached and they saw the backside of two full legs wedged up against the tree. "Deputies approaching," Upton said in an authoritative manner. "Don't move too quick or we'll shoot." They moved forward yet again and the full body came into view. He was covered with leafy branches and pieces of wilderness like the land itself regurgitated upon him. He was lying dead with legs perpendicular to his body as if he was propped up sitting against the tree and then fell over.

"I'm not sure he can hear you deputy," Wells said putting his pistol away.

"Agreed." Upton did the same. "You recognize him?"

"Not yet. Help me out here." They each put hands on the dead man's arms and propped him into the sitting position. They brushed away the dirt and leaves and threw the branches to the side. The body's position against the tree was an act of brevity and he began to fall to the side again. "Stubborn fella aye? Let's put him on the ground." They pulled the corpse from the tree and laid the dead man on his back. Layers of earth were caked on the face of the corpse. Sweat acted as an adhesive as the man's forehead and cheeks were blackened with dirt. The dead man's torso was plagued with blood. His shirt and jacket were crusted and stained a shade of brown with the metamorphosis from the dark red taking place over the hours. The deputies stood over the body and observed. "Got a gunshot there to the chest. Looks like the heart. Another one there in the lower gut. And another one up in the shoulder. I don't see any bullet in the tree. Must've moved him into the brush here."

"Got a graze of the arm here on his right too," Upton added. "They sure shot the hell outta this one."

"Surely did. Two more evenly spaced near his ribs." Wells said and he looked up at the sky.

"How come you reckon nothin's been at him?"

"Preoccupied maybe? They say critters don't like dark flesh."

"He one of them Mexicans?"

"Can't say. Maybe."

"Damn they shot the hell outta him."

"Not too good shootin' neither," Wells said returning his gaze to the body.

"What you make a' this?" Upton asked.

"Whatta you?"

Upton waited a moment and answered. "Hell, I'm thinkin' that rampant gunplay don't lead to aiming. That's why we got this scattering of the wounds. I reckon there was probably more than one shooter."

"I'd say that's right."

"It's got to be. Our dark skin's got it too many times for it to be one shooter."

"How's about one guy with two guns?"

"Didn't think of that."

Wells noticed a change in demeanor. "I's just thinkin' out loud. Only met a pair a' two gunners in my day, neither of whom could aim worth a shit. I'd say we're looking at two men plus."

"You recollect the sounds that night?"

"Vaguely. It's a distance, but it started with a hollow shot like a shotgun and followed with the small cracks a' pistols probably. What's your notion?"

"I say our man here drew first and set the whole thing off, but he missed and the others musta' finished him off."

Wells pondered it. "I'd say that's right. They tried to cover him up, but didn't fully bury him. So either they didn't care or were in a hurry."

"I wonder what the hell they was doin' up here."

Wells heard the man, but didn't say anything. He stepped away from the body and scanned his surroundings.

"What you say sparked the whole thing, Virgil?"

"Guessin' the intentions of others isn't usually an exercise of use." He paused a beat and shook his head. "Shit out here he coulda got shot for breathin' funny. Or him being of his color mighta' disagreed with his conference and they not taking kindly to said disagreement led to his bullet ridden demise."

"So what's our move here?"

"I suppose we gotta give the dark skin here proper burial. With the heat being what it is sooner is preferable. Let's get 'em on the horse."

They strained to sling the inflated body over the saddle. They placed him face down and his limbs draped heavily over each side rendering the body into the slack shape of the letter U. Wells took a rope and restrained the corpse to the animal. It let out a burdensome snort and Wells rubbed its nose in gratitude. He threw a blanket over the body concealing all but the lower half of his legs. He pulled the exposed rope with his fingers to check the tightness. The action confirmed his abilities and they returned their horses to the beaten path.

"If you ride slow he shouldn't move," Wells said.

"Jesus that boy was heavy." Upton's shirt was patchy with sweat and he removed his hat to look at the sun. He squinted and shut one eye. "Didn't seem this bad before we lifted him."

"That's the sad truth," Wells agreed. "We'll head back and let Tim know what we found."

"We goin' after them who done it?" Upton asked eagerly.

"They be long gone by now I reckon." He saw vexation grow in the young deputy. "Not every crime goes punished. You're best to learn that now. And who's to say this man didn't deserve what he got. The way we figured, we had him opening fire first. Might've been a matter of self defense for them others."

"I know, but dammit this is close to home. We're not but a mile or two away."

Wells sighed and rolled his eyes. "Upton, we don't have to like it and we ain't supposed to. These things occur and they've been occurring since God dropped us here. Killin' each other is natural as takin' in air, like the idea was here waiting eager for us for centuries, just waiting to be plucked. And it was plucked for sure. Almost immediately. And it'll keep on happenin' long after we're gone. It's probably so that God don't even notice much anymore and if he does, he likely shakes his head the way you do when a child cusses. Our kind seems meant for this, and people like us clean up the mess and wait for the next one. You can live proper yourself, but that don't change much outside yourself." His voice trailed off and the wind stole it. He turned and struck a gaze at the mark where they discovered the body. "Your deeds don't matter here and you're a fool if you believe that. Ain't nothin' a man can do to prevent the nature of another. It turns out a way and that's the way it is." He mounted his horse and started down the trail.

Upton remained. He watched the figure of his comrade diminish gradually as he made his way further. He came to and put his foot in the stirrup swinging the rest of his body over the saddle, careful not to loosen the ties on the corpse behind him. He avoided using his spurs and commanded the horse forward with a click.

The distance between the two men as they traveled the road to town was meager yet conspicuous. There was no chase in the strides. Upton allowed Wells his space while slowly covering the ground between them. Frequent steps of the horse brought reanimation to the limbs on the lifeless body though carefulness averted its jettison.

Wells looked back and caught the young deputy in his peripherals. He turned ahead again and allowed words to part his lips for the first time since his leaving. "What the hell you waitin' on back there?" The hooves behind him awakened and Upton approached his side in a few short moments. "I couldn't take sittin' here with you burning a hole in the back of my head."

"You flatter yourself old man." Wells made to ignore him. "I was back there contemplatin' on what you said."

"Oh you were, were you? Contemplatin' huh? And what'd you come up with?"

"Well I don't mean any offense, but I can't accept what you said," Upton said politely. Wells cocked his brow. "You said I don't have to like it and I damn well don't. But you said that folks can carry on and live a proper life to no effect except what effect it has on them. I say that doin' right by yourself and others can change outcomes a' what you call certainties. Shit I have to believe that and I know I ain't the only one. Them evils out there exist and they exist as what they're called because we exist as their opposite. They ain't nothing but ordinary if we don't counter it."

"And you think we counter it?"

"Hell yes we counter it," Upton said.

"And we counter it by livin' right?"

"That's right."

"You think you lived right this morning? With the dead man in the bar and the not quite shooter prospectin' the grave?"

Upton paused contemplatively before answering. "That turn of events was handled in the best way fit I reckon. Collie's the planner on it, but I would've backed his play had he asked me."

Wells finally turned and looked at the man before speaking and the man looked back at him. "And if you was alone, what'd you have come up with?"

Upton nibbled on his lower lip and shifted his gaze to the air, searching for an answer. The open sky was still and close mouthed. "I like to think I'd have been able enough to do the same."

Wells puffed through his nose. "Upton my friend, you are a true idealist."

"An idealist?"

"That's right. Don't worry none. That's a good thing."

"I'll take it. I have the mind to say you won't change yours though."

"I'd say you're ideal enough for the both of us. At least for now."

"I guess I'll take that too."

The sun continued to beat down inspecting the situation on high. The two riders came within view of Little Creek, only a number of minutes before it embraced them and they released the animals of their burden. "Sunnabitch," Upton said wiping his eyes. It's like it singled us out down here and its throwin' heat spears at us?"

"Heat spears is it?" Wells said. "Sometimes Upton I wish you weren't such a man of words."

"I say a drink'd do me just fine 'bout now."

"Ain't too early I suppose," Wells said in agreement.

"No I think I'd shrivel up to nothin' if I drank whiskey right now. Some water would go right though."

"If it's water then I'm buying." He waited a moment. "Water," he said to himself. Wells hooked his head to the right at his own comment and changed expression like a man struck by a fist.

"What's the matter there Virgil? You cheapin' out on a free expense."

"I think I'll have to owe you one." Wells angled off their route and brought himself to a one eighty opposite Upton.

"Everything alright?" Upton asked, concerned.

"You and your goddamn words itchin' at me." He crept slowly forward and Upton made the move to follow. "No you don't. I need you to go back to Collie. Give him the dark skin and tell him what we found as well as our theory."

"And you?"

"I'm back in them hills. If my notion pans out I'll be in Yankton by nightfall."

"For what purpose?"

"I'm settin' to make this right. See about our shooters. If I ain't back by night tomorrow, you send someone the seven miles down the way to see about my burial."

Upton opened his mouth to talk. Wells spurred his horse and flew hurriedly away from the young deputy before the words could reach him. "I sometimes wish you was a man of words," he yelled. He stared for a moment at vacant road and the dust trail thinned and settled. "Alright then," he murmured to himself. "Bout time we get back. Whatta ya say?" He lightly slapped the rein and rotated to his destination. With a dust trail behind him, he swiftly entered town with the uninhabited body flailing behind him.

Chapter 8

Billy Maple cussed under his breath when he picked up a splinter off the hitching post, yet the word hung in the air long enough for the female passerby to snatch it. "Sorry mam," he said with a wink and he tipped his hat to her. The woman scoffed and walked away unknowingly allowing for Billy to view her hips dance back and forth with each small step. A large grin stretched across Billy's face, his complexion a shade darker than the average man. He looked at the sky as if to say thank you to the almighty. "Damn I could use myself a piece," he said to the two men on horseback next to him. "Hot damn I'm jacked."

One of the men, a swarthy fellow with a gritty essence entered the stirrup and swung until his feet hit the ground. He had a towering presence, a hulk who might have been at home swinging axes in a Roman arena. Billy, who was facing the entrance of the saloon, turned and saw the brute's actions. Unconcerned by the man's prominence, he raised his voice. "What in the fuck are you doing Barton? Get back on your damn horse."

The second man remained saddled and answered for Barton. His pigment transcended white and delved into the realm of what some might have considered clear. Flecks of dirt infested the pits in his face, shrapnel from riding behind the others, and gave the appearance of a full grown Dalmatian. "Hell Billy we figured we camped outside of town last night just like you. We deserve ourselves a piece of what's coming." His voice contained a smoker's rasp.

Billy maneuvered himself back onto the street between the two men. His words were masked by a harsh whisper. "Jesus Christ Hix. Keep your damn voice down. We don't want no damn lookers knowing where it was we came from. Our business is ours and not for you to go announcing each time we set foot in population."

Hix leaned over the horse awkwardly until his ear brazed the horse's mane. "Hell Billy I ain't tryin' to get us nicked. I'm just sayin' it'd be nice to do a whiskey and a whore quick 'fore we set out."

"He's right Billy," Barton interjected. "We damn sure earned it."

"Now you both listen here. I ain't sayin' you didn't earn it. Course you did. But on account of the beaner we dropped in them woods, we gotta stay sharp." Billy huffed and rubbed his chin.

"No one's gonna find the beaner. And even if they did, no one'd see fit to avenge a Mexican," Hix reasoned.

"No more Mexicunts for us Billy," Barton added.

Billy cracked his back, tired of the conversation. "You think I don't know that? It's not my fault he drew. Son of a bitch got greedy and we gave him the hell he deserved. But no one here is changing the plan. Who does your planning for you? The thinking? The money you earned ain't been earned without me at the head. Remember that next time you find yourself shooting words in the middle of a street. You two sons a' bitches will get the lead put in you without me." He peered at them. "No one changes the plan. You got that?"

The two nodded almost discouragingly. "No one sees us together. When employees of the train we ripped start talkin', they'll be looking for a trio, which in our case includes the conspicuous presence of one with ghost-like affectations and a fuckin' bull moose walking on his hind legs. Won't take any law man who lays eyes long to realize it was us that done it. You two spread and you can have the run of the town minus this here saloon and that hotel across the street."

"We don't get a say?" Barton asked.

"No you goddamn don't. How a mind like yours doesn't keep you walking in circles is a marvel of science. I planned it then and I'm still planning. We divvied out our shares after our actions. You need to take that as an act of trust. If you can't do that, we'll have a different conversation." Billy caressed his Schofield with the tips of his fingers. He gestured a look that demanded agreement and the pair appeared to concede. "Five miles east, two days I'll see ya." He backed away careful not to turn. "Every goddamn time we have this same talk," Billy added. He stepped onto the saloon porch and kept his feel on the gun. Barton mounted his horse and Billy saw its legs buckle.

"Sorry Billy," Hix said and they trotted off down the street.

Billy kept his watch on the pair. Neither of the men returned a look and his body eased as they drew further. His fingers rose and he used them to adjust the belt on his pants. "Goddamn," he said to himself. He turned and headed for the saloon doors. A man of some age was sitting on a bench to the right of the entrance. He appeared looming despite his slender build.

"A man without companions is a questionable sort," the slender man said as Billy neared.

Billy stopped for moment in front of the man. He grinded his teeth behind his closed lips and squinted, overlooking him. The slender man did not shrink or allude to any cowardice. He simply raised his head to meet the stare and dropped it back again to the street. Billy unclenched his jaw. "Minding your own business is a staple of American fuckin' society." There was no reaction from the man on the bench, fixating on the street, simultaneously unaffected and entranced by the goings on around him.

"Then again," the man began, "companionship can be a man's downfall." He made no acknowledgement of Billy's remaining presence. "Pictures of life in front of me here. The cast in the foreground shifts in constant and the rest stays unchanged. Pictures of life."

"Crazy old coot," Billy mumbled and he entered the saloon.

The bar was occupied enough for midday while not giving way to the term lively. Billy scanned the area. They were all men, hunkered down around five or six tables. Whiskey bottles adorned the table tops, most were near half empty and judging on the consumers, would hit the finish mark shortly. The patrons with their tattered stained clothing alerted themselves to the newcomer. The air became heavy, weighed down by the beaming judgment of the onlookers. Billy saw himself being sized up by each pair of eyes in the room. He hitched his thumbs to his belt and gave a nod to the group. He maintained an idea of supremacy and stature despite the polite gesture. A few nodded back though most returned to their business.

The bartender removed the towel slung from his shoulder and wiped the area where he saw Billy approaching. "Can I get you something?" the bartender said flatly.

"Yeah I'd like me a beer," he said pushing his torso against the bar.

"A beer?" the bartender asked.

"There some kind of problem?"

"It's just not a common order. That's all."

"Not a common order. Well I'm a man who goes against the grain."

The bartender huffed and poured a beer from the keg. He pushed the mug forward. Foam erupted from the top half and crept over the side of the glass. "Not too cold," the bartender said. "No ice left."

Billy scoffed at the mug in front of him. "If I was someone else would there be ice left? Is this something of a personal nature against me?" He looked from beneath his brow and sculpted a mean feature of disapproval. "You know shifty cocksuckers often have a tone. A tone much like the one you displayed. I'm not one for tones."

The bartender looked away and twisted the edge of his mustache. He appeared rattled at the altercation. His skinny frame covered by an apron seemed like a slight wind would blow it over. "I don't know what I'm to say," he stammered.

Billy observed the man's actions. The bartender compressed himself, stepping backward like a scolded puppy and looked over his glasses back at Billy. The man behind the bar swallowed the lump in his throat only to have it re-emerge.

A smile slit the corners of Billy's mouth. "Hell I was only foolin'," he said in a tone that may have echoed insincerity. He reached forward across the bar and slapped an open palm on the man's arm.

"Jesus Mister," the bartender said.

"I'm sorry. Suppose humor ain't my regular strength," Billy said.

The bartender took a deep breath and rubbed a hand over his shorn head. "You still want this beer then?"

Billy laughed to himself for a moment and it was not contagious. He settled. "I want a beer alright, but not that beer. I'm supposed to drink it, not shave with it."

The bartender retracted the mug. "New pour coming out."

Billy turned himself to see the actions of the bar. "And put it in a pint this time. I could sure use it." He angled his elbows on the counter behind him and put his full weight into a lean. He heard the gentle pound of the pint hit on the wooded bar.

"That'd be fifty," the bartender said timidly.

"Fifty?" Billy said.

"On account of it bein' a pint and all."

"Seems fair." Billy reached into his pocket which afforded an audible jingle. He pulled out a small pile of rustic coins. He sifted through them without much thought and laid a dollar fifty in change in front of the barkeep. "For the misunderstanding," he said.

"Thanks mister," the bartender said brushing the money into his hands.

"Otis," Billy said. "Name's Otis Cuttingham." He looked to the bartender who was now focused on his register. "Say it." The bartender paused for a beat and stood confused. "Say it," Billy said louder?

"Say what?" The bartender asked, with a jump to Billy's volume. "Say your name?" Billy nodded. "Otis. Your name's Otis," he said and then stood as far away as he could.

He took a rather large, but slow sip from the brimming glass in front of him. It was that of the air temperature to the touch and Billy scrunched his eyes in mild disapproval. "Goddamn," he said. He gulped another small portion and then let the weight of the pint lower his arm to the counter. He again turned his back to the barkeep. He kept a relaxed yet alert posture. The population of the bar paid each other no mind and carried on in their separate ways with their separate business while Billy's stare cut through the small crowd scanning the entranceway like a sentry at his post.

***

Tim Collie entered the reverend's tent to find the man lying on his cot with eyes ajar. He clutched a black leather bible in his hands near his chest and made no acknowledgement of his visitor. He conveyed a hopeless appearance pale and despondent like a daisy petal thrashing down a river. His body was without tremor, but curled into the fetal position with protective vulnerability. Collie gave the reverend a moment and then cleared his throat when his presence went undetected. "A visitor," the reverend said at the sound. He moved his weighty head to the tent flaps and saw the sheriff standing hat in hand. "Sheriff Collie it is."

"Afternoon reverend," Collie said.

"Good afternoon my good sir," he said. He sat up and let out a groan. "Please forgive my informalities for I did not see your entrance." His suspender straps rested on his lap. He put an arm through each and snapped them over his shoulders.

"That's alright. Is this a bad time reverend?" Collie said.

"I'm afraid apologies may be an order depending on your query. I seem to have been afflicted with the burden of stomach sickness, no doubt brought on by the ill tasting elk meat I ingested last night."

"Mighta' spoiled in the heat. Have you seen the doc?"

"I have. He explained the very words I said to you only to me this morning. Lying as I was when you came upon me provides the only relief I've gotten since the early hours. All else leads to regurgitation." The reverend saw Collie's satiated expression. "I apologize Mr. Collie. Please forgive my cavalier words as a passing transgression brought on by illness."

Collie held his hands up in ease. "There's no need to keep apologizing to me reverend. It was I who intruded on you and believe me, I'd love nothing more than to leave you to your comfort, but unfortunately this is a call of business that requires a timely resolution."

The reverend leaned forward in an attempt to stand and then leaned back again promptly sitting. "A calling for Morgan Nutley I presume."

"That's correct reverend."

"I observed the commotion from afar this morning though was unable to make a complete inquisition without my body's upheaval."

"I take it most have heard by now."

"Most likely. And I take it all lawful matters were handled properly by yourself as the authority. I never knew the man well. Has he any family residing in these parts?"

Collie ignored the first part and shrugged at the second. "I did some askin'. It seems he mighta' had a brother out in Montana. No one could recollect his name or actual existence. 'Round here seems he knew little outside of the bottle and the poker table."

"A testament that our vices can overpower our sociability," the reverend said.

Collie pushed out his lower lip in thought. "Anyways, I've commissioned a coffin from Mr. Fairclough and I was hoping that you would preside over the funeral. His body's been keepin' cool by the creek. I was hopin' to get it done rather sooner especially in this heat and to prevent waterlogging."

"I understand."

"Bein' you're sick and all, I'll understand if you're unable to give words."

"On the contrary Mr. Collie, I don't believe the good Lord would hinder me from speaking for another over his final resting place." The reverend inhaled three long breaths and blew the air out of his ringed lips. He stood unsteadily.

"Are you sure you're able reverend?"

"I believe the Lord has righted me. Will there be anyone speaking for Mr. Nutley?" the reverend inquired.

"I don't suppose so and my thinking is that attendance will be slim."

"But you will in fact be in attendance."

"Correct."

"I see. Yet you yourself would not have voice at his resting?"

A sign of discomposure elevated in the sheriff. "No," he said.

"Very well," the reverend said. "Have you any thoughts on the reading for Morgan?"

"I'll leave that to your department," Collie said, replacing his hat.

"Perhaps a passage from Second Corinthians."

Collie began to back out of the tent. "I'm sure that what you choose'll fit just fine."

"It speaks of that which we cannot see in ourselves as the eternal and everlasting. Inward man is renewed day by day while the outer will perish with every passing breath." With each syllable the reverend uttered, his ailment was cast further into submission. He was upright and walking with only the slightest discomfort.

"That's a good choice," Collie said anxiously.

The reverend pushed the upper flap of the tent aside and left its confines. Both men were outside squinting in the angelic light. "Or perhaps based on character, Enter ye in at the strait gate: for wide is the gate, and broad is the way, that leadeth to destruction" the reverend said. Collie listened and rotated himself in the direction of his office. The reverend continued, "And many there be which go in thereat: because strait is the gate, and narrow is the way, which leadeth unto life, and few there be that find it," the reverend said.

Collie distanced himself from the holy man. He angled his head at the reverend as he finished speaking. The words seemed to sting as he paused in silence for a few long moments. "About an hour then to the hill?" he said quietly.

"I will be there Mr. Collie."

"Thank you," he said and strode away with his shadow following him stretching toward the place of religion.

As the sheriff station came into view, Collie noticed the attendance of only one of the deputy's horses. He swallowed hard at the body strapped on the back. He worked up a full run and burst into his office. Inside Upton jumped and the water from his glass ejected kinetically on himself and his surroundings.

"Upton, Jesus," Collie said.

"I damn near drowned myself sheriff," Upton said brushing the unabsorbed beads of water from his shirt.

"Where's Virgil?" Collie said concerned.

"Headed to Yankton last we spoke."

Collie appeared rattled and breathed heavy, making an active attempt to slow his nerves. "And who is on the horse?"

"Dead Mexican we found in the hills. Mexican at least we think based on its features."

Collie removed his hat and wiped his brow. "I must confess I concluded the worst outcome when I saw the horse outside bearing an ill equipped body." He motioned at Upton's newly saturated appearance. "Sorry 'bout that."

"No worries here, Tim. I'da done the same," Upton said.

"Gimme a minute to catch myself here," he said and ladled a portion of water into his own mug. He chugged it and ran a hand over his lips.

Upton placed his glass down. "I arrived near half of an hour ago. Where you been at?"

"I commissioned the coffin for Nutley and went to see Reverend Morris about employing a sermon over his grave."

"How'd it all come out?" Upton asked.

"With the coffin bein' simple and the lack of respecters, it'll all be on the hill in under an hour. What's that you mentioned about Yankton?"

Upton went over the details of their discovery in the hills and Collie listened. He spoke of the Mexican and how they ascertained his position as well as their theories about the turnout. "We was just ridin', him pissed about my disagreein' with him. He was with me, next thing I know he's changin' direction without explanation. Said he's going to make it right."

"What prompted the turn?" Collie said.

"I can't quite recollect." The young deputy rubbed his chin in search of an answer. Collie huffed. "I believe we were talking about havin' a drink upon our return. Said it was too early for whiskey and he offered to buy me water, cheap bastard. That's about when he decided to abandon his homecoming and rode out with haste," Upton said. The sheriff said nothing and thought for a moment. "I recall that bein' it," Upton added.

"You two reckon the Mexican and those that done him in to be thieving types?" Collie said.

"I'm not sure I'm qualified to make that guess."

"What do you really think?"

"Well I think that I can't think of many reasons a group of men camp in the hills and one of them ends up leaded other than the fact that they got some sorta' undesirable agenda."

Collie seemed to agree. "What were they to have robbed out there though?"

"It's just a notion, but it might not be far off if Virgil saw fit to ride out so quick without one of us. You said Virgil was keen to movin' after conversing about water. The hills where you found the Mexican ain't that far away from a water depot for trains. It's a short ways over the hills next to the tracks, not a mile from where you were."

"I don't know it," said Upton.

"It's used for trains en route to re-supply if needed. Most towns don't have 'em and the trains jerk the water from streams, but I suppose Yankton installed one in an attempt to modernize. The tracks run mostly parallel with our road from here to Yankton which would make the depot near a straight shot west of here as the crow flies."

"Shit," Upton said. "You're thinkin' the dead Mexican's group robbed a train when it stopped for water?"

"It's a possibility. Lot of money come out of the Black Hills. People headin' to Yankton with the railroad, tradin' in gold. Sometimes they'll hide the transports on lesser trains, hopin' they don't get robbed, but the riches transfer often with the finds increasing. Anyone scopin' those trains could see fit to rob it."

"They musta' dropped that Mexican up there over money."

"Money brings out the animal in people."

"So then what is Virgil's purpose in going to Yankton Tim?"

"I'm supposin' that he would first scout the depot and upon any discovery of our idea he would go to Yankton to confirm the reported robbery."

"Yeah, but that gang would be halfway to Cheyenne by now."

"I don't doubt it," Collie said. "But these outlaw types seek a haven of some sort and often need a fix. I don't reckon they'd come to Little Creek, hence the incident in the hills, but it's best to keep our guard up. Hell there might even be a picture of these sunbitches up the road. Virgil'll get it if there is."

"What we supposed to do in the meantime?" Upton said.

"We wait and hope they don't show here."

"Goddamn," Upton said.

Collie let out a breath and sat in his chair. He noticed Upton's discontented expression. He reached for the paper and opened it, masking himself to the deputy.

Chapter 9

The incandescent light of the hotel lobby muted in the stairwell and the whore's fragrance fluttered delicately in clouds above Billy, him shattering through them as he followed. He stopped for a moment. The woman continued and Billy leaned until his hands hit the stairs in an angled push up. He considered the sight of the woman's undercarriage. He twisted his neck and snickered.

"What's that laughing?" the whore said.

"I'm just admiring the view."

"You're gonna see it soon enough. You coming or not?"

Billy pushed himself and went upright. "Most definitely honey. I'm as excited as you're pretending to be." He hurried himself and keyed open the door.

When they entered the room, Billy brushed past her and surveyed the area. He walked briskly around, sticking his face against the window. He saw the view of the muddied road and saloon across the street. He squinted and witnessed the man on the bench near the swing doors, lips moving as they were when he left. He turned and saw the whore observing his actions.

"Is as you see fit?" she said.

He puckered his nose into the air. "Musty in here. Last occupant musta' been a goddamn dust farmer."

"I told you we could've used the rooms across the way."

"Nah, this here'll do me fine." He tugged his boots off without having a seat and nearly fell over in the process. "What you waitin' on beautiful?" He continued undressing. He tossed each article on the floor. When he was down to his one piece he hopped in the bed and drew down the covers. He sat up watching her in anticipation.

"Don't get too excited or you'll shoot early," she said.

"Don't you worry none about me. Let's speed this process up."

He watched her as she mechanically removed her clothes, stripping like it was pure business. "How old are you anyways Otis?" she said.

"They teach you to poke at the fuckin' affairs of others in whore school?" he said. She quieted, the silence mounting in the room. "I'm just foolin'," he said. "What you want to know that for anyways?"

"You just got a young face, that's all. I don't bet that you're my youngest though. Might've been a youngin' of fifteen as I recall. But you got a youthful face."

Billy rolled his eyes and then brought them right back at the girl, now naked. "Well I ain't no teenager I assure you that. I'm old enough to be able and willing. He held up the covers next to him, inviting her in. She doused the light and slid into the bed. "You're a good lookin' woman," he told her.

"Thanks," she said plainly.

He slithered his hands under the sheets and grabbed her by the hips. "It ain't that I don't like talkin' to you, but I'd just as soon get what I paid for."

"No argument here," she said.

The bed creaked like an old barn door when he rolled himself onto her. The room was black enough to mask her garb of disinterest and the jubilance rattling through Billy's face. He pulled his one piece down enough and prepared to enter her. "Ready or not," he said and then he performed, able and willing.

***

When Deputy Wells entered Yankton it seemed to emit life from every conceivable nook and angle as if the town itself harbored its own dynamic soul. There was commotion on the streets and the alleys off of the streets, inhabited by peddlers, merchants, residents, and those passing through. The people, mostly whites, moved through with an attitude of business as usual. It had a pioneering spirit and an energy that most other places could not possess.

Wells rode in unnoticed taking in the surroundings, not quite marveled, before hitching his horse. The first building he went to was the livery. He spoke briefly with the hand, a gruff fellow, about any new boards. He asked if he recalled putting up a group of horses for some men, most likely four or five who had a short term stay in town. The hand produced a lack of interest and memory and Wells in a brutal effort forced himself to move along without altercation.

He continued his inquiry through the focal stretch of the town. He formulated a pattern to his attention, looking out for wanted posters and sketches of undesirables that would have been nailed on the walls of certain buildings. His search came up short in the business sections aside from a penciled drawing of a bearded man wanted for the rape of a woman in Yankton. Wells gnarled his lower lip at the visual and then walked on.

He saw in the distance the office of the law, solitary and last in line as the final structure before a person's departure. He directed himself toward it, keeping an observation on the continuing population around him, careful not to stare. He carried on until his attention was caught by a man, elderly in appearance, though his age would have been hard to determine so squalid and used. His clothes were tattered and stained with a possible compilation of caked mud and excrement. There was a half torn sign of the Confederacy stitched onto the sleeve of his upper left arm. He wore an eye patch, flipped up displaying an insignificant naked chasm to the world. Wells's regard was magnetic. The Confederate's tough leathery eyelids hung purposelessly, a singular passageway to nothing, not even the rationally darkened soul of a man who may have committed or been victim to the horror and atrocities of an unfortunate life. The Confederate sat alone. His lonely eye passed across the people and met the image of Wells. The Confederate bared his teeth in a false smile directed at the deputy. Wells became aware of his encroachment and pulled himself away.

He entered his destination. The lawman, noticing the tin on Wells's chest, greeted him politely. He asked of the news and happenings in Little Creek. Wells explained without much detail the event of the accidental shooting and arrived at the point of his visit. He asked of any reports made from the rail company or monies lost en route to or from Yankton. Wells was validated to hear that a train was robbed two days prior and relieved of a large amount of money, cash most likely exchanged for gold mined in the hills. The lawman went on to explain that the employees of said train made the report hours after the robbery. They were hogtied and left next to the tracks at the water depot a few short miles away. They eventually freed themselves and made their way back to Yankton.

The lawman went on to explain that the employees were unable to discern any significant facial characteristics since the perpetrators wore burlap sacks over their heads. They claimed that the bags made them look like scarecrows, mangy and unkempt with vacant holes in the bags for their eyes. The report continued that it was a trio of thieves. Only one of them spoke throughout the entire robbery and he said little and said it well. He had a regular voice, with no specific qualities. The only useful thing the sheriff had heard was that one of the men was large enough to be noticed as large. The other two were "normal looking", as the most verbal of the employees noted. The lawman was told another fact, though he explained to Wells that he didn't much take stock in people's memories under duress. The conductor of the steam train said that the hand on one of the "normal looking" men was of ghostly white flesh, ghostly enough to see the blue vein superficially rising through the upper part of his hand. The conductor added that it was a short glance, but he remarked on it vividly.

Wells felt out the mental state of the employees. He was told that the men were a working class caliber and they explained their story in a matter of fact manner. The men were each slightly bruised and a bit bloodied, but none to an extreme or beyond. They were pistol whipped and punched initially to receive a point and one man received more for his tone. The trio and especially the talker in the trio carried out the scheme like old hands, never faltering or bickering in front of prisoners. And in fact, the talker even thanked the employees subsequently after threatening violence to them in regards to what would happen if they told the law about the crime. The lawman ended his account and Wells thanked him. He asked the deputy to pass on his best to Tim Collie, which Wells said he was sure to do. Before hitting the exit, Wells asked of the nearest saloon. The lawman pointed him in the right direction. Wells removed the tin from his chest and left the office.

***

Billy stared through his murky pint of beer, stained with the fingerprints of past drinkers. He was seated nursing his drink. The bartender stood behind the counter, careful to keep busy around his patron as to avoid conversation. The saloon doors opened and then skimmed past one another before coming to a complete close. Billy looked back sideways and saw Wells inspecting the mostly vacant room before approaching the bar.

He glanced at Billy on his way up and took some coins out of his pocket. He put two on the bar. "Whiskey," he said.

"Whiskey it is," the barkeep said and poured an ounce into a shot glass. Wells downed it and asked for another. The bartender obliged. The whiskey disappeared and Wells dropped the glass to the counter again. He held his hand to the keep to say he was through for now and then stood silently thinking with his head hung. "This place's vacancy don't ring true with the exterior."

Billy grabbed his pint and took a long slow sip. He produced a sour look after swallowing and tapped the glass to the bar. "That's something I don't reckon I've had in some time," Wells said to him.

"This sure ain't the place to reacquaint yourself," Billy answered, watching the bartender as he said it.

"I don't suppose it is," Wells said politely. "You in deep, friend?"

"That your clever way of askin' if I'm drunk?" Billy said sternly.

"It was more a question of tolerance, that bein' ill tasting and all. Sorry to hit a nerve."

A smirk crept onto Billy. "I was only fooling. And to answer your question, I am not in deep. Any man that can lose himself in multiples of this piss water is a braver man than me. Probably even you, though I'm not at liberty to make that judgment at the present."

"I'd say you're probably right," Wells said. "Virgil Wells," he said and stuck out his hand.

Billy seemed caught off guard. He wiped his right hand on his pant leg and brought it to Wells. He cleared his throat. "Amos Cuttingham," he said and they shook. The bartender was facing away from the men, drying out a glass with an already dirty rag. His ear caught the sound of "Amos" and he attempted a move closer to their conversation.

"You in business?" Wells asked.

"Was into freight for a time, but now I'm passing through. I guess you could say I'm looking for what's out there." Billy spoke and was careful not to let his eyes stray in search of an answer.

"Ain't we all." Wells reached back into his pocket and pulled out more coins. They clanged and spread across the counter in a perfect row. He pinched his shot glass with two fingers. "Barkeep."

The keep retrieved the whiskey bottle. He poured the shot and kept a watch on Billy as he did it. "It's only fifty sir."

"I know. Get him another," Wells said and motioned to Billy.

Billy appeared surprised at the gesture. "I certainly appreciate it, but I ain't much for drinking. I'll probably nurse this'n here long past your departure."

Wells stuck out his lip, understanding. "Leave it there anyway barkeep, for a change of mind. Keep it yourself if he don't want it."

"Yes sir," the barkeep said. "You let me know when you're finished Otis," he said, emphasizing the name. Billy took another slow sip from his pint, oblivious to the comment. Wells leaned in to see if he heard right. He watched Billy take his drink and then he looked to the bartender. The skinny man behind the counter slanted his eyes at Billy and then raised his shoulders to Wells as if to indicate that he could not vouch for the man with the pint glass.

Wells kept Billy in the corner of his vision, observing without staring. The young man kept a grip on his pint. Wells noticed Billy's youthful appearance coupled with a confidence embodied by those who have been around, been around the kinds of places that can alter a man. He saw Billy's firm grasp on his glass. He looked at his own hand, the one he shook with, and wiped it on his shirt.

"You through here Virgil?" Billy asked.

"Ain't decided fully," he answered. "Liable to fall off my horse if I keep at it."

"On the way to where?" Billy said.

"Little Creek," he said and waved off the bartender as he picked up the bottle of whiskey.

"Small town down the way?"

"Yep."

"Been there once or twice myself. Then again I've been to most places in the territory once or twice. Just can't bring myself to venture further I guess." Billy chuckled and raised his glass. As he did, Wells turned himself and saw the trivial browned blood stain crusted on the bottom of Billy's shirt cuff. Populating near the waistline of Billy's blue shirt were further dried spots of what might have been blood. Wells let out a long breath and felt tension echo down his spine.

"What'd you do in Little Creek?" Wells asked.

"Uhh," he sighed, "Let's see." He wrapped his fingers on the bar like it was a piano. "Went with freight. Hardware for your boys there and some pre-cut lumber as I recall. Couldn't unload it much though. Town full of workers. Haven't been there in some time."

"Good thing. Rough territory in them hills," Wells said.

"I'm told."

"End up dead in those hills if you're not careful."

"True enough."

"Fella could end up shot in them hills as early as yesterday."

Billy straightened though his voice kept cool . "Feller shot yesterday you say?"

Wells nodded. "Cyclical these things are. There's no end to violence. It hibernates. And when it wakes up it's hungrier than before. What amazes me is how surprised people are when it happens. It's all a wheel."

Billy snuck a look and saw the interrogative nature on Wells's face. Billy leaned back and pushed his shoulders as close together as possible. His back spoke with a few muted pops. He then turned on his barstool to face Wells. "You are a man of truth Virgil," he said and smiled.

"How 'bout you Amos? You a man of truth?" Wells said, accenting the name.

Billy puffed out his cheeks and exhaled slowly. "True enough when I need to be." He hesitated a moment and shook his head with a smirk. "Amos." Wells nodded. "I'm not sure if it's the beer or the whore that went to my head. Tell me Virgil. What business you in?" Wells reached into his jacket pocket and pulled out his star. He palmed it onto the counter. The star cast no reflection in the dank room, but remained prominent against the rustic darkened wood. "And what is it you think you know Deputy?"

Wells fixed his sight on Billy and spoke calmly. "I know you gave me a name that don't match up with the one you gave the barkeep. I know you're here in town with no certain business to attend to. I know you flinched when I mentioned the gunshots a' yesterday and I know your shirt's carrying blood on it." Billy maintained his stare at Wells. "The kind of blood that might come from pistol whippin' some poor bastard in the face before you rob him. And I bet you a burlap sack with holes for seein' that if I checked you or the horse you rode in on, I'd find at the least a small stack of money stashed aside from the piles you mighta' buried cause whorin' and drinkin' ain't free."

Billy continued to stare into the eyes of the deputy. He kept his mouth shut for the duration of the speech and now allowed for smile to creep through his cheeks. "You sure seem to know a lot." He turned and let out a chuckle to the bartender. "I should've known that seedy asshole'd sell me out. Called me Otis didn't he. You done said that loud on purpose. Shit." Billy rubbed his forehead with his fingers like he was massaging a pain. "Must've lost my charm on that one."

Wells righted himself from the bar. He stood straight with his hands at his sides, allowing the tips of his fingers to caress the butt of his pistol. Billy dropped his head and continued to rub it gently with his eyes closed. "You were right about one thing," Billy said.

"Oh yeah?" Wells said with close observation.

Billy lifted his head slowly like it weighed more than average and reopened his gaze at the deputy. "The wheel," he said and turned back toward his beverage. "I've just never been on the downswing before." He reached for his pint with his left. The beer was warm to the touch, a victim to the temperature of the room. He gradually brought the glass to his lips while he dropped his far hand to the pistol on his waist.

Wells noticed the younger man's shoulder drop slightly enough to be put to use. As the deputy blinked, Billy made his move. The glass stayed raised to Billy's mouth and with little motion he jerked the pistol from his holster. The flash of the gun metal caught Wells's eye. The deputy reacted and drove his open palm hard into the bottom of the pint. The lower rim of the glass rammed into Billy's lips. It split the corners of his mouth establishing a false smile inked with blood and large chunks of glass shattered into the roof above his tongue. The blood flow seemed on call and occurred instantaneously.

Billy's gun hit the ground with a thud and he brought his hands to his face. He delicately fingered the outline of his wounds and then hurriedly removed them. They came away soaked with crimson. He clenched his jaw and then opened his mouth to spit. Splinters of glass trickled out amidst the heavy stream like small boats and then fell into the pooled collection beneath him on the floorboards. "Wha the fuck id you oo a me?!" Billy yelled. He stood up, tightened his fist, and took a swing at Wells. The deputy raised his forearm defensively and blocked the blow. Wells then landed his own punch under Billy's chin.

The hit drove Billy's teeth together and forced his tongue against the roof of his mouth. When it did, he felt the shards of glass plunge violently into his tongue and he let out a scream with his mouth closed for a moment. The sound was grim and then he struggled to open it without pain. Fighting through the hurt, he was able to force it agape and then he shoved his bloody fingers in and grazed them across his tongue and palate. When he was able to grasp any piece of glass regardless of size, he pinched it and plucked it's embedment like a splinter. He fell to his knees in front of the misshapen pool of blood. He continued searching for fragments while the redness expelled from his wounds.

The bartender bent over the bar. His feet left the ground from his effort. He fell back as quickly as he went up and then bit down on his own finger in agony over the visual. He darted a look at Wells. The deputy slid his boot, toes first over the assailant's pistol and dragged it to himself before picking it up. Billy's blood decorated the hammer and various sections of the barrel. Wells paid it no mind and placed it barrel down into the front of his pants.

Wells glanced at the bartender and he saw the mortified expression in the man's face. It was a face that mirrored pure horror, an opposition to the indifference he had been accustomed to in the many faces exposed to certain violence. Wells turned and looked down upon his victim appearing disgusted and then reached back into his coat pocket. He dropped a few dollars' worth of coins onto the counter. One out of the many refused to remain idle and struck the bar loudly as an introduction to its rapid spin. Wells slapped his hand over it to stop the movement. "I'm sorry for what happened here," he said to the bartender. "I truly am." The barkeep saw that he meant it and nodded through his quivering.

Wells walked a few short paces to Billy and crouched down over him. The man with the youthful appearance had his forehead pressed to the floor in a downward fetal position as he recurrently spit from his wound. Wells grabbed the man by the shoulder, but Billy made no acknowledgement. "It's time to go now son," he said with mild authority.

"I can't ulee u kiwwed my fuckin' mouf," Wells heard, muted from Billy's awkward position.

Wells rose and stood over him. "Right yourself Amos." He waited a moment. "Right yourself and stand up. I'm bringing you with me." Billy rolled over to his side. The blood had formed tributaries like thick external veins stretching across the sides of his face. He was a man defeated, but not destroyed. He rolled to his back and stared up at the man who beat him. There was no light around Wells's face and his eyes were blackened by the shade from the brim of his hat. Billy saw the deputy's hand near, but not holding his pistol. He attempted a deep breath. There was a wheeze in his intake like a broken fireplace bellow and he turned again to his side, coughing up blood.

Wells looked on with pity and extended his hand downward to the broken man. Billy coughed again and ignored the gesture. He maneuvered himself onto his rear and pushed himself off the floor with his own volition. Wells stepped back. "Stay in front of me and walk out them doors," Wells said motioning to the entrance. Billy stared through the deputy, his eyes like a distinguished fire. He took his sleeve to his face and considered the blood on his clothing. The barroom was silent around him. The few patrons observed like an audience caught up in the last act of a play. Billy scanned the room and said nothing and then walked forward through the doors in time to see the depleting sunlight dip behind the mountain peaks in the distance. Wells exited the doors on their outswing and followed watchfully behind.

Chapter 10

The campfire was a beacon amidst the heavy curtains of the newly minted night. The stranger caught it refined in his view as the sun gave way to the moon and the black spread itself over the land. He had traveled the expanse aimless in a way, trotting over not one path, but instead moving like tumbleweed, a passenger in the wind, unhinged to any specific purpose to himself or the greater. The flames were at a distance and they grew larger and slowly as his horse pushed forward and the dark dirt waltzed beneath him.

As his arrival began to propagate, he saw a silhouette announce itself. It was that of a man, hat adorned and seated cross legged in front of the fire. The outline revealed the shape of a rotund and husky man. The stranger scanned the area around him. He blinked hard in the directions outside the flames. His pupils dilated and he rubbed his fingers across his fastened eyelids. He pulled back softly the reins of his horse and the animal halted. The stranger drew his gaze one last time upon the silhouetted man, a black on black painting all but invisible to any outsider if not for the kindled blaze afore him.

The seated man became alert to the disturbance and called from the ground. "Who's there?" he said, body stiffened. "Make yourself known or I'll be forced to use that which I have with me." The stranger watched as the man changed position, reaching behind himself to grab in his belongings. He was oafish and sloppy like a snail removed unwillingly from its shell. He squabbled on the ground hawing. It was a pathetic blur of a sight to the stranger, who was resting his head on his hand amused and observing from his saddled perch. The man righted himself on the second try and crouched ready-like. The stranger glimpsed the rifle in the firelight and nicked his horse to move forward. "Announce yourself," the man commanded.

The stranger rode forward and the mild conflagration teased and traced his features. He gracefully raised his arms. "You can lower your piece my friend," he said calmly. The man did not and cocked the hammer. "The need for weapons is then and later I assure you."

"Come in closer," the man said. He stood up, the act taking a toll on his body. The stranger flinched as he heard the popping in the man's joints off tempo like a drummer deaf from battle, but playing nonetheless. "I wanna see them palms up," the man added.

The stranger obeyed and moved forward. His hands were still raised. He tilted his head and mimicked a wave with his right. "You should know I'm carrying, but I've no intention of using it. I saw your fire and was hoping for respite."

"Come down off your horse," the man said with his rifle up near his shoulders.

"I need to lower my hands to do that," the stranger said.

The man hesitated. "O-Okay," he stuttered and took aim.

The stranger leaned back on the cantle and grabbed the horn of the saddle. He swung his leg effortlessly over the animal and hopped to the ground in one fluid movement. He was erect in posture and brushed his pants with his hands before bringing them back into the air as he walked toward the man with the gun. "I've done as you stated," he said politely. He approached and the warmth of the fire penetrated his skin and warmed his blood.

"You're white," the man said.

"I am," the stranger agreed.

"What the hell brings you up on a man's site in the damn dark in the damned middle of the night?"

"I had left a town called Monroe off to the east long after midday today. My journey across the trail led me to hunger. I came upon a coyote in the distance and shot it, though me not being one to exact gunplay often missed its vitals and it took to the open. I tracked it over the stretches, but the sun left before I could find it. I was ready to set camp myself and that's when I happened over your fire."

The man's eye twitched before speaking. "You was hopin' for what?"

"I was hoping for fire. Maybe some food if you could spare some," the stranger said with his arms still raised.

The man lowered his rifle to his side and his expression morphed into relief, contrasting the previous notion of vigilance. "Hell I'm sorry for the bustle. These parts, you can't always trust these parts. Thought you coulda' been a damn redskin heathen or some damned criminal agent or some other whatnot."

"May I lower my hands?" the stranger asked.

"Surely," the man said and waved him in near the fire. "Again, excuse my ill temper of before and make yourself of comfort here." He sat back down in his original spot, the ground dented from his back end. He dropped the rifle and situated himself. The stranger kept his eyes on the man and sat near, but not next him.

"The name's Dan," the man said. "Most folks call me Skinner Dan on account of my business."

"Your business?" the stranger inquired.

"That's right. Trader mostly. I trade hides. I hunt them hills and the plains. All over really. I salvage the meat I can for myself and sell what I can carry, but the hides get the top dollar. I gotta keep my trade up. With the increased movement in the territories bringing more folk, my competition increases. Seems by the hour. But I don't reckon I've seen a man with the stock I got. I get it all from elk to bear. Don't know many a man that will tussle with a bear out of straight business."

The stranger gazed at the indifferent stars as Dan spoke. "I don't believe I do either," he said.

"You'd be surprised at the living a man can make sellin' and tradin' hides."

"I can imagine."

"Let me show you this'n here," he said and reached into his pack. The stranger lowered his stare and watched him as his movements mirrored those pitiable from before. "Where the hell is it," Dan said under his breath. The darkness reached out and clouded him as he was turned away from the fire. He continued to meddle with his pack and the stranger was losing patience until Dan reemerged into the firelight wearing a hat made from the hide of a beaver. The creature was skinned, but its head remained intact, resting over the bald dome of the fattened man and the buck teeth mimicked an intrusive bite where a widows peak would have formed. The stranger made no expression for a moment. He stared at the ridiculous sight and then twisted a fabricated smile onto his face.

"That is some talent you have," he said through his teeth.

Dan removed the hide from atop his head. "Goddamn ridiculous looking on the head I suppose, but comfortable they are for certain. I didn't catch your name fella'."

The stranger stared into the flames. "Malcolm," he said. It sounded good.

"Malcolm then. I'd offer you a trade Malcolm, but you look like you'd be interested in other affairs." He took hold of a stick resting near the fire. The end was chiseled to a point and it had the darkened shape of an animal impaled through so that the tip of the stick was visible. He looked over and saw Malcolm noticing the meat. "Can I interest you in some rabbit my friend?" he said, rotating the stick with his hands.

"I would be obliged," Malcolm answered.

Dan pulled the rabbit near to his face, inspecting the roasted carcass. He rubbed his index finger over the charred flesh and then shook it briefly in pain. "Cooked to perfection it ain't. Might be damned close to eatin' ash, but it'll keep you goin' for tonight at least." He pulled the hind legs off of the dead animal. It made a sound like a heavy foot falling on dried grass. "Reach out here," he said to Malcolm who was waiting patiently. Malcolm reached out and took the legs from the host. They were hot to the touch and the grease of the meat moistened his fingers. There was a sting of pain from the heat on his flesh, though he did not wince.

"This is much appreciated Dan," he said and he bit into the meat. The outside was singed and the inner portions had a tough gamey quality, but he swallowed them down in gratitude. "I was wondering if you could tell me the nearest town from here."

"Nearest town? I'd say you're not too far out from Yankton. A bit east of here. That's a known one. There's little Little Creek, though you'd miss that'n on map. Deadwood. I'd say you travel east and hit the main trail you're liable to find what's in store." He stopped and pointed to the stick in the fire. "There's a slim bit more if you'll have it," Dan said before finishing his own serving. The stranger brushed his hand in the air indicating no. "It'll be saved for the morning then," he said and grabbed a skin cloth sack from his things. He placed his full hand into the pack and pulled the bottom until it was inside out. He then repeated the motion over the remains of the cooked rabbit and began to tie the sack closed. His head was hunkered down in concentration. One of the horses neighed and he brought his look back to Malcolm. The stranger had changed positions and was leaning on his side with an elbow in the dirt. Dan saw the empty holster at Malcolm's side and the stranger admiring the illuminated Schofield in his own hands. He was staring at the barrel with a pondering face as if the very weapon held him in a trance. The wind picked up and the burning reflected a departed beam off the stranger's piece and it faintly cut through the night across the area and onto the chest of the fat man. Dan paused a moment and inhaled deeply. The scent of the fire was muted from the breeze and he let out his breath. "It's amazing that man should suffer so much fear over an object so insignificant in size and bow to it and beg and turn another in the name of defense. It is so that I wonder now without that invention how man would have fared in their progress. Though I suppose we'd have stayed warriors in some way or another, killin' each other off with swords and spears. Hell I'd bet we could kill each other with pots and pans if the need struck right. It's easier now with what you're holding and objective and when killing becomes impersonal, it collects from those subject to it whether they're on the receiving end or just privy to the view and impersonality makes people forget their place and makes them entitled to that which they aren't." Dan cut himself off and swigged from the bottle lying at his side.

Malcolm broke off his stare. "Is it your contention that killing has become impersonal?"

Dan drank again and then corked and rested the bottle at his side. "Or maybe I had too much to drink."

"No, please continue," Malcolm said.

"It can get lonely here out under the stars. A man alone in his thoughts can solve all the problems of the world until he enters it again," Dan said. Malcolm kept his pistol in his hand though he held it as if he forgot it was there. Dan brought his eyes to the moon and then to the stranger next to him. "My contention?"

"Yes," Malcolm said.

Dan shook his head and massaged his temples. "Well I guess I was thinking that with the advent of particular combat, and the long rifle, and sharp shooting, it makes it so that killing a man could be as casual as a breakfast order. A shooter of some skill could poke a man from a hundred yards out and then ride away without ever seeing the face of the life he took. And that makes it easier."

"I suppose it would." Malcolm said resituating himself into the sitting position.

The skinner coughed and spit a batch of phlegm off to his side. "There was a time back a few years I stationed myself in the bush in an area populated by all sorts of critters. I had my rifle at the ready and hunkered myself down leanin' on a tree. It was a hell of a spot and I sighted myself some decent small game, but I figured if I could hold out, there'd be something worth waiting for."

"Time enough passed and my legs lost feeling. I got complacent and lowered my gun down and took to leaning on it. I musta' dozed as I watched the squirrels and rabbits scurry past. It's not like me to do that. I woke up later to a stick breaking. I don't know how long I was out, but it was still day and I startled myself by nearly falling over. I remember my eyes weren't quite cleared so I gave em' a splash of water and I looked out and there's this damned buck, not thirty yards out, twelve pointer. Now I've seen myself bucks before, but for this one to be out there just as I rise; it's like waking up in a bed and the woman's got breakfast all ready for ya'. Anyways I lift my rifle up real quiet like and poke the barrel through the shrub in front of me, careful not to spook him. The whole picture, me looking out at it, was just perfection."

"I clicked back the hammer and I remember that sunnabitch lifting his head up. I got anxious and moved my finger quick to the trigger. And this I'll never forget because it all happened in a matter of moments, but it seemed like hours to me."

"Just as that buck raised his head there was a call from behind me like an owl screech. I've heard calls, but this was skewed somehow. I turned my head round and saw nothing. When I swung back there was a mountain lion darting into view like he was slingshotted. He had a black and jagged line of fur over his ribcage like a battle scar. He moved like lightning and I froze up and almost pissed myself. He come right up and tore out that buck's throat with one swift lunge of his teeth. That buck didn't move once 'fore it happened. Just fell over and bled out. "

"My hands were shakin', but I was careful to keep a grip on my gun. That cat stood over his kill for a second like it was basking in glory and then lifted up his head to his surroundings. It was posed like some statue, darin' anything to challenge. The place was silent, as silent as I can ever recall. I stared at that lion from where I was, silently prayin' to the Lord up high to let me walk away. And then mid prayer that cat hissed and tore through his surroundings with the devil's hatred. There wasn't much game around, but it killed whatever it could. He stomped on squirrels and swiped at rabbit. It's face was soaked in blood like it dunked its head in a pool of it. And I just sat there watching."

"When the cat was done and there was nothing left to kill, he paused and looked over the area. I raised my rifle and put him in the sights, but I never pulled the trigger. I don't know why I couldn't do it. That lion reconnoitered what it done and then walked off. Walked off like it had done what it came to do. It didn't eat nothing or drag nothing off. It just walked on. I think about that sometimes. I don't know why I froze up. And I can't fathom what I saw. It happened." Dan sighed. "Ah well," he said and shifted himself a bit for comfort. He let out a chuckle and poked a stick at the fire. "Yeah I'm goin' on and on I guess. It's not often I get a visitor."

The stranger lifted his chin to the air and fire brightened his throat. The night sky was clear and present and the stars sprinkled overhead like so many listeners observing them powerless to the outcome though captivated nonetheless. He fixed his gaze above and spoke as if to the moon itself. "I don't suppose a person should be able to fathom something so intense. That which can be taken by a man is owned by man because he owns the option. Perhaps that's why some can kill without remorse. They become entitled with a false sense of power. Entitled, to use your thought from before. But I'd agree with you about the objectiveness being the problem. Killing is the most intimate thing out there. It's too important to be impersonal."

A line of drool happened from the corner of the skinner's mouth and he mopped it up with his shirt sleeve before bringing the bottle to his lips again. He swallowed down the liquor and wiped his mouth. He chuckled and spoke. "You sound like you mighta' spent some time alone too Malcolm."

The stranger let out a faint laugh. "And I haven't even been drinking," he said.

Dan offered the bottle and Malcolm declined. "I reckon this place and time can coax these things outta' ya," Dan said and laid his head back on the blanket behind him. "Damned whiskey is pulling me down."

The stranger again directed his stare on his pistol. He looked to the fat man who was lying flat with his eyes closed. His stomach shaped a portly hump in the air and would have been comical with a different crowd. The stranger scoffed and aimed at the man. The open hole of the gun barrel stood not ten feet away from its target and aligned with the skinner's throat. The stranger massaged the trigger without fully placing his fingertip over it. He mimicked the sound of a gunshot with his lips and jerked the pistol barrel like it had fired. He laughed to himself and took aim at the man again. "Are you sleeping Dan?" he asked in a quiet voice. There was no response aside from a snore. "I want to thank you Dan, if you can hear me, for the hospitality. I found you most interesting."

The skinner rolled to his side and opened one eye with a slit. "Whas that?" he said almost incomprehensible.

"Good luck out here. In a land of darkness your dreams become illuminated, but in that time it can open the gates to the reality of your nightmares." Dan said nothing in return. The stranger kept aim and his hand began to tremble. He looked up to the moon as if it would offer advice. There was friction between his teeth. His fingertip now eclipsed the trigger. He closed his eye distant from the gun sight and his target came into focus. His hand steadied and he brought his eyes back to the moon. It was crescent in the sky, ashamed. The stranger holstered his weapon. "Sleep well," he said to the unresponsive man, his large belly rising and falling with each breath.

The stranger rose and aristocratically brushed the dirt from his clothing. He peered down at his host and then to the fire and then back once again. The ground accepted his near silent steps as he made his way and mounted his horse. He raised his head to the night sky and the single brightest star presented itself. The stranger then twisted his neck to the side and it spoke with a few mild reports. The sound seemed amplified amidst the calm evening. His match cruised across the coarse strip. It came to life and he lit a cigarette. The orange tip glowed, but the smoke was invisible. He gently brought his reins down upon the horse and he headed east of the site, separating the dark curtains ahead with no effort like he had done a hundred times before.

Dan rose before the sun's first peak, his head weighted and his eyes struggling to clarify the landscape. The clouds hurried across threatening to open. There was no sign of his guest aside from the charred remains of rabbit bones in the now blackened firewood. There was not a footprint or body mark in any of the surrounding area almost as if the wind itself an accomplice had brushed away any trace of the traveler he met in the night. The skinner scratched his bald head and collected his belongings, making haste to clear himself of the impending storm.

Chapter 11

The newspaper was spread on the floor below the sheriff's chair. Collie occupied the seat. His head hung back off his neck like that of a dead man's and his arm was draped directly over the fallen paper. The office itself cast no sound outside of the deepening breaths of the sleeping sheriff. His chest rose up and down peacefully, though his breathing was at competition with itself.

It started near inaudibly, but had since turned unpleasant like it was revving to break through to Collie's lungs. This fight continued for a matter of minutes and then began to crescendo as the snoring ripped winningly through the room. With the final culmination of competing breaths, Collie jolted his head forward and sat up straight immediately. He looked about the room checking for witnesses like he had just committed a crime. There was no one. He wiped his mouth with his sleeve then coughed harshly and cleared his throat.

When he felt like noticing it, he saw the apple pie sitting on his desk breathing steam. Collie placed his hand over the significantly domed good and he pulled it back, his fingers moistened from the heat. "Hell," he muttered to himself.

The chair screeched across the floor as he rose from it. Outside of his window, the top portion of a woman's bonnet peaked into sight, relatively motionless as the person wearing it was sitting patiently on one of the porch seats. Collie shook his head then rubbed his hands over his hair and mustache, grooming himself presentable for the visitor.

As he pulled the office door open, the woman rose from the chair and entered the building. She greeted the sheriff with a kind and genuine smile. "Mornin' Miss Vandenburg," Collie said shutting the door behind her. She moved to the slight, but open part of the room and turned. She stood there with a dissipating smile. Her face was young and pretty, yet roughened. It contained the hints of experience and evidence of things she had seen and been exposed to that many of her age never would in their lifetimes. She was a girl of seventeen though her actions and appearance made her seem older.

"You saw the pie I take it Mr. Collie," she said directly.

"I did. Thank you."

"I'm sorry to have barged in. I did not want to wake you."

"Wake?" he said in false astonishment. "B-," he began to speak, but was cut short by the young girl.

"There's no need to explain to me sheriff. I know this job can take a toll and you're entitled to your rest. Especially in a place taken to tranquility as this one has."

"I..." he began again, though he looked at her face and knew there was no point in explanation. "Well I certainly appreciate the pie, but like I told you before, I don't want you to keep bringing me gifts. It's unnecessary."

Her hair, smooth and golden, draped over the right side of her face, parted intentionally in that direction. She raised her milky white hand and pushed the locks behind her ear. When she did, Collie could see the scar. The indentation was deep and the coloration was that of soft pink. It had healed over time, but its inception was wicked and brutal. He stared at it directly with brevity, the skin split for three inches continuing up her head across her hairline. The man made blemish was prominent at his angle. It was always a shock when he saw it; like an unwanted caller never threatening to vacate.

Collie looked away finally. As he did, the front door opened and Upton walked through. The sound was the catalyst and Miss Vandenburg swiftly pushed her hair back in place to mask the thin marred flesh. The deputy oblivious to the visitation had his head down in thought. He yawned and closed the door. He lifted his head. There was a startle in his face when he saw them. "Mornin' sheriff, Miss Vandenburg." Upton tipped his hat to the lady then removed it. "Sorry for the yawn. Bit tired this mornin'," he said pleasantly. Miss Vandenburg nodded.

"Yes, it seems to be a common affliction today," she said and smiled at both men.

Upton craned his neck around Collie and saw the steam rising behind him. "That your apple pie I smell Miss Vandenburg?"

She nodded. "Yes it is Mr. Smith."

"Much obliged. I admit I've had a hankering for one of these since your last," Upton said with a grin, though his mind seemed preoccupied.

Collie cleared his throat for attention and Upton straightened himself. "Deputy, why don't you check the locks on the cells for me. Make sure they're in working order."

"Heck, sheriff," Upton started, catching a look from Collie. "Yes sir. Thanks again for the pie Miss," he said and gave a nod of gratitude when he left.

Collie waited until Upton was out of sight before speaking again. "Well Miss Vandenburg, if there's nothing else, the deputy and myself have some work needs doin'." He moved to the door. His tone was polite, but his intentions direct. The door swung easily as he pulled it open and the young girl accepted the hint.

She was in the frame, then turned and put her hand on the sheriff's shoulder. His head fell and he sighed. "You'll never know how thankful I am," she said.

"Miss-"

"Just listen. What you did...The lord sent you as our guardian that day. That I'm sure of. And I'm forever grateful." She removed her hand from his arm. There were no tears in her face. It was strong and he admired her for that.

His nerves led him to tap his foot on the ground. He raised his head and met her gaze. "No more gifts. I'm asking you," he said with sincerity. "Please."

She swallowed. "As you wish Mr. Collie," she said and then opened herself to the town. She glided out from the shade of the porch and the perfect sunlight illuminated her figure. "Good day to you sir," Collie heard her say, as she drifted out of view amidst the crowds and carriages in the street.

"And to you," he said quietly shutting the door.

A cell clanged shut from the back of the office and Upton came back into view. "All well sheriff?"

"Too early to tell," he answered.

"Virgil ain't been back all night," Upton said heading for his desk.

"As to your statement yesterday, you mentioned that could be expected."

"Yeah Virgil said not to check up till nightfall."

"You worried?" Collie asked.

Upton manned up his voice. "Naw, ain't worried. Christ." He paused a moment and looked at the ground. "Can we eat that pie?"

"Have some pie," Collie said. He pushed it to the edge of his desk.

Upton pulled a knife from his drawer and cut into the baked good. Fresh steam escaped in heavy groupings, thinning as it crept higher. He took the piece in his hands and bit. The syrupy substance coating the apples dripped out the corners of his mouth and over the knuckles of his hand. "That's hot, but damn tasty," he said with a mouthful.

Collie arched his brow in a mixture of amusement and disgust. "It's a good thing you waited until she left."

"You may be right," Upton said wiping his palm on his pant leg. "Why'd you get her out of here so quick?"

Collie made his way to the pot and poured himself some coffee. "This ain't any place for a kid." He sipped his mug and exposed his upper teeth in approval. "Remember, kid, Upton."

"Oh I've had no impure thoughts in regards to that I assure you."

"You and me are in stride then," Collie said.

Upton shoved the remaining bits of his pie into his mouth and then brushed both hands across his pants a few times. Collie watched as the crumbs fell lightly on the floorboards. He indicated to Upton that he saw it and the young man grabbed a broom. "You still haven't ever told me why she brings you this stuff," Upton said, head down in his work.

"Shit," Collie said, drawing out the word.

"You don't gotta tell me if it's trouble," Upton said.

Collie's attention went to the window and his legs followed. "No, shit to this, not that." He squinted out the window. He could see the darkened outline of a man trotting in his building's direction. The sight would have been normal if not for the man hogtied and bellied over on the horse beside the other.

"I don't follow," Upton said.

"Stop the damn sweepin'," Collie said, waving him over.

"What we got out there?" the deputy asked.

Collie was silent for a moment, waiting for the figure to come closer into view. A few moments passed. They seemed long. "That's Virgil," he said.

"The one upright I hope," Upton said.

Collie grabbed his hat and ventured out of the office. Upton followed. They stood on the porch more eager than sentries as Virgil approached at a mild pace. They waited on the porch. Collie kept his hand in proximity to his peacemaker, though not on it. Virgil grew nearer. His teeth were brighter than his swarthy face and he bared them through the tight grin he was displaying. "You best prep a cell," Collie said to Upton.

"You read my mind," Virgil said when he was close enough to speak without yelling. The two horses approached and halted at the hitching post.

"Everything good?" Collie asked with one eye closed from the sunlight.

"I'd say so," Virgil said.

"There's no disciples of your passenger after you for a reason?"

"None that I saw. They'd have gone at me on the trail."

"I reckon," Collie said. He stepped off the porch and moved to the horse bearing the face down luggage. The man was wiggling pathetically over the animal. He teetered himself to and fro like an unbalanced seesaw, unable to meet any progression with knots in the rope tensed as they were. Collie moved opposite the man's foot end. The man was disheveled to say the least. His hair was matted in the front. Crusted lines of blood stemmed from his mouth and spread over the midsection of his face like darkened caricatures of the veins beneath it. There was a rag, fully reddened over the original color, shoved into his mouth. The man spoke vowels into the bloody cloth. None of the language was discernible.

"That ain't there on my account," Virgil said. Collie looked at him with a questioning face. "Doctor's orders, from Yankton."

"What the hell happened to him?" Collie asked. The man on the horse lifted his head. His skin was flush from the angle and time and he let out a string of syllables at the sheriff's question. Virgil dismounted his horse and hitched it. He moved to where Collie was and began untying the man.

"I met him over in the saloon. Looks like he's our man from the woods. Likely he or the fellers he was with killed that Mexican. He went to draw on me and met negatively with a glass of beer."

"Huh," Collie said. The tied man began ranting again into the rag. "You know we can't understand you." Collie said to him. "Let's get him inside."

They pulled him off of the horse. "Come on Otis," Virgil said. Billy's legs wobbled beneath him. "They're asleep," said Virgil and he took Billy's arm around his neck and the criminal leaned his full weight into him. They entered the sheriff's office and hobbled past the desks into the vacant cell in line with the doorway. Collie shut the front door and followed them from a few feet back. He wrapped his palm over his pistol, but kept it in the holster.

When Virgil and Billy were behind the bars, Virgil relieved himself of the man's weight. He dropped him on the cot, not violently yet not in a way one would call gentle. Virgil kept his eye on the man. Facing him, he backed himself out of the cell and then closed the gate. Billy pulled the rag from his mouth. It dripped fresh blood onto his shirt from the portion that was closest to his tongue. He lied down defeated and seized heavy breaths. His chest and stomach rose high in succession as he gradually calmed behind the bars.

"Does he need a doctor?" Collie asked Virgil.

"It's subsiding believe it or not." He spun around to find Upton who was standing right behind him. "Deputy Smith?"

"Yes," he said in anticipation.

"Fetch him a glass of water and a bucket. Keep the water coming if you can," Virgil said. He removed his hat and sighed like a burden of some proportion had been lifted.

"Will do," Upton said and retrieved the supplies.

"Thankee," Virgil said. He pulled out his chair and sat down.

Collie, relieved that the man was in the cell, replicated the act. He pulled his chair near Virgil. It squeaked across the floor as it always did. He handed Virgil some water and spoke. "Tell me everything."

***

There was an incessant pounding inside Billy's head as he lay on the cot staring at the ceiling. Herculean footsteps traced across his brain and his eyes twitched and he bit his lip to cure himself of the discomfort. He could hear Virgil from the office recounting the events to the sheriff. Billy leaned over and picked up the glass of water from the floor. It was half empty and lukewarm to the touch. He pooled a mouthful of water and then swished it around his mouth for half a minute before spitting into the bucket the deputy provided him. The redness in the fluid had dissipated through the repetition. He sipped from the glass again though this time he swallowed. It soothed his throat despite the warmth and he lay back down on the cot. His lids closed giving way to blackness. Remnants of the room light bounced side to side in his retinas painting rough and forgotten pictures; streaking paths, creating memories. He could still hear the voices of the lawmen arranging the groundwork for his subconscious. Their voices became distant like he was slowly rolling away. The conversation was interrupted when the office door opened. The sound swept Billy back to semi-consciousness and he was able to peel his eyes open long enough to see a man of business like affectations approach and enter his sight. However, the pain continued its marching and ironically the monotonous pattern led him to sleep.

He was awoken some time later by the rap of a stein across the procession of metal bars. It was quick like a rusted violent harp and he lifted his head to immediate attention. Billy opened his eyes wide, but they closed almost completely as even the dim light struck his vision. He looked to his cell door and saw Collie standing there holding the metal cup.

"You know there's a nice way to do that," Billy said freely, sitting up from his bunk. His swollen tongue marginally distorting his letters.

"Sorry 'bout that. I was just raisin' you so our keeper could turn down your linens and bring you supper," Collie said and then drank from the contents of the stein.

"I speak sarcasm too," Billy said and grinned only to retract it on account of the newly healing scabs ending his lips.

"Then I guess I got my message 'cross." Collie waited a moment. "You're talking better than I thought you might."

Billy went to stand. As he did, he crouched back quickly as if to sit again, his back in some pain. Collie watched this and sipped his cup again. "That'll ease as long as you don't strain it," he said to Billy.

"That's comforting," Billy said and made an effort to not show pain. "I don't see how I could possibly aggravate it here."

Collie bit the corner of his mouth and looked up like he had an idea. "Some feller's get it in their head that they're not into staying long. Their partners or kin will come and bust em' out. Hold up the law inside or maybe do worse." Collie straightened himself from against the bars and stepped back once. He drank the remains of his beverage casually. When it was drained, he held up the cup to his eye line and looked inside like he was reassuring himself it was gone. He made a sound of refreshment.

Billy moved forward and wrapped his hands around the bars of the jail. He pushed his face a few inches from the bar, but refused to rest on it. "Well I don't have any kin or partners to go bustin' me out."

"Now that don't hold water from what I hear."

"What'd you hear?"

"Let's cut through any semblance of bullshit."

"Sheriff, I'm not sure what you're getting at. Your deputy broke a pint glass in my mouth. Now I got a permanent goddamn smile etched in my face no matter how miserable the situation calls for. Can't open my mouth wide without reopening the wound and gushing blood and I'm not sure about eatin' anything solid for some time."

"Aside from a cocksucker there's no need for you to open wide."

"You callin' me a cocksucker you son of a bitch?"

Collie placed his stein on the desk. "Well I admit you sound like one with your speech pattern of late. And I'll call any man that throws down on one of my deputies, especially a conniving shit that don't have the balls to do it standing up, anything I want to. Now why don't you tell me why you think you're in here." Collie's voice was straight and unfaltering. His volume never rose above conversational.

Billy was red in the face. He gritted his teeth like they were mortal enemies and his knuckles were white around the cell bars. He stood, listening to the sheriff's words as they escaped his mouth like an irritable poison. "If I wasn't inside this cell, the outcome of this conversation would likely be different."

"Unfavorable to me you're thinking?" Collie said.

"No guarantees, but it'd certainly be a possibility."

"And I'd end up dead on the floor I suppose you'd say."

Billy scoffed. "Hell, I'm only foolin'. I've never killed a lawman in my life, but that doesn't mean you'd not end up on the floor in some fashion."

"Yet you drew on my deputy."

"That doesn't mean I was gonna kill him."

"Says you."

"What reason have I to lie in this situation? You said yourself I'm not going anywhere."

"So you're saying you pulled your piece on my deputy with no intent to fire it?" Collie arched his brow. "What was you gonna do? Talk into it?"

"A man can take the lead without dying, 'pending on the marksmen on the shooting end."

"So you admit you were gonna shoot my deputy."

Billy pondered with brevity before speaking. "I can't likely say exactly what I was going to do at this juncture, but I know I felt more comfortable at the time doing it with the gun in my hand. Surely you know what I mean sheriff. I mean shit I was threatened. You ever known a criminal to turn himself in? A man's gotta at least try and tussle himself outta any situation where his freedom's at stake."

"And look where that got you; standing upright with a restricted view, a sad man that can't wipe the smile from his face."

"I don't think I could've written the irony any better," Billy said, cringing in pain. With that, the office door shut and Upton strolled in. "This here the prodigal?" Billy asked.

Upton whispered something into Collie's ear, ignoring the prisoner. Billy hushed himself in attempt to listen. Collie shook his head regarding the information and then Upton moved to his desk. He sat atop it and stared at Billy. Collie cleared his throat and spoke. "Otis, this here's Deputy Smith." He pointed, indicating his colleague.

"He's smaller than the other one," Billy said. He squinted and gave Upton a once over. "Same age as me though maybe. Wonder how I'd have fared against him."

"No sense speculatin' on what ifs," Collie said. "Now Otis-"

"Not Otis," the prisoner said, cutting him off.

"What?" Collie asked.

"Name's not Otis. I got myself a real name. Never cared much for Otis anyways. Was my dog as a kid. Pissed all over the place."

"You volunteering that?" Collie said.

Billy laughed and stepped back in his cell. "Name's Jesse. No point hiding it now. Didn't work the last fuckin' time anyway. Might as well Christian myself up while I still got the chance."

Collie considered the statement. "Well if you plan on makin' amends with the Almighty, why don't you go ahead and state your crime for us."

"Seems like a waste of time, me statin' what you think you know."

"Think?"

"Yeah it's all speculation, using your vocabulary. You're working off a hunch. The hunch of that big son of a bitch. Virgil."

"When he inquired as to your purpose in the town and handed down the account of a criminal situation, you drew down, the result of which we're staring at presently. Brings us to the notion that what Virgil said caught your attention in a way you didn't want anyone knowin' about."

Billy shook his head. "I don't appreciate accusations of such. That's why I went for him."

"Then you goin' on the draw had nothing to do with the train got robbed at the water depot over the hill a mile out?"

"Listen sheriff, I don't know anything about that there incident. If I did, I'd be more than happy to help you out as I imagine it'd help me out."

Collie ran a quick finger over his mustache. "You familiar with a man named Morris Hixon?"

The color changed in Billy's face. He made an effort to stay poker, but the difficulty proved overwhelming. "I saw a man walk in before I dozed in here. Fancy man. Suit wearing fucker. Who was that?"

"Suit wearing man?"

"Don't play here," Billy said, annoyed.

"Fancy man was an agent of the Pinkerton's." Collie said, watching Billy closely as he spoke. "Rode down from Yankton with some information." Billy bit his lip. "Information regarding a pair of misfits, both encountering fates they likely didn't reckon of, and both separate events. Add you to the mixture and it seems like the whole bunch stepped in bucket of horse shit while their noses were in the air."

"Shit," Billy said sounding conquered. "Goddamn Pinkertons. Aristocrats."

"They're doin' what they're paid to," Collie said.

"You tell what he said?" Billy asked with general curiosity.

"You know a man named Barton something or other?" Collie waited a moment. There was no answer. "Big sunnabitch. Noticeably so."

"How's that?" Billy asked.

"Big enough to have it worth mentioning." Collie waited again, but Billy kept silent. "It ain't worth keeping quiet about at this point. You've been implicated."

Billy rolled his eyes, seemingly pondering his next move. "What about him?"

"Seems he got himself knifed."

"Jesus," Billy huffed, stunned and saddened. How bad?" he asked, lowering his guard.

"It was in the throat, so he's dead."

"How'd someone get the jump on that moose," Billy said.

"There's always someone bigger," said Collie, beginning to relax a bit with the prisoner talking. "Then there's the Hixon fellow." Billy sat back down on the cot. He hunkered down with his head nearly between his legs. His hands pushed back the sides of his hair like a madman at a dead end. "I'll take your silence to mean you know him too." Billy made no acknowledgement. "This dumbass threw down on a lawman same as you though for different reasons I understand."

"How's that?" Billy said.

"Heard he had a temper at poker."

"Always was a cheat," Billy said, raising his head finally.

"Nah, this was in relation to his voice. I guess he won good and sang like a schoolgirl. Man called him out on it and Hixon drew. Law tackled him before he got a shot off. Say his skin was so white, you could see the blood slithering through him."

"He's not dead then?" Billy said.

"He's in your predicament. Getting hanged in few, but not before he whistled a tune giving up you two cocksuckers in attempt to save himself, you and the moose. Referred to you by name. Billy Maple. I's only callin' you Otis to see how long it'd take you to come around. And then you came round with another lie, Jesse." Billy shook his head in disbelief. "Come on now," Collie said. "You really believe a man like that is above ratting? I've seen a man shoot another over a piece of bacon. When his neck's at stake, what you think that same man'd be willing to do?"

Billy continued to sit on the cot, waist bent with each brick of information stacking upon him.

"How long you been at it Billy?" Collie asked. "Thieving and such?"

"They gonna hang me too?" he asked.

Collie ignored the question. "You one of them that feels they had no other choice in the matter? You were driven to wickedness by some other person? Whiskey? Demons? Or are you one that can account for himself? I confess it'd be a welcome change of pace if you're the latter."

Billy hesitated for a moment and then looked to the sheriff, a man who appeared to be genuinely interested in answers to his queries. "I'm good at it. That's all."

"I'd stand to argue," Collie said directly, though without any hint of rudeness.

"You ever heard of Billy Maple, sheriff?" Billy said. He rose from the cot with quaint newfound energy. The sheriff shook his head no. "Deputy?" Billy asked, nodding to Upton, who responded in accordance with Collie. "You see now there's a reason for that. Some guys get out there looking to make a name. They hit a bank or train, faces out, words blazin' hotter than their pistols. Some go as far as to leave a mark or let them less fortunate know who it was that done it. There's some glory there. At least there is for those thick enough to think it. Fact of the matter is though, that it's a job like any other. And if you do it right, it's not for recognition, but the payoff."

"How long?" Collie said.

Billy couldn't contain the smirk that presented itself across his lower face. The right scab reopened and a blood droplet traced the singular memory of the past event down to his chin. He rubbed it off. "Make it about six years now. Started at seventeen."

Upton's jaw fell a touch. "No jail time or run ins with the law?" he asked, and then looked to Collie.

"No run ins as such. Sure we fled a few times, though the law had no avail in ascertaining our whereabouts. It's funny sometimes, whose side God picks." He chuckled.

"You do trains and banks?" Upton asked.

"Trains only." He answered.

"Why?" said Collie.

"Trains move. Information doesn't travel as quick when you're out of a town."

Collie pushed the chair nearest him under the desk. "What aches me is that you're still here in our jail cell."

Billy turned his head left and then straightened it. "You're only as good as you're help I reckon. Lapse of judgment on my part. Everyone lapses from time to time, only occupations like ours are more unforgiving in that matter."

"Why'd you go back to Yankton, Billy?" Collie said.

"What's your meaning sheriff?"

"I mean you don't come off as particularly dumb in nature from where I'm standing. Outside of them two assholes got themselves dead and jailed, you supposedly workin' six years plus at stealin' and not making a name for yourself carries some impressive stature. So why'd you go back to the town you robbed from?"

Billy shook his head smiling. "Sheriff, would you ever in your right mind go back to the very place you committed a crime in and chance any kind of run in with someone that could recognize you? It'd be damn crazy to do such a thing."

Collie listened and furrowed his brow. He then raised them as he snuck a smile onto his face for this was the first time he actually appreciated what the man in the cell was saying. He grabbed his hat off the table, fitting it to his head. "Let's go," he said to Upton.

"Where you getting off to?" Billy said, once again grasping the bars.

"Not too far off," Collie said looking back. "And we'll be back shortly for you."

"In what fashion?" Billy said.

"Gotta see about a dead Mexican." With that, the lawmen left the room hurriedly. The door shut, leaving Billy to himself in the office. The dimensions of the room never changed, but in the silence, the walls crept closer and closer until Billy forced himself to lay down with eyes shut to the world simply to make the creeping stop.

Chapter 12

There was the moon hovering luminescent over the grand plains as the stranger and his horse glided over the surface of the land. He had taken his time riding to Yankton, welcoming any distraction that arose in his path. His diminutive journey left no string of death aside from the carcasses of birds and rabbit, which he had shot for food.

When the town presented itself in the distance as the sun began to lose strength and the magic hour approached, the stranger slowed his animal and came to a complete halt, absorbing the sights ahead. It was only a town, but located in the vast expanse of the Dakota territories it inhabited some very features of a metropolis. There were people moving all around the streets, torches sparked and the flames brightening the roads. He remained on his horse overlooking the setup of construction and tents, his thoughts a mystery even to God. He nicked the horse forward.

***

He situated himself in the chair as the whore began to remove her stockings. "You sure you don't want to be touched," she asked.

"I'll let you know when," the stranger said. He took a long drag on his cigarette. The motion was meticulous and gentle as the ashes at the tip lengthened and refused to fall covering near an inch. He whispered the smoke out of the side of his mouth, careful not to interfere with his creation.

"Are we gonna get to fuckin' or what?" the woman said in the background.

Her shape came into focus as he shifted his gaze to her. When he did, the ashes fell abruptly to the arm of his chair. He shot a heavy breath through his nose. "What did I tell you?" he said.

"It's true what they say. The more handsome they are, the meaner they are. I don't need this brash shit from you."

"Sit down," he said. He rose from the chair smothering the cigarette with his boot. She paid no attention to him and began to redress. "Please," he said. "This isn't how it is supposed to go."

"You got that right. Who'd have thought I'd prefer being treated like a horse."

"Sit down," he said again with a raised voice. When she did not comply, he reached into the strap resting on the breast of his coat and unsheathed the Bowie. The pristine blade caught the flicker of the lantern and flashed over the whore's pupils. She screamed for only seconds before his palm cut off her airway, and his handsome face eclipsed her view.

He threw her onto the bed pressing his full weight into her. With one hand still over her mouth, he held the knife horizontally across her throat and pushed down hard. It punctured her skin and sunk past her windpipe down to her spine. She made an attempt to scream into the stranger's hand and the blood gurgled from her throat before her eyes rolled back into her head, lifeless. The blood was summoned from the wound and began to paint the bedspread.

When she ceased to move, the stranger let out a breath of relief. The Bowie had severed the throat in a particular way as to cut off the arterial spray from her jugular. He looked down and saw his work and then methodically removed the knife. When he did, the spray came forth with little power, speckling over the few remaining unstained portions of the linen. A bead of sweat fell from his forehead landing in the crimson gush from below the woman's mouth. He wiped his forehead with his sleeve and again let out another sigh. The room was silent, but the jubilant sounds from the lobby below remained.

He unnerved himself then moved from the bed. He gave himself a once over. His hands were reddened significantly and his shirt sleeves looked like he had just butchered a cow. Pinching the sheets together at the foot of the bed, he placed the blade between them and cleaned it. The blood streaked imperfectly across the metal. He repeated this until it was untainted.

A bird call in the distance removed his thoughts. He went to the window and viewed the town from his second story room. The camp was still in motion. Peddlers and passers occupied the streets with business and pleasure, the two sometimes mixed. The torches continued to blaze, replicating the passions and determinations of new lives desired. He looked up to the moon and stars. They were full of life, ever present, dependable.

His head rested against the window and then he brought himself to reality. The corpse of the woman appeared a shade whiter, clashing noticeably with the newfound artwork of the stranger. The room was completely still. She lay like a China doll perfect now only in death. "It wasn't supposed to be like this. But you just couldn't wait," he said to the corpse.

In one perfect motion, he spun the Bowie in his hand, the blade facing downward. He stepped toward the body and leaned over her, careful not to further stain his clothing. Her eyes were open, transfixed as a still shot replaying the last events of her life. With precision he inserted the knife point into her lower eyelids. The skin was frail and the blade penetrated easily. His hand was steady, inharmonious with the idea that the mind of most men having witnessed or been a party to a slaying of this nature might have raced around with only the ability to accelerate.

When the insertions were complete, he burrowed the knife at an angle behind her eyes. He lowered the handle causing the blade to rise. The eyeball crept slowly from its lair. "Shhhh," the stranger said. The stranger slithered his free hand and stole the eye with his thumb and forefinger. He did the same for the other and then placed them in a pouch inside his jacket. "I thank you darling," he said and slid the knife back into its leather holding.

From the lobby below he could still hear the sound of piano and patrons drinking. Two voices announced themselves more prominent than others. They were deep and belonged to men. He perked his ears and peered at the door. The voices were growing louder, closer. The stranger moved to the door and pressed his ear flush against it. There were footsteps on the stairs.

An alarm went off in him. He raced around the room scanning the floor for any personal traces. When he thought he saw nothing, he moved to the chair containing his belongings. There was a knock on the door. "Charlotte you done in there?" the voice yelled. "This ain't a goddamn hotel. Tell the John to finish and pay." The stranger winced and began to breathe heavily.

He fumbled the holster resting on the seat and retrieved the pistol. He grasped the handle until his knuckles turned white. The man rapped on the door again. "Goddammit answer me or at least fake a moan." His voice was commanding despite being hindered by the door. The stranger closed his eyes and touched his forehead to the top of the pistol, a move that made him look in prayer. There was a jingle of keys on the outside and he made for the door.

He could hear the key blunder its way into the lock. The stranger backed himself against the wall behind where the door would open. "I'm comin' in," the man said on the other side. "No damn answer," he said under his breath. The key positioned itself in the lock and the doorknob turned. The door opened slowly and the stranger saw the tip of the man's shoe enter the room. The opening reached forty five degrees. "What the-" the man gasped. He was cut off as the stranger slammed the door into him in a sharp motion. The man's head slammed against the door frame, disabling him momentarily.

The stranger pulled the man by the arm into the room. He closed the door and relocked it and spun to the intruder. The man was on the floor near the bed rubbing his head. "Son of a bitch," the man said and looked up in time to see the butt of the pistol crack his face. The stranger brought his hand down twice more. He wiped the butt of the pistol on the bed sheets, same as he had done with his knife. He rose and stared at his work. His victim sat unconscious though alive. Blood flowed from his skull over his eyes. The stranger blinked once, longer than usual as if taking a mental photograph.

He stepped back and moved to his belongings. The holster buckled easily around his waist. He placed his pistol inside. He then strapped the Bowie harness around his shoulders and covered his weapons and bloodstained clothing with his overcoat. His neck turned with patience as he scanned the room one more time. The delicate motionlessness of the scene inherited a surreal quality. He retrieved a cigarette. He pinched it lightly between his lips and then smirked in the slightest manner. The match moved across the strip, igniting a small flame. He lit the cigarette and inhaled and shook out the flame.

He pressed the ember to his wrist and then dropped the match. As the blackened wood traveled to the floor, the report of a pistol disrupted the moment. The stranger flinched and the noise from the downstairs lobby ceased. His glance traveled from the newfound bullet hole in the molding of the wall to the man on the floor, blinded with blood and barely holding the smoking gun.

The stranger's face was cardboard for only seconds. He scuttled to the male victim and crouched in front of him. He sucked a final drag of the cigarette and tossed it aside. He whispered gibberish frantically. The man mumbled before him unintelligibly, the pistol shot a last remaining instinct in a dying mind.

There was commotion from the floor below and footsteps announced themselves on the stairway. The stranger kept his wits and gently held the injured man's gun-hand in his own. He wrapped the victim's fingers around the weapon. The footsteps were getting closer. The man's fingers were stubborn and limp as the stranger placed the index across the trigger. The man on the floor continued to mumble as the blood oozed from his wounds. The stranger manipulated the man's arm like a marionette and positioned the barrel of the pistol under the owner's chin. "Jesus Christ," a voice said behind him.

The stranger turned to see an average man, mouth agape, staring at the scene in horror. "Shhhh," the stranger admonished and he pushed the victim's finger down. Muffled with the barrel tight against the flesh, the gun popped. The bullet sped through, splitting the man's tongue from the bottom and blowing a hole out the top of his head, inches from his crown. Fresh blood redressed the room. The stranger stood and saw the man in the doorway struggle for his gun. The man was older and mustached and seemed to be in a genuine panic. The holster would not give up the gun.

A smile of amusement graced the stranger and left in a second as he opened his own coat. His pistol revealed itself with the ease of a tender wind. He fired without aiming. The shot recoiled in the room. The older man fell backward when the hole appeared in his chest. He grabbed at the wound and dropped into the sitting position against the wall, framed by the doorway.

There was a discordant blend of shouts and vulgarities bouncing through the hallway from the lobby of the brothel, manifesting themselves through the greatest human fear of the unknown. The stranger did not stay to admire, but rather rushed to the window and pulled it open. It creaked as it slid through the frame. A succession of quick and heavy footsteps dominated the stairs. He could hear their words, commands of guns out and preparation for the worst scenario. The doorway revealed the first man as the stranger was straddling the window. His boot scraped along the roof of the awning and he snuck his head under pulling his other leg through just as they opened fire.

His body landed on the tilted awning with a thud and he began to roll. The concert of gunfire continued. Bullets whizzed overhead, ticking the wooden walls, exploding glass onto the ground below. "He's out the window!" yelled a voice from above.

Overwhelming anxiety punctured the stranger. The edge of the awning gave way to a thirteen foot fall in the night and he went over it. The drop seemed instant. He landed on the left half of his backside below his hip. He growled at the pain and hopped up as quickly as possible.

The streets were occupied, though not as wholly as he would have liked. The train whistle sounded from the depot near the edge of town. The stranger looked above, shielded from his predators currently by the dip of the awning. Eyes were on him at ground level from the townsfolk. He tilted his hat down and breathed deeply. He grabbed at his backside, seething in pain. He shot one more brief glance above and then bolted out into the streets.

Shots rang out immediately. Small clouds of dust emitted from the ground as the bullets refused to hit their mark. Under the cover of night, the stranger moved away from the building zigzagging his motions. With each six or seven steps he made to the right, he darted left the same. The shots continued and he could hear their voices becoming distant. There was shouting from the bystanders as they ran for cover and dashed into the shadows. A searing sensation rustled through his hip when he put weight on it, but he fought it.

Seconds passed without shots. He ran until his heart pumped acid. He could see the train depot in the distance. The trains rarely ran at night, though with the influx of robberies, they had taken to the habit to break the villains of theirs. He braced his leg and ran toward it. The streets were restless with the commotion, though the eyes on him earlier had ceased to rest on his figure. He had bolted down one thin alley after another, refusing to make the mistake of moving in a direct line. A thin passage between two businesses presented itself. He moved for it and ducked into the shadows.

He slowed his breathing, disciplined until it was dead quiet. He did not know how far he had run. The uproar had begun to simmer. People who remained on the streets were less hysterical in this area. The train whistled again, this time louder and in proximity. "Shut the fuck up!" he heard a man yell from an upper window. He crept further into the passage and knelt behind a barrel.

It was a straight shot to the train. The metal beast was huffing not fifty yards away. The stranger tuned his peripherals, he adjusted to the darkness. He kept to the alleyway. The train ahead began to chug. The stranger squinted. There were boxcars behind the engine, each without windows, indicating that there were no passengers. He crept to the edge of the alley walled in from his right and left.

They would be closing off the town as soon as possible. The crime committed, both passionate and abhorrent, little seen freshly to human eyes would awaken distant morals and shake loose the apathy stranglehold of this modern society. The stranger knew this and he knew he had little time for exodus. He removed his hat and peeked his head out from the alley, reconnoitering his surroundings. Upon his flight from the brothel, his pursuers had spilled rounds into the dirt, not one striking him. He thought about this for a moment. It was quiet. Only the train and the night creatures percolated the idea of silence.

The train chugged again and the stranger stood. He saw a man, drunk with a bottle and stumbling from across the street to the left of him. The stranger opened his jacket and pulled out the Bowie. Instinctively, he rolled back the sleeve of his jacket, exposing his bloodied shirt. He found a dry piece and began to cut away at it. He stole another look at the drunk. The whiskey sloshed through the half empty bottle. "Pssst,' the stranger let out from the shadows. The man stopped. The alley was pitch black from his point of view. The stranger stepped back further into the darkness and emitted the noise again.

He peeled off the shirt piece and placed it on the barrel beside him. There were footsteps on the porch. He knew it was the drunk. There was no cadence or rhythm, the man threatening to fall over in a stupor. With his back against the wall, the stranger waited until the portly figure came into view. The drunk was now there. He ignored the alley. As he was about to pass the stranger's hand eclipsed his mouth and he was pulled into the shadows of the alley. The stranger swiftly stole the bottle from his hands, placing it with the torn shirt. The drunk mumbled behind his hand. He passed the sharpened edge across the man's throat. Blood flowed and the man dropped to the ground, drunk no longer.

"Appreciated," the stranger whispered and then shot his glance to the train. It was moving at a creep, but the stranger knew he needed to close near fifty yards even if it were still. At the barrel he poured a bit of whiskey onto the shirt piece and stuffed the bulk of the material into the bottle. He struck a match and held it to the alcohol infused rag. It lit up, illuminating his face in the shadows.

He emerged from the alley a phoenix. "He's there!" There was a shout from nearby, no doubt one of the very men he fled from earlier. With great might, he launched the flaming bottle at the closest building. The bottle burst and the flash of light was brilliant clashing against the darkness. Shots rang out from each direction and the stranger sprinted to the engine. The engine's movement added yardage to his pursuit. There was a limp in his step, but if it bothered him it did not show.

Muzzle flashes popped like fireflies in the summer night outlining the men with smoke, incubuses stowing away in a dream state. The stranger continued his dash. He pulled his pistol in retaliation and fired at the varying flashes. He kept his gaze at the train as to maintain his lunar vision. "Go back for the horses!" one of the men yelled. "He's going for the train."

The stranger unconsciously looked toward the voice. As he did, his feet gave away and he tripped over an imperfection on the ground. The gunfire quickly became more concentrated. He was down for only seconds, but a bullet struck through the brim of his hat leaving an aperture not far from his temple. He bolted up and kept running.

There was a shape in the corner of his eye. One of the townsman's profiles lit up by a street torch. He saw the man raise his rifle. The train was twenty yards away. The stranger fired without aiming and the townsman's head jerked back. He holstered his pistol immediately. He breathed and made a final push for the locomotive. The chugging pulsated as he approached and the gunshots ceased to exist. The engine was exiting town and the surroundings were getting darker. He could touch the back car with his fingertips. The train was gaining velocity. The holding bar and metal step was visible on the side of the car and just out of grasp. In an act of faith, he leaped forward.

His arm near discharged from the socket as he wrapped his hand around the railing. He let out a cry of pain. His feet were dragging over the black dust. He looked back. With the town in the distance, he muscled himself onto the step and then climbed the side ladder to the roof of the train car.

He laid flat. The wind tunneled past him, cooling his body with a perfect sensation. He grabbed at his shoulder and began wheezing. From where he left, he could see the fire growing. Men were mounted on horseback. He imagined their words and faces as they saddled up to catch him. The sparks of the fire continued to rise to the heavens, some higher than others, dissolving when they drew too near the heavens. He watched the scene as it continued to withdraw. He lay back down and started laughing. He could not stop.

Chapter 13

The ceiling, cracked and splintered like his conscience, stared down in opposition to Billy. He had watched it long enough to see the mundane imperfections in the wood take on animate shapes that seemed to torture and scold him the more time he lay there. His mind wandered here and there, sometimes aimlessly, and sometimes reliving past events. He had tried to explain himself to the sheriff. How he was a party to the shootout involving the dead Mexican, but he was not the party who shot him.

Seeing the belongings of the Mexican at the undertaker's office and then the grave of the man whose death he knew he was directly responsible for was a new experience for him. He was shaken, though not to the point of entire regret, but rather to the point where unconscious contemplation was occurring against his will. Perhaps because when it was done in times before, they kept moving, not slowing enough to allow the faces of the dead to catch up with them.

The lawmen of Little Creek freed Billy from his cell not more than an hour ago to identify the body. He could have lied though what would have been the point. His counterparts were caught or dead and even if the lawmen had lied about those occurrences, Billy knew he had shown his hand too early. There was a respectful nature about the lawmen in Little Creek that pleased Billy. They seemed to set aside judgment. Or they at least pretended to.

Each of his arms was held by a deputy as the sheriff walked ahead toward the creek. Necks swiveled and faces turned from onlookers in his direction as he passed, prisoner of the town, less than human in the eyes of the rogue jury. Billy stared back at each one of them. Sometimes he grinned and other times he'd wink if the mood presented itself. Hanging his head in shame would admit to his failure and more importantly, his outstanding guilt in the crimes committed. Billy kept his head up, respectable as a man in chains could be, but the walk was long and the mask he wore was gaining weight.

He confirmed the identity of the dead man, yet could not recall his name. This was no false truth on Billy's part. The Mexican had worked a previous job with his crew, though he was an outsider from its inception and remained one until his demise. The lawmen brought Billy to the jail. Their walk back gave way to the same crowds only this time the onlookers could not have bothered with the sight of him in chains, them carrying about their business or conversations with him a distant afterthought. The world kept turning. It always did.

He lay there staring at the ceiling. The sheriff's voice altered to and from a muffle as Billy's attention drifted between his thoughts and reality. The three lawmen sat on the positive side of the cell bars, and Billy simply lay there with little observance to their presence.

His eyes moved across the ceiling playfully finding the discrepancies in the grain as if he were a child watching the clouds float by. The sheriff's voice was baritone and distant in his mind. He heard it get louder, repeating a phrase. He repeated it again. Billy shook himself.

"Billy!" Collie said, louder than the room required. "Goddammit. You ain't listening or you don't want to listen."

"I'm listening now. What is it?"

"I said you're set to hang on Friday."

"What day is it today?" Billy said.

"It's Tuesday."

"Why the wait?"

"There's things need gettin' in order," Collie said sounding concerned. "You have words I ought to give to anyone?"

Billy was silent for a moment as if in thought. "There's no one," he said robotically.

Collie rose from his chair and approached the cell. "You think on that and get back to me." Collie shook his head in frustration and turned to leave.

"That's it then? Final?" Billy said tilting his gaze at the lawmen.

The sheriff turned. "I don't see what I could possibly do for you. We have statements to the fact that you robbed a train and testament from you that it wasn't the first. We got you swinging on my own deputy and a body recently interred and put there allegedly by the very men you admitted to travelling with."

"Why'd you take me over to the digger anyway if you think you know the truth?"

"Strangely enough, it'd bring me comfort knowing that it was you that did the Mexican and not a band of Sioux," Collie said.

"The dead man brings you comfort?" Billy asked.

"Ain't the fact that he's dead, but knowing why and how? Yeah," added Collie.

"You afraid of them?"

"Afraid of who?" Collie said.

"The Sioux."

"You think on what I said. I'll be back with food," he said to the deputies on the side.

"I can do that if you want, Sheriff," said Upton eagerly.

"Naw I could use the walk," Collie said and sauntered out of the building.

Wells was staring down the prisoner as he had been for the entire conversation. He held a deep and inquisitive stare, carefully listening rather than waiting to talk. "You mighta let him help you," he said to the prisoner.

"Why Deputy Wells, I was wondering if I'd have the privilege of speaking to my captor before I departed off this wonderful stretch of earth," Billy said in a faux pleasant manner. "There you sit. The man that caught Billy Maple."

"You think highly of yourself don't ya," Wells said.

"Well if I don't, who will?"

"He may have a point," Upton said, eavesdropping from his desk.

Billy flared his nostrils at Wells and then in the direction of the table at the center of the office. He sniffed loudly, mimicking a curious animal. "You know deputy, I'm not quite certain that my mouth will tolerate the substance of solid food at this juncture on account of your actions to me previous, but that pie's been dry humping my brain since I noticed it." He saw Wells arch his brow. "You mentioned about helping me before, but you and I both know there ain't a help you can give me that'd be considered worth a damn outside of unlocking this here cell door and giving your backs a turn while I slip out and we all carry on with our lives. So I'm forced to focus all my attention on the sweet small things I can see with my separated vision from this abode I find myself in."

Wells rose off the desk and collected the remnants of the pie from the table. "This was made special for Sheriff Collie," he said, halting in front of the cell.

"Well he isn't eating it and I'm sure whoever made it will afford him same opportunity down the stretch." Billy reached his arms out through the bar, staring at Wells. "Please," he added.

"Step on back." The prisoner did and Wells slipped the metal plate through the horizontal opening above the lock. "Have at it."

Billy snatched the plate and scarfed what he could voraciously. Crumbs like boulders dropped and spread across the bust of his shirt. He gently pinched them and tossed them into his mouth, joining the carnage.

"You know you ain't dead yet," Wells said watching the scene.

Billy spoke, but kept his attention fixated on the good in front of him. "I know this don't taste quite right on account of the buds I lost, but I must be saying that if I had myself a fully formed tongue at the present, I might die of pleasure right now."

"Then where'd be the justice?" Wells asked with mild distaste toward the man's eating.

"What's the difference?" Billy said with a mouthful. "Dead is dead." A crumb shot from his mouth on the last word. "This from his wife?"

"Ain't got no wife no more," Wells said.

"She up and left?" Billy said, though he looked like he did not care.

"She passed, and you mind your mouth." Wells warned.

Billy scraped the remaining crust across the plate. It slid easily picking up the caramelized fruit and sugar. "Passed huh?" He shoved the last piece in his mouth and spoke. Wells could see the food moving behind his teeth. "There's no way any man on earth made this pie. It's got the touch of a woman to it. Who made it then? He stickin' someone else even in the face of his dearly departed?"

"I told you to watch your mouth," Wells said more sternly and fingered the handle of his pistol instinctively. Upton stood from his desk, hanging back somewhat.

Billy rose in the cell and pat his belly when he was upright. He saw Wells's reaction and noticed the placement of his hands. "When'd the wife go? Not too recent I hope. It'd make his current actions a bit more despicable." He stepped closer to the bars. And then closer again. "Why don't you go ahead and pull that piece? Finish what you started at the bar. Then you can get on with your life and Collie can go fuck that whore."

"I know what you're tryin' to do," Wells said, moving forward himself. "But I ain't gonna shoot ya."

"What am I trying to do exactly?"

Wells grabbed forward instantly reaching through the cell bars. He got hold of Billy's collar.

"Whoa, whoa," Upton said to his fellow deputy. Wells eyed him and he stood down.

Billy's face squelched against the thin pillars and he went cross eyed looking at the gun barrel pressed against his forehead. The cold of the metal contrasted the sweat beads newly formed on his awe stricken face. Wells kept the gun where it was. A thin squeal of pain emerged from the prisoner, who was noticeably trying to contain it. "I told you I wasn't gonna shoot ya," Wells said in a grisly whisper, the words invading Billy's territory. He cocked the pistol and Billy pressed closed his eyes. "But here's you knowing that I could."

Billy's eyes opened at the statement. "Then do it. Here and quick."

"We're better than that. Doesn't matter by how much."

The fear behind Billy had been replaced by acceptance and he nodded to the deputy. Wells loosened his grasp and pulled away his pistol, then let go of Billy completely. "You saddle them words about Collie. The man deserves better than the shit you been slingin' since he left. He ain't like what you're picturing."

Billy rubbed his face, adorned with two red lines, running parallel along the crests of his brows. "I was only foolin'." He brushed off his clothing and tucked in his shirt. "I don't wanna hang Virgil. I can't hang." He sat back down and hung his head. Wells watched and for the first time knew that the man was sincere. There was a patter on the roof. It began slowly and then picked up with aggression.

"Look at that," Wells said. "You made it rain."

***

Collie was caught in the streets when it started to downpour. He dashed under the nearest awning, covering the bread and bacon as best he could with his jacket. "Aw hell," he said to himself. The ground had been parched for weeks and the rain fell foreign to the turf, pooling up the uneven sectors of road, gushing from rooftops.

The streets emptied for the most part. To his side a group of children ran through the water, splashing and giggling like it was their first rainfall. They were foggy images to him getting older, the light failing and his eyesight in the early stages of betrayal. He could hear their laughter. He smiled. "Some night aye sheriff?" said the voice from the open door behind him.

"Sorry for occupying Myron. Was waitin' to see if it would settle. Got dinner with me ya know." He held out the bread, beads of water atop it.

"You want to wait inside?" Myron asked. He was elderly, holding himself up with the door frame. "I can make you food here."

Collie waited, considering. "Naw I'll head across. Press my luck. Appreciate it though." He tipped his hat. A thin stream of water flowed from it and struck his boot, its sound silenced by the surrounding noise. A train whistled in the distance. "You take care and I'll swing by tomorrow."

"Very well then sheriff. I'll wait till you cross."

Collie nodded and then sprinted to his office. It had been a while since he ran that fast.

Chapter 14

He had hit the ground awkwardly and was now lying on his back prostrate in the mud as the night sky opened and the rain fell stinging at his face like pincers. The stranger had ridden the train for only a matter of minutes before abandoning it. He leaped at the sight of the water depot, taking it on faith that it would be vacant in the weather. His head turned, mud squished against his ear. He saw the train continuing on without him. Its sight and sound were dissipating. The rain overpowered the canvass.

He made to get up, groaning as he did. Pain seared through his hip and he grabbed at it. He pushed off the ground and stumbled to his feet looking like a first timer on a pair of stilts. The stranger took his first step since his exodus. His groan matured into an anguished yell, masked by a simultaneous roll of thunder. His cry ceased and he began to laugh again, taking another step, and then another.

His boots plunged superficially below the surface as the water streamed down the hill behind the water tower. He made his way to the tower and grabbed one of the wooden legs for support. He leaned his head against it and relieved himself a long breath. The stranger planted his feet and straightened himself against the leg. He opened his coat. He moved his hands across his clothing before holding them out in front of his eyes against the moonlight. They were muddied though bloodless. He wiped the mud across his coat and inventoried.

The leather straps holding the Bowie were tight around his shoulders. He brought his hand around and palmed the handle of the knife. He then reached to his holster and felt it vacant. His head tilted downward. A small river of water fell from it onto his already saturated boots. He saw the holster empty. He looked above and the moon returned his betrayed glance. The stranger bit his lip and then wiped it with his shirt cuff.

The static sound of the rain and the water flow were omnipotent. Across the tracks he could see the terrain leveling before changing to treetops. It was downhill. He pivoted from his position and turned to look behind the tower.

The hill was steep, but not impossible. Water raced unwanted from the highest points. He nodded his head slightly. He needed to leave the tracks. With treetops and the way of simplicity behind him, he began his trek up the hillside. It was not the first place they would look for him. He moved upward with an admirable pace. The night was young. The rain fell and the water continued to flow in it's only forecast direction, disturbing the land and disguising tracks as if he and the weather were working in concord.

***

Watermarked boot prints aligned the floorboards of the office leading to the sheriff's desk. The lawmen were situated around Collie finishing off what was left of the bacon. The soggy bread remained untouched. "Really comin' down out there," Upton said.

"Hell yes it was. Is," Collie said, pointing a finger at his coat, now hanging on the rack near the door. Water collected on the floor beneath it. "Ain't seen it like this in some time. If the soil gets too lose, we could have downed structures." He brushed the crumbs from his shirt, still wet around the collar. He looked to the occupied cell. "How long has he been out?"

Wells peered into the cell to see Billy lying with his eyes closed. "Can't be too long."

"How's he even sleepin'," Collie began, "With all this goin' on?"

Wells leaned forward in his chair. "We had us some words while you were gone. Upton and me and him. Think he might have had some acceptance of what's coming."

Collie nodded. "Well I should be looking for a change here." He stood up. "Of clothes I mean. Goddamn chair is wet. This place is a mess."

"Tim," Wells said.

"Upton, maybe get the broom. Or maybe wait til it dries up some," said Collie.

"Tim," Wells said louder.

"What, dammit?" Collie said. At this, Upton moved to get the broom. "Not now. I changed my mind," he said to him.

"Tim," said Wells, "He in the cell there has been told a bit about you." Wells raised his brow in a serious manner.

"Told a bit by who?"

"By us," Wells answered. "Me."

"Told a bit of what?" Collie asked confused.

"A petty bit 'bout your time before here." Wells huffed. "I told him about the Sioux attack from back in the day and what you done." He paused a moment and sized up Collie's reaction. There was not one. "How you helped them settlers."

Collie dropped his head.

Upton interjected, "Sheriff, if you'd have heard his accusations about that girl sending you food you'd have wanted us to say something too." Collie held up his hand signifying that he wanted him to stop talking. He lifted his head and sighed. "Sheriff?" Upton said, concerned. "You alright."

Collie nodded. There was a long awkward silence. "Yeah, what's done is done."

"We meant it in the best, Tim," Wells said. "But we was wrong. I know you don't like talking 'bout any of that. I respect you keepin' yourself private."

Collie nodded to that as well. "You want that?" he said, pointing at the waterlogged bread on the desk. Both deputies acknowledged 'no' in unison. He picked up the plate and moved to the door. He pulled it and the wind helped with a push. The sound of the teeming rain invaded the office. With his right hand held low, he raised it swiftly, flinging the spongy loaf onto the road. He stepped back into the room and an image caught his eye. Fading in through the rain, he could make out a rider on horseback charging through the downpour. He shut the door. He squinted through the glass pane at the rider and his exhale painted a circled fog dissolving his vision. "Better the critters outside get it than the ones inside." Collie came to the center of the office, brushing his clothing again. "No sign of stopping it seems." He sat at his desk. "Either of you boys wanna head home?"

"You sure you're alright about the conversation that transpired here without you?" Wells said.

"I don't much want to talk about that. I'm sure there was reason behind it, though a habit it won't become. Now you's stayin' or goin'?"

"I'd just as soon wait 'til it slows," Wells suggested.

"Me too," Upton said.

"There's someone out there in this," Collie said, paying it little mind.

"I'm sure there must be," said Wells who was making himself comfortable again.

Collie cleared his throat before speaking. "Naw I mean literal like. Saw him when I was dumping the bread. On horseback."

"Poor bastard," said Wells.

"Damn right," said Collie, punctuating the thought. "I could do a whiskey on a night like this. Keeps you warm." He put out the feeler to the room and then pulled the bottle from his drawer. The deputies perked. "Only one though," he paused, "at a time."

Upton chuckled. The sheriff tilted the bottle over the shot glass, not an ounce spilling. As he tilted it over the second, lightning crashed and thunder boomed in the way that meant the gods were warring. "Christ," said Upton, and before another word could leave his mouth the door to the office burst open.

The figure of a man stood in the doorway. He was opaque and badly lit from the front. Water drained from his clothing as if he were the very cause of the rain. The lawmen tensed for a moment in anticipation. "Sheriff Collie?" the man spoke. His tone had the ring of business.

"Yeah I'm Collie," he said. He put down the bottle and rose. "Everything alright?"

"I've come with a message," the visitor said.

"Bring yourself in out of the damned rain," the sheriff said. Collie corked the bottle and dropped it back in the drawer.

Stepping forward, the visitor pushed the door closed with haste. He wore his poncho like a wooden stock. He turned to see the faces of the lawmen polluted with impatient anxiety. "I'll get right to it. Name's Miles Smith. I'm a deputy from up the way in Yankton."

Collie and Wells both turned back to Upton when they heard the name. "No relation," Upton said, keeping eyes on the man.

Ignoring the chatter, the visitor went on. "I was sent here with a warning from Sheriff Dougherty. We had us an...incident tonight." His voice shuddered. "Lot of folks dead, killed."

Their ears perked and bodies straightened at the words like they were poison, infecting the very air they breathed. Collie cleared his throat scratching away any notion of tranquility and hope of peace nocturnal. "Go on," he said measuring obligation more than want. He kneed the whiskey drawer shut and listened to the man.

***

Before the visitor's intrusion, he had lain silent and still printing memories across his eyelids, all the while listening to his captors and the cadence of their voices as they spoke and tended to know things both said and unsaid. His former boasting had become a youthful understudy behind apathy and the guilty receipt of his crimes. He remained motionless though amused as he heard Deputy Wells recount his error to Sheriff Collie and how Collie in turn brushed it aside with a tremor in his voice revealing his true emotion. Upon this interplay, an honest grin dusted over Billy's face for the first time since his capture.

Even when the entrance door broke open for the second time that night, Billy continued to lie there on his side eyes closed and his legs straightened fighting the fetal position. He heard the visitor introduce himself as law and attempted to pay him no mind. It was not until the man spoke of the death in the town he was apprehended in that Billy gave his full attention.

Not a soul seemed to notice Billy as he pushed himself from the cot and sat upright in his cell. From between the bars, he could see the rectangle of lawmen conversing. The sheriff and Deputy Wells were nearest the man listening intently to his words and asking questions of their own while Deputy Upton Smith looked on with fierce observance. Billy made a move to stand and then opted against it. The visitor had removed his hat. His hair was wiry and thin. Billy noticed a rough and almost secondhand look to the man's appearance. He was a deputy, but changed or haunted by the episodes in life around him.

As he listened on, he could see the startle in the other men's faces and the remorseful eyes of the messenger like a man who had to put down a wounded yet beloved animal. Billy's past was not one of merit, but the crimes conversed upon were bred differently.

When the messenger reached the point in his tale of the murdered woman, the disposition of the room formed into fury. Billy's own stomach churned as the deputy spoke of the woman's mutilation, her neck cut so severely that it severed through the spine, eyes removed, and the bed sheets inked almost entirely in blood. Billy drew his attention to Upton, who had jerked forward suddenly as if to vomit. It was dry and subtle to the others enough to not be noticed. He then looked to Wells. The older deputy had clenched his own lip between his teeth when the talk of the woman began and he had drawn blood, the small crimson stream inching its way to the upper part of his chin before wiping it away.

Images of the events swirled about Billy's mind disorderly like renegades bowing to no one and refusing to stop on the commands of any creature. He had left the conversation mentally and did not even notice when he said, "My God," aloud. The officers peered at him. There was no admonishment, the heinous and appalling story uniting the men in a more common than they knew code of humanity. Billy made his way back to the cot. When he did, he dropped his head in his hands as if overcome.

Before he left, Deputy Miles Smith warned the men to remain on guard against occurrences out of the ordinary, though he went on to assure them that Yankton was in motion to obtain justice. A posse had been dispatched soon after the massacre to follow the rail tracks and the fleeing train. Riders were sent to neighboring camps and towns as informers. The men agreed that Little Creek would be the least likely place for him to surface, it being neighbor to Yankton. Smith added that keeping a simple lookout was the best any outsiders could do. This did not seem to sit well in the room, especially with Wells.

With the door shut and the visiting deputy's presence gone, the air hung stressed and heavy. No one spoke for a time. When they finally did, it was not to Billy, who had taken on the display of a broken man. The cracked beams above his newest bed had once again come into full view and his mind sailed recklessly across his thoughts and memories. He reached his elbows out and then down toward the bed, pushing his shoulder blades together. His back cracked and popped. The mattress below him, devoid of any semblance of comfort, antagonized his body as the stuffing pressed to the edges where he had no weight. But still, he laid there uncaring, staring at the ceiling with eyelids gradually weighing as he lingered a prisoner in a cell, while others in the night roamed free.

Chapter 15

The stranger was on his belly at the edge of the hill. His clothes were muddied and degraded from the storm, which had ceased only an hour ago. In front of him was a squirrel, dead and skinned. Its minimal entrails rested beside it. Pieces of flesh were torn from the bone. He had eaten them raw. The bowie was motionless next to the animal's carcass, the edge crusted burgundy with the once fresh blood. The ground around him was soft and the mud had inched around him, molding an outline of his body.

He had reached that spot in the night after limping blindly through the woods. A path revealed itself almost accidentally and he had followed it a ways until he could make out the framework of the ridge. He moved off the path and rested there. The pain in his hip subsided. Lightning flashes offered glimpses of the town below and when the storm ended and the sun peeked over the trees on the hills ahead of him, it illustrated fully the the quaint settlement.

From his vantage, the stranger could see all happenings on the main road going in and out of the town. The road was L shaped and the sheriff's station was nearest him on his right. Neither lawmen nor posses could ride through undetected.

As the day passed along a bit slower than most, the sky had become clear contrasting the storm and the stranger continued his stay on the hill. There was little action in general, especially at the law station and he could make out the fact that there were only a few personnel. The men he ascertained to be sworn in, exchanged turns reconnoitering the streets, walking past the structures and folk along the road. They took their time. Upon completion of their watch, they would head back to their office where the next man was awaiting the same task.

Beyond midday a wagon approached with two men visible. They were carrying weapons. The stranger stiffened marginally and lowered his head near the dirt. As he crawled near the edge, he saw the wagon sink to a point where the mud swallowed the wheels. A number of settlers including some law came to aide. The stranger chuckled to himself at the sight. More than one person had fallen into the filth during the assistance, only to right themselves before falling again. The tribulation lasted some time before the wagoner and his partner were able to conduct their business. When they finished, they unhitched and carried on down the road. The stranger breathed easy again.

He had set himself away from the ridge and moved through the outskirts of the forest. He rubbed his hip as he walked and he walked simply to keep the blood moving all the while, keeping a bird's eye on the town.

Between the sunrays and exertion, his hunger was great. Life on the ridge was scarce, but existent and he was patient. He came to a tree with a berry bush beneath it. They were red and round. He picked one and held it. It popped and the juice, a pittance, stained the tips of his fingers. He picked another and threw it amusingly to the ground. The trees rustled above him and the shadows of the birds blackened the earth as they took flight.

The stranger moved back to the ridge in the place he had lain for hours. It had the mark of his body. The outline dried and solidified in the sun. He cocked his head to the side and laughed at the vacant blueprint and set himself near it. Beside him, a swarm of flies had settled over the squirrel carcass. He stabbed his knife through the body and flung it near the woods. The town was still quiet. He waited.

The day's course had begun to devolve. The stranger could see the sun staring back without having to raise his eyes. Across from him and the ridge the sky turned pastel, colored like flavored cotton and the closest star, orange-hued and centrifugal, journeyed downward imminently.

Lanterns and torches in the town had begun to spark. The streets were occupied, though much unlike the population in Yankton. As he observed the happenings from above, they emitted a familiarity connotative with small communities. There were problems in the town, like the wagon, but it was fixed and more importantly, fixed by the help of the people. There was nary gunfire, and no fights erupted. There were peddlers and businesses, passers-through and locals, drinkers and hunters and gamblers and traders, women and children and men and youths together, through the way things carried on, conveying to him a semblance of order and even amity.

He continued to examine, paying a close mind to visiting riders and the sheriff station in particular. Neither had raised alarm, but he watched nonetheless. From behind him there was a crow call and his eyes moved mechanically over his shoulder. He did not hook fully and then returned himself, occupied. It sounded off again. Twisting his arm over his spine, he removed the Bowie from its holster. It was tarnished and unattractive, though its look betrayed its arresting sting. He gently ran his finger over the blade. When he reached the knifepoint, he pressed down, indenting his fingertip without puncturing it. He heard another crow call and then a flap of wings. It was over the carcass of the squirrel. The knife flew from his hand, striking the crow and impaling it to a tree. The stranger spun. The blade split the bird between the wings through its chest. It called no more. The stranger moved over his kill. He freed the knife from the tree and held the dead animal near his face. He plucked the bird clean as best he could and when he was satisfied, he ate its parts raw in the dying sunlight.

***

"Time comes for us all, Deputy Smith," Billy spoke from his cell. "The thing about time is that it's got no prejudice. And it's the only thing strong enough to kill anything. I mean hell, time can kill a hundred foot oak, or even a rock. Time can kill a rock. It's the one thing that's gunnin' for us all." He slouched into the cell bars. "What you think of all that youngin'?"

"I think that we're about the same age so youngin' don't apply," Upton said from his desk without looking.

"What you think of time?"

"I think you mighta' actually been thinking too much in that there cell and its rottin' your brain."

"Now how can thinking rot your brain officer? You even hear yourself?"

Upton kept his face in his book. "No, see, that's the problem. I can't hear myself. I can't hear myself think and I sure as hell couldn't get a word in if I wanted to, you been talkin' so damn much."

Billy rubbed his nose and sniffled. "Well what else is there for me to do?"

"Why don't you think about why you're in there and what it is you done?"

"Hell, my friend that's all I've been doing. Getting myself straight in here. What you think led me to my 'time' conversing?" Upton huffed. Billy pushed away from the bars. "Time's a funny thing it is. It never moves quicker or slower, but we feel it does. Never bows to anyone, never stops coming. It always leads to tomorrow. No matter what."

"Not for everyone," Upton interjected and then Billy shut up. The deputy noticed the silence. He stopped reading, but did not reveal this to the prisoner. He remained quiet a moment longer and then peered at the cell. Billy's gazed at the floor, despondent. The deputy pushed his chair out and as he did, Billy moved to his cot.

Upton walked slowly approaching the cell. "I'm sorry 'bout that. It was out of order."

"Not to worry none, Deputy."

"Still, you bein' in there is no cause for me to disrespect."

"I must say, this is the politest damn group of lawmen I've ever met." He saw Upton was holding something between the bars, shaking it to draw attention.

"I brought this over for ya'," Upton said. The prisoner rose and moved to the bars. "It's a book. About Kit Carson it is."

"Kit Carson?" Billy asked. "He that army scout?"

"Yeah. Fights Apaches in this one here. It's a good one. I liked it at least. Thought it might help pass the time for ya."

Billy reached for the book. The pages were curled up around the edges, yellowed and worn. "I'd rather it stopped than passed."

Upton waited a beat to respond. "That's what you said it couldn't do."

"Thought you weren't listening," Billy said with a smirk. There was the sound of footsteps on the porch outside. "Looks like the sheriff's back from his prowl. You fella's even know what you're looking for out there?" Upton gave an irked expression. "I mean guy shoots up a town and no one gets a look enough to describe him. You don't know if you're looking for a dwarf or a giant."

"He's about average size they said, and it ain't none of your concern, Billy."

"Come on now, I'm just a curious man by nature. You don't deem it a waste of your time to go looking for a man, a criminal, in your own town, that of which is located not ten miles from where the crime took place, who is neither tall nor short, light or dark, fat or skinny, and who hopped a train from the previous town to a place called far away?"

"I know that I'm wasting my time now. Enjoy that," Upton said pointing at the book. "I'm going for some air."

Billy raised his eyes in faux enthusiasm. "I'll meet you out there. I just want to get a few chapters in," he said, holding up the book. The door to the office shut and Billy sat on the cot holding the dime novel tightly around the edges and brought it to his face. He fanned the pages. They sent a cool breeze and the aroma of old paper filled his nose. He closed his eyes, bringing back memories.

He breathed a sigh and then regarded the book's cover. "Kit Carson, the fighting trapper," he said to himself. The cover featured the main character, rugged and bearded suppressing two Indians, one under each hand. Billy ran his finger over the outline of the caricature and then remained staring as if his mind had wandered off without permission.

Shaking his head, he snapped out of his trance to see the sheriff enter the building, his face worn and his conscious deteriorating. "Why don't you let me take a turn out there sheriff?" Collie sat down without answer. His eyes were at his desk and his profile to the prisoner. "Forgive me sheriff, but it seems I've been deserted here. What say you and me have ourselves a conversing session. What you make of the concept of time?"

Collie leaned back in his chair, wearing an expression of deep regard for the prisoner's words. He cleared his throat. "Time's a funny thing Billy..."

Billy's face dropped, sore as the sheriff spoke his own words back to him nearly verbatim. "He tell you that out there?" he asked, perturbed.

"Who?" Collie said suspiciously.

"Smith."

He held his breath a moment. "Yeah I guess he did."

"Well they are thoughts. My words. I thought 'em myself."

"Huh", Collie said, amused and wrinkling his nose. "He pawned 'em as his own."

"That doesn't seem fair."

"That's the trend."

***

The stranger began his descent from the ridge. The hill declined sharply and he was slow and careful as he advanced. The cover of darkness offered permission to operate more freely. When he reached the base, he squatted down to get his bearings. There were buildings not thirty yards before him and he could see people's shapes lit by the firelight of the road torches as they passed across the alleys.

Upright, he inched to the nearest structure. It was two stories and built from pine. He could tell from the knots in the wood. From the edge of town closest to him, there were six buildings side by side, all occupied by what he ascertained to be businesses. Cornered at the L in the road was the seventh, the sheriff's station. The stranger hunkered down with his back against the third building. Its sign was to the road and he knew not what purpose the structure held.

He removed his hat and peered around the corner. The alley was lit only at the front end by the flames of the torches as they licked their way sultry at the shadows, curtaining his end in blackness. He gazed above and saw the night sky overcast blinding the moon and stars. It was brighter when he closed his eyes.

Ahead of him was a collection of crates, piled without care against the side of the second building. The stranger kept his watch from the corner. He paused his breathing a moment. A woman walked by followed by a man. Neither drew their attention to the alleys. He stayed in his place and waited for another passer. One came, portly and dawdling, perhaps even drunk stumbling from porch to porch. He too paid no mind.

The stranger exhaled and crept serpentine to the empty crates. He kept low as they grew larger and then kneeled when he had reached them. Halfway down the alley, his field of vision grew. He could make out the scene of the road and those populating the storefronts across it. The town was by no means lively, nor was it vacant. There were a handful of folks, mainly men, scattered across the streets. Some held bottles and some smoked in conversation with others. Horses were hitched at various posts, though they were few and there were few wagons. He had seen the livery and stable at the far side of town from the ridge. It was a distance from his current standing and he was armed only with his knife. He sat down and let some time pass.

His back was to the wall of the second building and he sat on his rear with his knees to his chest. He rolled mud between his fingers waiting and watching as it eroded and flattened in his pinching grasp. As people walked past, he paid close attention. He used his peripherals for the women, but stopped and carefully observed the men in the glimpse he was given. Each had moved too quickly up to this point and he was unable to discover if they were carrying. He picked up another batch of caked mud and began rolling. Patience was a virtue.

His assiduity was returned with the sound of a slamming door. He peered through the crates and saw a man across the road. His outline was difficult to make out with his distance from the torches. The stranger comprehended certain grit in the man's posture and squinted further through the crates deeply focused. The man struck a match and brought it to his face and the orange tip of the cigarillo glowed insignificantly through the thickened night. The stranger lifted himself to see over the crates. His weight dug into the cheap wood as he leaned ever forward.

The man dragged off the cigarillo and then turned, flicking the match to the street. As he did, his coat shifted and his gunmetal flashed catching the firelight for a split second. The stranger missed nothing and then stood like a tall stalk in the alley. He pressed himself toward the lighted half. As the stranger became dimly illuminated, he stared down at his ragged disheveled self, clothes in tatters stained dirty from events previous. His presence in the street would cause alarm so he acted accordingly, skillful in his steps.

He approached the edge of the outlet. Others in the road were distanced as if this happening was predestined and the two men's paths were cut off impenetrable to outsiders. The stranger saw the cigarillo tip dead on from a distance of twenty yards. The man was facing his direction. As if on cue, the stranger reached the intersection of the alley and road and then immediately tensed his spine and bolted his hands in the air as if he were threatened to do so. The man across the street removed himself from his leaning post and postured his curiosity. The stranger laughed sardonically and deliberately spun himself keeping has hands raised. He began slowly heading back into the deep stretch toward the caliginous ridge he appeared from like a lone man forced into a death march. He kept his hearing acute for the footsteps of his mark. The man would follow. Not all men respond to those in need of aid and for those men that do not it is often in their nature to scavenge off the victims in cause of their own betterment. The stranger knew not which type the man was, though he was intent to discover.

He reached the ebon half of the alley where the grasp of the flames ceased. As he stepped past the worn crates, his pace quickened to a near run until he made the back side of the second building. The stranger pressed his face against the pine, skimming across it until his right eye was naked to the alley. The silhouette of his mark was present and moving steadily toward him. The stranger readied his weapon, holding it firmly though in a way that the blade was parallel with his forearm, hidden from a glimpse.

The man grew ever closer. The stranger heard the gun cock and his knuckles whitened around his knife. "What the hell's going on down here?" the man asked. Anger and bravado sheltered the tremble in the man's voice. The stranger noticed and greased a divided smile. "You let the man go!" he added, again to a vacated audience. The stranger was still. It was difficult for him to make out the figure of the man with his shape bleeding into the surrounding nightfall. The outcome of a knife throw at this distance in the current conditions would be uncertain.

The stranger allowed his head and a portion of his body to emerge into the passage knowing well that he would not be seen immediately. A fidgeting unveiled itself, likely the retrieval of the gun. "Pssssst." The stranger hissed the sound across his pallet and stepped completely into the open.

"Who's there?" the man said. The stranger could tell now that the gun was pointing directly at him.

"You scared him off," the stranger said.

The man kept his gun raised. "What's going on back here?"

"He tried to rob me, but you scared him off," the stranger said, inching his way toward the man.

The man bent his arm at the elbow, sinking the gun. "Where'd he go? You alright?" His tone suggested suspicion as well as inquiry.

The stranger stepped closer again. "I'm fine. Thank goodness you came." He paused for a response. His vision was dulled and he could not see when the man uncocked his gun, but the sound seemed amplified, betraying the secret. "Samaritan," the stranger began, moving within an arm's length. "I need your gun."

"Hu-," was all the man was able to muster before the stranger's blade sprinted over the man's throat, opening it and shedding the outer darkness over his lifeblood. The man grabbed at his own throat in a pitiful attempt to close the wound. The stranger could see that the victim was still holding the pistol and the blood pumped over the barrel as the man fell to his knees and then to the ground.

"I must thank you again," the stranger said. He crouched and turned the body so the man was on his back. He extracted the gun from the dead man's grip and placed it in his own holster. He then rolled the lifeless body over the mud against the building, moving with determined quickness. As he rose, there were voices from the street near the lit end of the alley. With their current dance completed, it was as if time had suddenly regained itself. He darted toward the voices and concealed himself behind the crates. Through them he saw two men stroll by leisurely. One bellowed a laugh as they crossed and then their voices faded.

The stranger emitted an audible breath of relief and abruptly noticed he was sweating. He wiped his brow. Inhabiting the dark for such a time, his eyes had adjusted and he removed his new pistol from the holster. He clicked open the revolving chamber. The weapon was black against the muddied earth and he could see nothing. He rubbed his thumbs over the cartridges determining that all but two had been dispensed. He needed ammo. However, the night was young and full of opportunities.

Chapter 16

They were standing on the porch, the three of them, speaking while the wind whispered under their voices in the cool crisp evening. The streets carried fewer passengers than usual. Storm clouds had again gathered, masking the sky's inhabitants from the onlookers below and dampening the clarity of the full moon. The lawmen were huddled together revealing their tins openly on their chests.

Wells stood with a double barrel shotgun pointed downward while Upton held a Spencer rifle. Their adornment had brought looks from the town's people as they sauntered over building fronts, armed sentries at the ready. "You want us to keep up the rotation Tim?" Upton asked. Collie hesitated, regarding the question, and noticed their similar looks of bridled concern over the futility of the situation.

Collie huffed and tapped his boot lightly on the porch. Wells broke the moments of silence. "Chances of that man that done what he did in Yankton pushin' over to our side is slim at most. Guy'd have to be thicker than a herd's worth a' cow shit in a mud river."

"I tend to agree with ya," Collie began, "But I can't justify the risk of not doing."

"You're the boss," Wells answered. "I'm talking too much nowadays. Too much talk is bound one way or another to lead to statements of stupidity. Remember that," he said nodding to Upton.

The young deputy gestured to the interior of the sheriff's office. "Well I've seen it first hand from that one in there."

Wells spit tobacco onto the road. "So that's how he's taking it?" He asked, putting the question to both men.

"Taking it?" Upton asked.

Collie continued scuffing his boots over the porch as if impatience had gotten the better of him. "Imagine that you had a timeline put to your life. How'd you respond when the end got closer?" Upton shook his head, his eyes traveling distantly for an answer. "Some men don't say a word. Others externalize every damn thing that pops through their skull."

"Some get goddamned defiant," Wells added.

"Some do," Collie said. "But almost all of them try and make a deal."

"He hasn't yet," said Upton.

"No he hasn't," Collie said and then spit on the ground himself. "But it ain't over yet." As he finished, the wind picked up. It was a pleasant respite from the night's heat which drew sweat as they patrolled.

"Where was this ten minutes ago?" Wells said, scanning his eyes a final time over the road.

"Upton and me will head out for this one. Your turn with the talker," Collie said to Wells.

Wells shook his head in amused disbelief. "Figures the temperature drops for you two."

"Some men are favored," Collie said.

With that, Wells opened the door to the office. Before even attempting to enter, the prisoner's banter had begun. "Why mister Virgil Wells," Billy said in faux excitement. "I've been waiting-."

Wells closed the door as quickly as he opened it. "It ain't me that's favored," he said and latched his foot to the porch rocker, pulling it toward himself.

Collie and Upton laughed quietly. The young deputy let out a yawn which was then echoed by Wells. "Little Creek's finest," Collie said with a hint of sarcasm. "Come on deputy. Let's get goin'." The sheriff's words were punctuated suddenly by the sound of gunfire. He jumped a start, a move quickly repeated by the others. "That's damn close." He stepped off the porch with Upton and came to a sudden halt as his boots struck the mud. He spun back to face the office. Wells had already thrown the shotgun and Collie mechanically retrieved it in mid-air. "You stay here in case there's a group. Shut the door and man the armory." Gunfire erupted again in short bursts. "Shit," Collie said firmly. "I'll send back the word when I can."

"Be careful," Wells insisted and then moved inside with haste. He shut the door. Pausing a moment to collect his thoughts, he then moved to the center desk to extinguish the lantern. "I know you ain't said nothing Billy, but keep your mouth shut til' I tell you not to." The room did not dim, but pitched itself charcoal and silent. Wells could hear himself huffing louder than usual. He crouched and tried to control his breathing. Through the window, he could see the barren overcast sky, a mite more illuminated than his current placement. Remaining prone, he progressed to the door. Wells's raised his head deliberately until he was able to see out the corner of the door window. The streets were empty and his partners were nowhere in sight. Where moments ago there were gunshots, the night had since turned silent. Wells squinted and shook the nerves from his head. He removed his pistol from the holster.

"What's going on Virgil?" he heard from the cell behind him. Electing to answer non-verbally, he cocked back the hammer of his gun.

***

They pushed their way toward the sound of the gunplay. Townsfolk were beginning to press their faces against the windows. He and Upton were moving across the building fronts with their guns ready in tandem. Shots rang out again. The cracks blared contradicting the elements of the once peaceful evening. This time though, they were close enough to hear the laughter following the shots.

"That's at Bollard's," Upton said at a whisper.

Collie agreed. "Outside though. With the echo. I'm gonna kill him. Twice in one week with this." Two buildings down, Bollard's chain hanging saloon sign creaked with the sway of the breeze. Collie and Upton lowered their bodies and crept swiftly to the next building. They ducked in front of the entrance.

"Goddammit," Upton said.

"What?" Collie asked, flustered.

Upton motioned to the nearest window. The corner of the curtain was raised and small eyes peered through. The drape fell before Collie could lay his eyes. Upton shook his head. "They're more concerned with knowing than their own safety."

Collie tightened his grip on the shotgun and pressed the gun butt into his right shoulder. He kept a whisper. "Have your pistol out and ready. If I fire off both barrels, I'll be disarmed for a few seconds. It's on you then til I'm set."

"Don't take too damned long."

The gunfire sounded off, pulling the men's attention away from their plan. Once again there was laughter, only this time it was riotous. "What the hell's going on?" Collie grunted. "Let's go." He stood with his deputy following and moved down the alley adjacent to the saloon.

Collie held his hand up, indicating a stop. A hazy fog of gun smoke caressed the hanging air between the structures. The laughter was now more prominent. They heard voices from around the corner. "You miss again I'm liable to leave here a rich man," a voice said.

Collie turned to his deputy and dropped his brow. "These assholes," he said, losing the whisper. The tension in his back loosened and he lowered the shotgun while still allowing his finger to lightly graze the trigger. "Bollard or any you dipshits can hear me, it's Collie. Coming from the alley here. Don't shoot," he yelled. He pushed himself from a lean against the building and pivoted into the open behind the saloon. Upton made a nervous motion to grab at the sheriff. When Collie moved out of sight, Upton pulled his pistol and followed.

There were two men side by side and armed standing roughly ten yards from a row of empty whiskey bottles. The bottles were lined across a trough which was now riddled with holes, streaming water from nearly a dozen places. Bollard's heavy figure stood amongst a crowd of five, all men and giggling like hyenas in the twilight. Collie stepped closer still while Upton trailed quietly behind. When the sheriff approached within a few feet, he lowered his shotgun.

"What in the sweet shit are you fools doin'?" Collie asked. His voice was plagued with both anger and relief.

Bollard opened his mouth to speak, but instead heaved a wheezy laugh in all directions. It lasted longer than it was welcome. Collie kept his stare on the fat man while he lifted his shotgun one handed. The double barrels stared down the glass targets. All aside from Bollard had given Collie their attention. Collie pulled the triggers and both barrels thundered. Upton saw the sparks ignite their faces for a brief second. The largest bottle exploded simultaneously with the gun blast. The sound startled Bollard and his laugh turned to a choking cough before he tumbled over onto the ground. There was a moment's hesitation before everyone realized that no one was hurt. Collie's eyes never moved. They remained on the fat man. Collie's trance held within it a sense of steady authority and Bollard felt the burdensome gaze.

The saloonkeeper struggled to push himself from the mud. He reached out for a hand. He did not receive one. "Hell with you all," he said. Struggling to level his feet, he finally lifted himself from the mud. A conspicuous stain clung to the entire left side of his body like a parasite and reignited the laughter of the men in the crowd. Collie opened his shotgun exposing the ejector and retrieved two more shells from his coat pocket terminating the laughter. The sheriff standing tall and unyielding finished loading his gun. The men jolted in unison at the hollow click of the now readied weapon.

"Now any shit bird present can give answer provided it's comprised entirely of intelligence. Anything less will meet with unkindness." Seconds passed. Time seemed to slow up by double. "Chrissakes," Collie said with revealing irksomeness.

"Well hell sheriff, there ain't much to it." The man stepped forward from behind Bollard. He was tall and skinny with a shirt that draped excessively around his limbs.

Collie made a gesture to get on with it. "Say it Slim 'cause the kid and me are losing patience."

"Ok. Well Pete and Emmett here bet each other about who's the better shooter. Only Pete's claim is that he gets better the more drunk he gets. So we waited while Pete shitfaced himself and Emmett sobered and took it all out back and here's about where you come in."

Collie looked to the heavens in disbelief. "It's damn near midnight."

Bollard cleared his throat before interjecting. "If I may Collie, I'd like to offer myself up to blame for this here incident."

"You're goddamn right you're to blame," Collie answered.

Bollard huffed. "Well it wasn't me that did the shooting."

Collie turned to Upton and shook his head. "You think any mind would be paid to us shooting him?"

"Now Collie that'd be a violation of my-"

"Shut up," Collie said, cutting off the fat man. "What'd you hit Pete?" There was a chuckle in the audience.

Pete raised his head. A drunken pool swished from eye to eye as his head swayed side to side. "Ifink Ihirtit all." He exhaled the words as if the dialogue itself was an accident before falling onto the ground. Collie squinted at the specimen and then hid a smile, revealing it only to his deputy.

Collie waited to collect himself before he addressed the men again. "It's late dammit. Y'all head home and get his drunken ass out the mud. I oughta lock every last one of you up." Slim and another man moved to retrieve Pete.

"Wait just a minute there Sheriff," Emmett said with his eyebrow cocked upwards. "You a bettin'man?"

Collie ignored the question and turned to go back up the alley to his office. "Next time y'all get locked up. Pullin' this shit." He and Upton began walking.

Emmett placed his hand near his mouth and raised his voice. "I's just wondering. Since we's already got this place woke up, how'd you like to try for the title. You hit that whiskey with that damned cannon of a shotgun, but how's your aim with a pistol? Been a while for you hasn't it? Best see if you've gone soft."

Collie planted his feet and stopped moving. "You got yourself some nerve. Challenging an officer of the peace after nearly getting' arrested."

"Come on sheriff. It won't take but a minute," Emmett said.

"I ain't runnin' myself against you like this. I got nothin' to prove." He waited a moment, deep in thought. "But Deputy Smith will take you on." Upton shot a look at Collie then the men and then back to Collie. "6 shots only. Load 'em up. 6 shots only and then fuck off home." He gave a confident nod to his deputy. "Before it starts, I need Slim here to run past my office and tell Deputy Wells of what's occurring." Slim jogged forward unable to mask his excitement. He reached the edge of the alley, about to disappear from sight. "Slim," Collie called. "Make sure to announce yourself to him. Otherwise you'll end up shot."

***

The stranger watched with startle and intrigue as the streets emptied at the sound of gunfire. The people scattered like mice. He had jumped at the cracks himself. The shots, as they so often were, entered boldly and unannounced. He moved himself to the intersection of the alley and road, butting his head out carefully. He remained ready to bolt back into the shadows at the first sight of men on horseback. He waited and no one came.

The triangle of lawmen at the office entrance had dispersed at the gunfire. Two had fled to the scene leaving one behind, assumably to guard the armory. The stranger honed in on the lone officer crouched in the shadowed building. "One two," he whispered quietly referring to his own stock of bullets.

The guns championed again from the opposite side of town. The bullet whaps were sharp and steady. It was pistol fire. This time he did not flinch. He simply held his stare upon the sheriff's office, unaltered and refreshed at the glimpse of new possibilities.

His virtue of patience was nearly betrayed as the stranger felt himself shaking in anticipation. A thunderous boom echoed from the same focal point. A shotgun. He played the imagery of hypothetical scenes. A quiet burden retook the night.

The casual slip of conscious so often takes control when progression folds. The stranger's imagination commandeered his thoughts as the situation unexplainable continued until he was brought back. From the corner of his eye, he caught the movement of a man approaching the sheriff's office. He was slender and tall. The stranger angled his head like a curious dog. The approaching man sped urgently and then came to a sudden stop at the sheriff's front door. The man spoke, though it was impossible for the stranger to hear at his distance. Whatever was said must have worked. The slow growth of illumination emerged from the interior of the station. The door was opened by the third law man, his shape recognizable to the stranger by the lantern in his hand. They conversed briefly.

The stranger watched on like a limited narrator imagining what was being said. The voices were still too low even in the hushed night. He paid close attention to their body movements as they spoke. Their conversation was brief and was concluded by the visitor being shooed off of the porch. The stranger moved for the first time since the gunfire, perking up and unknowingly digging his right heel into the mud. The law man shut the door forcefully, but remained outside. The sound echoed boisterously through the streets. "Huh," the stranger muttered to himself.

Through the thick cut of night along the road, the stranger tread as the law man scratched the rocker across the porch to sit in recess. The deputy appeared steamed after his meeting. The stranger could offer relief. The man ahead of him had taken to a tranquil sag in the chair stretching his arms outward as if unburdening himself of the day's events. The torches along the street had begun their slow demise and their weak orange hue strained to reach the center of the road. The stranger walked peacefully along the dark path, his gun removed and in the sanctuary of his own hand as he drew nearer to the judicial center of Little Creek.

***

The changeless curves of the oak rocker rolled delicately over the hollow porch creating a low rhythm metronomical to Wells as he pushed softly off the boards with his toes. The contentment held in his eyes after Slim's account of the gunfire had begun to dissipate. He was relieved at first to understand that no one had been injured, but annoyed to learn of Collie's allowance of the incident. He would wait to vent himself until they got back. For now, the night had matured and he intended to enjoy whatever else he could amidst the twelve more shots he was told were coming.

He lifted his chin to the sky. Thin streaks of clouds revealed themselves only over the moon while the rest hid among the black meridian. His body had let go of all tension except for his hands. Wells gripped the arms of the rocker ignorant to the fact that the blood had fled his knuckles. He inhaled and six shots in rapid succession followed his exhale. "Goddamn," he said under his breath. His body jerked initially, yet he stayed right on rocking.

Wells shook his head and breathed an audible sigh. The shots had brought his attention back to street level, where a noticeable vacancy had lent itself. There was faint laughter from the saloon to his right. "6 more," he said to no one. He leaned back again with his head resting against the oak. Straight ahead, he thought he could make out a man's figure, growing as it approached. The firelight sniffed the figure's edges as he continued forward through the blackened tunnel. Wells straightened in the chair and hunched forward. There was a rumble in his gut. As he squinted and started to rise from his chair, the final shots from the saloon rang out. Ahead of him was a muzzle flash, an instant pop of fire before the bullet struck him in the face, an inch beneath his eye and all to him that was earthly vanished in a split second without cause or introduction. His body like a scarecrow's fell onto the rocker which subsequently banged against the office wall. His arms hung lifelessly over the sides as his head and body slid downward, stopping before he was leveled completely. His hollowed eyes open to the world cast their despondency outward in one final statement.

The stranger stepped through the gun smoke maintaining pace. His boots knocked on the pine boards and he stopped before the entrance. He stared down over his kill. He rubbed his thumb over the pistol hammer and replaced it to its origin. His brow lifted upwards and had there been a witness, he could attest to the look of pride that gleamed apparent in his face as the connection between the two men was now complete.

The door creaked in a pitch like a gopher's cry as he opened it and moved inside. A lantern stood on a desk projecting dead shadows of the room's objects against the walls, their shapes gothic in their distortions. He kicked the door closed and scanned the room. His gun was readied and he stepped forward into the foreign lair. He paced around the room, its contents indistinct in the poor light, muttering to himself as he went. He stumbled in frustration. "Where are you," he said rhetorically.

From behind him came a voice. He jumped, startled at the presence, spinning to ascertain its source. "You're him," it said straightly.

In the corner of his eye, the stranger caught the indistinct movement from inside of the prisoner cell. "Him who?" he asked. The prisoner approached the bars, as did the stranger and their distance closed. "I was expected, I take it."

Billy swallowed the hard lump in his throat. "You killed him didn't you? I saw the flash." The stranger stared without response as if he were considering something. "They're all looking for you. Everywhere."

The stranger creased his eyes and huffed in a disapproving manner before turning from the cell. He continued searching the office while Billy looked on in bewilderment. The stranger's mouth contorted in a wicked smile as a less than sizable door to his right came into view. He opened it and it creaked in the same way as the entrance. Four rifles and an equal number of shotguns stood side by side while six revolvers lay on a shelf beneath them. There were two gun belts with boxes of ammunition stacked low on the floor. The stranger peered outside. It was clear. He scurried through the supplies relieving the sheriff of two pistols, and a rifle, along with ammunition for each. He removed the gun he used to kill Wells from his holster and placed it, still warm, into the armory as if it were a payment.

He kicked the door shut and strapped the other gun belt, struggling to move quickly. He placed the new pistols in the holsters on each side of his hips. "They'll find you," Billy said through the bars.

"Not here they won't. Not this close to where it happened." The stranger cleared his throat and raised his rifle. The barrel leered across the room to Billy who stood his ground uncaring. "I appreciate the concern though." He took aim. "Sometimes things just fall into place."

Billy stared straight into his future, the long pit of the barrel withholding all hope. "Do it already. I'm finished here." The stranger opened his aiming eye and stared inquisitively at his target. "What are you waiting for? I've been doing nothing but waiting. Get on with it!" he yelled.

The stranger kept the rifle at his shoulder, lowering the business end away from his target. He laughed once through his nose. "I must be going," he said and turned his back to Billy.

"What do you mean?" Billy said.

"Your path is set."

"They'll come for you. They have to come for you. And I hope they give you the hell you deserve." Billy's volume increased as the man grew more and more distant.

The stranger reached the door, peering through its window before opening it. The streets were inhabited again though only slightly. He cracked the door to change his angle and noticed a small group of men stumbling across the road from the saloon. The door opened fully with the same creak. He looked once more to Billy whose position had not changed though his features were now unrecognizable from across the room. "I giveth," the stranger said just above a whisper and then fled the office, sprinting out of view like a windblown fog.

Chapter 17

"Why'd you let them go?" Upton asked Collie as they sauntered through the saloon alley.

"I guess I figured that in light of what happened in Yankton, this was on the side of innocence."

"I just don't want it to become a precedent."

"We'll lay down hard on the next crew."

"I hope that works."

Collie swatted at a cluster of mosquitos near the road torch. "I don't know what you're complaining about. Ya hit every damn bottle with your six."

"So'd he."

"Yeah, but you did it quicker."

"I guess I got a reputation now?"

"I'd reckon."

"That keeps the assholes away."

"I didn't say that."

"Wishful thinking I suppose."

They were not fifty yards away when they curved around the store front adjacent to Bollard's. Their pace was slow and meandering. Collie yawned and started speaking before it finished. "I think we can all call it a night when we get back. I reckon them shots would scare off anyone lookin' at comin' here. Intentions true or not." Upton stopped suddenly. Collie took a few more steps before noticing. "How'd I offend you now?" he said, raising his arms. Collie's own brow creased when he saw Upton. The deputy's mouth was agape in horror before he closed it to swallow the lump. Collie followed the line of vision until the image of the bereft body hanging over the rocking chair on their porch presented itself. "Jesus," he said. They started their sprint to the body. With each step into the mud, the gap between them and their destination seemed to widen. Their boots kicked up filth as they ran.

The body became less of a profile as they approached and Collie, who was in front, slowed as he recognized his friend. When he was near ten feet of Wells, Collie stopped, hesitating. Upton ran past despite his superior and halted in front of the dead man. Collie picked back up in a walk, perhaps with the thought that by slowing the process, the outcome would change.

"Oh my Christ," Upton said. He brought his fist sideways to his mouth and bit down on his clenched index finger.

Collie's face transfigured from the irony of hopeful doubt to certitude. His boots thumped onto the porch leaving an insubstantial mud trail. Upton remained on the road, distant from the scene. The sheriff dropped the shotgun to the ground, unable to grip it and then stood over the body. Wells's eyes were open and unmoving, cast at the sky like they were admonishing a god. The bullet hole in his cheek bone had given way to a thin trail of blood appearing like a single extraneous tear drop that had leapt unwanted from its origin. There was no exit wound. Collie was breathing heavily from the short run. Both men hesitated to speak as if their voices had flown with their tranquility. Collie's chest heaved in and out while he shook his head, the movements small and appearing like a nervous tick. He looked to Upton who was cupping a hand over his mouth. Then simultaneously like they were shaken from a trance Collie said, "Billy," and Upton motioned to the front door.

They burst in with their guns up. Collie stepped straight ahead while Upton moved along the wall to the right. The room was virtually black aside from the inevitably vanishing light cast from the lantern Wells had lit. "Billy," Collie said authoritatively.

A figure bolted to the bars from inside the cell. "You just missed him Collie. Hurry." It was Billy's frazzled voice.

Collie looked at Upton. "Out back," he said. Upton nodded and swiftly departed the office. "You armed Billy?" He continued to inch forward with his pistol leading the way.

"Why the fuck would I be armed?"

"Put your hands around the bars above your head." The lantern flicker ebonized Billy's shape painting his silhouette. Billy raised his hands and slapped the bars before gripping them. "In my situation if I was able to retrieve a gun do you not think that I would then be able to relieve myself of the situation?"

"Keep them up til' I say."

"It ain't me you're looking for."

"Is there anyone else here?"

"I don't know where he mighta gone off to."

"There ain't nobody else here?" Collie verged upon the illuminated section of wall. The light brought shadow duplicitously to his face as he progressed to the cell. "Come on. Answer me dammit."

"No nobody's here but us."

Collie refused to lower his pistol though the tension in his forearm decreased. He was only feet away from Billy when Upton returned. He was announced when he banged his shoulder into the door. The sound was startling and Collie pivoted instinctively. "Whoa don't shoot," Upton said pleading and Collie brought his gun down with a burnt out sigh.

"Just stay there and don't move," Collie said to Billy. "I mean it." The sheriff stood straight, twisting his neck back and forth between the two men. "What?" he asked to Upton.

"Virgil's horse is gone Tim. He's gone too, whoever done it."

Collie dropped his look to the floor. It was too dark for the others to see his consternation. "Raise that lantern Upton. And light another one. Bring some damn light into this place." His tone was out of character. In the background he heard Upton searching for the lantern. "You can lower your hands Billy."

"Ain't you gonna frisk me first."

"You'd have shot me by now if you had the means."

Billy did as he was told. "I'm telling you Collie, it wasn't more than ten minutes ago that son of a bitch came in here then left."

Collie lifted his head in unison with the gradually intensifying light. Upton came from across the room with a lantern in each hand. He placed them on the desk nearest the cell. Collie nodded a thank you and then cocked his pistol and stepped toward the prisoner.

Billy jerked back in surprise. "Whoa now there's no need for that."

"You gotta tell us everything and make it quick," Collie said through his teeth.

Billy lifted his hands using them to shield his face. "I'll speak. Why wouldn't I? I seen some fucked up event tonight. Put it away."

Collie did not put it away, but he did not aim it either. "You said it ain't been ten minutes since he came in here and left."

"Yeah that's right."

"Why'd he come in here?"

"Took your guns from the closet there." Billy pointed at the pantry door.

Collie motioned to Upton who then opened the door. "He ain't lyin'," Upton said. "We're light."

"Shit," Collie said.

Billy slipped a glance through his fingers and then lowered his hands recognizing that Collie would not shoot. "Course I'm not lying. I couldn't see the whole thing, but I saw the barrel flash outside and then your dear departed crash against the wall in his chair. I knew he was dead when I saw his arm draped in the entrance over there."

"Who did it?" Collie asked.

"It was him," Billy answered.

"Him who?"

"Him who I heard about when eavesdropping. Him that came from Yankton. Butchered that girl and some others."

"You can't know that."

"I know it."

"How?"

"I just do. I saw his eyes. I just do."

"You saw his eyes? You saw his face?" Collie looked back to his deputy for a reaction. "Upton, what was that description the deputy from down the road gave us?"

"No description. Not from one damn person. Waltzed in and out like a wraith."

"That's what I remember too." Collie said. "Not a single witness from a town shot up like a war saw the person responsible. And the ones that did ended up dead. Yet you saw him Billy, and you're still alive."

Billy shook his head, disgusted. "Yeah I did see him and I see what you're getting at too. I am still alive. He came right up to me pointing the gun at my face. I asked him to do it. Said I had nothing to lose. Death is nothing more than a change of scenery. And he listened and walked off. Wasn't in his plan I guess."

"You talked to him too?" Collie asked.

"Not much talk other than what I told ya."

"And you know it was him that," Collie struggled, "shot Virgil."

Billy noticed the stressed tone in the sheriff's voice. "I'm sorry as hell about that. I saw the muzzle flash and heard him fall. All things considered, he seemed like a decent man." Billy hesitated a moment. "For a law man that is. You've all been fair with me."

Collie listened attuned with his prisoner. "We gotta move Tim," Upton said from behind. "He's got the jump on us." Collie rose trapped in congeries of possibilities. He backed away, thinking. "Tim?" Upton said urgently.

"Hang on," Collie ordered. "We can't just leave him out there." He pointed to the doorway and his fallen friend.

"But he'll be-

Collie cut off his deputy's words. "We're going to bury our friend. Go wake Fairclough and the Reverend if they ain't up already in this commotion. I have to sort this before I go."

Upton stirred dubiously. "The longer we wait, the farther he's gonna get."

"Just do it. I'm gonna ready supplies. Enough for two and then ready the horses."

"You got it," Upton said eagerly. He left the room. It was quiet. Collie paced to his desk and sat down. He retrieved a pen and paper from a drawer and began writing.

"What happens to me while you two are gallivanting?" Billy asked. There was no answer. "What are you writing?" He was again ignored. "Well when you two head off, you go ahead and leave me the rope. I'll stretch myself. There doesn't seem to be any other way outta here. Just make sure you send him you're after straight to hell."

Collie halted his scratch on the paper. He lifted his head. "What?"

"What do you mean what?"

"What'd you say?"

"Which part?"

"The last."

"I said to send him to hell."

"That's thinking that we ain't all headed there ourselves."

Billy scoffed. "The breed's different."

"From who?"

"From us"

"Us? As in you and me?"

"Yeah why not?"

Collie lowered his head back to the letter and moved the pen across the page. "Maybe you're right." The friction between the pen tip and the desk grew louder as he finished what he was writing. He placed the pen on the oak top and folded the letter in half. It was a careful deliberate act. The drawer made a hollow sound as he opened it and placed the letter inside.

Billy huffed from his cell. "Seriously Collie. What happens with me?"

"Same thing that happens to all of us."

The prisoner rolled his eyes. "I'd prefer it be someone from here that does it."

"What's the difference?"

"Feels right I guess. Are you two leaving immediately?"

"It ain't gonna be *you two*."

"What you mean?"

Collie stood, his figure prominent in the incandescent hue of the candlelight, and walked to the prisoner's cell. Billy sidled away unsure of the man's intentions. The sheriff pressed in against the bars and considered the confines before speaking. "I mean I got a deal for you."

II.
Odysseys

They rode out, the two of them, the town in hind view. Their pace was steady and their saddle bags bounced on the animals' ribs in unison with their strides. There was a rope tethered from the horn of Collie's saddle to the other horse's neck. They moved parallel to one another. Billy held the reins awkwardly, his hands fastened together with rope. His horse bore plenty of supplies, though nary a weapon.

The strawberry sky smiled down and the sun hid shyly behind the clouds in procrastination. The town grew continually smaller before moving out of sight as the path dipped and then circumvented the eastern ridge. Collie spurred his horse and the side horse followed. The two men were the only human life for miles and the surrounding artisan landscape threatened to consume them whole. They rode on peering hawk eyes over the impending trail. Billy tried speaking. They continued on in silence.

Hours passed and they increased their distance from Little Creek. Billy, now a free man in certain terms, kept a graced appearance of relief, though he was smart enough to keep it humble. The rocky slopes to the south and east had begun to taper and Collie slowed their pace. The land in front of them opened up offering a sudden and lesser known panoramic view of the omnipresent glory of nature.

The horses slowed coming to an eventual stop and the two men took pause, absorbing their extraordinary insignificance. Collie squinted ahead into the sun. "You're eyes good?" he said.

"Good enough."

"You see him out there?"

Billy raised his bound hands above his creased eyes. "So damned bright it's hard to tell. Wish the sun was behind us."

"He'd be only a speck I s'pose."

"We waited too long leaving."

"Notion of friendship is lost on you. And tracking in the black coulda' brought us further away anyway." Collie paid attention to Billy's tied hands as he lowered them back to the saddle horn. "I reckon we stay on the trail here," he said looking forward. "You reckon the same?"

"Your call."

"I know."

Billy waited for the sheriff to say more. He never did. "I haven't seen a single track that'd lead me to believe he hopped off the road."

"Forward then," Collie said and they took off side by side.

Hours died along with the miles, muted spectators, mere blotches on canvass. The rope connecting the animals remained tied, though Billy's horse had dropped behind as if in respect to the sheriff's authority. Or perhaps it was because Billy could not take the silence any longer, observing the older man and his pitched straight stare echoing not despondence, longing, or content. Collie simply kept on forward.

Up ahead the vast expanse narrowed giving way to a forested region and the green caps of the pine filled their view while the distant sounds of birds and wildlife echoed across the dirt. They slowed to a trot. Collie became alert at the bottleneck. He angled downward, feeling for his weapons. Two rifles, a Spencer and a Henry Lever Action, were encased in leather and slung over the left side of his horse while his shotgun lay along the right. He gripped the Henry by the handle, keeping his fingers away from the trigger and unveiled it. He moved it to his other hand so the business end was away from Billy. "Whoa," he said and the horses stopped.

"What's wrong?" Billy asked. "I don't see anything."

"You don't always see what's about to kill ya."

"There's not a track that wanders off the beaten."

"It ain't him I'm worried about."

"Sioux isn't likely in these parts."

"You know that?"

"I do."

"How can you be sure?"

"These parts belonged to others. Not Sioux. Though I don't think they're around anymore either."

"Well it ain't only Sioux that'll kill ya." Their eyes met. Collie shook his head. "You can tell that all from tracking our man?"

"Not just that."

"Jesus Christ. You sure he went through here?"

Billy huffed and looked at the ground. "May I?" he asked and jerked his head in a motion to dismount.

"Why?"

"Just to be sure." Billy put his weight into the stirrup and swung his leg across the animal. "Ya know this'd be easier if you untied me." Collie spit in his direction, though not at him. "Alright then." He took a few paces in front of the horses and lowered himself to a squat. The rain from previous nights had aided their quest. Molded lightly into the ground was the trace of a hoof print, stressed by an iron shoe. "It's gotta be him Collie."

"You sure."

Billy glanced back down, rubbing his fingers over the track. "It's got that same horizontal etching in it as Virgil's. That can't be no damned coincidence."

"I shouldn't think so. Get back on your horse."

Billy stood and sighed. "You're welcome," he said sarcastically and moved to his animal. He put his foot in the stirrup and quickly stumbled, losing his grip on the saddle. He looked across. Collie stared in the opposite direction. Billy attempted to mount the horse again and succeeded. "He must've gone through there." Collie placed his hand on his pistol and ran his thumb over the hammer without cocking it. "You know, we run into anything, how am I to defend myself?"

"How'd you plan on defending yourself from the rope if I left you there?" Collie said. Billy bit his lip as Collie looked down to fiddle with his holster. He stopped. He was pinching a bullet between his fingers. "Here you go," he said and tossed it to his prisoner.

Billy jolted faintly and caught it in his cupped hands. "What am I supposed to do with this?"

Collie raised his shoulders. "Try throwin' it."

"Hell," Billy scoffed. He placed the bullet in his shirt pocket.

"Let's go," Collie said and spurred the horse.

***

The forest was thick and dark compared to the open land and the sun struggled to bleed through, casting only anorexic beams sporadically to the areas deemed worthy. The two men continued forth, soft and careful. Collie had even shushed Billy despite the fact he hadn't said a word. The sheriff's right hand was near purple as he gripped the handle of the rifle and both men kept their attention savvy to details.

Collie did not know how much time passed, but it seemed to be racing. The trail had become increasingly obscure in the dense forest with fallen brown needles and he found himself stealthily looking to Billy for signs of guidance. The young man never seemed to notice and was doing exactly what Collie brought him along to do. There was a dichotomous blend of discord and harmony as they continued on listening to the wild chorus echo around them.

"It's opening a bit," Collie said sounding relieved.

"It isn't much further."

"How many times you been here?"

"I told you. I've been everywhere in this territory and probably the next at least twice."

"Thievin' the whole time I s'pose," Collie said.

"Something like that."

"Only something?"

"Well sheriff, you only know what you know."

"And you know more?"

"I know different."

Collie loosened his hand on the rifle, allowing it to breathe. "Well we'll have to rectify that." He took a deep breath and brought the rifle to a firing position. He took aim, moving the barrel toward Billy. He fired. Billy jumped as the gun erupted before his eyes.

"What the hell Collie?"

"Dinner," he said pointing to the dead rabbit in the brush.

***

He picked up his kill and rode hurriedly until the trees scattered and the land opened up again. They built a fire near the edge of the forest. The sky was clear and the stars stretched across the sky. Collie had the rabbit on a spit and he turned it slowly so only the most determined flames could get to it. When it was done, he removed the spit and shared the rabbit equally with his prisoner. They ate what little tough meat there was without talking. Billy licked his greasy fingers when he finished. "You still hungry Collie?"

"There's some sausage and jerky in my bag, but I'm inclined to save it until necessary."

"This'd be my best meal in days believe it or not."

"I can get another in the morning. Supposin' they ain't in hiding." Collie leaned back on a rolled up blanket resting his head and stared at the fire.

"There's nothing like a meal under the stars."

Collie peered up at them. "You find yourself a good woman that can cook and you might change your mind."

"Your wife can cook?"

"She could."

"She died?"

Collie nodded acknowledging yes.

Billy looked confused. "I knew that. Not sure why I asked."

"I don't want to talk about her."

"That's fine."

"Not with you I don't."

Billy chuckled to himself. "Why'd you let me go?"

"You ain't let go."

"I was swinging in a few days. That railroad, Dakota Southern and them Pinkertons could rest easy and you and yours go down as heroes."

"Is that how we go down?" Collie tipped his hat over his eyes. "Heroes?"

"So why then?"

"You saw his face. Who the hell knows how many outfits our killer here has got after him and our Pinkerton visitor claims no one knows what he looks like. But he walks into our prison, has a bonafide conversation with you and lets you live. That's just too damned perfect. I don't trust perfect, but I don't tend to mess with it either."

"Why not get an artist sketch and take Smith?"

"I need him back in town for this to work out."

"You think it will?"

Collie hesitated a moment and huffed. "I hope so." He rose and stepped toward Billy. He pulled a rope short in length from off his belt and placed a hand on Billy's back. "Lean forward."

"Is that necessary?"

"I think so. Lean forward."

Billy hunched and put his wrists together behind his back. "You best remember what a sport I'm bein' through this."

Collie bound the hands together and then tied the remains to a branch off the thick log behind Billy. "You do the same for me. Now go to sleep." He moved back to his side of the fire and brought his hat brim over his lids once he hit the ground.

Billy lay down near the fire opposite of Collie. He was restless, unable to find comfort. "You trust me not to do try anything huh?"

"Like what?"

"Like wriggle outta this," Billy said, waving his fingers behind himself.

"You couldn't wriggle free of that if you tried. Billy, you seen the same shit that I did at Creek. It musta' made an impression. Plus a man sticks to a deal. Plus you're tied to a log."

"Untie me then."

"You could earn it soon enough."

"Thanks for the trust."

"Billy,"

"Yeah?"

"I sleep real light." His eyes were already closed when he said it and his consciousness drifted off defying his final statement.

***

He woke to the snapping of a twig and raised himself on his elbows. His hat was still slanted forward and he brushed it back. The fire in front of him was in its downfall. It took a moment for his eyes to adjust. There was another sound. Only this time it was more like a dull clunk on wood. "Billy," he said in a loud whisper. There was no answer. He reached for the gun in his holster and found a vacancy.

"Other side Collie," said a quiet voice.

A jolt ran through the sheriff. He turned to his left in the dying firelight and saw Billy crouched not three feet away from him. He was staring directly into Collie, holding the Peacemaker in his hand with mild exuberance. Collie opened his mouth to speak and was forced to clear his throat when no words formed.

"You best calm yourself there sheriff and don't do anything stupid like run. You have no idea what kind of dangers can be on the prowl come nightfall."

Collie swallowed hard and pushed himself upward slowly until he was sitting. "Billy-"

"I mean it Collie. I'll put one in you and not think twice. Understand?"

Collie nodded, clenching his teeth together. "How'd you get out?"

"I wriggled free," he said shaking his head in amused disbelief.

Beads of sweat began forming on Collie's hairline. "Please don't shoot Billy. I have to finish this."

Billy brought his stare down to the Peacemaker as if mesmerized by its presence. "Sorry," he then said matter of factly and cocked the pistol. He started to lift it gradually. The seconds felt as heavy as the gun. Collie tensed and closed his eyes and in an instant, Billy let the hammer back to its resting place. "I was only foolin'," he said. In a fluid motion, he turned the pistol around in his hand, holding the barrel. The butt of the gun was now facing Collie.

"What?" Collie said, unable to contain his heavy breathing.

"Take it," Billy said, pushing the gun forward.

Collie hesitated a moment and then grabbed for the gun. Billy pulled it slightly out of reach. "What is this Billy?"

"This is me showing you that I can have a gun and not use it. And this is me telling you that I won't be tied up again." Collie placed his hand out, palm up, and Billy gave him the pistol. "You brought me here to track that son of a bitch and I intend to do that. Just like you intend to let me be when it's all complete, assuming that you weren't lying. I'll keep my word if you keep yours."

The sweat was running despite the fact he had his weapon again. "My intentions remain," he said, putting the weapon in his holster. He placed his hand over it securely.

"Good," Billy said. "Now I suggest we get some sleep while the night still has us. What you think?"

"I think that's good."

"Ok then. I'm going back to the log. You comfortable there?"

The entire scene was almost surreal and Collie nodded his head. "Y-yeah," he stuttered. "Comfortable." He kept his head up and watched as Billy positioned himself on the ground. There was a blanket rolled beneath his head and another between his knees. Collie squinted through the fire, flabbergasted. "Billy," he said in a whisper for some reason.

"What?"

"You ain't gonna try and run?"

"I'm sleeping."

The sheriff lifted his questioning gaze to the heavens and pondered for a few brief seconds. He laid down flat on his back, unsure of what else to do. His hand remained latched over his pistol like a fastened leather belt. He tried to close his eyes, but they bounced open each time as if the world were telling him not to.

***

He awoke before Billy and before sunrise and the young man followed suit. They collected their belongings and saddled the horses hastily. They spoke not of the incident in the night, but it hung there omnipotent and unavoidable and the men developed an understanding of how things would play out from that point on.

Collie mounted his horse and found the satchel containing food. He waited for Billy to mount as well. When he did, Collie threw him a piece of jerky. "Thankee," Billy said and began to gnaw.

"Got some ground to cover," Collie said.

"What's his distance daily you think?" Billy's mouth was full and a chunk of dried venison expelled from it. He picked it from his leg and tried again.

"I couldn't say." Collie ripped at the meat himself. He salivated. "Him bein' the hunted and all, some fellers go day and night. But they do that and they crash before long. I can't say I begin to know our sunnabitch, but if he's steady, we're in for some hurt."

Billy acknowledged him, seeming to agree. "Coulda' left the trail at any point too."

"I reckon. Probably obliged to, knowin' what's after him."

"He's got cajones though."

"What's that?"

"Because he doesn't seem afraid."

"No, what's cajones?"

"Oh. Balls."

"Oh."

"You never heard that? You been around a long time too Collie."

"What language is that."

"Spanish."

"Well I've never run with no Spaniards or Mexicans."

"But you're aware of them."

"Yeah I'm aware."

"And you've heard 'em speak."

"Yeah I heard 'em speak, but its not like I was listening. It's like one long line of dialogue. No separation."

"We probably sound the same to them."

"I wouldn't presume to know what they think."

"You got a problem with Mexicans Mr. sheriff man of the people?"

"I'm not the one that left one dead in the woods."

Billy's eyes lit up and he beckoned an irregular smirk. "Well touché on that one."

Collie lowered his head as if in shame. "Well touchy right back."

"Touche. Kinda like the word *shade* without the D."

"I said before, we got ground to cover." Collie took off moving.

Billy noticed his untethered horse. "Isn't that something," he said to the animal and nicked it on after his former captor.

Chapter 19

It was magic hour when the sun is neither up nor down and the world is in transition either preparing for imminent transgressions or shaking them off. They carried on the trail in tandem with the anterior prisoner leading. His eyes scoured the surface as they progressed keeping in stride and the class system falling by the wayside. Collie followed closely with diminished suspicion only to concur or deny the propositions set forth by the superior tracker.

It was hotter this day than the last and the air was heavy and their clothes matted to their skin. The discomfort led to crestfallen conversations and demeanors easily agitated. They rode on ignoring all but their initial purpose.

The horses were sweating beneath them. Their pace slowed. Collie brushed his animal's mane, calling it by name. Billy noticed the action and considered it. He licked his lips. The perspiration was salty on his tongue and he looked to the sky and the sun stared back unblinking with its passionless force. Billy replaced his hat on his head. He looked to Collie and saw him hiding signs of fatigue. "Water hide Collie? Carry it myself."

Collie gave a yes and untied the second canteen off his satchel. "It ain't from hides," he said and threw it to Billy.

He caught it. The tin was not even cool to the touch. He drank displaying a berating expression at the contents and then tied the canteen to his own saddle bag. "Obliged. The horses need water."

"We need to press on."

"I know," Billy said.

Collie waited in thought. "Yeah I s'pose. We'll stop at the next we find." He peered down at the trail and then to Billy. "You sure this is the right way?"

Billy scraped his upper lip with his teeth, pondering. "I believe so."

"Even with the fork back yonder?"

"Tracks go this way."

"I don't see any tracks."

"You don't know what to look for."

"Maybe you ought to tell me."

"If I did that, what use would I be?" Billy laughed to himself.

"What?"

"It's funny the way things turn out."

"What things?"

"You needing my help and all."

"It's a deal is all it is. A fair one mind ya. You get something out of this too if I recall correctly."

"Might not seem fair to the folks I allegedly wronged. I wouldn't think they'd think so."

"Everyone does a penance for something. Not to mention, I cut you loose, doesn't mean you're free."

Billy shifted in consternation. "What you mean?"

"Pinkertons won't quit if there's a price on you."

"But we're straight after this."

"*We're* straight. Not you and the railroads."

"I figured as much."

"What you think I left Deputy Smith behind for?"

Billy shrugged.

"They're gonna come callin' to see you hang. Make sure it's done and tender the reward to my office. But Upton's sayin' that you escaped when that asshole killed Virgil. He let you out. And that you had no part in the killin'. But you took the opportunity to flee. And why wouldn't you?"

"Smith is gonna say that?"

"He's gonna say that."

"You sure?"

"I'm sure."

"You trust him."

"I do."

Billy lifted his cheeks to squint against the perspiration and it appeared he was smiling. "I guess things are different on your side of things," he said.

"I hope so."

The trodden road meandered through the territory and they followed it lightly as Billy dismounted his horse intermittently inspecting the markings and unnatural damage left behind by their target. Billy lead, with his apparent heightened senses and furthered experience ill matched for a man his age. Collie followed closely, a move that relinquished most of his legally ordained authority. However the gun at his hip and the incident at the camp fire placed both men near level.

They came to a pond after some hours and brought the horses to the edge. The animals lapped up the water. Billy jumped to the ground with thud and submerged his entire head like an ostrich. "Thank you lord," he said to no one including the Lord, and then shook out the water from his hair like a dog. Collie dismounted and dropped meekly to the water. It was still and tranquil with a greenish hue. He brushed the algae aside with his hand and lowered his canteen, filling it. He brought it to his lips and his body gave an audible yet unknowing thanks.

"Tastes fishy don't it?" Billy said.

"I don't care much," Collie responded and gulped more. "We'll stay for five."

Billy nodded and dunked his head again. Five minutes turned into fifteen. Collie reconnoitered the pond fighting the sun glare to spot fish. He took his time. He kept eyes off of Billy and the young man appreciated it without saying anything. Billy sat at the water's edge. He leaned forward and caught his reflection, scrutinized by the image bouncing in the measured ripples. The man staring back had aged some. His complexion was swarthier like a native's and his hair was ratty and unkempt. The skin on his body looked worn and borrowed. He ran his knuckles over his cheek and spat in the water. Across the pond, he saw Collie stretch his arms to relieve back pain. The older man began moving again and the movement was betrayed at the start by aging knees. "The beauty of youth is short lived," Billy said to his horse and then stood ready. "We set?" he asked Collie as he approached.

"Yeah we best go. Stayed longer than I hoped." Collie opened his satchel and tossed a moist piece of jerky to Billy. "Even the meat is sweatin'."

They made their way over the grassland and fell back in line with the road. It was well beyond midday. They moved with an even trot carrying out their routine like it was second nature. Collie scoured the land around him, while placing what little faith he had in Billy whose skills in this realm were largely anecdotal. Yet he held his doubts in check. His time in the wild had ceased years ago and his abilities had become unsharpened through the domesticity of a quaint town life. The young man had been brought before him through uncertain coincidences and he could not overlook that, but he was troubled by overlooking his own incertitude.

They approached a section of raggedy shrubs, overgrown and riddled with weeds and the thin branches extended like skeletal fingers impinging on the pathway. Billy slowed his horse and hopped to the ground before Collie could say anything. He stretched his young legs over the worn earth and to the bushes. Billy crouched in front of them and ran his palm along the weathered leaves. He leaned forward as if to whisper to the plants, but said nothing.

"What is it?" Collie asked from his horse.

Billy was too engrossed to answer. He tilted his head and brought his attention to a faint patch of fur. It was hanging off an extended vine being gently brushed by the passing breeze. Billy pinched it between his fingers. "Same color as Wells's horse. We might be in business." He stood up and ran his eyes over the ground in front of him. "Hard to make out, but I think he's still moving forward. We need to look close though. Can't imagine he'd be dumb enough to stay on one road for long. Surprised we haven't moved to open land yet."

Collie blinked hard and squinted at what Billy was holding. "Ok," Collie said.

Billy grabbed the saddle horn and swung his leg over. "Onward?" He posed it as a question though the answer was already known. Collie nodded and they rode on.

A short time passed and Collie remained some paces behind his guide. He held a look of contemplation, but this gradually morphed and his face tensed and he wore a dubious expression as he burned a hole in the back of Billy's head. He began to voice a thought. He hesitated. "You say something?" Billy asked.

Collie bit his lip and looked around. "What'd you mean the other day when you said 'not just that'?"

"I say a lot of things."

"Before the night we camped by the forest. Before we went through it. You thought I was worried about Sioux and you said they weren't around these parts. And I asked if you could tell all that from your method of tracking. You said not just that. What'd that mean?"

Billy turned and shot a smirk at Collie before continuing forward. "I'm reticent to tell you."

"Why's that," Collie said as if offended.

"Back in Creek I was mouthing off to your deputies, if you can believe that, about you and that youngin' of a girl who brought that pie. They told me some about you to set me right."

"What about me?"

"When I tell you, you'll understand my reticence to explain myself."

"That's alright. Say it. A man should know who he's riding with."

"They told me how when you came to Little Creek, it was just a mite camp. Ruffians about mixed with prospectors and business folks and families looking to settle. And before you became sheriff, you loaned yourself out as security-like to families and wagons on their way in. That girl happened to be on a wagon with her sisters and all that you were watching."

"And?" Collie huffed.

"You were attacked. Sioux came out from the hills looking for blood. They said you fended them off damn near single handedly and everyone white came out all right. No one else though. You saw to that."

Collie cleared his throat, appearing distraught at the words like they were daggers. "Brother of the fella whose father to the girl took an arrow. He didn't die though. Lost the arm, it was in beneath the elbow."

Billy seemed unfazed. "Well almost all right then." He peered back to the sheriff who was staring off into the distance. "They told me after that you stopped lending yourself out. Hardly left camp for much of anything. Then when Creek built to a town and was annexed, you ended up sheriff based on whatever past law experience you had. You and Virgil straightened the place out to be respectable.

Peaceful, if you could call it that now. Ran out any, what would you call them? Undesirable elements. That all true?"

"Depends who you ask," Collie said. "In essence, yeah I suppose. So what's any of that have to do with you?"

Billy pulled back the reins on his horse until he was beside Collie. They were still moving. "What's this?" Collie asked, uncomfortable.

"Increasing my vantage."

"What?"

"Where's your gun?"

"What the hell are you talking about."

"I'm talking about wanting to know where your gun is."

"It's holstered."

"It's gonna stay that way?"

"Why wouldn't it?"

"Based on what I tell you. It's going to stay that way?"

"Chrissakes."

"I don't want to get shot over honesty."

"I might shoot ya now for getting on my nerves." Collie distanced himself from Billy by a foot or two. "You got something to say? Say it."

Billy smirked at the move. "You know my uncle once ran a pharaoh game in some shit saloon in an even shittier camp. Kind of place that makes you want to bathe. It was a tight game. He didn't let anything pass. You know, took no shit. So this one time, some fellas are into a session going on maybe thirty hours. The money was coming in so he let the game continue. Now my uncle's shuffling when he notices the deck's light. He mentions it to the four playing and no one blinks. So he asks again. Again no one says anything. They all just stare back at him with blank eyes saying nothing. That's why he knew they were lying. They didn't need to say a word. So he proposed to them that if whoever's stowing cards admits it here at the table, the law won't be called in and that man will give up his winnings and be asked to leave. My uncle sat there watching their eyes watching each other. They must've sat there ten minutes before an answer. Then suddenly the fella in the middle says ok and he pushes his chair out. He pulls a card from each sleeve and lays them on the table. Then he pushes his stack of bills forward towards my uncle and says he's gonna head out now. My uncle nodded to him like it was ok. Then he pulled out his gun and shot that man in the chest."

"So what's your point?" Collie asked like he was half listening.

"My point is there's a man who might've been better off on the low road."

"That story true?"

Billy let out a snicker. "Sorta."

Collie shook his head. "You ain't gonna end up dead. In fact, had I known I'd have to listen to ya this much, I'd probably have kept my mouth shut." Collie waited a minute before his curiosity got the best of him. "How can you track the way you do? How'd you know about them Sioux?"

Billy shifted his stare to Collie. "Because I'm half."

Collie faltered, taken aback a moment. "You're half. Half what. Half Sioux?"

"Not Sioux."

There was a false chortle from the aged man before the blood in his face came near the surface. "Not Sioux. Some other goddamn one of them I take to be your meaning?"

"Some other, yeah," Billy said calmly.

Collie tore his eyes and the hatred behind them away from Billy and looked through the trees to the sky. "Jesus Christ," he said and sped forward with a trail of dirt and grass behind him.

***

Billy came across the sheriff's camp near sundown. It had not been hard to find. Collie had chosen not to deviate from the road before him and while keeping a moderate distance away from his targeted disappointment, was careful not to dip out of his view. As Billy drew closer, he opted to give the man an ample berth. He steered his horse under a hickory not far off of the road and some hundred yards away from Collie. He saw in the distance the fledgling blaze of a fire and then licked his lips with an appetite.

Billy dismounted and went to the ground weak-kneed. He made fists and pounded on his quadriceps for blood flow.

"Falling apart," he said aloud to his horse. He tied the animal's leather rein to a low hanging branch and removed supplies from the saddle. He grabbed the tightly wound wool blanket and threw it to one of the hickory's protruding roots. He turned and again snuck a look over the horse's saddle to his partner's more inviting campsite. "Son of a bitch," he said. The bag hanging off the saddle was devoid of any food, but Billy checked it anyway. He sat down under the tree with a mildly wounded spirit. When his back hit the grass covered earth it was the first coolness he felt all day. He let out a tone of content and then stared at the sky through the leaflets to the stars and though their luminance had dissipated from nights previous he allowed the beauty of their detachment to overpower the incessant nudging of hunger.

Collie speared six links of sausage and the fire was flinging its spittle at them while the meat hissed and snapped. He had noticed Billy's arrival minutes ago, surveilling for it for over an hour. The solitude had given him time to collect himself. The image of the half Indian swayed and distorted in the distance through the proprietary haze of the fire. His frame appeared as that of a mirage in the desert, but it was real, and Collie acknowledged it. He would likely not admit to being surprised, but his expectations of the young man had grown muddled. He grabbed the spear with the largest link and then rose. His ankle and knee emitted a crack and he grunted. Then he got on his horse.

As he approached the hickory, he dropped his brow. He appeared stern. Billy did not move, though Collie could see the slight gleam of his sclera and knew he was awake. "Good spot," he said and threw the sausage to Billy's gut.

Billy brushed at it and sat upright when he felt the warmth of the food. "I didn't want to cause no bother." He took a bite and then another.

"There's more," Collie said and then turned with his horse back to his camp.

They sat there with the fire between them, speechless with mouths full of food. The mood mellowed with both men fed. When it was gone, they licked their fingers and wiped the remnants on their shirts. They wished for more, but were sensibly conservative. The deadness of exchange weighed heavily and Billy was the first to make comfort lying the better distance from the fire. He pulled his hat over his eyes and made no effort to converse. Collie on the other hand remained upright. He tried not to stare at the half breed.

Guilt for some men represents a dilemma because it idles apathetically in one's conscious while its very existence lays the foundation for the type of irksomeness that one believes should not exist in the first place. He cleared his throat. Billy made no movement, so Collie spoke instead. "That day it all happened was the type of day you wish you could capture and let out whenever you wanted. Not like it was today. The sun was up, but it was cool. The wind was playful-like. You know." Billy lifted his hat brim a mite and began to pay attention. "I was out there like you said. There was no sheriff at the time, but me comin' out of Kansas like I did, a lawman and all, figured I could lend myself and whatever skills I thought I had to others who might need them."

"You come out of Kansas?" Billy asked.

"Yeah."

"Tough towns in Kansas. Texas too. At least I hear so."

Collie dropped his head concurring. "My wife and I had come to Little Creek some months prior. It was just a camp at the time, but we took a liking to its quaintness of location I suppose. Figured we could make a stay of it. When I done buildin' what'd become our home, I rode with the wagons for pay. The threat of Sioux was legitimate, them not takin' to any treaty right off. So I'd link up with any that wanted me and travel as a gun hand."

"That girl that you saw was in the back of the wagon with her two sisters. They was out of," he paused a moment trying to remember, "Minnesota I recall. The dad rode the wagon front and his brother rode a solo horse beside. They were hardware men, taken with the idea to prosper out here with the gold strikes selling prospecting tools and whatnot. They offered me trade of supplies for services rendered and that seemed fair. They were two grown men, but, I think they had some spare worry more for the little ones behind in the wagon. Said the mother died of pox the previous year."

"Well we was a distance away from camp, maybe a half score of miles. They was pleasant enough and I was too. I warned them to keep a guard up, but that attacks had been on a decline with more folk comin' settlin' and the calvaries clearing territory. We continued on and I dropped back some to reconnoiter. That back flap of the wagon kept opening up. Them youngsters stealin' looks at me who was a stranger. They'd make faces. Wife and I didn't have any ourselves. But they had a look to them. The kind that forces you to smile."

Billy dug his heels in the dirt and pushed himself up slightly while Collie continued. "We couldn't have been more than three miles from camp when it happened. There weren't none others around. That's maybe why they chose us. Bout three miles out, you mighta noticed on your way in," Collie let a quick huff, "then again maybe not with you bein' slung over a horse. But the road in has an openness to it. Ain't much on the immediate sides. However, some hundred yards out on either side you got the hills overlookin' on one and the forest on the other."

"I was back some ten feet when the brother let out a grunt. There was the softest damn whistle right before, but I couldn't attest if it was real or not or if I placed it in my head due to circumstance. It stunned me right quick. But I pulled my pistol and got my head right. I saw it was an arrow. I yelled to them girls to stay hidden and galloped up to the brother. Another arrow came and pierced the wagon horse's throat. It fell partly, not all the way since it was harnessed in, but it was dead the way it dropped. The brother was alive and conscious, but that arrow hit him in the arm and passed through enough so that it pinned it to his side. His gun hand and all. 'Thomas,' I yelled, Thomas bein' the name of the father, and I saw him readying his rifle when they come down off the hill."

"There were four of them total. It wa'nt no war party. They'd not send a war party after one wagon. They mighta' been scouts or stragglers. Scavenger's even. Who knows how they live? They were Sioux alright though. Two of 'em had the war bonnets on. I'd seen 'em before. Their kind. Dead though. And they had them long braids and I knew they were local to Dakota. Well they rode down like hell from those hills two by two and then spread out four wide. They got that horrible squawkin' to their cries and it grew loud quick. Thomas raised his rifle and they slung a rock more fast than he could fire. He fell clear off the wagon when it struck his head."

"I pulled that brother from his horse and told him to get beneath the wagon. His pistol was drawn. He held it in his left on his weak side, but he held it nonetheless. I yelled to the girls to stay beneath the canvass and when I turned they were yards away. Had I thought, I probably wouldn't have done it the same, that bein' the detriment to all involved parties. I fired my peacemaker from my hip, fanning my palm across the hammer three times. I hit two of them with the three shots and they fell. The other two kept on."

"One had the bonnet and the other only braids and they were damn close to naked other than them nether cloths. They was painted up with whatever heathen signs they wear. The one with the braids leaped in stride from his animal and ran around the wagon to finish the father I thought. The feathered one swung some goddamned club at me and when he did, I dodged left and I fell from the saddle. He was off his horse in no time. I was on my back and the wind left my lungs and I coughed on my first breath. He kicked my face from the side and straddled over me. He grabbed me by my hair and lifted my top half upright. I grabbed at his hand. There was blood in my right eye from the kick, but I could see he had a knife in his other hand."

"The fall had me disoriented, but I grabbed for that knife anyway. He brought it to my head, trying scalping me before the kill. When I grabbed for it, he brought it down into my shoulder. The knife was of stone not metal and I never felt pain like that before. It was jagged goin' in and I could feel it tap my bone. He had me pinned with his knees. My head dropped down to the side and the Indian pressed his hand on it so I couldn't move. From my angle I saw the brother tendin' to Thomas. But then there was screaming from the wagon. One of the girls. I couldn't see none of it. The brother yelled for that heathen to put her down and then there was another scream. Made ya cringe. And the rest here happened quick."

"The brother raised his weak hand and fired toward the back of the wagon and it jerked his whole damn arm and that savage came at him. The girl was alive still because I heard her screaming and cryin' by the wagon's end. He fired again and missed again. And did again twice more. Then they were both in my view and my guy still had me pinned like he wanted me to watch. That Indian stopped not two feet away from the brother and began to laugh and he put his red hand on the arrow in brother's arm and pushed it through, harder. And it pressed further into his side and that squeal that the brother let out was something outta legend. It was headin' to his lungs. I don't know how to explain it, but somehow that man fought through that pain. They say that sometimes a person can get strength from emotions. I think that's what they say. Well he musta' got that strength. He brought that pistol left handed under that savage's chin so he wasn't in missing distance and blew the top of his head clear off."

Collie paused a single moment swallowing the lump in his throat. "So that shot makes my guy let up a split second and gawk at his newly dead friend. I saw an opportunity and I swung on him with whatever strength I could muster. I hit him with my fist right near his eye. It was my wounded arm, but he still went down. He went to his back beside me and I rolled over and got up quick as I could. I was distorted now that I was standin', but I could see him makin' his way back up. I was half blind from the blood in my eye and my pistol was somewhere on the ground. Another shot rang out. It was the brother tryin' to help, but he hit the hind wagon wheel from where he was. He shot though he was damn near passed out. That bastard savage was comin' to and I simply reacted. I brought my boot down hard as I could on his throat. Crushed his windpipe I reckon cause he started this terrible wheezing." Collie cleared his throat again. He seemed uncomfortable. "Then I..I stepped my boot to the side of his head so it was sideways at it, like it was making a T if his head was flat. I had spurs on. And I rammed my foot heel first, backward, as hard as I could and the spur went right through his temple. He couldn't make a sound with his neck crushed and all. His arms went up, reachin' for whatever god he could and then he laid there twitchin'. The twitchin' stopped when I pulled the spur out."

Collie reached for his bag and retrieved a bottle of whiskey. It was mostly full. He uncorked it and took a swig then held it out to Billy. "No," Billy said, barely getting the word out. Collie drank again and replaced the cork. "You protected them best you could."

Collie made a motion like he was considering it. "I heard stories in the past about what they do to folks. White folks. Don't matter if its woman or child."

Billy stared at him with a sadness. "They ain't all like that." He thought about who he was speaking to.

Collie wiped his lips with his fingertips and gazed into the fire. "When I pulled my spur from that Indian's head, I looked around at the scene. I couldn't see none of them movin' and I remember feelin' glad right quick, but then I saw one of the girls little feet pokin' into view behind the wheel and I rushed over to her. She was crying on that ground real hard and her white dress was dirty and had blood near the collar. It had flowed there from her head. I picked her up and pushed her hair back. That sunnabitch ran his knife across her forehead near her hair. Tried takin' her scalp in front of her uncle and father. I looked into her eyes and she looked into mine and I held her tight as I could. It was only a few seconds, but it felt like more. I pulled open the canvas flap to the wagon. The other two girls were all hunkered down, clutching at each other in fright. I saw they were ok, but they were in shock, not knowing what happened fully. I placed their sister next to them and told them she was ok, but that they had to be quiet. I gave them the shush sign with my finger and told them not to come out unless it's me that opens that flap. Then I tied it shut, tight as I could."

Billy heard his tone go sour as he heard the last words spoken.

"I stepped over the body of the one I killed with my spur and I found my pistol near the front wagon wheel. It had three shots so I reloaded it to its full six. I moved to over to where the brother was and the father and saw they was both still breathing. The brother was minutes away from passing out, but he told me they were alright and to just make sure they were all dead."

"Guy in Kansas once told me what Indians believe. Something about them needing their eyes to wander in the afterlife and without them, they're blind. Lost eternally or some story. Now I don't believe that. But I thought that maybe it don't matter what I believe. It's what they believe that will happen to them."

"I thought of that little girl's face and the blood streaks across it. The hatred just overtook me." Collie turned from the fire a moment and the blaze no longer reflected off his pupils. "I walked up to each of them lifeless assholes and I put one through each eye. I started with the one I spurred and then moved over to the brother's. Then I walked the short distance to the other two. The one I put two bullets in wasn't dead so I waited on him. I took the eyes of the other one and then stopped and reloaded again. I put six in anyways. The last one was crawling backwards on the ground, kinda pushin' himself along with his heels. I glanced back at the wagon and thought of those kids. I got a real hate on so I knee capped him and he let out a scream. I remember laughin' at that, but not the kind of laugh that's because something's funny. Ya know. It was some other kind. He was flailing around so I gut shot him. He stopped moving for the most part and I aimed my pistol real good and fired twice in his lookers. Then it was over."

Wind whistled past in a hurry like it was waiting in the wings for him to finish and it fanned the sparks away from the campsite. Billy stared at Collie who was somewhat expressionless. The younger man did not interject. He rather sat there with a pondering glare embracing the newly appropriate silence and perhaps it was the horror of the unfolded tale that Billy contemplated, or maybe it was of the man burdened with carrying the polished memories of the pain he suffered and inflicted. They both were silent for some time.

"Ya know my wife became sick after that day," Collie began. "Not right away. A few months after. Took to coughing up blood. Doc said it was tuberculosis, but he hadn't seen a case like hers. One that seemed to come out of nowheres with a... 'rapid deterioration' is the way he put it. It was punishment maybe for what I done."

"Did she know the extent of what you did?" Billy asked.

Collie motioned a no. "She died less than a year later. Never was sick before. And just like that, the world turned on her. Her insides rotted and she spit 'em up and got nothing except worse." Collie prodded at the ground with a stick and spoke in a way uncaring of any audience. "Sometimes I think it's them I killed. Wondering around blind like the stories say. They found her. In all that darkness in all the world, they found her."

Billy gulped. "I don't think it works like that."

"Well, you ain't been dead," Collie said objectively.

Billy inhaled deeply and hesitated to voice his thoughts. "I seen the way they treat you in that town. The way they look at you," he said after a while.

"How's that?"

"Don't know exactly. Like they respect you I guess. Like you were a hero."

Collie breathed a short laugh. "Ya know what's funny about that. Sometimes at night when I wake up and she's gone from my side, I wish I never helped that family in the first place. Like maybe she'd still be alive."

"Yeah, but then you wouldn't have helped those girls. They would've been killed in the worst possible way."

Collie appeared like he was thinking. "I don't rightly know who is best off any more." He rustled in his place and moved to lie down. "I'm sorry for the way I treated you," he said.

"It's alright," Billy said, caught off guard.

"I want to try and sleep."

"Okay."

Collie turned away from the fire and stared out into the distance unknown. The vibrancy of the fire inevitably dwindled. They tried to sleep.

Chapter 20

On the third day they came across a merchant. The surrounding clouds were hued in purples, making the sky like candy, and the sun was only a fingertip on the horizon, but it silhouetted him enough to be spotted in an open field far off the road. He was prepping his wagon as they approached. He was a man of unpronounced height with a hearty beard and an appealing disposition. His attire spoke more to that of a business man than to a rugged frontier type.

The merchant moved around his wagon hastily packing his belongings as if readying for the arrival of his guests. He had one horse and it was already unhitched. By the time Collie and Billy arrived, he was buttoning his overcoat above his three piece suit. He waved his hands in a welcoming gesture. Collie nodded to Billy and they moved forward.

Piddling smoke slid out of the ashen wood pile on the ground. Collie craned his neck and saw the words "King's Things" printed in large text on the side of the wagon with a middling "Consignments" below them. The merchant lowered his hands and then climbed to the wagon bench and sat and placed his boots on the footrest. A Spencer Rifle hung from two brackets on the wagon panel behind him. He grabbed the horse's rein and held it loosely with his thumbs, the rest of his fingers pointed upwards. "Good morning gentlemen." He had an accent.

"Mornin'," Collie said and Billy followed.

"Allow me to introduce myself. My name is Milton King."

"Tim Collie," he tipped his hat. "And this is-" he paused.

"Bill. Hendershot." Billy said. Neither paid heed to the fiction.

"Mr. Collie, Mr. Hendershot, the pleasure is mine." The merchant wore a stretched smile and he fully removed his hat when he bowed from the seated position. "And you have no doubt already ascertained from the sign on my wagon, I am something of a salesman."

"Sales of what?" Billy asked.

"Oh a variety of things. Objects of interest depending on the party concerned. Let's say, my merchandise consists of the items I've picked up along the way."

"Way from where?" Collie asked.

"I hail from Germany, though I've been here in your states for two years and three months. I arrived in Boston by ship hoping to bring to these territories a taste of my foreign culture and there I developed affection for collecting tokens of this culture as well. And I decided that it would be my duty to bring all the flavors of the world to those not fortunate enough to experience them first hand. To provide you with the much expedited version, I ventured my way to the places described in those adventure dime novels, the wild frontier. Places like Texas and New Mexico, and then I wandered your country through its heart. When the great color was struck here in the Dakotas and the mining camps not only set up, but prospered, I surmised that this would be the next logical place to journey." He breathed deep and showed his teeth with his grin. "From here, who knows where?"

"What's in the wagon," Billy said with genuine curiosity.

"Well as I said before, things that I've accumulated being a journeyman. What interests you my friend, Bill?" He continued before the answer. "Say it was weaponry. What if I told you I had a Devisme Revolver all the way from France in semi-used condition? Or perhaps a Mauser from my own country?" Billy shrugged. "If not weaponry, how about art? How about an original of the Irish William Cuming? Or a pencil sketch done by Van Gogh completed in a book page and snatched by a lowly worker who was simply taken by it? Or memorabilia? Like a bullet casing dispensed from the very rifle of Davy Crockett at the battle of The Alamo. And that's simply what I have today. Tomorrow may be different. You see, I take what I can carry and sell and purchase as I move. This allows me the freedom of non-conformity. Though critics may say it makes my stock unreliable, I rarely stay in an area long enough for grievances to arise."

Billy rubbed his stubble and arched his brow inquisitively. "Can I take a gander at that French pistol?"

"Why certainly." King made to move off of the wagon.

"Enough on that," Collie interjected.

"I don't understand Mr. Collie. It won't take but a moment."

"We ain't got the time for this."

The merchant's smile thinned and disappeared as he read the altered deportment. "Mr. Collie, has the atmosphere given you reason for alert in any way?"

"Not yet. The reasoning in our approach, we're looking for someone."

"I see. There's many people in the world."

"Yeah, well the feller we're on the scout for is important."

"And why is that?"

"The world needs him rid."

The merchant's aura changed. "He's killed a lot of folks," Billy said. "Without cause. For pleasure like."

King seemed to consider it. "And you stand to reason that this man has ventured out here?"

Billy nodded. "He'd have been preceded by a posse perhaps. Pinkertons likely. Maybe a day in advance."

"Preceded?" King said. "Seems counter to the basic philosophy of a manhunt."

Collie spoke sounding impatient. "Billy and me tracked him this'a way, but we ain't seen many folk for a time. Been that someone seen the one we're after it'd be encouraging and if not we'd as soon be on our damned way."

A cocksure grin came over the merchant. "I understand fully Mr. Collie, Mr. Hendershot." He nodded to each as he said their names. "And I'd just as soon help you if I indubitably believed your story."

"What the fuck does that mean?" Collie said through his teeth.

"Indubitably?" The merchant asked.

"The whole damn thing."

"It means you say you're after a man. A killer you claim. Which may be true. Which means it may also not be true. And perhaps this man you're after is himself the victim."

"He ain't," Collie said.

"As you're inclined to say." King removed his pipe from his pocket and placed it in his mouth. He struck a match and puffed until the tobacco ignited. "Just as I'm inclined to disbelieve. For all I know this poor devil did nothing in the wrong and for me to tell you his whereabouts could lead to his unwarranted demise. And this predicament brings us to the figurative crossroads." Billy reached for his pistol, holding it without removal. Collie gripped his horse's reins, but left his weapon alone. "Mr. Hendershot, if you're under the impression that turning a gun on me will in some way shake me of my character than you might be more naïve than your young face conveys. A man who hasn't had a gun cast in his direction in this country is a man who has never left the comforts of his own house. So let me ask you gentlemen something. How much money do you have?" They looked at each other and King watched them do it. "Between you. Total."

"You trying to rob us?" Collie asked.

"No I'm trying to sell to you."

"Well this is one hell of a pitch," Billy said amused.

The merchant ran his thumb over the end of his pipe and spoke through his teeth as they clamped down over the mouthpiece. "You men are seeking an alleged fugitive and I am simply seeking a sale. You say you have money, you purchase an item of moderate expense and I will give you the information you desire."

Billy removed his pistol from his holster, but did not turn it on the merchant. He held it comfortably and ready. Collie opened his overcoat enough to expose his star. "You believe this?" Collie said, drawing the merchant's attention to the tin.

"I may," King said. He turned his interest to the burning tobacco in his pipe. "Mr. Collie, you may not be able to see from your vantage, but Mr. Hendershot is placed perfectly to confirm my next claim. Mr. Hendershot?" King removed the pipe and whistled. "Mr Hendershot, do you see the slight bulge in the canvas of the wagon cover?" Billy forced himself to look. King turned, directing his voice behind the wagon. "Show them son." The bulge in the cloth slid down and then poked at the canvas. Billy looked to Collie and acknowledged it was true. "Now gentlemen, the author of that movement is a double barrel shotgun currently being wielded by my son Karl. He can no doubt make out your shape Mr. Hendershot in this light and with a cannon like the one he has at this distance he barely needs to. So the question is Mr. Collie, do you believe me?"

"Chrissake," the lawman said. He waited and his face reddened. "You're gonna threaten us with an imp holdin' a peashooter from behind a piece of cloth? For all I know it's a goddamned dog or a pokin' finger."

"Karl," Milton yelled behind him without taking his eyes off Collie. "Out front." There was a rustle from inside the wagon and Billy flinched at the sudden stir. "Gentlemen, do not make this worse than it needs to be. Please do not aim any weapons." From the rear of the wagon came a thud and a child emerged. He could not have been more than ten and he was in fact holding a shotgun. The item vertically would have measured near his height though he held it without awkwardness at the two strangers.

"Oi poppa," he said, his voice not yet broken.

"Stay calm son. No need to worry. Say hello to Mr. Collie and Hendershot."

"Hello," he said with little affect. He was dressed similarly to his father, wearing a relatively untarnished suit for a boy.

Billy tipped his hat giving an amused simper. Collie did nothing except speak. "You'd arm a child?"

"You do your best to show them a better world, but it's best to prepare them for this one." King leaned over and rubbed his son's head, ruffling the young one's hair. When he was done, he palmed the small crown and forced his son to turn. "It's ok," he said gently. "Show them." The child brushed back his hair from where his ear would have been revealing gruesome scar tissue. It was tan and yellowed, from the past. Collie and Billy winced. King read the men's faces and patted the boy's head again. "It's ok," he said to the child. "You can go back in the wagon." The child exhibited neither relief nor disappointment and then backed away as if he was called for chores.

"How'd it happen?" Billy asked.

King shook his head like he was blocking a memory. "It's from a time before we were prepared. From a time prior to reality. When we still believed," he cleared his throat. "When I still believed in others."

Collie breathed deeply before he spoke. "I can part with up to five dollars."

"And him?" King asked.

"I got his. And the number's still the same."

"Too many vices," Billy said pointing at himself.

"Very well," said the merchant. "Produce it."

Collie clumsily pushed his hand into his coat and sorted blindly through the pocket. There was a faint jingle of coins. He removed his hand in a fist. "You don't do your part, this won't end well."

King sniffled. "I'm not a bad man. Just a careful one. And while you sit there mistrusting me, if you for an instant turn your glaring suspicion in the other direction, you might realize that for me to mistrust you, the two strangers that happened upon me before the hot sun was even over our hopefully civilized heads, would be well within my rights and in addition would be considered not only careful, but intelligent." Collie opened his fist. "Five? What can I interest you in?"

"I don't give a good goddamn," Collie said.

"Go for the gun," Billy said.

"It is beyond your means," King said as he waited for a suggestion from Collie. "A thought sheriff?"

Collie leaned over and spat. He wiped his mouth and then flipped five coins to the man in the wagon one at a time. Each landed in the man's lap, though he only collected them at the end of the sequence. He inspected them and grinned. "I will tell you what. If you've no preference in the matter, allow me to make the decision." He bent forward and picked up a satchel from the footrest. "Arrest your suspicions gentlemen." He rummaged through the leather quickly extracting two items. "Here," he said and tossed something at Billy. "And gently," he added before doing the same to Collie.

"It's chocolate," Billy said.

"Correct. And for you Mr. Collie, it is jelly. Brambleberry I believe."

"That's five bucks?" Billy asked a bit dumbstruck.

"You will understand when you taste it."

Collie pocketed the item without even a glance. "And the rest of the goods?"

"Right you are." King clapped his hands together cheerily. "To prove my worth as a man of business I will speak only truth. Not more than half of yesterday I came upon a man. He was alone and I almost certainly cast him as weary from travel expecting him to venture forth. Though his deliberate attempt to evade me gave me startle causing me great discomfiture as I was in need of respite from the monotony my journey. We were approaching one another head to head, bound to meet before continuing in opposing directions. As he neared I noticed he was hunched over. I thought perhaps in pain. And when he was truly in sight I could make out his tattered appearance. His head was down and his face was hidden as if he were sleeping, which he may have been. I called out to him in a friendly way. That was when his head rose and his traveling halted. I offered him to approach and exchange words of travel though he provided no response. So taking the initiative I brought the rein and moved forward. At this he abruptly bolted off of the road and into the open."

"He said nothing?" Collie inquired.

"No. Simply took off like a demon was giving chase."

"You didn't aim to follow?"

"Why?" The merchant scoffed. "In that man's condition it would be fetched rather far to think to ascertain a company of money on his person."

Collie dragged his fingers over his coarse stubble. "I supposed it's too much to hope for that you got a look at his face, but did you notice what he was riding?"

"Gentlemen, a man in my position pays heed to the details. The horse was white for the most part, but patched brown in places like a cow would be. A rather queer design I remember thinking."

Collie looked assuredly at Billy. "You're sure?" he said to the merchant.

"I would give away my stock if I was wrong."

"As for Pinkertons?" Billy added.

King shook his head. "I cannot attest to seeing them or not. I left a fledgling mining camp across the plains two days ago. You say they preceded your inquiry. For me to provide you with a definitive answer would be misinformation. Please accept my apology."

Collie began drawing deep breaths. "Which direction was he headed when he rode away?"

King looked to the sun. He closed one eye at its brightness. He then looked behind his wagon. "From where I was stationed," he paused, thinking. "It was west."

"West you say?"

"Indeed. You know what lays that way don't you?"

Collie waited while the thought oscillated. "I do."

King raised his brow in concern. "It is most certainly not any of my business, but it may behoove you to give second thought to your pursuit." He could see his meaning miss the mark.

"If you're positive about the direction, we'll be on our way," Collie said.

"As sure as the sky is blue."

"If this turns out to be a lie," Collie began.

The merchant smiled. "You'll arrest me. Or maybe hang me. How about decapitation as a response to my low lying purpose. Mr. Collie, do you really want to end our parting with idle threats?"

"No I don't. Thank you." He tipped his hat and rode off.

Billy lingered staring at the man.

"Your friend's blinded by his mission."

"He's not my friend."

"Nevertheless, you're in for trouble."

"I know this territory better than most."

"And yet you follow. Vengeance makes a man cloudy."

"It's not mine. I just have a debt to pay."

The merchant puffed the final tobacco flakes and rested the pipe on the wagon seat. "Then I bid you adieu. I doubt very much we will meet again."

"Stranger things have happened Milton King," Billy said with a grin. He peered at the wagon canvas and then tipped his hat as well. "I like your style." He nicked at his horse and then spurred it to gain on his companion.

The merchant watched the dust collect behind the two as they fled. "Poppa." He heard the boy's voice and turned to discover him out of the wagon.

"What are you doing?"

"I wanted to sit here with you."

A spark of welcomed content graced him. He tapped the bench next to him. "Up you jump." The boy leaped from the footstep and plopped himself playfully down next to his father.

"What will we do today poppa?"

"Let's see where the day takes us."

"Are we heading west as well?"

"No Karl."

"Why?

"This way is safer."

The information aligned with the boy's understanding. "That's where those men are headed. That's silly of them."

"Why's that silly?"

"Because we know their country better than they do."

King placed his arm around Karl and gazed at him with admiration. "You're a smart one you know that?"

"Will they be alright poppa?"

"It is hard to imagine." The merchant brought the rein down tenderly on the horse. The boy lost his balance a beat, but righted himself. They headed toward the road. The wagon clanged and wobbled over the rough terrain, but when they reached the road it leveled.

"Will we be safe poppa?"

"Of course we will. We have each other."

***

They pushed forward into the early night making headway until they were forced to stop with the lacking light. Billy had determined that the way off the path loaned itself to tracking much more than the previous route. Their target had knowingly done this. And this position made them uneasy in their pursuit.

The current evening was much cooler than the last. They lit a fire. Collie insisted they keep it small. They hunkered down closer than usual holding their collars tightly as they shivered with the frigid breeze. Collie reached into his satchel and brought out more jerky. He threw it to Billy without looking and they ate in silence.

As dusk continued to fade the firelight took prominence capturing the men's attention and they watched and listened as the kindling cracked and the flames lifted. Neither man lay down nor did they make any attempt to converse. The brisk air was simply too much. They kept their strength.

In the distance was a brief reflection of light like a mirror catching the sunrise. "Wolf," Billy said unmoving.

"I know." Collie scanned the area.

"That's odd, skulking around by its lonesome."

"Probably starving."

Billy agreed. "Never seen one away from the pack before."

The animal moved closer though kept a distance. Its figure caught the lunar glow and the firelight. The wolf's frame was emaciated, the bones nearly protruding through the skin. The flesh was loose, hinting at its once dominant primordial self. And the animal's movement was sluggish out of necessity rather than deliberation. The creature's being emitted a resonance of an era past, not forgotten, but faded like so many things in the world that would continue to fade into extinction. It stalked the perimeter finally sitting aside a tree. He stared at the men as if in envy. The men saw the beast's eyes and the eyes displayed the longing of when it could not only kill with its brethren, but relish in the act itself. The men remained sensitive to the animal's presence. They soon let their guard down. It saddened them that the creature once hungry in life and able to lead others of its kind to victory could no longer muster the force to lead itself. When they would wake in the morning it would be gone.

***

The stranger sniffed at the night air. It was cool, crisp, and unfilled. He had seen their fire the night before. They were following him. Their numbers and identity still enigmatic. They would not stop. He had collected too many for them to stop. He allowed himself to break out of necessity only. It had been a long time since he rested properly and the pain once relegated to his hip had crawled down his entire leg perpetually flaring and never losing purpose like a great predator. With each new incursion he gripped Wells's animal beneath him which was now in a state of constant tired distress. Its head drooping like it was attached to a loose thread. He pushed forward.

Their pace always slowed in the darkness. The animal leery of what lay ahead. The stranger encouraged it, running a hand through its mane. Surrounding them was a choir of crickets and assorted inhabitants. He halted occasionally listening for water. He licked his lips. They were desiccated and crusty and he could taste the salt of his dried sweat. He brought the rein down upon the horse. It did not move. "Come now." The head hung. "Move." The heel of his boot dug into the animal's ribs. It neighed and progressed.

They navigated their way over the land which to had the feeling of being untouched. The terrain was wide and clear from what he could gather under the hinted light. When he heard the plunge of the animal's hoof through the skin of the ground he dismounted and drank from the formed puddle. He drank deeply, gagging on foreign solids. He cupped his hands and brought the water to the horse. He repeated this for some time before pressing on.

The stink was horrid and grew as he neared. He was in the midst of it. He left the horse and approached on foot. The soft ground gave in under each footstep. He moved slowly and with curiosity. The body lay before him. It was that of a man, chained by his hands to a tree, though one hand was absent. The lifeblood abandoned the flesh. It had been there long enough. The stranger paused in front of it. He sat. Cross legged, he winced audibly. "What's your story?" he said to the corpse. "Mine's more interesting." He saw the missing hand. "Or perhaps not."

The foul decomposition invited the small fauna, usually ignored, to the open surface. They explored the territory, taking what they needed to survive and in a way so instinctual it was a wonder they were not held in higher regard by those with reason. It was as though they had been there for millions of years in that same spot doing as they were time and again with the same unfortunate soul who may have in truth been there only for their survival. All the while the stranger slept soundly and not far away.

***

They had woken abruptly to the hollowed popping sound of a woodpecker against a black walnut tree. They ate a meager portion of dried beef and cleared the camp. It had rained during the night. Their clothes were damp and they could hear the suction of the hooves from the earth. But they rode with determination for Collie glanced down at the tracks beneath him as evident as a smoking gun. He smiled and they went from trot to gallop.

They went steadily and for some time. The heat of days previous no longer lingered and the wind shooed them at their backs--.. Billy no longer maintained point. They rode side by side with an unspoken rapport and had an onlooker caught sight of them in the distance he might have thought they had been riding together for years.

They rode through a wooded area densely populated by firs. They slowed and Billy proceeded on foot. Collie huffed, grizzled, observing as the half Indian displayed his superior tracking skills in front of him. He huffed again, but then breathed lightly and chose not to speak. "Won't be but a moment," Billy said. He grasped a patch of low lying branches, half snapped and brushing over the ground and then ran his fingers over the smooth needles of the fir. From their ends he pinched a small collection of hair. He brought it to his face inspecting it. "I see you," he said and he rubbed his fingers together. The surviving breeze from outside of the forest carried off the tuft of animal hair and Billy watched as it danced across the ground. "Let's keep this way," he said.

When they reached the edge of the forest Collie spoke and the sound of his voice startled the younger man. "How come you ain't run still?" Collie asked. Billy chuckled. "I'm serious."

"You're not a trusting man are you?"

"Are you?"

"No I'm not." There was a smugness in his voice. "What if we were simply acting like human beings were intended to?"

"That might be the problem all along."

"And that would mean that to be inhuman would bring the world to harmony."

"I guess it would."

"That sure is a point of view," Billy said.

They came upon a field garnished with blossoms that overtook the landscape and they were tall and full and the wind came and stole the flowers gliding a pink snowfall atop the wild grass like a pastel drawing quiet and untouched. Collie moved forward. "It's not that way," Billy said, but the older man either ignored him or did not hear and in the midst of the wind and the trees he raised his arms grasping at the flowing pedals like a child catching snowflakes on his tongue. He looked above and squinted at the light peaking through the foliage. He laughed and kept on doing so like the action itself was cathartic. And then he brought his arms down. He opened his palms and the prisoner blossoms grew unrestricted in his hold. He blew at them and they joined their peers amongst the grass.

He took a breath. "Okay. We can go."

Billy regained point. "They're cherry blossoms," Billy said to Collie who was trailing behind.

"Is that right?"

"Yeah. You've never seen em'?"

"Can't remember."

Billy waited a while. "Does it bother you? That I know more about this place than you do? And at half your age."

"Lot's of things bother me."

***

The ambiance stirred when they discovered the body. The skin of the corpse like dried leather was fractured and compressed, the face was yellowed pages of a long book handed down through generations. Collie dismounted first and approached the body without recourse. Billy was hesitant.

He left his horse and stood some yards away. "I don't think he can use an assist. How long's it been here?"

Collie scanned the vacant body. "A while. His stink ain't much." He peered leisurely at the surroundings. "Flies ain't botherin'. Looks like the sun's been at him longer than anything."

Billy moved closer. "What happened to him?"

"Starved to death probably."

"How do you know that?"

He waited a moment. "He ate his own hand."

Billy was chewing his own lip aimlessly and stopped in disgust. "Say what?"

"I'm sure it was an attempt to free himself firstly, but I'd bet on the notion that three or four days without any food or water makes unkind thoughts run afoul." Collie tapped his own head as he said it.

Billy moved closer. He came to Collie's side and cringed. It was slight, but audible. "How do you know it wasn't some critter? Coyote maybe."

The sheriff crouched. "See that brown from his chin to his lower lip?" He brought his finger close in order to point without touching. "It's smeared like," he said waving his finger, "and dribbled here. It ain't red cause it's weathered. Old blood looks brown on the skin."

"Holy shit," is all Billy could muster.

"Whoever shackled him made it secure, that's obvious. But look here." He raised the chained arm of the dead man and the coagulated stump came into view. "He was out here for a good while. His wrists and forearms are beat to hell all scratched and bruised. They ain't in the vein of defensive so he tried to fight loose. Probably tried it a few hundred times before the next idea started itchin' at his brain. Almost certainly started small, you know, like an inkling. A little speck. And he shook it off. But then it came back. And then back again more often 'til he couldn't shake it off no more. Then that speck burst. I'm sure by the end it even seemed like a good idea. The ground is soft and you ain't gonna break through bone by cuttin' it with tree bark. So he used the sharpest thing he could find. Teeth. He wasn't so smart though."

"Why's that?"

"He saved the thumb for last. Can't figure on that. The other four fingers are gone, but he only got the top half of the thumb. Didn't even crack the bone." It protruded from the top knuckle like a twig. "He eats that first, he slides that wrist out and maybe he makes it. But who knows the state of a man willing to eat his own self? Maybe I'm too judgmental."

"Takes a mighty lot of will power," Billy said.

Collie nodded. "For him and the one that left him."

Billy kept staring at the body. "The one that left him got off easy. Never saw the lights go out. Anyone can do that."

"Let's get out of here," Collie said and began walking away. He made it to his horse and looked back. Billy stood beside the corpse though his attention was elsewhere. He was staring at a mark a short distance away. "What?"

"He was here," Billy said. His boots skimmed across the dirt as he moved carefully to his destination, dust streams trailing his heels. "It was him I reckon."

Collie approached. His face turned angry. "Yeah?"

Billy held up his hand motioning the sheriff to stop. "There's tracks here," Billy said. "Not from any walking or passing through." He stepped back, still observing. "They're longer than that, like he bed down here. Who else would sleep near a corpse?"

Collie sauntered away a bit. "That'd make this his evacuation," he said motioning to the ground.

"His evacuation?"

"His shit."

Billy hopped up toward Collie. "Makes sense it's his. That means he's eating."

"We ain't seen no fires."

"He's probably eating raw what he can. If he gets small game he's likely burying the carcasses or their bodies are small enough to get picked up by scavengers. It's his only choice if he wants to leave a lesser trail. Otherwise he'd starve to death."

"We'd have to catch him before that happens. You tell which way he went?" Collie asked. Billy pointed a direction. They were quick to mount the horses. "If you're right, you're good."

"How's that now?" Billy said amusedly.

"You heard."

"If I'm right you say?"

"We'll see soon enough. I'm willing to trust you."

"That's mighty kind of you sheriff." They began to ride. "What if soon enough never comes?"

"It'll come."

"You're sure about that?"

"The surest I've been about anything."

"And when we find him?"

"I'll kill him?"

"Just like that?" Billy said snapping his fingers.

"Should I pray first or something?"

"You're not going to ask why? Ask him anything?"

Collie blew at a mosquito. "Back in Kansas I arrested a man. Farmer. Came to town to purchase a frying pan. His shirt was speckled with blood and it was smeared over his hands. When the shop keep glimpsed him, he sent a boy to come get me. I got to the shop and the farmer held two pans, one in each hand. He had the shop keep backed into the corner, shouting questions at him about which was better meaning which was probable to cook a better meal. The keep was cryin' and beggin' for the man to leave. Anyways, I pulled my gun. Didn't use it, cause I was able to get him down on my own. Back in the lock up I asked the farmer what happened. Said he killed his wife. I asked why. Said he didn't like her cooking anymore. Said she burnt everything to the damn pan something awful. Food tasted like ash and that he knew what flavor the color black was. So after a breakfast not to his likin', he took that pan and beat his wife to death with it. Then he brought her outside, dug a hole, and threw her and that pan inside it."

"That a fact?"

"That's a fact."

"So?"

"I'm telling you that the why ain't important. It doesn't undo anything and it don't make people feel better. The world works better without some folk in it. That's all." Collie spit. "This man we're after killed my friend. And from what I gathered, killed a whole lot other than Virgil. He did things to women too. Cut 'em up. Kept parts. This world's got no cause for a man like that. I'm gonna kill him. And my why don't matter either. But when it's done things'll be right. And I'll know it. You just keep pointin' the way. That's why I brought you."

Billy huffed. "That's fine. I'll do what you brought me to do, being I owe you. But know that this isn't my cause. However your thing turns out, I end up away from this place on my own."

"You don't have to remind me of a goddamn thing."

"Well the elderly have their limits," Billy said taunting a reaction. "I was only fooling."

"I see now that your accomplices may not have gotten killed on account that they were dumber than hammered shit, but maybe it was due to the notion that they couldn't stand the proposition of working with you ever again."

"I'm inclined to say fuck you sheriff."

"Not giving in to every inclination is something that comes with age. This'll be a good test to see if you're pubescent."

There was no stalemate and they fled. The two men sat tall in their saddles and for a brief time they loped in tandem before moving side by side.

Chapter 21

(*This chapter's italicized words are Spanish translated into English.)

He spotted them through the handheld scope. There was blood caught in the tracks of the retractable shaft. He had missed some when he cleaned it. He positioned himself on his stomach at the edge the ridgeline overlooking the plains. The view was clear. Two men were in pursuit. He watched them for a brief while. They were miniscule even through the telescope. They were closer than they had been in days.

The stranger watched as the more slender one left his horse. He could see the man moving his hands over the ground and remounting his animal and they headed slowly in his direction. The hills were tall and rocky and the road through them serpentine. It would buy him time. The stranger removed the lens from his eyes and pushed himself away from the ridgeline remaining prone. When he was far enough from their vantage he rose and limped to his failing horse. He rode out at whatever pace he could muster.

Night arrived. There were three of them, four counting the fat one, but he was sleeping and his rotund distended belly ascended and fell to the rhythm of his snoring. The others were drinking. There were two bottles between them. With each swig they seemed to grow more cantankerous with one another.

The stranger crept forward. He was alone, his horse at a distance. The sound of his mangled body dragging across the rugged terrain was masked by the puerile belligerence of the three drunken philistines. He moved, slowly and heavily like a large slug, pushing across the ground erratically. His injury made him cringe in the blind. As he grew nearer, the firelight brought clarity to their faces and he could hear their foreign words as they spoke childishly of women and the honor of men and how that honor was manifested and assessed through the tolerance of alcohol and sexual conquests. He seemed enraptured but for a moment. It arrived when one spoke of food and reached for a pair of sticks near the edge of the fire, each with small game on them. From his angle, the stranger could not make out the game and whatever distinguishing characteristics there may have been were now charred. When the man placed the overdone meat on the fire again the stranger's captivation broke.

It was dark. They would not be able to see him. Not at first. He perched, staring at them triangulating the fire. He listened and observed.

There lacked a hierarchy. The man centered at the camp was bearded and wore a dark bandana around his neck. He seemed to hold ground over the quartet at times, berating the others and then yielding to his own laughter. Yet the others did not give in to subjugation, hurling back each insult with a quip of their own. The stranger sat in judgement over the scene.

"*You two don't fall asleep tonight first,*" the bearded on said. He swigged from the bottle. "*I'll slice your nuts.*" He bellowed a laugh and drank again. He spit the alcohol into the fire and it swelled. He laughed again. The others reciprocated.

The one on the left squinted through one eye at the man with the beard. "*That is the excuse you use to try and see them. Isn't that right Jeffe? What you think of that?*" Jeffe on the right belched and snickered, though said nothing and the bearded one's demeanor changed.

He pulled out a knife and held it out at a full arm's length. He closed one eye and then opened it and closed the other. He did this a number of times. "*How much blood you think is inside a horse?*" Jeffe and the other did not answer. Their minds appeared elsewhere. "*It must be gallons man. Buckets worth.*" His gaze remained on the blade.

"*You drink too much, Luis,*" Jeffe said.

"*I don't drink more than you. When a horse is tiny, he's got some amount of blood. But then he gets big, big like four of us together. Does he just make more blood or does the original thin out? Where does it come from? He just makes it I suppose.*"

Jeffe scoffed. "*It's not just horses. It is true of all living creatures.*"

"Aye, but I'm talking about horses."

"Why horses?" Jeffe said.

"Because we killed a horse today," Luis said. He ripped a piece of the charred meat from the skewer with his teeth.

"I killed a horse today," the one on the left said.

Luis exhaled around the piping hot meat. *"Shut your mouth Cesar. We all did."*

"It was not a group effort," Cesar said. *"You two shot and missed the vitals. You got the horse, but not the kill. I got the kill. I exposed your incompetence."*

Luis spit the meat on the ground. *"Incompetence?"* he yelled. He lunged the knife forward, still a distance from the other men. *"Incompetence? Fuck you!"* Jeffe tensed, glaring at Cesar.

A moment passed before Cesar cracked a smile. *"Fuck me. Okay Luis. I'll go fuck myself. I'm the only one with a dick long enough anyway."* He took a drink. They began laughing slowly. Drunkenness was apparent. *"Shut up about horses. Always going on about nonsense...blood of horses. Who cares?"*

There was a thud from outside their circle and they stopped talking. They heard a voice. *"There's roughly twelve gallons of blood in a horse. Which is roughly twelve times more than that of a human. Cows are similar to horses depending on the breed, perhaps take a gallon. And pig blood? Pig blood is relative to the size of the pig, but they swing closest to the human."* It was perfect Spanish with only a hint of an accent.

"Who the fuck is that?" Luis said and scrambled to his feet. Cesar and Jeffe followed. They pawed at their holsters for their guns.

"No need for all that," the stranger said.

"Come into the light and prove it," Luis said. He kicked at the ground anxiously. The fat sleeping one caught a face full of dirt and roused. His one eye went crescent and he jerked himself upright as the stranger stepped into the camp. To the inebriated men he glided across the terrain despite an

injury like a graceful and gothic specter. When he entered the light he appeared tainted and abused, though his face shrouded a sense of a conniver or perhaps entitlement as a smile lay calmly camouflaged like an experienced predator across the lower half of his countenance. His hands were raised in submission as he moved forward to the four men. He stopped at the edge of the fire and looked over his hosts. They stared back and he wiggled his fingers playfully in the air.

"*May I offer my sincerest apologies if I've given any cause for concern. I am armed only with hunger.*" He began to lower his hands.

"*Keep them up.*" Luis shouted.

He did. The stranger scanned their faces again, this time slower. There was fear unmasked coupled with brash chutzpah. "*An odd combination,*" the stranger said.

"*What you say?*" said Jeffe holding his gun out further. It shook as his wrist bore more weight.

"*Sorry again. Thinking out loud.*" He read the hesitation in the air. The concerned men shifted both their gazes and feet in discomfort. "*I can pull out my pockets if you like. Raise my shirt.*"

"*Yes do that,*" Luis said.

"*I'll need to lower my hands. Is that ok?*" The stranger asked. He received a nod of approval from two of them at once. He pulled out his pockets and disrobed enough to show them he carried no weapons. They were reticent to accept that they were appeased, but they were and the weapons lowered and the tension withdrew to a point.

Luis jutted his chin at the stranger as if sizing him up. "*You are no Mexican, stranger,*" he said. "*You seem to be no Spaniard either. Just a gringo with our language. How's that?*"

"*A little knowledge is a dangerous thing. Why not do things the right way?*" He eyed the food near the fire. He licked his lips and brought his attention back to the men. "*I wonder if...*"

He was cut off by Luis. *"Why are you out here? Why did you approach our camp? We might have killed you. Not so smart to be sneaking up on people in the night."*

"Killed by us," Jeffe said. *"Not him. He can't shoot,"* he added.

Luis stabbed with a spiteful gaze. The stranger noticed. *"I doubt that's true. Competent men I'm sure you all are. Been enjoying the drink though I see."*

"What of that?" said the fat one. He spat on the ground and the remnants lingered on his chin.

"Don't let it get the best of you," the stranger said and put a hand to his stomach.

Luis squinted, emitting derangement through intoxication. *"You have explaining to do."*

"I'd say that's true."

"We don't like what you have to say," Luis paused and circled the barrel of his pistol at the sky, *"This is your last midnight."*

"Seems fair." The stranger tilted his head and moved his eyes to the spits near the fire. *"You don't suppose I could have some food do you?."*

"Speak first," Luis said.

"I'm quite hungry. It's the reason I approached your camp."

Cesar shook his head. *"You can eat when we're satisfied."*

"Again, that's fair. It's only that the man who has reached contentment is often the man with the clearest mind."

"For chrissakes give him some goddamn food," Jeffe said as he made his way to the fire. He picked up a spit and brought it to his face. He sniffed at the meat. He wore a face of mild disgust. *"Here,"* he said handing the spit to the stranger.

"Very much obliged," he said and blew on the scalding meat before tearing into the burnt carcass. He ate the game. It scorched his mouth, but he consumed it callously. As he ate, he watched the men watching him. The hunger overtook him

and he focused on the meal. When he finished, he thanked them again.

"*Now you speak,*" said Luis.

"*Shall we sit?*" The stranger said, brushing his hand across the view of the fire. Luis nodded, his suspicions not dwindling. He backed toward the camp. His gun was on the stranger. "*I am a man who never takes advantage of the hospitality of others, so it is with great and humble gratitude that I ask if there is any more food to eat.*"

Luis's eyes closed for a brief moment as if he were getting into character. "*You ate your share. You speak now and answer our questions or I'll blow a hole through your face and cook you and eat you.*" The others stared knowing better than to question the comment at this stage. "*You've come to our camp unannounced and uninvited. We've been kind enough to let you have the food we hunted. You've been courteous and that means precisely dick in this territory. So again, I say speak. And speak the truth. I'm no fool. We're no fools. Lie and we'll know it. So tell us a story. Speak stranger.*"

The stranger read the eyes of the gasconading host. He arched a single brow and leered transiently beneath the shadows cast across him like small crows drifting over sun beams. He inhaled deeply with confidence. "*My story you say?*" He scanned his audience a final time. "*I'll speak of the gold.*" Their ears perked. "*I assume I have your attention.*" They leaned forward simultaneously, eager children in a classroom. Their weapons became benign accessories growing heavier and more burdensome until they eventually dropped them in the dirt as he told them his story of riches, betrayal, and flight.

Chapter 22

She sits in the soil between the rows of corn drawing pictures in it with a short offshoot from the nearby bushes. She buries the stick inches deep as it glides and the soil is soft and moist from the morning mist. In the distance is a call from her mother. She ignores it staring at the man in the sun she has created in the dirt beneath her. There is a call again, this time louder. She pauses. Her attention is broken. She opens her mouth to answer, but says nothing. She begins to move the stick through the ground making earthen rays. Her father now calls for her. The voice is stern. She applies pressure to the twig and it breaks over the sun's perimeter, the rays unfinished. She stands. The corn is a foot above her and she can see the upper half of the stalks dance with the youthful breeze. She kicks over the dirt and the sun man dies and she leaves the corn field in a hurry.

At the edge of the field she halts and looks to the great maple atop the hill above the corn. There are riders there, two men on horseback. The wind is unaccompanied and the men are motionless. They are backlit and look like her drawings in the soil. She can see their hats outlined. They are not of her tribe. Her father's voice is raised once again from the village. She turns toward her home. When she looks again to the maple the men are gone. She takes deliberate steps and then advances to a run in the direction of her parents' voices.

In the lodge she sits with the other children as the warrior dances. She speaks to them as they watch the ritual. Through the smoke she sees her father. He does not seem pleased. She says something to the child beside her. The child drives an elbow into her side. She sighs. The smoke escapes through an aperture in the ceiling. She watches it rise and becomes fixated on the blue headdress of the warrior. It moves aggrandized by the billowing grey clouds and she travels with it as it transforms emboldened and alive. She is away. The other children laugh and she is brought back to the present in a clarity or obscurity dependent on the beholder. The boy behind her whispers something in her ear. He is a mite younger. She turns and he whispers in the other ear. She pulls back and peers into him as if searching for a greater truth and they both laugh softly.

Outside of the earthlodge her father speaks of responsibility. Although amidst her later youth, she has duties the same as other tribeswomen. His voice is not raised, but his words are commanding. He is tall and his frame great from years of work and battle. He is a tower to her petite being. His sermon continues. She drifts. She stares at his beard. Most native men did not wear them though many of her tribe did. He catches her wandering. He slaps her face. She is jolted, but not in pain. And he continues speaking.

Later the cornfield is dry and the aura stagnant. Her instrument is to the side and she is painting in the dirt with her finger. The sun and the moon are in congress. They have faces and a man walks atop each one. The man is only a stick figure, but she has drawn each in identical motion as if staring at a reflection. The only inconstant being the great star and the moon. There is a rustle behind her. She does not stir. It happens again. She turns. There is nothing. She leaves the cornfield, this time before a beckoning. At the edge of the crop she stops again. There is something beneath the maple. It may be a person. The sky is overcast. There are no silhouettes. If it is a person he is crouched as if hiding. She steps forward to examine. Her second stride is heavier. The thing beneath the tree shrinks and disappears. She runs to her village.

She helps her mother with the corn meal. The women are quiet and their motions habitual. She drops her pestle. Her palms are reddened. She clenches her fingers into fists and does this repeatedly. She is chided for lagging. There is no mention of the occurrences at the maple.

Her family eats from the deer slain by her father and the other hunters. Silence is predominant but for the slight words spoken by her father and brother. They sit in a tight circle. The unseen space is vast and cavernous. She watches her brother watching her father, mimicking his moves worshipfully. Her eyes roll. She is admonished. This time by her mother. She lifts her hand to her mouth. She watches her brother watching her father. The venerable man speaks to the boy. He suggests the work of the days following. Her mother points to her plate and tells her to finish. She eats lacking pleasure. Her brother gives her a half smile and touches her hand. The man and boy stand and leave the women.

She is drawing a map of their village on the large rock with a smaller rock she found outside of the lodge. The bird's eye is accurate. Outside of the pictorial home she draws her version of a forest and beyond the forest another village. She colors the other village with berries from foraging. This is not from memory.

In the evening she lays with a girl of her age on a blanket of animal skin outside of her own lodge and they point to the stars and trace with their fingers the celestial and fantastical beings that arrive each night unheralded and they tell stories of the endless stretches of black and the small piercing light that penetrates it. They giggle and are joined by another girl and boy, both younger than them, but they too partake in the view of the natural canvass. They are wordless for stretches and playfully take turns with their tales.

Her father sends her to collect the food that has ripened and to nurture the seedlings. She drops her basket when it is half full and approaches the small mounds where the seeds have been planted. There are rows and rows of tiny humps. She lowers her face to one of the mounds and blows gently on it, whispering. The superficial dirt is weak, but beneath it stubborn. She leaves to collect more.

Her basket is now full and lays outside of the corn field. Between the rows she sits and views the clouds lightly masked by the stalks and she draws the sky in the dirt. There is a rustling behind her. It is not the wind. She begins to turn. She is enshrouded by an umbra. Her eyes are down. She closes them hard. And when she opens them the once meandering shapeless form that was the incubus of her subconscious has fully manifested itself pillaging her earthen rendering and she screams and it is abrupt as a filth ridden hand covers her lips stifling her violent desperation. She tries to scream through it. She tastes the skin of his palm and heaves dryly. Her body wrenches beyond her control, but she cannot break free. He speaks in a foreign tongue. There is another voice behind his. It is the same, foreign. They are talking and she kicks at the ground pushing her body weight into the man. He is strong. The attempt, futile. He says something again to the man behind him.

With his hand still around her mouth he rises from his knees bringing her with him. He shifts his right leg around hers and pulls back on it bringing her to her stomach. The blow to the ground takes her breath for a moment. She is parallel to the ground. There is a small mound of an unborn seedling directly in her view. She moves to see her attacker. He pushes her face into the ground and she feels it creep into her ear and she inhales the dirt. She no longer tries to scream. He hikes up the animal skin dress she is wearing and enters her. He grunts and does this repeatedly and her breath pours out to the inconstant rhythm onto the seed mound which diminishes in size with each exhale. Her mind tries to drift as she hears the words from the second man behind her. She knows not what he says and she cannot understand the laughing.

She is pale and her eyes heavy. She moves through the field bending to collect the squash, the move awkward with her now showing belly. She is alone in an apportioned section. The other women are near though seem miles away. Their eyes are down on their work and she can hear them giggle in punctuation to sporadic comments. She has accepted this.

She is alone in the teepee sitting to the meal she has prepared. No prayer is said. When she is done she lies back and stares blankly and a time later she finds herself meandering digging her nails into her distended belly.

She receives a visit from the girl she used to watch the stars with. The girl has brought generous strips of smoked bison. She makes to refuse them, but then grabs them like they were the last pieces in the world. The girl smiles and puts her finger to her mouth telling her to keep quiet.

She is on her back. The pain is severe. Her mother places a band of leather in her mouth and tells her it is so she will not bite her tongue. She bites into it immediately. She squeezes her mother's hand. Another woman of the tribe enters the teepee. She is her mother's age. The woman has brought water and cloth. She seems kind, as does her mother. They calm her between contractions.

She spits out the leather when the baby comes and exhales like a drowning victim who has just been revived. She is explained to that the baby is her responsibility, none other, and the baby shall walk two worlds. She nods although she does not understand. They hand her the child. She rises upright as best she can and she stares into the newborn's eyes and the child stares back at the foreign cosmic pupils in wonderment. Her throat swells and she weeps.

Her father enters. He scans the scene and she wipes her eyes of tears and brow of sweat. He tells the woman of the tribe to leave. She does and his wife remains. He walks toward his daughter and stands over her and looks down to the child making no expression. He tilts his head in curiosity as if discovering an ancient writing and then bends down to pick up the child. She gives it up willingly. He says it is a son and hands the infant to his daughter. He leaves the tent.

The child sits among the others in congregation with the teacher and his mind escapes as she speaks and he stares at the others, their black hair and swarthy hides a constant reminder of his seeming alien body and when the children gaze back at him he cannot help but envision what they may be thinking, internalizing the possibilities. He is snapped at by the teacher. He is startled and straightens himself as the children laugh.

He is collecting wood with the other boys for the fire they will use in tonight's ceremony. When they have collected enough they are given hatchets as rewards. The excitement is seen chiseled in their faces despite their wordless respect. It is hot and the work is hard. He wipes his dusty brown hair from his forehead. Later they sit as a group on a downed log while the man he is told is his grandfather demonstrates the stringing of a bow. They are silent. The warrior speaks and his voice travels suggesting an invariability without regard to an audience. He has them pick up the bows. He does not make eye contact. The boys listen and act on command.

The boy makes clicking sounds with his tongue as he travels to his mother without detour. The abode is distanced from the tribal camp. When he arrives he is given food and she kisses his forehead. She asks about his learning. His answers are square and he begins eating.

He and the girl sneak into the woods after lessons. They should be working. There are many chores for each family and for the tribe. Beyond the treeline into the depth of the forest it is still light with twinkles of sunlight descending and the beams themselves are thick enough to appear to be grasped. She leans openly on the tree and accepts his proximity. He brings his face close and he smells her lips and smiles and they kiss and giggle and kiss some more. She removes the top half of her garb and drops her head shyly. He reaches to grab her breasts. His hand is swatted away and she clothes herself and explains that it is wrong and as she begins her walk to camp she promises not to say anything if he does not. He is confused and remains in the forest for a while.

His sense of curiosity grows over time and his quest for knowledge becomes an ever present feeling like an itch in the throat that cannot quite be vanquished. He questions his mother about the tribe and their estrangement from their people. Her answers are like shields. He is not satisfied. His questions become incessant. He wants to know how his father died. He asks why the man who is his alleged grandfather refuses the title. The boy is never satisfied. He stops asking.

He loses himself in hunting and tracking and he is able to cultivate relationships through the training with the fellow young men. He is sometimes physically slower than the others, but his knack for cunning exceeds theirs'. He is often called Half Moon, though not maliciously. They hunt as a group. He leads the tracking when they receive their inaugural weapons. The first kill is made. The boy who made the killshot is praised and the group is congratulated by an elder upon their return.

The men keep him at an arm's length. He is dichotomous in his loyalties. He seeks resolution. He ventures further and further away from camp. Sometimes alone.

His mother grows increasingly distant. She no longer has any contact with the tribe. She is a shut in. Her health is failing. He now prepares the meals. He hunts and gathers. His own connection with the tribe is beginning to dissolve.

It begins to rain and the day's rain transforms into rolling thunderous storms and the skies are ashen, gunmetal and soot. The forest stands before him a waking dream in all of its raw and uncompromising wonderment hooking a finger in invitation like an enlightened and venerable seductress and an ancient wise god offering an uncharted path into an unnavigable subconscious. His point of embarkation into the forest is densely lined with compact brush and thickets of thorny arms. The young men are stationed individually around the camp waiting for the call. The warrior behind him explains that it is said a dog caught in the rain can often not find its way home. He examines the perimeter. His closest peers are more than one hundred yards away. They must remain gone for two moons and return with something useful to the tribe. His grandfather is watching with unbiased eyes. He is reprimanded by the warrior for losing focus. The horn sounds and the boy enters the forest and from the camp the miniature frames of the small boys grow less and less and their bare backs once clashing among the life of the woods are camouflaged as the nature swiftly envelops them.

He emerges from the forest upon the eve of the third moon, his presence announced by the cracking of the underbrush beneath his feet and the withdrawn sounds of muscle strain and exhaustion. A buck is strewn over his shoulders. His feet sink into the ground as he moves to the center of camp. The young hunters are gathered on the downed log. He sees them rise. They are instructed not to assist. As he continues his journey forth, his right knee buckles and he drops to it. The buck's hind side now angled down. The boy presses his teeth together and stares into the elder warriors' eyes and grunts his way into a stand. He approaches the assemblage. The members are silent. He can see the mixed looks of the boys, both proud and beaten. He squats and drops the buck to the ground. The boy rubs a laceration under his eye. His knees are bruised and his feet bloodied. He breaths heavy though says nothing. One of the elders pats his shoulder. The pat is hard and the boy nods his head. He scans the group. His grandfather is not present. Two boys are ordered to pick up the buck and prepare it for cleaning. Outside of the smoke tent, he sees the other kills. There is a string of birds, squirrels, rabbit, and an undersized doe. He is told to clean himself. There is a comradery near visible for the first time in his life. He leaves the village to see his mother.

The girl is looking at him. He has noticed her before. She is older by only two years. She smiles and he does as well. At nightfall they enter the woods together. She speaks in foreign tongue when she wants to. The language is broken.

She tells him it is English. He is intrigued. She teaches him. Their congress continues.

There is blood settled in the dirt outside of the teepee mildly congealed through the tributary leading inside. He tenses but for a moment and breathes deep and walks inside. His mother is on the ground lightly gripping a stone blade painted in dark red and her eyes like a doll's stare openly above, unblinking and lifeless. Her color has started to fade. His throat grows, but he does not cry. He leaves the tent. His steps seem lighter than usual. He looks over the village. A home that has been marginally out of his bounds for his entire young life. He examines the lodges and homes of the families of strangers and acquaintances. A single tear develops. He brushes it away as if it were a pest. He goes back into the tent. He slings his bow over his back and gathers his satchel. In the corner of the teepee is the stock of smoked meat. He collects all that he can carry. Before leaving, he stops over his mother's body, over the woman so terrified of witting ostracization that it had consumed her beyond redemption. He places his hand over her eyes and closes them and he tells her how much he wants to hate her for her choices. He tells her he loves her and then leaves the teepee. There is a girl outside. They have been intimate. She is near enough, but not close. She waves to him. He shakes his head and lowers it, perhaps in contemplation and then waves back. She is jovial for a moment then her expression changes as she senses his despondence. She takes a few steps forward and he turns and enters the forest from the village for the last time in his young life.

He sits beneath the pine, bow beside him cracked, paired just away from equal. He turns the spit and the middling meat blackens in contrast with the middling fire. He licks his lips. They are cracked like barren ground. He turns the spit. The aroma is charred and off-putting. He stands. His waistline is diminished and he stumbles as he walks to his shelter. In his shelter, he spreads the soft needles in relative coverage. When it is even, he kicks it up and does it again and then returns to his supper.

He moves about the land in brush and shadow. The nights seem extended. At the arrival of eventide he finds himself yelling at the moon. There is no answer.

The campfire cuts through the black for miles. He creeps ever closer. He sees the group. It is a family. There are five of them, all women and the father. They are speaking English. He can make out portions of their speech. He positions himself so he can hear without straining. They are telling stories. He listens. A smile graces him for the first time in a long time. He waits until they are asleep. When they awake, their food will be missing.

He is drawn to the sounds in the distance. They are man made and raucous. He flattens himself, skimming the soft earth to the treeline. It reveals itself and he squints and rubs his eyes and peers harder. He sees the camp and it is beautiful.

The clothes lack the proper fit, but they are stolen so he does not complain. His gash is wrapped in a piece of shirt and he hides his hand in his pocket. He watches the people around him and listens intently. When he is alone, he mimics their patterns.

He holds his own in the fight. They call him a savage. He says nothing. The three of them are not much older than him. They talk and boast and he grows tired of listening. They call him the son of a whore. He is in the dirt in the alley and the ground is cold and hard. The blood on him is not completely his own.

He picks his first pocket. It is not clean. The blood spurts forth from his nose as a result of the strike to his face. The owner kicks him as he lies on the ground and then walks away with his wallet. He spits blood from his mouth and moans and the moan transforms to a laugh as he removes the fresh money from his inner coat pocket.

The dapper man sees him from the poker table sitting near the bar. He notices that the young man would be considered well dressed had the clothes been washed some weeks ago. The dapper man is called by another player. He folds and continues watching the young man at the bar. He sees him take the money from his mark. It is swift though imperfect. The dapper man is intrigued.

On the road adjacent the saloon the dapper man stops him. He says something to the young man about what he saw and the young man begins to run. The dapper man shouts that he does not care and the young man stops reticently. The dapper man says his name is Andrew Fisk. The young man says nothing and Fisk lifts his hands in wanting. The teen waits and says to call him Billy. It sounds good. Fisk extends his hand and tells him that he is pleased to meet him.

He sprinkles the tobacco ritualistically across the paper and then licks the paper and rolls it. He offers it to Billy and Billy accepts. He coughs on his first inhale. Fisk laughs and tells him to try again and then to continue trying until he does not cough any more. They smoke together on the street outside of the hotel. Billy strains to hold the smoke. Fisk watches and smirks and suggests they go inside.

Billy sits in the dining room as Fisk speaks to the hotel manager. He keeps quiet as the men talk. He sees the manager enter the kitchen and Fisk approaches the table. He sits and tells Billy to drag on the cigarette. Billy ignores him and makes to stand and leave. Fisk asks if he is hungry. Billy's silence conveys his true answer. He is told to sit if he is hungry and drag on the cigarette. He sucks in the smoke and the tarry taste fills his lungs and he explodes it out violently, coughing like a victim of fire. Fisk tosses him a napkin and grabs the cigarette from his hand, stamping it out on the floor. The hotel manager returns with two large plates of food. He explains that his nephew had the tuberculosis and how it took him up to God much before his time and how he cannot abide the suffering of youth. He pats Billy gently on the back and tells him to eat up to build strength. Billy nods. As the manager is about to leave, Fisk takes him by the wrist and asks the man to join them in prayer. When they are done eating, Billy groans and belches. He is told not to lose the sale. He coughs in succession and thanks the manager on the way out. No money exchanges hands and it is the best meal he has ever eaten.

He has never seen a boat before, let alone one of such size. Steam bellows out the stacks and he steps back almost frightened. Fisk approaches holding two tickets. Billy asks how they were paid for. Fisk says with an honest dollar. Billy says that they do not have any of those. Fisk says that someone did.

Billy fixates on their expressions as Fisk takes each one down and his fascination grows in how willing they are to part with that which they earned when the cause appears right and there were times when it was as though God was their third partner. Sometimes his job is to smile. Other times he is to seem despondent. Both are simple. He is paid well. He takes to drinking. Fisk does not mind as long as it is private. Billy continues his part. And over time, it grows tiresome.

They work the alley outside of the strip in San Francisco. Billy's youth and looks carry them beyond what Fisk is capable of by himself. Billy sees two children asking for money from every passerby. Billy struts past them and turns when they ignore him. He asks why they did not solicit him. They have lost heart. Billy tells the young boy that his sister looks pretty enough and they should use what they have and that begging and breathing do not jibe.

Fisk is pushed from the barbershop. He stumbles as he hits the street. There is a half chugged whiskey bottle in his hand. Billy excuses himself from the girl he is speaking to and helps steady the older man. He has never seen Fisk drunk and he has never seen him sloven. Fisk shrugs him off and Billy remains alone in the street with a thousand strangers of the city.

Billy sits on the bar stool nursing his water. He alludes to his Pa at the poker table when the sale needs it. The bartender tells him it is no place for a kid. Billy says that his Pa should not be long and that he is no more a child than the bar stool. The chair screeches in the background and hits the ground with an intense thud. The man standing has his pistol on Fisk. Billy sprays the water out and the gun fires before he can turn. The acoustics make a cannon of the gunshot. Fisk's cheeks well out like he is holding in vomit. He grabs at the hole in his chest, pawing at a phantom itch. Billy takes a step and Fisk falls off his chair in unison with Billy's first stride. The man holsters his pistol. They reach the body at the same time. Fisk's eyes are wide open and still. Billy inhales and goes through the dead man's pockets. He pauses a moment and stares into Fisk. He is about to close the man's lids. He does not. He continues through the pockets. He pulls a wad of bills from Fisk's jacket. He is told by the shooter that the money is rightfully his being that he won it. Billy says that it cannot all be, but hands him the whole stack anyway. The shooter fans it and takes what he wants. He hands Billy the remnants. He tells the boy that his Pa was a cheater and then asks if it was in fact his Pa. Billy says he was something like that and he leaves in the wind.

The round head of the dandelion seed's image is disrupted with the varying ferocity of the breeze and the breeze steals, unbiased, parts of all things great and small. And each solitary floret drifts in what seems aimless fashion at the mercy of their new master and they skim across acreage and are deposited at sectors along the way. And the uncharacteristic stubbornness is manifested in those that cling against the drift, but even those are stolen when enough force is applied. And when they take root it is often at the behest of the master and some never root and are passed through this counterfeit freedom until they are discarded elsewhere. And elsewhere is a place of sudden death where nothing grows and

*nothing flourishes and nothing ever has to know the truths
and lies of the universe.*

Collie bent up with a shock from a deep sleep. He awoke
to the sound of silence. It was a dawn indistinguishable from
dusk and the sun and moon were both at odds in attendance.
He closed his eyes and pushed his palms into his sockets hard
and the phosphenes danced and he followed them sidetracked,
forgetting the present for one sublime moment. It was as
though nature had taken pause. The discord of even the
insects was dormant. Collie cleared his throat and blinked his
eyes in a progression and peered around his camp. The
blanket across the fire was slept in, but empty. He pulled his
own blankets off and jumped to his feet. The inharmonious
chorus of nature began their cries as if on cue. He stomped to
the other side of the fire pit and noticed that although their
shared supplies remained, Billy had taken his gun with him.
Collie reached for his revolver. He kept his hand on the butt
while the rest laid in the holster. "Goddamn savage," he said
to himself and he kicked a lump of dirt in front of him.

"What's that you grumbling about?" Billy said. Collie
spun and saw him. He was holding a dead rabbit by the ears.

"I didn't hear any shot," he said removing his hand
from the butt of the gun.

"No need," Billy said and he spit a pebble from his
mouth. "Got this'n with a rock."

"Got it with a rock," Collie said aloud, but to himself.
"We gotta get on the move."

"You wanna eat this then?"

Collie patted his stomach and his brows went up. "I
could do for some food. Best make it quick though." They sat
and ate and left with the sunrise.

Chapter 23

(This chapter's italicized words are Spanish translated into English)

The clouds rolled in dulling all semblance of vibrancy and it began to rain and the road was wet as they traveled forth. "It won't be easy with this," Billy said with no response from his company. They stuck to the road. "You see them rocks up ahead in the distance?" Collie nodded whether he saw them or not. "It looks a short way because the terrain inclines, but it's not. We can move up to there at least and figure our bearings."

They saw the blackened circle where the fire had been. The weather had extinguished it. Even the smoke had ceased. They moved cautiously. "You don't think he'd have lit fire, a man in his spot do you?" Billy asked.

"I don't reckon." Collie said. He reconnoitered. "This ain't him." He got off the horse and moved to the site. Billy dismounted as well. Collie bent down over the charred logs and picked up a thin metal spike, blackened at the end. There was another adjacent to it. "More than one poker," he said. "And our fella's been going raw from what we gathered. This ain't him."

"I'd tend to agree," Billy said.

"On account of my intellect I be supposin'," Collie said.

"No," Billy said and Collie looked at him sideways. "On account of him."

Billy pointed in the opposite direction. Collie rose and grunted and his knee made a snap. There was a man wearing a gun, his posture enervated. He was bearded and disheveled like the current storm had retched him out. "He just get here?" Collie asked. Billy nodded.

"You just keep your fucking mouths shut until I say otherwise," the man said.

"Christ what is that Mexican?" Collie said to Billy from the side of his mouth.

"Spanish," Billy said. He kept his eyes on the foreigner.

"There ain't no difference."

"Mexican doesn't exist," Billy answered quickly, almost annoyed and he raised his voice and spoke, *"Who are you and what do you want from us?"*

Both Collie and the visitor appeared astonished at the young man's language. "You half Spaniard too then?" Collie whispered staring ahead.

"I'm not, and this fella in front is Mexican."

"What did I just say?" The man placed his hand centimeters from his holster. *"You both need to put your hands up."*

Billy lowered his eyes and stared at the man and waited a moment before answering. *"I need to talk to my partner. He doesn't speak Spanish."* The man said nothing and Billy slowly put his hands up. "He wants us to raise our hands. That's all he said so far."

Collie discharged a long breath and raised his hands no higher than his shoulders. "What's this about?"

"What is it you need from us?" Billy said.

The man began to laugh a toying laugh. Collie tilted his head and bit his lip. *"We want the gold of course."*

"What'd this asshole say?" Collie said. His gaze never left the man.

"He said they want the gold."

"What gold? Who the fuck is they?" Collie yelled to the stranger.

"We have no gold friend. You are mistaken." With Billy's words, two more men peeked from behind the rocks. Their double barrels were already aimed.

"Oh Christ," Collie said.

"You need to tell your friend to stop making noise. I'm becoming frustrated."

"He wants you to stop talking."

"We don't have time for this. Tell him I'm gonna rip his neck out."

Billy cut him off. *"There is no gold senor."*

The disheveled one who seemed to be in charge now gripped his gun. Collie lowered his hands an inch. *"No games. You fast as lightning? Our guns are down on you and you ask questions.*" He giggled and removed his pistol from the holster pointing it at the ground. *"Your world is sideways...friend."*

Collie made a sound as if to talk, but Billy again stopped him. "This is in my purview. Trust me. I got it." He breathed deeply. *"Why do you think we have gold sir?"*

His crooked smirk departed and he raised his gun and his arm looked like it bore much weight. *"You get to ask one question before we put holes in you both."*

Collie clenched his teeth together and began to speak softly through them. "This guy is either three sheets yesterday in need of a nap or hammered like flattened cow shit as he stands before us. He's shaking like a rickety old tart."

"And tell your friend to shut his fucking mouth. He has no use," the man yelled. His face convulsed and Billy and Collie jumped, startled at the sudden interjection.

"Don't talk again. He'll shoot you," Billy said sincerely. "He said I can ask one question. I already asked it though. I'll ask it again I suppose. *One question. Same as before. Why is it you think we are holding gold?"* His last word softened and trailed off and the time and the world seemed to stop for Billy and a nascent smile began to crease before his scars. He looked at the ugly Mexican who knew that Billy knew the answer before it was uttered. Then it was uttered anyway.

All the while Collie remained sturdy with the rain pouring down streaming off the brim of his hat, the kind of rain that batters more forcefully with each thought that it could not possibly do so. He watched with superior observation at their unsteady motions, their limp hazy bodies struggling to remain upright in an alcoholic murk, and their greasy profusive sweat beading through the raindrops. He grit his teeth as Billy and the Mexican shouted at one another in the foreign tongue. Me moved his stare to each of the three potential hostiles and he saw when the one on the far right unknowingly gave up the position of the fourth. Collie held. The one on the left, heavyset and grubby lifted his non trigger hand to his nose. He wiped the snot and rubbed it on his poncho. He then whispered to the one in charge. With that, Collie bent his eyes, but not his head and he strained and at the absolute edge of his vision he saw the boulder and the dark unfocused head behind the rifle. And in that situation, adverse with gibberish permeating incessantly, Collie brought himself to the grey sky and began to laugh.

His action was quiet and went unnoticed at first. But then Billy could not help but look over. He attempted to continue to speak until he was shockingly interrupted. "Hey now," Collie yelled to the boss. "You gonna kill us?" The guns were all pointed at him. He brought his right hand down slowly and patted his chest with the word "us." "Us. You gonna kill us?"

"Que?" the ugly one said.

"We ain't got the time. Are we gonna die?" Collie made a pistol with his fingers and brought them to his head clicking his thumb three times. "Bango Bango?" The one in charge went from malicious to amused and when he chuckled to his two partners, Collie swiftly dropped his shooting hand. The gun was out of the holster and the bullet discharged and the only thing any of them saw was the boss's absolute bewildered state as he peered at the newfound gaping hole in his chest. Collie ejected the second shot and struck the boss in the forehead and the boss fell like a sledge on a railroad spike. The Mexicans froze, befuddled, objects in a painting. Collie hit the minion on the left in the throat with the third shot before Billy had his pistol drawn.

The blood mixed poorly with the rain on the only standing Mexican. Billy drew quickly. He pulled the trigger and the man bent forward with the blare. He discharged his shotgun into the air. The boom echoed. He fell to his knees. Billy turned to Collie who was peering off in another direction. Billy took a step forward and shot the man three more times and the man fell and his face sunk halfway into the surrounding mud.

"There's one more," Collie yelled.

"Where?" Billy said, disoriented.

"Why the fuck didn't he fire?" As if on cue, the fourth pulled his trigger. The click was barely audible amidst the teeming rain, but Collie noticed it. He halted and exhaled before firing. A shard of rock flew from the boulder. The prone Mexican then rose and attempted to fire again and the gun gave off another click, misfiring a second time. He stared at the bolt, his expression one of hysterics. Collie stepped forward three paces and when the man fixated on his personal reaper, Collie shot him through the eye. The Mexican fell backward onto another rock and remained leaning slightly upright for a brief moment before his weight pulled him to the side and then parallel to the ground. He twitched once and went still.

Collie kept his gun aimed and he heard Billy's voice in the background. "You get him?" the voice yelled. Collie moved over the dead man who was staring with a begrimed and hollow socket. The rain was thinning out the blood draining from the wound so that the spectrum of red seemed infinite. Collie heard the splashing of boots behind him. "You got him." Billy said. Collie turned ninety degrees. Billy was there. Collie swallowed and nodded.

"You good? You ain't hurt?"

Collie shook his head and continued looking at the last man he killed. "Clowns," he said. "Pathetic."

"One round off between the four of them. That's something else. How's that even possible? That's not even possible." Billy removed his hat and closed his eyes and lifted his face to the sky. The droplets showered over him and he howled at the clouds elated. The eruption of the gunshot rattled him from the moment and he turned as the smoke dissipated from the barrel of Collie's Peacemaker. Collie holstered the weapon and walked to collect the horses. Billy was breathing more heavily and when he looked down at the body he saw the second bloodied aperture where the lone remaining eye once resided. "Why in hell did you do that?" he yelled and followed the sheriff. Collie mounted his horse before Billy caught up. "You think that was necessary?"

"What's the goddamn difference?" His voice was rather tranquil.

"Waste of a bullet if you ask me."

"I don't recall askin'. Times like this, I wish I smoked. We gotta get movin'. But you already know that."

Billy stood and he lowered his head and as he did the rain let up allowing the sun to slice a crevasse in the clouds. "Everything ends," he said and mounted his own horse.

"That was good back there," Collie said. Billy waited, acknowledging wordlessly. "Where'd you learn that Mexican? Spanish I mean."

"I'm a student of many."

"Picked it up along the way?"

"Something like that."

"Fair enough. What happened in all that conversin'?'"

"I have confidence in your guesswork."

"That simple huh?" Collie removed his hat and ran his hand through his hair. "I'd say our feller came upon these misfits last night and talked his way outta gettin' shot and swindled them outta something, probably food, with the return payment of information. That information relatin' somehow to our possession of a fortune in shiny gold. And judging from the gunfight ensued and partook in, this crew was drunk enough to buy the bullshit." He returned his hat and pulled the front of the brim forward. "And the bullshit's gettin' deeper. How's that now?"

"That about covers it from what that one said." Billy said pointing at the body.

"He give any notion about where our mark made off to?"

Billy shot spittle from between his teeth. "Couldn't rightly say. Didn't go there. But he mentioned a town near here, in passing, like he paid it no mind."

"You know it?" Collie asked.

"The town?"

"The town."

"I do." Billy wiped his brow and pointed to his right, beyond the incline of terrain. "Some miles that way. Five or six I'd say. Been some time, maybe years, but that seems right."

"I'd bet our man discovered that same information and headed there himself."

"You conclude that positively?"

"He's resourceful. Well hell that's where I'd go." Collie brought the rein on his horse and the creature moved forward. "And if it ain't right, I'm sure you'll find the way for both of us." They increased their pace, the horses slinging mud behind them with each beating stride.

"What'd you mean back there when you said you wish you smoked?" Billy asked, his voice raised over the passing breeze.

"I sure hope he's there."

"I guess I'll just go fuck myself."

Collie looked over at Billy after the sarcasm. "I'm sayin' I wish I smoked 'cause it's quick and simple and it'd be here now if I had the hobby. And I could light up and ease the tension. But I don't and as it happens I could do for a steak. So he best have gone to town. To kill two birds, so to speak. I could do for a steak. That's my necessary."

"Lots of people eat steak."

"Yeah, but I'm saying that's my necessary."

"Collie, you're old and prone to senility."

"Boy, I'm just older. Ain't old."

"Then explain what you're shitting out your mouth for me."

"I'm worried that words are gonna distract you on the off chance he ain't stickin' to road at this point."

Billy chuckled bitingly. "Billy Maple doesn't distract by the likes of elderly meanderings." He glided his hand through the air as if offering the stage. "Proceed."

"It ain't much. It's that everyone's got a necessary. A thing's gotta get done after what we just done. Some kinda necessity after the deed is over. I'm sure you know what I'm talking about. Got a space needs fillin'."

"Like a void."

"A what?"

"Doesn't matter. I know what you mean. I got that. Hell I got that in spades."

"Well what is it?" Collie said, sounding genuinely intrigued.

"Well snatch of course. Surely not uncommon. At least in my line. And I'm sure wearing a badge doesn't make a man a saint. Snatch. You know, like a woman."

"I know what the hell it is," Collie shot back. "I told ya I ain't old."

"So a steak and a woman when we get to town then?"

"Ease yourself youngin'."

"I'm only saying you never know what's around the bend."

Collie's demeanor changed as if he was considering it. "He ain't far. We know that. Maybe only six hours or so. And if he went to town, he may still be there and we'll take him. If he's beyond, but he passed through, we'll have to do the same. But how bout we make a deal?"

"I'm listening," Billy said.

"When we're done with our thing, we come back. I get my steak, and you get your woman."

"You mean in lieu of me getting stretched by Pinkertons?"

"I told ya when we set out, if that happens it won't be from me. I'll keep my word."

Billy angled his head and then nodded it a few times. "I'm in then. No sharing though. You get your own woman. Wouldn't be nothing but a disappointment after me anyways."

"I ain't after a woman. Not one that would be subject to you 'specially."

"I may just partake in one of those steaks though."

"Don't push it kid." He exhaled as if it were a great relief. "You were good back there." And with that, he spurred his horse. It whinnied and moved ahead.

"Ya know, sometimes I wonder what it would be like to be your actual friend."

The sun was at their backs elongating their shadows into thin black caricatures, almost serpentine if not for their bulk. They remained in that formation, Billy following while Collie rode on ahead. Not once did he turn his head. He simply moved forward away from the great star, away from previous combat. And then suddenly he stopped where the road began to decline and the land angled down and he was overlooking their destination. It was a town not unlike the one he abandoned for his friend. It lay ahead, resting in dawn and awaiting the imminent light of day. Billy stopped beside him. "That's it," he said.

"I done figured," said Collie. "What's its name?"

Billy scratched his head. "Red Falls as I recall. Yeah that's it. Red Falls."

"On account it's by water? I don't see none."

"See them trees out yonder past the church?" He pointed past the town. Collie nodded. "Behind them is the lower part of the river, descending from the falls."

"Red Falls." Collie turned at the waist and peered down the path they had just traveled. He adjusted like he was considering something and then looked back at their objective. "Got a ring of peril to it don't it?"

"Anything's possible," Billy said.

"Ain't that the truth."

They slapped their reins simultaneously and made their way to the main road through the town. The hooves of their animals plunged into the mud with the sound of suction on repeat. As they grew closer, their shadows vanished and they entered the fading dawn. Had they waited mere minutes, they would have continued following the adumbrations.

Chapter 24

The interior lanterns push the slow orange light through the window of the humble cabin, illuminating the brink of the dense forestry. Its penetration impossible past the tensely violent thickets. The stranger stands statuesque, a pillar of the forest amongst the tall pines, fixated patiently on signs of occupancy within. The building is only strides from the oddly makeshift yet inviting church and it is dark and has been since his arrival.

There is a rustle in the tree above him. The owl calls. The stranger's gaze remains on the window. It sounds off again. A shadow develops from the interior of the cabin. The stranger inhales and holds his breath. The owl shrieks above him and it takes flight producing a crepitation as it departs the tree limb. Its sudden liftoff brings the man to the window. He is a priest, adorned with his collar. He cups his hands around his eyes and presses them to the window. The stranger is beside a tree leaning like an old man tenderly pondering his life. In daylight his visibility would be unquestionable. The priest presses closer to the glass. His pink hands turn white against it. He is squinting. The stranger is motionless aside from the half smile that begins to grace itself. The priest pulls away and exits the window and the stranger moves toward the cabin.

When the priest comes to his mouth is open, though he cannot speak with the rope between his teeth. The room is near black but for a few lit candles. He looks about the room. The blood in his eyes mixes with the hue of the candlelight creating a dense red orange fog around the rim of all that he can see. He stops on the corner of the room where the candle waltzes, caressing its faint light at the figure standing there. The shape comes forward. The priest pushes himself back in his chair, instinctive yet fruitless. He attempts to speak through the rope. The words are muffled and unintelligible.

"Don't try to speak," the stranger says. "There will time for that shortly. That is my hope at least." He approaches and halts when he is close enough so the priest has to raise his head to make eye contact. "I'm sorry about the wound." The stranger touches his own forehead above the brow and points at the same area on the priest. "You see I cannot risk detection. And although these quarters are uniquely set somewhat away, I gauge the rest of the town within shouting distance. It's interesting. I would have thought that if one was building a church, he, both the man and the universal, would like it centralized." He pointed to the ceiling when he said universal. "I wonder what was the thinking behind this location." His voice goes up, making his last words sound like a question.

The priest blinks trying to clear his eyes, but the blood tracks disobey and travel over his eyelid. He bites on the rope and straightens in the chair.

"How ridiculous of me to pose a query to a man in your state," the stranger says. He steps away and grabs a candle from the nearby mantle and brings it to his previous location. He bends down. He is now crouching looking up at the holy man. He brings the candle to his own face and the firelight sweeps titian across his left side while shadows envelop the opposite and he moves the flame and the shadows shift hither and thither playing games of children and the priest watches hypnotically until he lifts his head to the heavens and presses his eyes shut as if they were weighed and lingering to spring open. The stranger extends his arm and places the candle under the priest's chin. The man groans behind the rope and drops his head again to his captor. "I'm sorry for that, but I need you here."

The stranger clears his throat. He looks across the room to the door and then behind the priest to the window he himself was idling at. "I do not have all of the time in the world, but I do have some." He laughs for a moment. "Yes I do have some." He leans forward. He reaches his free hand behind his back and when it returns he is holding his knife, the weapon soundless leaving its sheath. He taps it on the rope between the priest's lips. "This doesn't hurt does it?" The priest is sweating profusely and his breathing becomes rapid and powerful. "Shake your head or nod to acknowledge. I mean my goodness, do something," he says twirling the blade. The blood from the priest's head wound has forced him to close one eye. He slows his breathing. He shivers and then shakes his head "no". "Though it is uncomfortable I'm guessing." The priest nods.

The stranger stands in a movement not fluid and he places his hand on his hip and strides away to the center of the room. There is another chair. It is a rocker and he grabs it by a rail and drags it over the oaken boards and it sings gratingly with each step until he stops in front of the man who again presses away from the stranger. "I'd like to remove your gag," the stranger says though his voice trails as he speaks to the center of the room as if to an audience. "Though I'm reticent due to the nature of this situation." He turns avoiding the priest and stares down at the curved rockers beneath the chair. He places his left foot at the edge of the floorboard and shifts the chair against his boot until it is aligned perfectly. "You understand our situation, yeah?" He glides in front of the rocker and sighs relief as he drops himself into it. It leans behind him and he freezes the sway forward with his boots. "I'm sure you must. I've never met a stupid priest. Fools yes, but not stupid." With that he leans forward and fixates on the face of the man in the chair like he is examining a crime and the man closes his crimson soaked eye and swallows hard and looks down to the floor breaking the attention. "Look at me," the stranger says. "Look at me and listen." The man raises his head.

The stranger lowers his brow and lifts his cheeks into a deliberately faux smile and the priest recoils only marginally and then returns stoic as a ruse brought on by the uncertainty before him. The stranger begins to softly hum the melody of

Camptown Races. *He stops as quickly as he began.* "I'd like you to be able to speak." *He again taps the tip of his blade on the rope between the man's teeth.* "But I can't have you yelling. If you yell you will cease to be. Now I want you to swear to yourself that you will not scream." *He rises from his chair, standing over the man of God. The priest appears confused.* "A nod will suffice. Do you swear to yourself that you will not scream?" *The exhalation of the priest amplifies and the moment seems to hold before he brings his head down twice.* "Now I want you to swear to God that you won't scream." *The stranger's gaze is concrete. The priest nods again, this time without hesitation and before he is done the stranger yields the candle under his face and presses in close. He smells of fire and the elements.* "Now swear to me. Swear to me you won't scream. You won't make a sound past the necessaries of conversation. This is ultimate." *There is a pause.* "Am I communicating?" *The priest acknowledges and juts his chin to the stranger and nods the final time.* "Fine then." *He places the candle on the floor, away though not far and moves behind the priest.* "That is three times you swore. Twice to man and once to myth. Potentially. It would be quite the broken oath if you," *he begins untying the gag,* "Well you get it."

The rope falls. The man opens his mouth wide and his jaw pops and he lowers his lips to his shoulders alternating between them wiping away the spittle. "Thank you for that." *He speaks through rough phlegm and then coughs and coughs again in succession until he calms.*

"An Irishman. I can tell from the accent." *The priest indicates agreement.* "What's your name?"

"Callaghan. Father Callaghan."

"Father. Not to me. But trifles."

"And your name?"

"Eli," *he said unaffected.*

"You sound so sure about him being a myth. How can that be?"

"I'm absolutely unsure as a matter of fact. Hence the word potential."

"Yet you just exercised compassion."

"Yes."

"Where does that come from?"

"A decision I came to on my own."

"Yes I do not doubt that you pondered the options and freed my speaking capabilities for a reason, but I'm talking about the concept of compassion. The very notions of good and evil. Morals. Feelings. We have what the beasts do not. How is that? Who instilled that?"

The stranger tilts his head amused. "You're suggesting that humankind is or was incapable of the realization that certain things are wrong and should not be done? That the only rational explanation is that an invincible deity imprints virtues and ethics in our brains at birth like the way we brand cattle? Is it not possible that we as a species have arrived at these conclusions on our own? We deduced that certain things, sins as you may call them, slow down our progress or evolution. We simply," he snaps his fingers, "Figured it out."

The priest appears to not be phased. "You've killed I take it."

"A question?"

"No, an assumption," the priest says, the words like arrows. "And after your kill you felt something inside in a place no one can touch. Now I cannot attest to what went through your soul, but before or after you committed the act, a voice undoubtedly spoke to you and if it was remorse, regret, terror, then you heard our lord. Anything else, you only heard yourself. And that is an inherent disconnect between your soul and the almighty."

The stranger wraps his hands around the arms of the priest's chair and squeezes and beneath the encrusted dirt his knuckles go white. "You know that voice in the back of your head, the one that may be whispering to you right this second? That's not God. That is you. And mine is me. And it is filled completely, brimming with our own flaws, desires, and agendas. Conscience evolved and some have evolved past the conscience." He decreases the tension in his grip. "Tell me, are you afraid?"

The priest hesitates and then shakes his head and says no with conviction. The stranger arches a questioning brow. "No," the priest says again.

"Child of God. You know you'll be with him, the creator, that sort of thing."

"Yes. That sort of thing."

"God made man in his image. And he made me. If I am in his image, what does that say about him?"

"Everyone can be saved. It is never too late," the priest says and oddly he smiles.

The stranger straightens himself. "Perhaps I've simply evolved."

"Blaspheme at will. I can only control myself."

The stranger chuckled. "You're twisted at my conviction of uncertainty where you are just as uncertain of his existence."

"I've said no such thing."

"You don't have to say it. I'm telling you you're uncertain. That is something I know."

"I know in my heart what I feel. Even in the company of you I can feel his presence."

"Believing is not the same as knowing. I'd expect an educated man to know the difference. And what you know in your heart is singular, pertaining only to you and cannot be conveyed to any outsider. It can be a contagion I'm sure to the dimwitted, but a so called fact conjured out of your own making is no fact. A belief is simply a belief. Intangible and unable to be proven."

"It's faith," the priest raises his voice. "It's faith," he repeats more quietly.

"I'm not sure why that is good."

"There are places in us that no man can reach. It cannot be smitten by other people or forces of evil. It can only be smitten by our own selves and when we finally reach our conclusion, that immovable force, and we stare it in the face those places within us either become engulfed in shadow or light. It is not until that moment occurs that we truly know ourselves. So no sir, to again answer your question from before I am not afraid. I can feel the light, the sun coming up inside me painting even the darkest corners. And your words, your actions have not penetrated or steered me off course and that makes me know my destination. Regardless of your judgments, regardless of your upper hand, you have not won. I have won this. I already have. It cannot change." The priest rights himself in the chair and looks to his counterpoint. The stranger stares at the candle on the floor. "Have you nothing to say?" There is no immediate response. The priest is patient. "Why have you come here? Of all of the places in this town, you missed the saloon, the livery, the hotel. You came to the priest's cabin behind the church. Why is that? What do you want?"

He gains the stranger's attention again. "One not need look too closely to see that I'm in tatters. And its destitute of life here seemingly."

"Let me help you."

"Help?"

"Yes."

"What help can you provide?"

"No one is beyond saving. Tell me what you've done. Tell me your sins. What has led you here? I cannot help you escape the law, but I can help you escape your torments, those internal."

"Confess," the stranger says and he steps back enveloped in the shadows in such a way that his body is uniform against the black and his face a phantasm amidst the night. "Confess to you and you'll put in a word with God."

"I will listen to you."

"A question to you."

"Very well."

The stranger moves forward again. *"Why are any of us here? If being with God is so great, and our destination in the afterlife is heaven, why did he bother with the middle ground? Why not place us there to begin with? Many would tell you that paradise here is all but lost. Makes living a paradox, knowing that the best comes after."*

"He wants you to choose. If you played a game of chess in which you foresaw each move beforehand from both you and your opponent, what would be the point of the game? Love is meaningless if everyone loves the same thing. He wants you to want him, but to force it is tyrannical regardless of good intention."

The stranger brings his knife forward prominently and kneels before the priest. *"Now understand that I've listened, heard, and understood you. And you claim you've won. And I say you haven't. Therein lies the conundrum. Which I believe is infinite. You're not afraid of dying. I believe that also. You think that he can do anything."*

"Infallible," *the priest interrupted.*

"Yes, well, if he can do anything, he can move my blade. He can stop it if he wants." *The priest begins praying. His words are so faint that they are barely audible.* *"But do you know what will make my blade fall? It is not misfortune, it is not fate. It is not even gravity. And when it falls you'd say it is his will. But it is not. It's actually mine. It lives or dies on my say so. I am the reaper. I am the savior. I am all that I can be and all you will never be. So why don't you pray to me?"* *The stranger places the tip of the blade beneath the priest's chin and lifts the man's head in mid prayer.*

"And yea though I walk through the valley of the shadow of the death, I will fear no evil," *the priest grins.*

The stranger's knife remains in place. He whispers, *"You see, God doesn't love you. And he doesn't love us. He loves himself. There is no God if there is no people."*

"What can man do to me if God is with me?"

With those words the stranger stands and flinches alternately and grabs the candle from the floor. He returns to the priest and without announcement or affect he stabs the man shallowly beneath his ribs. He removes the knife. The action is quick and practical like swatting a fly. "People with small minds see in small pictures."

The priest shivers. He does not look at the wound. He does not even blink. He stares into the eyes of the stranger and the orbs reciprocate. They are human after all and the priest smirks and says, "I told you I won."

The stranger begins to laugh and he twirls his knife and after a while his laughter slows and he speaks. "I like your shirt."

The priest is caught off guard. "What?"

"Your shirt. I like it. Do you have others? And how about a bath?" He poses his questions and promptly waits. His face is calculating. And then the priest answers and his words are his final anything.

Chapter 25

_____They hitched their horses to the post outside of the sheriff's building which was smaller than most and curiously out of square. A hand chiseled sign adorning the official title hung above the doorway and the letters were spaced unevenly proving the work was done by a hobbyist at best. Collie went first stepping onto the porch. The boards greyed and weathered creaked underneath sketching the images of an enduring difficult past. He knocked once on the door, an obligatory formality and then turned the knob and entered before invitation.

The man in the chair behind the undersized desk was elderly with somewhat long and stringy hair that seemed achromic rather than white. He had a crooked beaklike nose and his back and shoulders were hunched despite the attempt at proper posture. He placed his fountain pen in the inkwell. "Who is that? Announce yourselves please." His words resembled authority, though he emitted an air of inviting softness. He pinched his glasses and creased his eyes staring at the two men.

"Name's Tim Collie sir. And this is my deputy Bill Hendershot." He pointed at Billy and then removed his hat. Billy did the same. "You the sheriff?"

"That's what the sign says don't it?"

"It sure does."

"It damned well better. Otherwise somebody made off with it. Made it myself some time ago I did," and his voice trailed off a mite at the end.

"It's fine work for sure," Billy added.

The old man stood up and grabbed at his lower back nimbly before pulling his vest down over his belt. The star on his chest bowed as if nodding. "It right the hell isn't. But it's spelled correct though. I can vouch for that." He sidestepped the desk and stood beside it. "If Mr. Hendershot is the deputy I take it you'd be the sheriff Mr. Collie?"

"That's correct."

"Elias Milburne," he said and stuck his hand out, first to Collie and then to Billy. Each reciprocated. "From where do you hail?"

"Little Creek," Collie said. "Sheriff elected."

"I know it. Little Creek. Not well, but I do know it some," Milburne said. He reached into his pocket and retrieved his watch. He arched his brow and lowered his glasses and then put the item on his desk. "Mr. Collie, would you do me the courtesy of producing your tin?"

"I surely will." He reached across his chest and pulled away his coat revealing the star.

Milburne squinted and flicked the star with his index finger and the metallic ding lasted less than a second. "That's it there. I thank you. It ain't that I'm not trusting, but even careful can get a man killed so I find it's always better to be more than." His lips stretched a faux smile. "And you Mr. Hendershot."

Billy lowered his head and sighed and then looked Milburne in the eye. "Can't do that sheriff." The old man's demeanor changed though almost unnoticeably. "It's not intact."

"Ain't intact you say?"

"That's right sir. You see it stopped a bullet."

Collie's brows raised and the old man began to convey discernment. "That's right it did. Million to one shot. Million to one. I told Bill here after it happened he might best begin attending church more regularly him bein' favored and all by the up above."

"Huh," Milburne said. "And how'd you fellas, you in particular," he said pointing at Billy, "find yourselves in the non-fortuitous path of a stray bullet?"

"Wasn't any stray," Billy said. "It was most certainly intentional."

"I see," Milburne said.

"It was indeed," Collie added.

Milburne straightened as best he could. "Well I'm hoping it wasn't due to the fact you seem to have the appearance of a God forsaken heathen. No offense intended. It's just what I'm able to see. You being cursed with that complexion." Collie examined Billy as he absorbed the nature of the old man. He could not gain Billy's attention.

Billy lifted his brows and slid across half a smirk. "No offense taken sir," he said cooly. Collie exhaled a slow breath of relief.

The old man squinted appearing confused for a moment and then he shook his head as if the motion would rearrange his thought bank. "Then I'd further query as to what kind of event transpired and I do mean including up to and the aftermath of the discharged bullet in your direction."

"You see sheriff, that's one of two reasons we are here," Collie said. With that, the door opened and the breeze kicked in the room and a man entered. He was young, but tall and built and clean shaven except for a pair of long wide sideburns that laid trimmed neatly against his jaw bone. There too was a star that displayed prominently on his black vest.

"Morning strangers," he said. "Sheriff," he added. He marched to the vacant desk across the room and laid his hat on it. "Business occurring?"

"That it is," the old man said. "Gentlemen," he brought his hand out presenting the man. "This here is my deputy in town and I suppose you could call him my deputy in life as well. That being that he happens to be my son. This is Michael Milburne."

The young deputy paced forward with his hand out. "Michael," he said.

"Tim Collie. Sheriff. Little Creek." They shook hands.

"Bill Hendershot. Deputy." Billy did likewise.

"How do you do?" Michael said.

Collie scratched at the thick stubble under his chin. "Glad to be here speakin' with you both and in such an upright manner as it turns out." Michael's head twisted upward in curiosity. Collie continued. "I was just gettin' on with it, the purpose of our visit that is, with your father here before you walked in. Though bein' that you're sworn like the rest of us, it seems a welcome coincidence that you happened in." Billy shook his head in agreement.

"No others in your party?" Michael asked.

"Only us two," Billy said.

Michael crossed his arms. "Continue please."

"I'll give you the reasons in tandem if it suits ya," Collie began. "Back up the road a piece not much over five miles...that right Billy?"

"That's right."

"Roundabout five miles it be for sure long as he says it is, we come across four banditos in our travels. Now they wasn't on the road per se, more to the side a ways, but noticeable. We approached their camp for introductions and information and three of them turns out had different intentions. They were armed and at the ready. Now Billy here is able to speak Spanish."

"Isn't that something? And the relevance of that?" the old sheriff asked.

"They were Mexicans," Billy said. "He left that part out."

Collie huffed. "They were Mexicans is right. So anyway Billy here is translating for their leader I guess you can call him and it's clear they are looking to take whatever they could from us. And then I saw the fourth Mexican savage in my peripheral. That's when I knew. We knew I should say." He twitched his finger between Billy and himself.

"That they were gonna loot your bodies rather than take it and leave ya," Michael said.

"That's for damn sure," Collie said. "So understanding our predicament, without announcement we opened up on them and were lucky enough to drop all four. Billy here took one in the chest after he eliminated two. Wasn't till it was over that we saw the tin absorbed the brunt. Hell I don't think he knew he was even alive," he said and laughed and the others chuckled softly. "Point bein', there's still four bodies down that trail as far as we know. You bein' the closest in proximity, I figured I'd report it to ya."

"Well it ain't in our purview sir," Elias said. "That distance out."

"That's right," his son added. "In fact why tell us at all? Seems you could have left it out if you wanted."

"You're probably right. But any swingin' dick walks through and reports it, it'll save you the hassle of having to worry what's around the corner. Not to mention, bandits, Mexican or not often make a career out of thievin' and may likely carry a reward. Figured if you's or anyone in town were so inclined, you may be able to collect a profit off them four bodies. Truth is though, I don't give a damn what you do."

Michael cleared his throat. "That's mighty generous of you. Well Mr. Collie, Mr. Hendershot, I do, we do appreciate you bringin' it to our attention and I do reckon that'll be added to today's necessaries. And forgive me sir if my next question sounds as if I'm displeased by your visit because that would be the opposite of my intention, but my father and I are only two and we have work need's doin'. Red Falls is a small town, yet that doesn't mean the duties are less. So not to rush, but if you could enlighten us with your second and seemingly main reason for being here, it'd be duly appreciated."

"I like the way you talk deputy," Billy said with a hint of condescension.

"Thanks deputy," he reciprocated.

"I understand the haste," Collie said, "and now I hope you can understand ours." He paused for a moment and the moment hung in the air and he commenced. "We're after someone. A man who we believe may either be hauled up somewhere here unknowingly to you or maybe passed through after taking whatever it was he needed. We're looking for any information you might be able to provide us with. Things out of the ordinary. That kind of thing."

"What's he to you?" The sheriff said and for the first time he straightened and held the posture of youth as if his body forgot his ailment amidst the inquiry.

"He killed my friend," Collie said directly. "My deputy for years and friend for longer. This asshole shot him in cold blood."

Billy spoke up. "And a killer of women from what we gathered. Cuts em up. Does things to em they say."

Collie started sounding impatient. "Shot up Yankton is the word we got before he come to our neck of the woods. And now we're after him. Same thing any man of conscience would do. You see, a happenstance near identical to this came across us back in Little Creek where a law man showed up and warned us of this killer. Didn't do nothing ourselves until it was too late. I'm hoping nothing happens here like what happened there." He paused and read their demeanor.

"There's a string of decimation following this fella," Billy said in the interim.

The two lawmen of Red Falls stood listening and the old man held a look of impassivity, the story impotent in unearthing any sort of empathy, perhaps because of credibility or maybe it was simply one small insignificant tale in a lifelong history of tales, one that he would pass over if it were laid on pages in a book. The young Milburne however brought his hand to his mouth and bit at his thumbnail and stared at the cracks in the floor for a moment before speaking. "I'll tell you both this and you too pop since I was coming here for this reason anyway. Out there this morning for my saunter I seen Mr. Faraday outside of his place lookin' frantic. And he was vexed about something. He was fiddling with the handle on his stable door and cussin' like he was just cheated at a hand of cards."

"Who's Faraday?" Collie asked.

"He's the proprietor of the livery," Michael continued. "So I approach him and keepin' it short, seems someone made off with one of his stock in the wee hours."

Billy and Collie laid waste to their over exhaustion. "He's here in town now? This Mr. Faraday?" Collie said. Michael nodded. "He say anything else?"

"Matter of fact he did. Said he went around the town looking for signs of the horse, thought maybe he mighta' just wandered. Couldn't find the animal anywhere. But when he looked out in the woods some, a good piece away from the church, he found another horse dead on the ground. Looked like it was worn to death."

"What'd it look like?" Billy asked.

Michael stared unblinkingly at the two men. "Didn't say. Didn't ask." He clenched his jaw and his eyes narrowed. "This town ain't lookin' for trouble. We keep the peace round here however necessary. So if this fella's here, we will put him down. But this fella turns out to not be here after my inspection, I expect you two to follow suit. There is such a thing as too much help. And we're more than capable. No disrespect to y'all. Simply what I deem best for everyone I reckon."

"This here a professional courtesy?" Collie asked.

"It is."

"Real hospitable goddamn town," Collie grumbled. He put his hat on. Billy did the same and they moved to the door. "We'll be takin' our leave now. I apologize for the swift departure, but we've business to attend. I thank yee both for the time." He opened the door and stood halfway outside. "I assume there's no disrespect in us askin' this Faraday our own questions." Neither man responded and Collie tipped his hat and stepped out the door.

"Sheriff," the old man called. Collie was already in the road. When he turned, the elder Milburne was framed in the doorway wearing a cocksure grin. "Is there anything else we can do to help?"

"Ain't lookin' for any more help," Collie answered. He began to walk away and stopped suddenly. "You got a map?"

The old man laughed and held his hand out and it trembled like a flag caught in a strong wind. "Spilled coffee on it a time ago. Rendered unreadable." Collie bit his lip and turned his back for the last time. "Don't get too old Mr. Collie. Age comes to us all, but *old* age doesn't necessarily." And the old man laughed again and the waning guffaws grew fainter and fainter to Collie as he drew away from the office.

Billy stepped down from the porch onto the road. Michael moved past his father and leaned over the railing. "Tell your friend to head to the saloon before ya leave. They got a map there."

"Alright then," Billy said. "I'll do that Deputy."

"How'd ya get them scars? If ya don't mind my askin'" Michael said pointing to his own mouth.

Billy peered upwards to the sky and squinted at the sun half hidden in the clouds. "Too much damn smiling," he said.

"That a fact? Ain't much to smile about nowadays."

"Matter of perspective," he said and went to meet his partner down the road.

When Michael stepped into the office he found his father already seated at the desk breathing heavier than normal. The old man's hands like a sepia cloth fidgeted through his pockets. "Pop, what in hell is it you're doing?" The old man kept fidgeting. "Pop," he yelled.

"Don't raise your voice to me," Elias said. "Story sounded familiar didn't it?"

The son nodded. "Not two days ago, that right? That other party wandered in here?"

"That's right. Sounds like these two missed the party. Fools they be."

Michael pulled his pistol and spun the cylinder. He holstered the piece. "I gotta go check on things."

"Do that. And when it's well, then leave it be. It ain't our problem. See that they leave though. Don't go puffing that chest of yours out. Observe only unless is necessary to stop observing and do something. Then report. You understand? Yeah you understand." He brought his quivering hand over his meager hairline and then down again to his pockets. He felt at the tiny compartment in his vest and then the sides of his pants.

"What is wrong?" Michael said sounding agitated.

"It's my watch piece," the old man said. "I swore I had it with me."

Collie entered the saloon and the door swung shut behind him. The interior was underlit. He scanned the room. It was two stories with a vaulted ceiling and a rail that wrapped around the entire second floor so that who was entering and leaving each domicile above could be viewed by the company below. The building itself was a considerable enough size, perhaps too considerable for a town this small. There were six round tables spread evenly across the floor, all vacant minus one that held a pair of stayers. The kind that seemed never to make it home. They were upright though it was up for debate as to how long.

The bartender, the only other occupant, threw his rag over his shoulder and it whipped in the air before landing. He gave a welcoming gesture and then placed his palms across the bar. Collie approached and halted an arm's length from the counter. "Can I get you something friend?" the bartender said.

Collie ran his hand across the edge of the bar. It was burnt, blackened yet sealed and he tipped his head forward and to the side until he could see a straight shot down the entire bar top. He ran his fingers delicately over the smooth pine and then knocked twice. "You do this for effect?" he said referencing the rustic edge trim.

"I did," the barman said.

"Damn fine work."

"I thank you."

"You did do it yourself?"

The bartender nodded.

"And it's all one piece? One length I mean?"

"That's correct." The barman smiled. "Not the milling, as far as my individual effort. That's eighteen feet. Did the milling with my brother. Before he passed that is. We finished it though. Tree came down in a storm after we put the walls up here. A record storm I'd bet. It come down in it, the tree did. Like it had fallen just for our purpose. Fate one could say if you go in for that sort of thing."

Collie knocked the bar top again. "Very impressive. Best I've seen and I've seen a number."

"You a carpenter by trade sir?"

Collie snorted a laugh. "Not by trade. Only by hobby. I can hold my own. I'm envious though."

"Well I'm sure you've done things I haven't, and that'd make you the expert on those over me. A man can't be an expert on everything."

"And avoid those that say they are," Collie said.

The barman pointed at the sign behind him for fifty cent whiskey shots. "It doesn't have to be too early sir."

Collie shook his head. "Naw."

"Coffe then?"

"Please," and he nodded in conjunction. "Listen," Collie began and he exposed the star pinned to his vest. "Name's Tim Collie. I'm the sheriff of a town called Little Creek. Few days ride from here."

"I've passed through," he said. He went to the stove and poured the coffee from the pot into a metal stein. "A fine little place."

"We thank ya. I don't mean to be cuttin' you short Mr-"

"Kennefick, Lucas Kennefick," he said and placed the stein before Collie.

"Ok Mr. Kennefick." He gripped the stein and imbibed without savoring. He coughed as if he drank too quickly and it dripped onto his chin. He wiped it away with his hand and then rubbed his fingers across his pocket. "That's good. Thank you." He sipped again, this time cleanly. "We came here, my partner and I who should be here shortly, because we was told you are in possession of a map." It sounded like a question. "Chartin' this territory. This true?"

"Is this official business?"

"It is. Though not pertaining to you. Just looking to get our bearings." Collie brought the mug to his face. The coffee was strong and hot and it pained his cracked lips and he could not help but wince at the pain. If the barman noticed, he played it as though he did not. There was a mirror mounted behind the bar along the wall and it ran roughly half the length of the counter and at the far end off to the side near the piano Collie saw it framed on the wall. "That it?" he asked.

"I'm sorry?"

"In the frame down there."

"It is indeed."

Collie put his mug down, loosened his grip and then let go of it completely. The front door opened behind him and the sunlight invaded the room in stark contrast for a few rapid seconds and the shadow, a black caricature, overpowered the rhomboid illumination until the door closed again vanquishing all shadows and revealing only a man. It was Billy. He forewent any form of observation and moved directly to the bar. When Collie saw who it was he returned to his business. "Would you mind takin' it off the wall so we might have a look?" he said. Kennefick ignored him, looking to the new customer.

"Ooh wee, what have we here?" Billy said stopping at the counter. He clenched his hands into fists and brought them down on the bartop. He leaned over, peering into the remnants of Collie's near empty stein. "Not partaking in the firewater I see."

Collie ignored him and asked about the map again. Kennefick quickly shook his head as if he was snapping himself from a trance. "The partner you mentioned I take it. Can I bring you something sir?"

"In a minute," Collie interjected.

"Yes, the map. I'll bring it over," he said and left them.

Collie faced forward and downed what was left of his coffee. "Well?"

"Well," Billy began. He relaxed his hands and tapped on the wood with his fingers. "It's him."

"How do you know," Collie said as he watched Kennefick remove the map from the wall.

"I found the horse."

"Which?"

"The dead one. That prick deputy mentioned. Been worn to death."

"Virgil's?"

Billy brought his head down once in a yes. "Out near the church," he said and his words were rushed as the barman neared.

Kennefick spun the map so it faced his patrons and he laid it on the bar in front of them. "Excuse the dust," he said and he brushed it with his towel.

"It's fine," Collie said and hacked out the residual dust. "It's exactly what we need." He squinted and brushed his fingers over the flat mountains portrayed over the browned sheet. "She's big alright. Looks a funny sort on paper."

"You feller's know what you're looking at?" Kennefick asked.

"We know," Collie said not making eye contact. "I been here a long time. And Billy here knows the territory."

Billy smiled like a salesman. "Been everywhere worth going at least twice."

"So I've heard," Collie added.

Kennefick left and came back with another stein and he filled them both with coffee. The steam spiraled over the rims. "No charge for these sirs."

"Obliged," Collie said.

"You been everywhere you say?" The barman said to Billy.

"Worth seeing."

Kennefick rested the coffee pot. "I admire that in a young fella like yourself. Wish I had done the same."

Billy's attention went to the map, ignoring the musings of the proprietor. He pulled the frame closer. Collie who was leaning on the drawing jerked at the pull and gave an expression of tired irksomeness. "Give me this for Christ's sake," Billy said. "See, we're here." He pointed on the map to the penciled house labeled Red Falls.

"Well goddammit I know that," Collie said.

"I know you know that." Billy was calm. He halted his speech, taking a minute to peruse the entire drawing. "There's no legend," he said to the barkeep.

Kennefick shook his head. "It ain't to scale either. It's a rendering. It was made for me as a gift."

"A gift?"" Billy asked.

"Correct."

"Well halle-fucking-lujah."

"Enough," Collie said in a tone of admonishment. "It ain't to scale you say Mr. Kennefick. But it's accurate in terms of what is where. Am I correct in saying that?"

He gave a grading stare from behind the bar. "The layout is accurate. That is also correct."

Collie looked to Billy and then the barkeep. "And you'll swear to that?"

"Gentlemen, what is drawn there is what is out there."

Collie drank a bit of coffee. Billy did not touch his. "I apologize if we've been curt in our time here," Collie said.

"Road weary," Kennefick responded. "A man can travel a path well traveled for days on end and still manage to lose himself somehow. May I ask you gentlemen what it is you're looking for?"

Billy chimed in. "It's not a what, but a who rather."

"A who rather," the barman repeated and the front door opened. Two men, frontier types, sauntered in. They walked to a table and removed their hats and one man collapsed onto a chair like a burden of secrets had been lifted. The other approached the far end of the bar. "Excuse me for a few. I'll be back."

"Take your time sir," Billy said. He and Collie hunched over the frame and although the map lacked the accurate truth of the area, a great inherent beauty lay in the meticulous attention to the images as if each pencil shading and stroke of ink was made with a love of the country. "What do you see?"

"The same goddamn thing that you're seein' I hope. Can you pick up his trail out there or not?"

"I believe I can."

"Then why does Billy Maple who has traversed the planet wide twice and thrice need a map?"

Billy grabbed the handle of his stein and slid the metal cup away. "Because I needed to see I was right about something."

"Are you?"

"He's coming back."

"How can you tell lookin' at that?"

"No the bartender. He's coming back."

Kennefick approached and stood in the same ready position as when the men had arrived. "Any use to you?" He said pointing at the map.

"It has been," Collie said. "Let me ask you something. You see anyone strange here last night?"

"Strange," Kennefick repeated.

Collie shifted his weight. "Yeah. Out of the ordinary or any kind out of sorts. Maybe made you think twice at some point."

"Would've been late. Quite a ways past sunset," Billy said still eying the map.

The bartender crinkled his nose and peered upwards as if he was catching an escaping thought and then blew a breath through his nostrils. "Hmm. Well I'll tell you that you both ain't the first two in the last few days to be in here searching for some fella."

"Pinkertons?" Billy asked eagerly.

"Yeah. Some posse mixed in. Not too professional on the whole. Though some were. All over some evil fella they say, shot up a whole town. Yankton. Like a ghost is the term they used."

"Might be its related," Collie said. "Can't confirm it. The fella may have doubled back or gone in any sort of direction. We're doin' our own legwork."

"I see," the barman began. "Seems serendipitous, I believe the word is, that you sirs would be here today askin' these very questions."

"Why's that?" Billy said.

"Because last night near midnight came a man into the bar. There were folks here, more than there are now, but not a crowd if you understand what I mean." They both nodded. "This fella come in late and he was cleaner than a woman before her walk to church on Sunday. He was shaved newly. He had a nick on his neck where the blood was dried and his hair was slicked wet with water, like he was fresh out of the bath. And he...he...I'm reticent to say." His face grew red.

"Come on out with it," Collie said. "Reticent why."

"I'm ashamed to say it, him bein' a fella and all."

Billy smirked. "No judgement will be passed on to you by us my good man. I assure you," he said.

"Well," Kennefick cleared his throat. "You see, he smelled rather nice. Fragrant. Like he'd come from a madam's tub."

"Smelled nice. Anything else?" Collie said.

"He wasn't friendly or in any mood to make acquaintances. And let me clarify that although he may have appeared like a theater man, he gave me the impression he'd cut a man for breathin' wrong. Anyway, he come in real late. And he drew looks, but paid them no heed of any kind. And he came to the bar and asked if I had women to buy. Ya know, hourly. I told him this wasn't that kind of establishment. And he peered around like I was lyin'. I told him there weren't no place in all Red Falls like that. Which is probably why the traffic here ain't nothing but light. I offered him whiskey. He didn't acknowledge. He just walked over there to the corner." He pointed, indicating where. It was cast in shadow the way the light bounced across the upper terrace. "He pulled a chair there and sat. Alone. And I remember some minutes went by and then his face glowed orange. It was only a match. And he smoked a cigarette. I watched him, but made sure not to stare."

"How'd he go?" Collie asked.

Kennefick rubbed his chin. "He couldn't have been here longer than a half hour. But brothers, it was a long half hour.

When I saw him sittin' there like some kind of stone critter, I worried myself. So I retrieved my pistol from the end of the bar, bringing no attention. And I stuffed it in the back of my belt and when I turned around he was gone."

"Nothing?" Billy asked.

He shook his head. "A cloud of smoke at the door. Hung around like it was left behind for a reason."

"No disturbance made though," Collie said.

Kennefick gestured no. "That helpful to ya?"

"It may probably be," Collie said. He shifted his weight and looked down. He began tapping at the glass pane over the map where Red Falls was located and then stopped and traced a straight line north of that point. "Tell me, what is this here?" He brought his finger down hard. Inked on the page was a representation of a cluster of hills protecting a great plain which stretched on before giving way to the mountains. Billy leaned over, his brow furrowed. "It ain't labeled. Hell of an area." He pushed out his lower lip.

"I be supposin' not everywhere then," Kennefick chimed in to Billy. "No offense intended deputy."

"Perhaps it'll come back to me."

"That there is Sioux country," the barman said.

Billy pinched his forehead. "I figured as much."

Kennefick gave a half smile. "I figured you'd figure once you heard it."

Collie's face seemed to drop in a cold uncalculated expression. "You sure?" He said, though it did not come off as a question.

"I am Mr. Sheriff," Kennefick said and Collie sighed. Kennefick opened his mouth to speak then said nothing. He looked to his other patrons and then to the two men before him. He removed the rag from his shoulder. "I'll leave you gentlemen for a bit. It would appear you need to mull some things over."

Collie masked his lower face when he leaned on his fists. "We'd sure appreciate it," Billy said speaking for both of them. The barkeep moved to the end of the counter out of earshot and went about his business. "It is what I thought it was. What's your play then?"

"It don't mean that he went that way," Collie said bringing his hands down, elbows on the bar. "It's there on the map, but he coulda gone elsewhere."

"Here though," Billy began pointing at the map. "The mountains box in the territory here. And they're thick enough that a horse won't make the inclines. Not that I'd reckon anyway. And south is the river that will not get crossed without assistance. He may very well do that. But to ferry across he'd need money or one hell of a threat of violence. If he takes the ferry himself that puts him vulnerable past any logical person's desire."

"I'd venture to concur," Collie said.

"That leaves this." Billy targeted two small parallel lines through the eastern mountains. "This," he said to the road they traveled in on. "Or this." His index finger went over the Sioux lands.

"Operatin' under the idea that he ain't floatin' like a goddamn feather in the wind and he has at least a general workin' knowledge of the region, I'd leave out the mountain pass. One way in, one way out. It's disadvantageous any way you look at it. Now him heading back the way he came, that ain't particularly far fetched. He ain't exactly done it before. But we know that he hangs around longer than a thinking man might."

"True," Billy said.

"But he also knows we know that."

"Also true."

Billy noticed the tension in Collie's fists as the older man dug his thumbs repeatedly across his index fingers. A parched breaking noise emitted as a result. "You think he knows what's up there?"

"There?" Billy said, jutting to the map. Collie nodded. "I don't believe I could attest to the knowledge of others. Particularly not a man as such. He's been more than lucky through most of this. If he went that way with knowledge of what's out there and he went alone, that makes him a fool. And if he went that way with no knowledge of what is there, that makes him a fool as well."

"Because of what's out there."

"That's right."

"You say that about your people?"

Billy chuckled. "They are not my people. I don't have a people."

"The hell they aren't."

"The hell they aren't." Billy straightened in a snit. "You trying to get a rise outta me this late in the game? I'll tell you what is the same. And it sure isn't all Indian folk. What it is is old men. Sitting around pondering how the world got the way it is. How things were different when you were young. And you all think it was better back then. When the truth of the matter is that nothing changes. The world's the same damned irritated dirt it was a hundred years ago. Damn near everything out there wants us dead. It's not any greyer now than it was then. And the big bright futures ahead of all of you get greyer and greyer as the time passes. And as your future gets closer you realize there's a ceiling. You build it yourselves. And you look down resentful on the youth that don't have one. That makes you wistful. And intolerant. I've seen dozens of you."

"Wise beyond your years you think."

"You have it in your head that you peaked. But the one thing that sets you apart from all those greybeards out there is what you did for me."

"You mean breaking the law?" Collie toyed with his stein. "Or at the slightest, marginally ignoring it?"

"Quit acting angry Collie. You broke through your ceiling. Smile. Smile like I've been for the last few days."

"I wish you'd written your speech so you could read it when you're my age."

"You and I, we'll catch up then."

"Fair enough." Collie pushed the map away from himself. "He went that way." He used his thumb to point over his shoulder.

"You can't be sure of that."

"He went toward the reds. I am sure of it."

"How?"

"It's all been shaping up that way. Do me a favor Billy." He stepped from the bar. "That fella from the livery. Can you track the stolen horse?"

Billy nodded.

"Yeah?"

"It had custom shoes," Billy said with a twinkle. "Easier than the last I'm certain."

"On foot, why don't you gander outside at the possibilities. His possibilities that is."

"Say he went up there Collie. You're planning on following him. I can tell. Why do that? You and I know Sioux won't greet him with a smoke pipe. He'd be done for. Why don't you just let it lie."

"I can't. I can't do that. I have to know its done. I need to be the one to do it."

Billy's brows raised and he nodded his head at the expected response. "Very well then. You'll be here?"

"I will. Gotta see about a few things."

"Okay. I shall return."

"Do that."

And with that, Billy left and the outdoor light adorned the room in the brief seconds that the door swung open. Collie leaned again on the bar. "Mr. Kennefick," he said and the barkeep approached. "I thank you for your services in regards to this here map." He lifted the frame and handed it to the owner.

"Glad you found it useful." The barman turned to replace it, but halted at the next request.

"Would you have any food sir?" Collie asked.

"I have only jerky in the stores," Kennefick said. "But I'm partnered with the hotel across the way. Which means I'm partnered with their kitchen. It's limited though. I'd have to check what they have today."

"That'd be fine, unless you know they have steaks."

"I know that and I know that they do."

Collie pulled some bills from his coat and rested them on the counter. "Can you put in an order on my behalf?" He queried. The barman agreed. "Two of your largest best quality steaks." He pulled more bills and laid them on the others. "And I do mean best quality."

Kennefick appeared distracted for moments. "Is everything alright Mr. Collie?"

"It will be. You just fetch them steaks."

"I certainly will. And you can pay when you're finished."

Collie acknowledged a thank you. "That's fine. Why don't you take some now anyway." He shaved off the top two bills. "What's your finest whiskey Mr. Kennefick?"

The proprietor pointed to the bottles near the register. "I'd stand by that stock there."

"You got any not on display? The kind the frontiersman won't ever ask for."

His crow's feet began to show as he crinkled his eyes. He walked a few feet down and retrieved a bottle from under the bar. "This is scotch Mr. Collie. Straight from Scotland. Got it in a trade."

"Any good?"

"I've never tried it."

"Huh, look at that. You're right. Right under your nose and never even been opened. Why don't you go ahead and open it." He did and his hand began to shake and Collie grabbed it. "Go ahead and pull down three glasses."

"But sir, it's five dollars a glass."

"Make it four dollars and the third glass is for you." Collie said and he watched as the edges of Kennefick's lips stretched enough to reach his ears.

When Billy returned he opened the door to find Collie at the table nearest the bar. There were two plates in front of him occupied with a porterhouse a piece and golden brown elixir residing in the glasses beside them. Collie sat admiring the untouched meals. He slid his heel across the floor planks and hooked the chair with his boot and angled it in invitation. Billy accepted and set himself down. The second plate was in his reach though not directly before him.

"So it would appear-"

"Hold on," Collie interrupted. He composed his posture and pulled his plate in position and then lifted the second and placed it in front of his companion. He rested the other fork beside it. "Let's be undisturbed."

"Alright," Billy said.

"Can't go on out on just jelly and chocolate." They began carving and the seasoned juice from the meat brimmed over the cut and pooled along the edges of the steaks. Collie separated a square and held it on his fork at the height of his mouth for moments before eating it like it was his lifelong ritual. Then he carefully brought it to his mouth and sank his teeth slowly into the portion. He savored it. His eyes closed. Billy watched the old sheriff. He opened his mouth to speak then tasted his own instead. His second bite came before Collie's.

Collie wrapped his hands around the two fingers of scotch and situated it. Billy stopped mid chew and looked into the glass. "I don't touch it," he said.

"You're foolin'," Collie said and Billy shook his head. "No kiddin'."

"No kidding."

"Not now or not ever?"

"Ever."

"What do you want then?"

"A beer would do me fine. One though."

Collie turned to an eager Kennefick. "Mr. Kennefick. A beer for my friend please."

Billy watched as he poured the golden ale. He filled it two thirds and scraped off the frothy head with a stick and filled it the rest of the way. The barman lifted the hinged portion of the counter and served the beer to his customer. The mug thudded on the oak. Billy nodded a thank you. He raised his glass to the man who was once his captor and the man reciprocated. Men are capable of being many things. Sometimes all at once. They ate and drank like gentlemen and the meal was good.

They saddled from the livery. The horses were fed and watered. Collie paid the owner and they mounted their steeds and started down the road. Townsfolk appeared in the shop windows and doorways to watch the departure. It seemed a superficial curiosity though the undertone rang eerie. The two men rode parallel. They approached the office of the sheriff. Young Milburne stood outside, his hands hitched cooley in his pockets, a grass blade between his teeth. Billy reached into his coat and pulled out a small silver watch. He checked the time and sent an exaggerated smile in the deputy's direction. He pocketed the piece and tipped his hat to the lawman. Milburne unbent his leg off the post and stormed into the building. Billy chuckled. "Not so friendly a kind in this town. Wouldn't expect that from a small place," he said.

"Small places tend to be tight knit," Collie said. "And when a people are that close it makes everyone else an outsider. And outsiders bring change. The best way to avoid outsiders is to make them feel unwelcome. That's the first step at least. Some people have a real friendly way of bein' impolite."

"Change is certain," Billy said.

"That it is."

The road to the hills hooked left after the church and they began to approach it. They passed the inelaborate building and saw the priest resting on the front porch with his head down, hat pulled half over his face, and his shirt unbuttoned to his chest. The area was shaded. He seemed at peace. The sign out front was hand painted and it read *Welcome Any and All.* "That looks at odds," Billy observed.

"Friendly way of bein' impolite."

They reached the bend and began to arc out of sight of the main stretch and the proprietors and settlers who espied with masked vexation abandoned their mediums and returned to their business and the stir of excitement was quelled. It was only the priest who garnered nary a notion of the visitors' presence as he remained motionless in his rocker on the front porch of the church since before the sun announced itself that very day. And had any parishioner or lost soul the inclination to pray or rejoice that morning or simply wish the father pleasant happenings, he or she would have gathered a growing suspicion over the unreturned response. And if the curious party were to tilt back his hat and let the light of the morning sing clearly, he would be privy to the blatant truth represented by the lifeless sockets and word of the day which was *Fool*, as it must have been, being carved into the holy man's chest in all capitals.

Chapter 26

The town of Red Falls was long behind them and the trail began to open up fading its definitions. They stopped for tracks. Billy picked up the marks of the custom shoes. As they rode on the heat of the day became oppressive. They lost their coats and continued forth.

The morning was nearing its passing and the horses at a gallop rendered more and more trail at their backs. And as the sun reached its pinnacle the road became the vast expanse before them and they halted and stared into the sea of tall grass that stretched on for miles leading into the rolling hills in the distance. The horses neighed in concord. Collie stared ahead with a scrutinizing look like he was chasing an elusive destiny. The land was still and soft and the wind grazed its noble hands over the tips of the blades and they responded in a successive waltz until the entire fields were dancing harmoniously and the sound of the tranquil ocean permeated and conquered all that was around them.

With acute and patient senses the remnants of the paths long gone could be seen amidst the flowing turf and the ghosts of the travelers before them could also be seen, the shape and history of the land offering itself, questions answered, yearnings quenched. And the way things were, right or wrong lay unjudged because they happened regardless as things would continue to happen forever until the end of time. The stories lived in the wind and the earth and were there in all encompassing truth for the taking. Only they were never taken and the ghosts left in the wind and remained interred under ages of soil and their stories lingered hidden.

"I'll cut you loose," Collie said.

"What?"

"I'll cut you loose. You done your part the way I figure it. It all adds up. Askin' you to head into them hills, that's something else. We're square."

Billy faltered. He pondered the phrase. He placed his hand on the rear of the saddle and turned to peer down the road into their past and then to the future in the hills ahead of them. "I have a debt and it's not paid yet," he said staring forward.

"Ok," Collie said and waited. "Thank you." He nicked at the horse and it started to trot. His pace quickened in the open terrain. Billy followed. Collie kept one hand on the rein. The other hung loose near his sidearm for the duration. The hills grew in scale as they approached. "Billy."

"Yeah."

"Before we head into this, tell me something about yourself."

"Why?"

Collie sighed. "No reason in particular. I'm not sure why I said it."

"Alright. Like what?"

"Anything. I don't know. Anything I guess. Tell me how you came to be everywhere. Why'd you leave your folks?"

"They left me," he said.

"Hell," Collie said.

"It's alright. I don't mind." He wiped the beads of sweat from his brow. "See my dad, I never really had a dad. He was just the man who raped my mother. I would venture to say he was never aware of my existence. So I suppose he gets a pass for that part. And even if he did know, I assume a man of that sort lacks a sense of follow through. And my mother," Billy started and cleared his throat. "She took her own when I was young. But I was old enough to understand what happened. And then I left."

"That is a raw deal."

"It was the only hand I had. How bout you?"

"My folks?"

"Nah not folks. How about marriage," Billy said. "Never really understood it myself. Tell me something real though. Something good and something bad."

Collie leaned and spat and wind carried it. "Something good huh? Ok. At the end of the day, when you can bare your soul to someone and she still lays happily beside you and you know you can do the same tomorrow with the same outcome, you know you found yours. It's realer than anything out there. If it happens once count yourself lucky. And I was in fact lucky."

Billy kept his smile. "Something bad?"

"Well this is more a simple truth than it is a negative."

"I'll accept it."

"A woman...a woman needs to be told by more than just her husband that she is wrong. Otherwise the information don't stick."

Billy began to laugh at the comment and Collie smiled and they rode on with the wind skimming across their faces. They reached the base of the first hill and their demeanor changed. They waited. The perspiration was rampant, the heat like an anvil weighing them down. The air was stagnant, dichotomous to the flatlands they had traversed. They craned, looking at the hillcrest. Billy rolled his sleeves to his elbows. Collie squinted from the despotic sun. He pulled his hat down further creating a shadowed blade across his eyeline. He bit down on his lower lip. His knuckles went white as he gripped the saddle horn. "Here we go," he said and he spurred his horse. The animal darted up the incline without warning and Billy's horse leapt on its hind legs.

"Easy now," he said patting the animal's neck. The horse came down. The hooves fell with an empty thud. "Here we go," he whispered. He slapped the reins and they took off running.

They slowed at the base of the third hill and the ground planed for acres. There was a tree line to their right with a quiet body of water behind it. "That's the creek from the picture," Collie said.

"Everything we've seen is in accord with it," Billy agreed.

Collie took a moment to scan the territory. He blinked and the sweat diverted around his eyelids. There was a chorus of robins about giving way to harmonious echoes. It was almost peaceful. Amidst the songs of nature Collie tensed and jerked his head, startled. The motion made Billy jump. He lowered his hand over his weapon. Collie stepped down from his horse and drew his own pistol.

"What is it?" Billy said. He hunkered himself in the saddle, but remained on horseback. "I said what is it?" He was ignored.

Collie progressed forward deliberately before moving to a jog. His lower quarter was lost in the tall grass. He stopped suddenly and crouched on one knee. Billy was behind him. He mimicked the aging sheriff. Collie looked out, his eyes level with the verdant blades and their tips pierced, invading the picture of the veiled wagon ahead. "To the right. Behind them bushes near the water," he said in a soft exhale. "You hear that?"

Billy listened. "Like a rustling. Yeah."

"Ok. Good." Collie rose. "It's gonna go quick, this. Stay behind me ten paces. I'll venture to the blind side. You hang back on the other until I say so." He stepped forward and then hesitated. "And watch for an ambush. Ready?"

"I am that."

Collie started. Billy inhaled and counted and they brushed through high stepping the wild ground. Their strides were long and heavy on the dry earth and in the idle scene their boot steps were like mallets. Collie quickened. He halted before the wagon and held his gun out. With his free hand he pointed to the exposed side. Billy hit his mark and on cue Collie skirted the front wheels and jockey box. "Oh God," he said. Billy angled his head around the wagon. He could see the back half of Collie's profile and nothing else. "Billy," Collie yelled.

Billy rounded the wagon and saw the man on his knees, vagrant and disheveled rocking back and forth in no observable pattern like a tattered flag in a windstorm, with Collie's barrel considering him intently. The sheriff's arm was angled down and controlling and his weapon swayed in accordance with the chaotic ataxia. The dilapidated figure was moving his lips in rapid succession, his words near muted and his eyes transfixed ahead staring across a vast and empty crevasse in his mind. "Stop moving," Collie said.

"What's he saying?" Billy said.

"I said stop moving," the sheriff commanded again.

The man's monotone repetition grew louder and he began twitching. Billy looked to Collie who kept his aim on the threat. The old man's hand was now steady. "What's he saying?" Billy said, this time to himself.

The volume increased again and kept doing so at the pace of the man's own will. He was still rocking and staring in place. "All together now all together now all together now all together now...," they began to make out. Billy leaned in. "All together now all together now all together now,"

"What the," Collie began and he was cut off by the man whose words now morphed together taking on a form of dialect that sounded like tongues.

"Togethanow togethanow togethanow togethanow." His convulsions shifted violently. Collie stepped back. Billy was dumbstruck. "Togethanow togethanow togethanow nownownownownownownow." The words crescendoed until his voice sounded like tearing paper and he went hoarse. Collie's gun hand dropped. He looked to Billy who appeared to have have his thoughts ripped away.

"He's still goin'," Billy said. Collie turned. The mouth was moving as before sounding like a dying dog. And then it all stopped and the robins' songs commenced and the world once again embraced them. The man was motionless.

"What the fuck is wrong with him?" Billy said. He was next to Collie. "Look at him," he pointed at the face. For the first time a clear display. The beard matted with substance seemed to be a growing retraction, looping back into the worn skin like a collection of frightened earthworms returning to the ground. Every chasmic line whether from age or violence was caked with filth. He had been beaten. His knuckles bruised. And his brows arched down like a V above his eyes and above those the dried rusted flow of smut and putrefaction was painted as if he was struck by a rain cloud of soot that was manifested only inches above him. Blood and soil were one. There was a flat charred nub where his nose had been. His hair and skin were missing at the widow's peak. They had been torn off and packed with mud. There was a semblance of man residing in the shell beside the wagon, shaken and spewed forth from a cyclone. Yet survived he did, a personification of misery, and he kneeled catatonic before them.

Collie swallowed the lump in his throat. Everything around him seemed to pause like photographs he had seen though never admired. Billy tapped his shoulder. It spooked him. "What is this?" Billy asked.

Collie wiped his mouth with his back hand despite holding the gun. "He's half scalped," he said. "The mud on his head. He packed the wound to stop the bleeding."

"Jesus Christ," Billy said.

"And he cauterized the stump after they cut his nose off."

Billy placed his hand on his stomach. "Who does that?"

"He did," Collie said and pointed to the rear of the wagon. Billy turned and peered down at the headless body on the ground.

"Buckskin," Collie said.

"Sioux."

Collie nodded. "Though I don't see how there is only one heathen shuffled off while this sorry sack remains alive." Collie pondered amidst foreign confusion and neither man noticed the broken trance of the tattered man as his eyes lifted to his superiors and the V above them angled deeper. He stood like a tensing rope and approached the pair and at the sound of the bending blades Collie thwacked the man with the butt of his revolver. He dropped to the ground unconscious. "Watch him," Collie said, stepping over the fallen and moving to the rear of the wagon.

An opaque cloud of what looked like ash hovered above the torso. Thousands of moving insects clamored at decomposition so erratically that it took on a frozen appositional form. The incessant hum of the flies blossomed until it was all Collie could hear. He reached the end of the wagon box and stood over the body. The front of the torso was grounded and the stump at the top of the neck had been pushed slightly into the ground and there the ground had turned cinnamon after the earth's drink. Collie cringed a mite and blew the excess air from his nostrils attempting to rid the stink. He holstered his weapon and pulled down the hinged tail of the wagon box. A metallic creak cut through the buzzing and Collie retreated a step with the drop. He sighed and regained his footing and searched away as if some unanswered truth would welcome him. There existed only the sound of the dining fauna and he continued his gaze at the decaying head of the native inside of the wagon.

When he came to they lifted him to his knees. There was a nascent ruby globe where Collie had struck him. He began rocking again compulsively. "Knock that shit off," Collie said. He placed his hand on the man's shoulder and the man pushed forward and then slowed until the rocking ceased. The tattered man raised his eyes to Collie and peered into him and Collie reciprocated discovering only clouded distortion, the narrow obsidian pupils glazing over conveying nihility. The recent history depicted superficially across his face was all that was written.

"Together," the man said.

"Who? Who is together," Collie said.

The man started rolling his head, untwisting it. "Together now."

Billy spat next to himself, amused. "This fella should write a book. It'd be riveting."

"Shut up," Collie said. Billy snorted and moved away from the wagon and into the field in solitude. "Who's together?" Collie repeated.

The man opened his mouth and paused and the recess lasted some time. "They are," he said.

Collie was impatient. "Who is they?" He shook him, the body frail. "Come on. Who?"

"The girls. They're with their mother now. The girls. My girls."

Collie peered over to Billy who perked up at the sign of coherence. "What happened here?" Collie asked. The man hid his face quivering. "We know you were attacked. We see that. What were you doing out here? Huh? Why are you out here?"

The man began crying . "It comes for everyone."

"For chrissakes," Collie said. "No more riddles."

Something in the distance behind the treeline caught Billy's attention. He started to walk through the field in the direction of the creek.

Collie was about to yell when he was interrupted. "Death," the man said. The word oozed from his mouth.

"What?" Collie said. He placed his hand over his pistol.

The man's brow altered to the narrow V and a thin smile creased to one side. "We can't help it. It's in us all. You've only just missed it."

"Missed what? How long ago?" His diligence was drawn between the enigma before him and the gradual disappearance of his partner, who was no longer in his view.

"Time doesn't attach itself to such a thing. It exists for all, human and not. I know it now intimately."

Collie grit his teeth together. "We're after a man, may have be you've seen him in his passing through. Answer that and we are on our way."

The man twisted. "There he goes," he said referring to Billy. Collie looked and saw nothing, but he remained. "Discoveries."

"Billy." He raised his voice and he was answered only by the sound of a mellow splash and wading water.

The man laughed and the laugh grew into a tantrum. "He is no man. So they and all that belonged to them went down alive and the earth closed over them and they perished from the midst of the assem-" The rest was unintelligible.

"It's hard to talk with a gun in your mouth. Inn't it?" Collie said, his finger pressed on the trigger. A single bead of sweat trekked down the forehead of his target. "You tell me what I need to know." The man made an indication of understanding and Collie removed the gun. There was more splashing in the distance followed by a hollow plunge alerting Collie. "Speak," he said. He lowered his pistol. "A man came through. You saw him," he stated, though it sounded like a question. "Was it he that took your women?" The dry cracking sound of pressing stalks grew closer.

"He found them," the man said and looked at Collie. The sheriff appeared confused. "A man can travel the entire world and find the same people everywhere he goes. The dead will be raised imperishable, and we shall be changed."

The beating treads sprouted in rapidity. "The man," Collie said. "Tell me," he yelled.

"I did it for them," the man said. "They wanted to be with their mother, and now they'll know no evil. I had to do it for them." He closed his eyes and raised his head to the sunlight painting him in warmth as Billy came around the wagon sidestepping the headless corpse. Collie noticed Billy, but was too engrossed to pay much heed.

"Speak," Collie yelled and the shot rang out in unison with the crimson burst through the man's face and the man blew forward and fell to the ground like a cumbersome slab and the deep red pooled around his fragmented visage in contrast to the wheaten yellow blades beneath them. Collie stood breathless staring at the smoking barrel of Billy's discharged sidearm while the water dripped almost poetically from his lower half. Billy seemed a man possessed, studying his kill and continuing his aim as if the mark might suddenly arise for vengeance.

Some things at times are best left unsaid when truths and mistruths could collide and breed. The smoke hung at the end of the gun and rolled slowly, an unwilling soul repudiating its order to depart. Billy's pistol was trained still while Collie holstered his and moved to the edge of the field at the treeline. The grass and thickets became greener as he approached the creek. He saw the bent stalks and muddied prints from his colleague. He reached the treeline and moved to the clearing where Billy had entered the water. It stank of ragweed and algae. The ripples abated and finished their dying wades.

From the shore he searched the water with his eyes starting in the middle and then across. A new breeze was born and it picked up and ran across the water and through the trees and the trees swayed to the lyric and the maple above Collie released its grip on a cluster of leaves. He followed their descent into the creek as it fell with a most simple swell near the bodies. Collie grabbed his chest and shuddered probing at his heart when he saw them. They were face down. Their dresses surrounded them flowing outward like nourished lily pads, each with a different color, and the white, green and orange were the only vibrancy in the calm collected water, blossoms from the new spring taken without warning by the wind and abandoned as the wind like everything in the world passed. He dropped to his knees and vomited in the grass and wiped his eyes and mouth. When he was finished he stood again and stared at the stolen youth. The ardor first encompassing them had purged itself along with him and now appeared pastel and faded.

"You okay?" Billy said behind him.

Collie kept looking at the girls. "He did it. He told me."

"They were drowned."

"They were his daughters. He did it himself."

"I'm not sorry for this. You should know that."

"You don't need to be."

"There's just no telling who is worse. There's no logic to any of it. No pattern to this kind of wrongdoing." Billy said.

"I suppose if there was it would cease to be so. Wrongdoing that is. There's no gauge. No gauge at all." He stepped back from the creek next to Billy. "He told me before you shot him. They wouldn't know any evil any more. That they'd be with their mother. Maybe it ain't the worst thing. Things don't get no better. We seen that. Maybe it ain't the worst thing."

"It is the worst thing," Billy said and walked away.

The breeze left and the scene again became still and they remained silent, pondering or praying or perchance both. And neither disturbed the other as if the spoken word would collect the souls of the departed and hinder their journey elsewhere. The report and echo of the gunshot came from the distance beyond the hills. It was followed by another. Collie turned in that direction. A third shot did not arrive. He looked to Billy. His faux smile rendered from the scars could no longer mask the authenticity of the young man's turmoil. Collie began his slow march to the horses. "Let's finish it," he said.

Chapter 27

The once capacious scope of the land had diminished as they rode and the surrounding terrain folded in on itself tunneling them and that which it was a part of existed solely on the exterior offering whatever awe and significant wonder it held only to the inattentive. Collie led. Billy maintained a distance. He was tracking, though Collie's instincts had been correct thus far. And never did the lawman or the thief turn into the past upon the five bodies left behind. They traveled only forward as if possessed, across the natural meridian and the vigorous life of the wild that had existed for thousands of years kept its calls and cycles with no mind to the human disturbance. They would endure as they had endured. The world of men was simply that, of men, and the illusion of comity between man and nature remained.

The incline of the hill was stubborn and as they made their way closer to the sun it glared down unrelenting forcing their heads to bow. Billy could hear exertion from his animal as it grunted and panted with each pace. He called to Collie, but the sheriff went on. As the older man crested the hill he stopped and stared at the route ahead. He was breathing heavily close to unison with his horse. Billy arrived next to him. "They could use water," Billy said.

"They'll make it," Collie answered. Two hills remained, each decreasing in stature and giving way to a unique fork. West presented the open plains and grasslands for what could have been miles. To the east the earth inclined gradually to a ridge clustered with oak and pine varietals overlooking the grasslands, and the pine dominated after the introduction at the ridge and lived connectedly to the woods where the dense forestry overtook the entire field of vision on that side. Collie looked west and east then did so again. "The shots came from the ridge I'd reckon. Doubt we'd heard them as we did had they been in the open."

Billy rubbed his horse's mane. "I'll be able to tell if I stay up front."

"Okay," Collie said and spurred the ribs and he and Billy moved together. They trekked the decline and as the land opened between the hills the graceful strides of the animals lengthened and the clubbing sound of their hooves on the dried earth stretched apart. The miniscule dust clouds left behind each landing was the only evidence they had been there. Had they wings, they may have taken flight.

They covered the hill before them and then the second and as they reached the final slope before ascending to the ridgeline they picked up a speed surpassing nearly beyond capability and the cool wind struck their backs propelling them downward. The hearts of the animals pumped acid. What the men had once seen as broad strokes had now curtailed and the lone point ahead sharpened despite the contrast of the unfocused surroundings and as they drew on further it became clearer, their destination. The journey like all things was ending and it could be felt, colossal, lingering in the air.

At the base of the final hill, Billy's horse halted without command and fell to the ground as if its legs had snapped. Billy jerked forward and was thrown from the saddle. He struck the ground skinning both elbows. His face peppered with dirt. He shook his head and ran his fingers over his eyes brushing the soil away. He rose and looked ahead without missing a beat and saw only the dust trail behind Collie as he rode toward the sparse forest before the ridgeline. "Collie," he yelled to no avail. He exhaled heavily and checked his holster for his pistol and gripped it and then let go. He kneeled beside the horse. It lay on its side, breathing with its head resting on the ground. Its eye, the large black orb, held the sun and the clouds, and Billy peered into it and he touched the animal's mane. He grazed it gently and repeated. It lifted its head taking comfort and Billy mouthed the word sorry. From the leather skin along the saddle he pulled the rifle. The horse dropped its head again, breathing at a simmer. Billy moved to his feet. The ascension presented itself boastingly. He twisted the rifle and began to run.

The call scattered missing Collie's ears as he hammered the reins continuing forth with the ethos of a great ocean beast. He could feel the wind circumventing his body and still it seemed like quicksand. As the forestry began to occupy and surround him he lifted himself in the saddle. The darkening trees came into view on his right. He was nearing the edge and noticed in the distance the treetops a thousand yards out from the ridge. There was no evidence of the gunfire. Though the area radiated some feeling of significance and as the sunlight shifted above the thickets and the shadows of needles and jagged leaves penetrated the brown earth beneath him his attention was drawn to a shape prone at the cliff in the distance.

Struck by the object's foreign nature, Collie grabbed the saddle horn with both hands and placed all of his weight on his right foot in the stirrup. He swung his left leg over the saddle and leaped from the horse as it was moving. The animal kept on and then slowed and stopped without its owner. He drew his pistol. Marching to the horse, he pulled the shotgun from the leather along the saddle. He could hear the rapid beats of Billy's footsteps from afar. He slapped the rear of the horse and the animal trotted away.

The figure lay some fifty yards out unmoving and twenty yards further beyond it lay the final step before the escarpment. Collie trained both weapons on the figure and progressed forward in a serpentine pattern finding cover in the trees as he moved. The shape on the ground was motionless, alien in all aspects from his vantage, and what started as a speck developed in scale as Collie neared until he could ascertain that it was in fact a body. And that of a man.

He heard his name at a holler. It was Billy's voice. Collie spun to see him sprinting. Billy yelled again. Collie placed his hand on the tree to catch his breath ignoring the shouts. He stared ahead at the seemingly lifeless outline. It evoked the concepts of both predator and prey. There were no rock walls to climb or seas to cross. For the first time the odyssey presented a definitive portrait of destiny. And life as it seldom is was solvable. The sheriff could not wait.

A powerful mass and burden belabored each step as he ran to his target. The pain in his back reminded him of his age. When he was only paces away he hesitated as if restrained and exercised a measure of caution. He holstered his pistol and gripped the shotgun properly. The body lay before him face down, arms stretched Christlike and the head positioned away overlooking the plains. He held the gun barrel close to the body and approached until the man was at his boots. "Do not move," he said pressing the barrel in between the man's shoulder blades. A shudder polluted his voice. He poked the gun at the body. There was no acknowledgement, no recoil and he crouched and listened to the sounds of the world as the lump swelled in his throat and a single tear fought through the weathered terrain of his face. His jaw opened at the realization of the body's lifelessness and he began to take in air as if it was nearly unbreathable. The steps in the background were gaining and he wiped away the tear, but more came. Enraptured in the blinding nature of all vengeance, he spoke arbitrarily. "I'm Sheriff Tim Collie. You killed my friend." He sniffled and tightened the hold on his weapon. "You hear me? You killed my friend. His name was Virgil Wells. And you got what was coming to ya." His hand trembled and he wiped his tears and this time held them at bay.

Billy reached them panting like a dog lost in the desert, hunching over and grabbing just below his ribcage. His respiration conspicuous, unable to speak. Collie lifted the end of the barrel from the body. The indentations in the dead man's shirt like memories lingered moments and then faded at the edges and then disappeared altogether. Billy straightened and collected himself. He moved over the body. Collie stepped away. Billy paused regarding his elder and knelt at the corpse. "That'd be him," Collie said. Billy leaned across, able to see the profile. Collie shook his head. "He's like the barkeep described. Pressed clothes and shaved at his departure. Better than most."

Billy ran his hand along the stranger's coat patting the material sporadically and then held his palm to the sunlight inspecting it while Collie stared into the distance. "No blood yet," Billy said. He pushed aside the orphaned hat and grasped the stranger's hair at the crown and wrenched it with the indelicacy of a butcher and raised the head into the air giving birth to the revelation of the peeled skin, scalped at the side and matted with soil. He let it fall again into the dirt and then rolled the body. The wound across the chest from the cutting edge of the tomahawk spewed forth blood further bedecking the attire while the laceration at the neck made crimson along the collar and the ground beneath it. Billy looked away a moment and stood and saw Collie's attention to the body, particularly to the eyes, white rondures rolled away peering into an eternal abyss. If the stranger adorned the fangs of the devil it would have been expected, though he was there forthwith existing as nothing more than a broken vessel, as soulless and inanimate as the string of death that he himself had rendered. There was no exodus of foggy apparitions nor the heralding of celestial phosphorescence upon the passing. Death in its utmost simplicity was all that prevailed.

Collie placed his finger across the trigger and aimed the weapon at the corpse. "What are you doing?" Billy said. "I'm sorry Collie. I know this wasn't the plan, but he's dead and we have to go."

"This wasn't justice," Collie said.

Billy stepped away from the body, his attention drawn to the surroundings. "Listen I know. Death waits for everyone. Whether its patient or not I suppose depends on the day."

Collie shook his head. "He'll never know. He's never gonna know why we're here."

"What does it matter?"

"It matters," Collie said.

"He's gone. Why?"

"Because he got away with it," the sheriff yelled and stared at Billy. "Don't you see?"

"He's laying there dead. Killed. Just like we'll be if we don't skidaddle on out of here. He is dead."

"By the wrong hands," Collie said and he lowered his weapon. The cloud coverage masked areas of the sun making beams through the treetops. He turned to Billy, the young man exhibiting an unsure composure. "I don't know what else to do."

"Listen-," Billy said. The arrow made a whisper through the air striking Collie with a meager pulse. The sheriff coughed as if he had swallowed an insect and looked down in astonishment at the wooden shaft protruding from his upper pectoral. All life and movement desisted for the eternity of that moment. Sounds, thoughts, and actions destroyed in some vacuous element, and then as the moment ceased, like a man surfacing from a deep water, the situation crystallized and the components rushed forth at the two men bestowing an unlasting state of hypersensitivity as their minds acclimated. Collie pulled his eyes from his wound in time to see Billy in flight. The young man leaped and grabbed Collie bringing them both to the ground with the sound of gunfire. The bark of the trees exploded around them. The gunfire continued. "Can you move?" Billy yelled over the shots.

"Yeah," Collie confirmed. Billy fired his rifle in the direction of the forest and dispensed the cartridge and fired again as soon as the round entered the breech. The shooting ceased a sudden instant and they crawled to an old fallen tree. They stopped, exposed in front of it. There was a native call followed by another and the light pounding of feet closing in. Collie let loose his revolver, firing three shots at the unseen enemy. "Fire again on-," his words were drowned by the report of the guns. "Fire on three and we'll hop it," he finished. Billy acknowledged by cocking the hammer. "One, two, three." They could see the smoke clouds hovering not thirty yards ahead. They fired in unison and rolled to the other side of the log. They hit the ground with a flattened thud and were pelleted immediately with bark and earthly shrapnel.

Billy pressed his back against the log, his head just lower than the surface. He grabbed Collie's arm and the sheriff managed to right himself using the forestock of the shotgun. "You okay?" Billy asked loading his pistol.

Collie leaned to his side and spat. It was free of blood. He dropped his weapons and grasped the arrow tight to his chest with one hand. With the other, he snapped the long shaft and threw the feathered end to his feet. He picked up his pistol and emptied the spent shells paying no more attention to the three inch shattered bolt sticking in his body. "Can you make how many?"

"No," Billy answered. Collie held his shotgun over the log and discharged the double buckshot. All went quiet. The grey and white haze of smoke permeated the view exaggerating the sun rays. Billy tilted his head and peered over the log into the forest. He squinted despite his youthful eyes and there ahead between a pair of centennial oaks he noticed the row of custom scaffolds, garnished and feathered, facing south. "Chrissakes," he said.

"What?" Collie moved to his knees to see.

"It's a burial ground. Out there," Billy whispered, pointing.

There was movement in the smoke, blackened forms like malevolent spectres bouncing between the trees. "Listen," Collie said no louder than his leaving breath. An incessant whir captured their attention, growing louder and more rapid and the sound seemed to echo perpetually until it stopped and the uneven cumbersome rock hit the barrel of Collie's shotgun twisting his fingers at the grip and trigger guard causing him to drop it entirely. He grunted at the pain and saw Billy prostrate beside him taking cover. Collie opened his mouth to speak and as he did he heard a battle cry. The steps battered the ground like cudgels and the shape emerged from the smoke. The Sioux broke the cloud at a sprint. His tomahawk raised, he howled again. Collie gripped his pistol in his good hand and fired. The Sioux jerked to one side, but did not fall. He picked up speed. Collie tensed and fired again, missing the target and the Sioux crashed into the log before him. He struck the downed tree with his legs and his upper half bowled into Collie. Disorientation took hold. He swung his tomahawk as if blindfolded. Collie could see the dark maroon off center in the man's chest. He pushed away from the log, remaining low and fired at his enemy. The head jolted in unison with the shot and the target fell from his sight.

Smoke prowled from the barrel with a smooth caress. Collie was statuesque, his gun still aimed ahead and when he finally broke and looked right for his companion all he could see was vacancy. Billy was gone without any mark of evidence. Collie held a moment confounded and then touched the disturbed earth as if the act itself would conjure that which was lost and in doing so he did not hear the second native until the enemy breached the cover catching his foot on a rogue appendage of the downed tree. He stumbled and his misfortune allowed Collie time to swing himself around. The Sioux extended his arms, palms out as if ready to push something. Collie fired. The report seemed louder this time. The Sioux already on his knees fell forward crouched like a fetus and moved no longer. Collie inched carefully to him and lifted the head by the long coarse black hair and saw the eyes no longer inhabited. He forced the body away. The head flopped and a line of blood from the mouth whipped like a pendulum illustrating a half moon of the future. There were no encores.

Collie kept low and scuttled parallel behind the fallen pine to where the evergreen needles were thickest and had begun to amber. He tossed the spent cartridges from his pistol and reloaded. The sweat poured over him. He thumbed back the hammer. The weapon clicked and as the chamber came into alignment he noticed the silence around him in great absolution, a pact between nature and those he was fighting. He was the foreigner. He was the unnatural.

He gazed through the branches. Not even the wind dared break the stillness. Collie near frozen opened his mouth to silence the sound of his breathing. The idleness cast an eerie tension over the modest battlefield. And then as if given direction there was faint movement. At a moderate oak he saw the ivory feather amidst the dusky mane appear to glide up the bark as the warrior straightened behind it. Collie raised his gun deliberately. He closed an eye taking aim and with the other in his sole peripheral he became suddenly engulfed in the realization of their method. A burst of fire from behind a tree opposite his mark flashed and he felt the heated sting across his brow and through his temple before he heard the shot. He strained to keep his vantage. The warmth spreading down the side of his face and around his ear was oddly comforting. He could taste the metal in the air. The grip on his pistol loosened and he tottered backwards to his rear. The world spun.

Collie encased in the newness of his muddled state left the wound untouched. He moved about, his head vacillating searching for signs of the enemy, the entire picture granting rouge distortion. There were sounds everywhere. The steam chugging of all trains occupying every cranny and their subsequent derailments bestowing an omnipotent anarchy. He palmed his temples, pressing tightly against his head. He kicked at the ground. The hand from his wounded temple came away shades darker than ruby and he pressured again over the gash. A mammoth turmoil and chaos ripped through him and he looked to the sky his mouth agape preparing to scream. Though all he emitted was silence.

He fell onto his back, the ground soft and peculiarly inviting. His breathing slowed. His arms lowered. The blood now leaving the wound reluctantly. Catharsis perhaps and Collie closed his eyes and witnessed a sea of bodies, Indians all of them, living and dead, standing and lying, men and women. Tribeless in his mind. They are faceless, heads like blank canvasses. The dead are strewn across the ground in front of the living and the living shout and flaunt weapons at a gruesome force unseen. As the dead increase their stock the bodies layer and the layers grow higher as the once living fall in shocks of horror becoming the spiritless numbers around them. They stand. They want to fight. The world is open. There is nowhere to run. They continue to fall. There are so many. Even the warriors wail. And then all is hush. And a group of living parts and the child emerges from their ranks. She is so very young. The child beautiful. Savage though she would be called by some. Her face is distinct. Soft and featured. Swarthy and wholly untainted. She is holding a flower. The white petals penetrate through the red earth and sky. No one is screaming anymore. The universe stops to behold her. She steps over the fallen regarding no one. She moves in a drift. They lower their weapons. There is no more fear. She lowers her head and stops and rests over a particular fallen body. She holds her survey over the faceless soul and bends at the knee and drops the flower on the chest. A tear streams to her cheek. The others circle her. She looks at no one. She raises her head to the blood red sky. Her feet hover above the ground. She is lifted into the air. She floats above them, above everything. And they watch as she departs. It is all they can do.

The one who followed lay between Billy's feet grasping for air, a landed fish helpless for the clubbing. He was a man drowning without a drop of water in sight. Prone on dry land. His own knife protruding from his neck while his killer cast a shadow over his dying body, hovering like a casual hunter admiring a well earned trophy. The Sioux cast his eyes upwards to the heavens. The eagles were circling. Their small dark bodies soaring in and out of the leaflets. Beautiful creatures. He pawed at the knife handle.

Billy tarried for reasons unknown and while the time existed in only a few mere moments, they seemed to hold and linger like constructed thought for as long as he desired. The Sioux would become a kill. The body beneath him limply holding on. The death rattle. The attempts pathetic. Billy met the Indian's eyeline. He too saw the birds. Above, the patient surrounding buzzards perfect in their ugliness. He bent down. Their eyes met and he expelled the knife from the jugular. The blood stream followed. The Indian clasped the wound and his eyes rolled into his head, his arms lifeless at his side. There were no dying words. He had only the strength to emit one slow passive breath, like the creak of an old wooden door, exiting remorsefully a disappointing coda.

As the child ascended making her exodus into the clouds Collie shook himself awake. The Sioux was straddling him, knife already in hand and alarmed at the sudden return to consciousness, he brought the blade to Collie's throat. The sheriff clutched the armed hand and pushed with all of his might. The warrior was strong and full of vigor. The knife remained inches from his neck. Collie pushed again though the blade came closer. The warrior battle scarred and sinewy leaned in and whispered to his prey and the words though unknown to Collie rang ominous. Collie stared through his blood coated eyes, the enemy reddened in the meridian, and Collie saw a raw and boasting smile grace the face of his executioner. For a split second Collie gave in, his fight decaying. The euphoric aura of acceptance pervaded. And like that, a crack of thunder, it was gone. Collie inhaled flexing his strength and smashed his head into the warrior's nose. The Sioux at once straightened and grabbed at the sharp pain. Blood spurt between his fingers. Collie bolted up. He scanned for anything that could be used as a weapon. The Sioux respiring heavily no longer smiled. He grabbed his knife from the ground and ran his tongue over the freshly formed blood on his upper lip. Collie clenched the soil desperately and as the Sioux moved forward to attack, the sheriff swung his arm opening his hand and showered his enemy with the dirt. It pattered the warrior's eyes blinding him impermanently. He crouched and abraded his face with his knuckles. Seeing his foe disabled, Collie cracked him in the chest with his bootheel.

Billy saw the four of them standing in a semblance of a line like a group of off duty sentries. They were watching the death match with relative ease. He marked one on the end with his gunsight. The shot unobscured and the distance short. However, the reload capacity of the rifle would not be fast enough for the entire quartet. His ammunition was depleted. He lowered the gun and peered at the surroundings. The Sioux remained engrossed. He moved to another tree further off center from his targets. He raised the rifle and sighted again. This time they were more tightly clustered. In the distance he could hear the groans and wails of the savage duet. Collie was alive, though in what condition lay the mystery.

Billy opened the cylinder of his revolver. Three were lethal. He ejected the other half. Between that and the rifle were five bullets. He cocked the hammer of the pistol and laid it at the root of the tree and then pulled the tomahawk and knife from his waistband. Blood adorned both instruments. The handles were notched by the former owner. He placed the tomahawk next to the pistol. The knife he sheathed and clipped to his gunbelt. The ground was soft at the tree base. He dug in his boots and steadied himself against the tree. The butt of the rifle was nestled into to thick portion of his shoulder. The Sioux at the far left was chosen and if the man adjacent leaned forward, the dual targets would become one. The warriors keen on the outcome were loose and cheering. Billy closed an eye and smiled and while the song of viciousness played in sets across the fertile landscape he revealed an irreverent laugh, a punchline divulged from a joke that only he was in on.

Collie lost his footing and fell to his back. The Indian pounced and struck him bare knuckled in the face. Collie could feel the pressure behind his eye socket, willing it to close. The Sioux grabbed him by the collar, straddling his torso. Collie clung at the man's wrists keeping the noxious hands from his throat. The veins in the native's arms were popping, definitive. He held the look of a man about to summit the tallest peak. His upper teeth pressed into his lip. Collie's strength was diminishing.

When man is pushed to the outer reaches, the absolute jagged limits of his mind, there comes a moment when he is bestowed with the bitter clear cognizance that he has a choice in the matter. Collie strained his head forward and bit into the man's knuckle. The blood flowed between his teeth bringing newfound warmth across his face. The Sioux screamed and slammed Collie's head to the ground. Collie loosened his grip. He turned his head and felt the rough skin of the enemy's fingers clench around his neck. The warrior had amassed the strength of all the men who had lived and died on the land before him, he drove his thumbs into Collie's windpipe, his knuckles casting impressions in the soil. Collie dropped his arms to the side palms up. There was no wind to caress them. His air was near exhausted. He began kicking at the ground. His hands turned, nails in the dirt clawing in desperation. He could feel something. His world was darkening.

The Sioux men yelled from over the tree, the foreign tongue harsh to Collie. The warrior on top of him acknowledged his people. Collie could see them through the cardinal layer covering his vision. They were looking on, boasting. He was the final obstacle. One of the Sioux yelled again. His war bonnet heavily feathered conveyed the essence of leadership. The warrior turned and said something and the smile reappeared. Collie pawed at the dirt. He felt the object. He worked his fingers around it and held in his grip the broken shaft of the arrow whose point had been mapped inches from his heart.

The rifle clapped but once blowing the jaw off one of the natives causing him to fall like a slab of rock and inking the leader with blood and fragment. The war chief was stone for a moment and patted his torso and face checking for wounds. He looked down at the newly massacred and cocked his head to the mouthless man as if confused and then noticed his other man on the end, teetering, struggling with levity like a pyramid turned upside down. A fine mist sprayed from the through wound to his jugular. The injured Sioux, stunned, dabbed at the wound with two fingers and then stared at them, the blood black like oil. His eyes rolled upwards and then he staggered and fell.

The world froze and went mute until the hideous click of the rifle's misfire snapped all again into being. Billy threw the weapon to the ground. He grabbed the pistol and tomahawk. The war chief and his soldier were dazed. Billy rose and the chief turned. They locked eyes. Billy raised the pistol a mite quicker than the soldier raised his bow.

The sudden burst of violence left the warrior entrenched for seconds bewildered, drawn to the carnage swarming his comrades. Collie felt the force inflicted on him subside. He too gazed upon the war chief accented now with human gore carrying an expression that he was next in line for the abattoir. Collie allowed no effect. He pulled the arrow shaft from the dirt. The warrior commenced his death hold and as he did, three pistol shots whacked the atmosphere stealing him away again. And as he cringed and lowered his head intuitively, Collie stuck the rugged stem through the warrior's throat. The Sioux's hands went immediately there. Collie gagged for air, the life giving breaths causing ironic pain. He kicked the Indian off of him. The native fell on his back. Collie pushed himself up, massaging his neck in the process. He traded former positions with his combatant. The man was writhing, ripping at the arrow. Collie pressed his knee into the Sioux's sternum and compelled the arrow deeper. The Sioux's hands fell. His eyes met the sky. His breathing slowed and Collie watched until it came to a standstill, and the clouds and shadows glided across the deserted pupils and the writhing stopped and the body went calm. Collie witnessed what he had seen before, what had held the truth unknown to anyone fortunate enough to have never see it first hand. That the preciousness of life and the instinctive nature to preserve one's own is upheld until the very small seconds before it ends. And death rolls in. And in those nanoseconds before it encompasses all in its newfangled omnipotence, it is in fact welcomed.

Collie leaned back sucking in air, his throat swollen and unsanded. He rolled beside the dead man. He tilted over and vomited, his stomach unsettled, his body convulsing with each heave. He could hear Billy and the impending fight. It was far away, at least to him. It could not be further. The blood droplets rained in languid fashion from his head and chest around the pool of his sick. He coughed and spit blood and bile. He peered off at the horizon and into the sun, soft and low, and the storm clouds gathering like petty vultures in the distance pestilent and uninvited, denouncing beauty, though with the fortitude to move about untested. Collie placed a hand on the ground. He pushed and steadied himself until he was upright. He wavered. He stepped forward and looked once more over the dead warrior, subject never again to pain or tribulation. The man's face transmitted relief in a way synonymous with Collie's. The sheriff mimed the tipping of a hat to the deceased and then limped away from the battleground.

The soldier hit the ground gutshot, but the chief remained unscathed. The wails of the wounded native high pitched and childlike echoed over the terrain. The chief pulled his tomahawk and stared down the aggressor who appeared notoriously to be one of his own, acclimated to the white world. He squatted as if to sit, flexing his quadriceps. He shifted his weight from leg to leg and commenced with low successive whooping.

Billy rose from the tree. The pistol still smoking in his hand. He too held a tomahawk. His knuckles paled around the handle. He observed the chief and the war dance with amusement rather than fascination and when the moment presented itself, Billy lowered and caricatured the man. The chief stopped in a blink. His brow narrowed and he charged without warning. His hide wrapped feet pounded the earth the twenty yard distance. Billy dug his boots in. He raised his pistol to his prey and dry fired it. The chief charged on. Billy flipped the gun and held it by the barrel, the great Sioux only feet away. The hallowed thumps growing. Billy could see the crow's feet and suffered flesh, the tortured history drawn in the man's movements. The chief bellowed a final cry extending the crafted axe and as it reached skywards Billy with an intrepid grin threw the pistol, and the clumsy shape whooshed uncalculated striking the chief. It bounced aside in his trail. The chief hied unfazed, but it was enough to change his footing. In killing distance, the honored fighter brought down his tomahawk and it clashed into Billy's before it could even whir. They were paused a moment, their weapons in a state of perpetual stagnancy against one another. The chief leaned in and whispered something to Billy and clutched the young man's throat. He was strong despite his age. He grit his teeth and spoke again, only this time not a whisper.

Billy pushed his tomahawk with all of his force against the chief's. His breath was ending. He heard the words of the Sioux. They could have been anything, hanging apathetically in the air for no particular audience. Billy's thoughts raced across his mind, the possibilities endless. And as he stood there, his own life escaping his custody he smiled and the chief saw and tilted his head and tightened his grip on the boy. And as each individual finger rushed into Billy's larynx, the thief slipped his hand to the sheath behind his hip and pulled the blade all the while staring into the eyes of his venerable killer.

The chief did not notice the knife until it was plunged half way into his neck, the edges sharp and graceful. Billy had slithered it around the man's shoulder and drove it in gently. The chief's hands dropped to his side. His weapon fell. He tried to step, but Billy retained the knife. The chief opened his mouth to speak and his lips moved yet sound never followed.

"I can't understand you," Billy said and he sank the knife in deep to the handle. The life vacated that instant and the body went limp. It began to slump and the blade in turn revealed its complete self in Billy's hand as the chief hit the ground. Billy stared down at the body of the elder native. The land was quiet. Only the sounds of the birds and the labored breathing of the gutshot warrior. He looked at the knife coated in red. He wiped it clean on his pant leg. In the distance he could see Collie walking. Billy stepped over the chief's body and moved to the downed tree where the Sioux soldier lay. The blood was thick and pooling around the soldier from the wound in his stomach. Billy watched as the man's belly ebbed and flowed spewing blood with each series. He shook his head and peered off to where he had last seen Collie. There was only the escarpment and the trees and the horizon. The Sioux was muttering beneath him. Billy said something in Hidatsa and dropped the knife at the man's side and the

Indian looked at it but did not take it right away. And when he did Billy regarded the grounds of the battle and he held no sympathy, he scouted it only as an artist might if he was committing a picture to memory. And when he had absorbed all he could he exhaled a long breath and made his way to the ridge line.

At the hillcrest stood a proud oak which surveyed miles of valley as it had for over a hundred years. Collie sat at its base enthroned between two protruding roots, his breath sweeping rhythmically in and out while the tame rays beamed warming his skin and the humble fingertips of the wind flicked by. His wounds were packed with dirt. The sky was clear but for the storm clouds in the distance, and he viewed the sky and valley below until he grew tired and he leaned his head on the trunk and closed his eyes.

Billy sidestepped navigating the titanic roots like veins flexed spreading across the earth. He leaned and saw Collie's feet at the opposite side of the tree. He approached with care and found the old sheriff unmoving and seemingly at peace. "Jesus Christ," Billy said and removed his hat and peered over the cliff.

"Only me," Collie said.

"Thought you were dead," Billy said a bit jolted. Collie shook his head. Billy crouched next to him and inspected the wounds. "You look dead, no offense given."

"I had a feeling I appeared that way."

Billy pulled a handkerchief from his pocket and whipped it open through the air. "Its nothing." He pressed against the laceration.

"That Indian fought like hell," Collie said. His eyes watering as he allowed him to soak away the blood.

"You must've too."

"You got 'em all?" Collie asked. Billy nodded and he wiped his hands. "Helluva thing. Thought you left when the shootin' started."

Billy cleaned the remaining blood and placed the handkerchief on Collie's leg. "Hah. I could have. You would've been fine."

"Yeah?"

"Hell I'm only fooling. You could've never done that on your own," Billy said. Collie laughed and it rattled deep in his chest. He spat. The blood and phlegm mixed with the soil. "You alright? Hell we better get you out of here." Billy straightened reaching for Collie's arm. "Up you go." Collie made no effort to move even when Billy grabbed his arm. "What's this now? I'm not carrying ya, that's for damn sure."

"Its nice here," Collie said. "Isn't it?" He looked off into the plains. "You ever seen the pronghorn run?"

"What?"

"Before you made your way here, I was just settin' trying to collect myself. And that Indian's face clouded over me and I couldn't see nothin' else regardless of how hard I tried. I tried thinkin' about my wife and I couldn't see her face. Even tried thinkin' about this fella back home, ugly sunnabitch. Billiard man. But all I could see was that Indian and the way he looked when he knew he was gonna kill me. Don't know if it was excitement or pride or I don't know what else. But he wanted to do it." He wiped his eyes and sniffled. "It's repeatin' over and over like some moving picture painted across the sky. And then I look out." He pointed at the valley. "And down there I see the pronghorn runnin'. All my years, all my time in the territory, I never seen one in flight. You believe that? It was the fastest thing I'd ever seen. Not a care in the world, them animals. I could see the grass kick up behind him. You seen one?"

"Yeah, I've seen a few."

"I don't reckon I'd move that fast even if I could. But it sure was something to see."

"I bet it was. You'll see more," Billy said attempting to pull him up. "Come on goddammit."

"This is some spot."

"I'm taking you out of here," he said, his voice raised.

Collie smiled. "That's some kind of code you got."

"Well I made a promise. It was to myself, but anybody would have done the same."

"No they wouldn't." Collie grabbed the handkerchief using it to slow the blood flow.

Billy started to speak and cut himself short. He looked at the ground and the valley and then Collie again. "I can carry you a ways."

Collie shook his head. "You gotta get the hell outta here. You're a wanted man. That ain't changed. Pinkertons will realize you been through the places we been through when they finally double back. They ain't full stupid. Think about the attention we'd draw, me lookin' like this. Nah. You take off. In the wind. I need some time. I'm not sayin' I'm shufflin' off, but if I do this place is as good as any."

"Doesn't seem right...leaving."

"Don't even know what right means anymore. Take my horse. You holler for him at the bottom of this hill, he'll come round."

"You saved me. From that cell. You saved my life. I'll remember."

"We're even."

Billy hesitated for what seemed like minutes. The storm clouds were growing nearer. He lowered in front of Collie and extended his hand. "Well hell, you did put me there. Alright," he said. They shook hands. "Even."

"You ain't all bad," Collie said. "What will you do with yourself?"

Billy stood up placing his hand near his holster. "Hah. You really want to know?"

Collie gave it a thought. "No I suppose I don't."

"That's how to be. Sometimes not knowing is the merrier." He chuckled and took the time to tidy his appearance. When he finished he walked to the edge and looked over. "It is something." He came back to his heels. "New beginnings and all that." Collie nodded. "I'll be in the wind like you said. You make it out of here. Take care of yourself, you hear?"

"I hear."

Billy began descending the trail. "Ya know something Collie?" he said in stride, his voice outlying. "You got no ceiling."

Collie twisted peering over his shoulder to see Billy, his dark outline shrinking like a pebble dropped from a bridge. He sighed at the fading sight of his friend and then rested against the trunk closing his eyes for a time and when he awoke and looked again Billy was gone. Collie creased a conflicted smile and attempted to swallow the lump forming in his throat.

The storm clouds gathered encircling the sun the way children would to hear a story. The bright star distinct and luminous despite the impinging threat. Collie emitted a laboring breath and stared into the duplicitous heavens and the greys and blues collided in unsettling complexions and as if on queue the skies opened and a hundred thousand translucent globes fell and settled hanging in the air as the sunlight fired through them delivering kaleidoscopic rainbows to the lone and humble gallery. The ground moistened. The drops cooling over his body. He looked upwards and let the rain cascade down his face and wet his tongue. He began to laugh and he laughed until he could no longer remember why. He drifted between the conscious plane and the unconscious, each as real as the other, traversing the hallowed roads of eld where shapes and stories appeared and spectres confronted those who trespassed. He glided as a seer, passive and forgotten.

When he roused the sky had turned giving way to an ashen landscape and the rain conquered rapping the pads and leaves around him like a long and echoing drumroll. His lids fluttered under the falling drops until he surrendered opening them all together.

For the longest time there was only darkness. An endless void stretching into infinity as if all that was ever known had been swallowed and existed now in the belly of some omnipotent species. And amidst the eclipse unannounced at the deepest comprehensible boundary gleamed a single bead of light like a distant star in the overcast night. And the bead moved forward sucking in the dark matter as nourishment growing stronger in stride until its light was blinding and brilliant and it burnt his pupils just to look and it warmed the world around him. In the fully illuminated canopy he saw his wife in crystalline perfection. As beautiful as the day he met her. She graced him with a smile, delicate and ambrosial. His legs were rubber as he approached her. He wanted to tell her all of the things he was never able to, but his words carried no sound. He cried and her smile turned to sympathy and when he reached to her she lifted her hand rendering the aura ravishing. It was glorious, and as he flitted toward her she whispered and he felt a push.

The rain had stopped. Only the clinging droplets on the leaf points and the opaque puddles scattered about were evidence it had ever started. Collie squinted at the newfound blaze of sunlight. He wiggled his toes in his boots. There was strength returning to his legs. He peered into the heavens and muttered to his wife and then grinned delighted. He grasped the enthroning roots on either side. The bark coarse like his hands. He rose and after a time he steadied himself. His attention cast to the east. It was the way home and he had a long walk ahead of him. Though he remained fixed, straddling quite literally the line between the places he'd been and the places he hadn't, gravitating toward the unknown, drinking in with a most porous certainty the benign and ancient congregation of all things. And the land like a picture that had come to life breathed with vigorous energy, the pronghorns skimming across the wheat while the birds soared and sang melodic, the vibrant greens of the pastures blanketing the earth's flesh and the cherry blossoms and purple hues of verbena, and the soft lyrics of the wind carried bringing voice to the trees and gifted him the fragrance of time. Collie stood and watched and felt the world around him, the emittance of its untamed majestic wonder. It was as it had been and it might have been beautiful.

The End

Made in the USA
Middletown, DE
18 January 2020